T0116531

HARLEM MOON
BROADWAY

also by bertice berry

harlem moon

broadway books

new york

the haunting

of hip hop

a novel bertice berry

This is a work of fiction. The names, characters, incidents, and most places are the products of the author's imagination and are not to be construed as real. Although part of the story is set at the very real, very hip House of Tina restaurant, the actual restaurant is not in New York City. There is also no Tubman Terrace in New York City. While I am often inspired to use names and qualities of folks I like, none of the characters in the book is based on an actual person, and any resemblance to persons living or dead is entirely coincidental and unintentional.

The figure in the Harlem Moon logo is inspired by a graphic design by Aaron Douglas (1899–1979). HARLEM MOON and its logo, depicting a moon and woman, are trademarks of Broadway Books, a division of Random House, Inc.

Visit our website at www.harlemmoon.com

Designed by Dana Leigh Treglia

The Library of Congress has cataloged the hardcover edition as follows:
Berry, Bertice.
The haunting of hip hop: a novel / Bertice Berry.
p.   cm.
1. Sound recording executives and producers—Fiction.
2. Harlem (New York, N.Y.)—Fiction. 3. Haunted houses—Fiction.
4. Afro-Americans—Fiction. 5. Hip-hop—Fiction.   6. Drum—Fiction.
I. Title.
PS3552.E7425   H38   2001
813'.54—dc21
00-057006

ISBN 978-0-767-91212-9

146721804

For Jeanine Chambers, Keith Chandler, Diane Dickenshied, Selena James, Janet Hill, David Mayhew, Earl Nicholson, Melissa Rivera, Ph.D, Victoria Sanders, Roberta Spivak, and all other assistants, agents, editors, and just good folks who give of themselves so others may shine.

the haunting

of hip hop

prologue

No man can put a chain about the ankle
of his fellow man without at least finding
the other end of it about his own neck.
—*Frederick Douglass*, Life and Times of
Frederick Douglass, *1881*

Ngozi sat behind his wife, Bani. His legs were wrapped around hers. She leaned back, and he rubbed her large belly. "She will deliver soon," his mother said. Ngozi nibbled Bani's ear and then whispered into it. "We will have joy. Don't worry." His wife had wept for most of her pregnancy. She felt that something terrible was going to happen. Ngozi tried to persuade Bani differently. On nights like this one, calm and still, Ngozi would rub her belly and speak to his unborn son. "Yo Tayembé.

Yo Tayembé, and then you say 'Ye oh Ye Ba Ba,'" he said to Bani's stomach.

Bani laughed when Ngozi first did this. *"The child cannot hear you, and you know he cannot respond."*

"Yo Tayembé, I'm calling you, son. 'Ye oh Ye Ba Ba. I hear you, Papa,'" he said again. *"How do you know he cannot hear me?"* Ngozi asked.

"How do you know it's a boy?" his wife responded.

"Woman," Ngozi said playfully, *"did I not tell you that you would be my wife? Did I not tell you that I would bring you happiness? Have I been wrong? I also told you that you were with child. I knew the moment it happened."*

Bani laughed. *"Your mother was right to give you a woman's name. You have the thoughts of a woman."*

Ngozi smiled. He'd heard this many times before. Never was he offended. *"Yo Tayembé. Yo Tayembé,"* he called to the child. *"Someday you'll answer me and my stubborn wife. Bani, you'll remember this moment."*

Bani was soon lulled into a sweet sleep. She would not wake up and feel Ngozi's arms wrapped tightly around her as she had on past mornings. Instead she would come to know the reason why she had been crying. Her husband, her love, would be gone from her forever.

When Ngozi saw that Bani was deeply asleep, he quietly moved himself from their embrace. He had to find the piece of wood his mother told him to look for. He had to make the drum for his unborn son. But he was making it for the son he would never see.

The drum had always been important to his people, but this one would be special. It had to be. Ngozi's mother had told him everything she had seen. Her visions started on the day he was born. On that day the memory of her grandfather appeared to her. *"Name him Ngozi, for he will be a blessing."*

Ngozi's mother laughed and said, "The others will think me crazy. Ngozi is a name for a girl child, she who is a blessing."

"Yes," the spirit memory of her grandfather said. "He will be a blessing, but he has been chosen to give birth." And then he was gone.

His mother had many visions after this one, but the last one, the most important one, she shared with him just before he was captured. She told him how to make the drum, what materials to use, and when to use them. The drum would be the last thing he made. "You will make this drum for your son, but you will not see him play it," she said. "Your life here will be short, but your task is great. The drum will keep you connected to your people and your purpose. You must do it, son, and you must do it right."

Ngozi was searching for just the right piece of wood for the body of the drum. Just as he bent down to touch the hollowed log that almost spoke his name, he heard something behind him. Before he could turn to see what it was, Ngozi was attacked by human hands, connected to an unnatural evil. He was carried away into the thing that his mother had spoken of. Some called it slavery; he called it death. Unfortunately for Ngozi's son, and many sons to follow, the magic of his drum would not be heard. It would be several generations before that power would be felt. Once that drum was found and played, however, it would send the wrong message.

part

one

1

the birth of Freedom

And before I be a slave, I'll be
buried in my grave and go home
to my Lord and be Free.
—Negro spiritual

*H*arry "Freedom" Hudson saw the old house and wondered why it had come to mean so much to him. He'd driven by this place many times, and it always reached out to him and called him back. Something in the boarded up corner house wanted him there, even in the midst of all the gentrification and the onslaught of yuppies. It was white flight in reverse. The park across from the brownstone was filled with children, mostly white; an odd thing in Harlem.

Harlem belonged to him, to his people now. As he slowed and pulled up to the curb, he had a feeling that one day he'd own this house. What he didn't know was that this brownstone would come to own him.

Freedom, as he was known by the hip-hop world, was born Harry Hudson on the coldest October night New York had experienced in over one hundred years. "I'm not going to let the Devil steal my joy," his mother, Earlene, had said as she tried to start the engine of her old Chevy. The pain came suddenly and passed just as quickly. By the time she reached the hospital, she could feel Harry trying to make his way here. She drove up to the emergency room, blowing her horn and screaming in the Southern accent that had long been replaced by Brooklynese. The emergency room attendants who ran out to help her were shocked to see the crown of the boy's head on her seat.

"That boy always knew how to make his own way," Harry's mother would say later.

Harry never knew his father, and was raised by his mother and grandmother, who instilled in him a fierce independence. As a young boy, Harry always felt, even if it was not apparent to those around him, that he'd been born to do something major. He had no idea what that something was, but he knew he had to be ready. Thankfully, he was good at just about everything he put his hands to. Not just good; he mastered any area of study quickly, but he got tired of it quickly, too.

Harry finally found his "freedom" in music as a hip-hop producer, and it was his style, or "stylo" as he called it, that everyone wanted. Freedom was being pulled in so many directions now that he had little time to create. But he wasn't convinced that the record companies truly wanted or understood his creativity. They just wanted more of what had made them rich and him famous; the phat sound that put all of his artists on the charts and brought renewed prestige to a sinking music corporation. KMB Records paid him the crazy fees he asked for. Freedom laughed at the fact that his fees were based on whether or not he wanted a job. If he didn't really want the work, he charged a higher price. He'd gotten joy out of charging mad fees for tunes he made up on the spot and rejoiced when he charged people who didn't remember that they'd once told him he would never get work in the recording industry. When he first started out, he heard every rejection for every reason possible.

Initially, the industry people told Freedom that his sound was too repetitive, then they said his music didn't have a hook. After a while, Freedom ignored the criticism and just did what he felt. "Go with your heart," his mother had always told him. And it worked almost all of the time. Almost.

Freedom had many women in his life, but he only allowed his mother and grandmother into his heart. To say that Freedom was unlucky in love would be like saying Phyllis Hyman could sing. Both statements were true, but were grossly understated. Phyllis Hyman did more than sing. She ripped out your heart with every note and phrase. Phyllis made you feel all her sadness, and she made you feel like it was yours. But she warned you just the same. "Be Careful How You Use My Love" was the song Freedom thought of whenever he thought about the concept of love. There was a wall around his heart that was as ancient as the pain of black men. He wore that wall like a stick on a kid's shoulder, daring anyone bad enough to knock it off. Freedom loved women; he just didn't know how *to be in love* with them. He'd allowed himself to fall in love once, a very long time ago, but had no intention of making that mistake again.

Freedom was raised by women before psychologists had a chance to declare that not having a father was dysfunctional. For Freedom, it was heaven and he loved the balance provided by his mother and grandmother. Still, something was missing.

Shy, self-conscious, and an only child, Harry had very few playmates, so he filled the gap by creating his own imaginary ones. But to Harry these playmates sometimes seemed real, like long-gone relatives come back to play.

His grandmother was never bothered by these "playmates," but his mother didn't like it. "Stop talking to yourself, son, and go out and play," she'd tell him.

"Leave him alone, gal," his grandmother would argue, "he's talking to his people."

Sometimes at his mother's request, Harry would try to shut out the voices he heard—deep, lilting voices that told him stories and sang him songs. One day a voice called him to the window.

"Yo Tayembé," he heard the voice say. Harry didn't know the meaning of these words. They sounded familiar to him, but he couldn't exactly remember where he'd heard them.

"Yo Tayembé," the voice said again. Young Harry walked toward the window looking for the source of the voice, but didn't see anyone. He climbed into the window seat and threw open the window and stuck his head out. Still, he saw nothing. Quietly but suddenly a wave of sadness enveloped him, and he began to cry.

"Where is my father?" Harry said aloud. Just as he said this,

his mother entered the room. "Where is my father?" he repeated as he turned to her from the window seat.

"He's gone and he's been gone for a long time. Now come down from there," she said, trying to remain calm.

Harry wanted to do what his mother said, but became dizzy and lost his footing. His mother rushed to him and pulled him back in. "Ye oh Ye Ba Ba," he chanted before losing consciousness.

From then on Harry's mother forbade even the mention of an invisible playmate. Earlene argued for days with her mother, before she told her about the incident at the window. Harry's grandmother responded as Earlene assumed she would, by going into a mode of prayer and fasting, saying that little Harry was under spiritual attack. Finally, though his grandmother was too proud to verbalize it, she silently relented and decided to go along with her daughter. Grand would no longer indulge her grandson and his belief in his imaginary playmates.

Around this time Harry started communicating without speaking. He would play drumbeats on any surface with any object. In school he'd use his pencil and beat out rhythms on his notebook. At first, he played so softly that no one noticed. But the playing was accompanied by what appeared to be daydreaming, and it grew louder.

"Hey, Little Drummer Boy," his fifth-grade teacher yelled. The entire class laughed at the name and began to use it with a vengeance as children do. "Drummer" was slowly replaced with "Dumber," and so he was known throughout his school career as the "Dumber Boy," which put him just above the most unpopular boy who everyone called "Stinkweed."

Despite his nickname, Harry continued to play his beats,

luxuriating in the steady waves of music ever present in his head. One day he felt the rhythm in his heart swirl and dash whenever a certain little girl was around. Stacey Brown. For days he let her name move around in his brain, dancing in between beats. *Stacey*—*"ba ding ding"*—*Brown,* he would think, *was cute*—"ra dat dat"—*smart, and popular.* He didn't care that the main reason the other boys liked her was because she developed early.

"Hey, Harry," she whispered as she passed him one day in the hall. He usually heard his name from older adults, rarely from children, so when she spoke to him, he couldn't believe it, and couldn't respond. For weeks after Stacey first said his name, the shy Harry allowed himself to dream about what he'd overheard other boys say they were doing with girls. Harry imagined what it would feel like to kiss Stacey and touch her all over. Then he imagined doing "it."

Finally, after a great deal of mental preparation, Harry worked up the nerve to ask Stacey to the movies. He approached her at the end of their sixth-period class. "Stacey," he stammered, "would you . . . would you . . ." Harry was so taken with her he was unable to complete his sentence. Instead, he began to tap out beats on the books he'd been holding.

Stacey had liked Harry, but popular girls like to stay popular. Talking to Harry when no one was looking was one thing, but just as he began to drum, a group of her friends walked up and created within her the need to be nasty. "Spit it out Drummer Boy, or should I say Dumber Boy?" and without any concern for Harry's feelings, she ran off.

Harry stood frozen in the hall, and remained in the same spot until the school building closed. During those painful two hours, Harry made plans to take revenge on Stacey and all the other women he would ever come into contact with. "Someday, they're gonna want to be with me, and *I'll* be the one to run away."

It would take Freedom his entire life to realize that too often childhood wishes become the motivation for the misbehavior of adults.

2

the Devil's wages

he cell phone in Freedom's car rang, and his thoughts faded back to the tune he'd promised someone.

"Peace," he barked into the phone.

"Somebody page me?" the familiar voice asked.

"Peace," he said, smiling. "Ava, I need you to get on something right away."

"What you trying to say, brother? Don't I always act quickly? That's the way I handle all your shit."

"Don't cuss. It ain't ladylike," Freedom said to his attorney.

"What do you need, my brother?" Ava Vercher was a Harvard-educated lawyer with a Brooklyn style. She was an excellent attorney and could have joined any of the top firms, but she chose to do her own thing instead. "Besides," she had always told the white recruiters, "my behind won't fit those little suits y'all have to wear." Instead, she wore African-inspired clothes such as the kind designed by Moshood that allowed more than ample room for her larger than average body. In downtown Manhattan she was considered overweight, but in Harlem and Brooklyn she was fine. Ava felt beautiful when she was with her own people, so that's where she stayed.

When Freedom told her about the house and his need to have it, she responded by saying, "You don't want that run-down piece of shit—I mean stuff—choir boy. Besides, that whole area is white as the North Pole. I happen to know on good authority that the only reason that place is empty is because it's haunted."

"Yeah, but I'm gonna haunt *you* if you don't get me that house." With that, Freedom hung up and drove off. He always knew when Ava was pulling his chain. Back when he first hired her, she'd told him that a white woman was suing him for child support. Most of her other clients would have gone into a rage, but Freedom just laughed and told her she'd better start working on a countersuit.

"How can you be so sure the kid's not yours?" Ava asked.

Freedom laughed and told her, " 'Cause I don't put my stuff in no stuff that don't look like the stuff I came from." They both laughed, and from that point on, Freedom was one of her favorite clients, and Ava by far his favorite female—not including family, of course.

As he remembered that encounter with Ava, Freedom thought that this haunted house business was just another one of her crazy pranks. But he didn't have time to think about it all now. He needed to get to the studio. He had work to do.

Freedom considered his real "work" the tunes he created for himself: music that no major record label would ever release because it was filled with the messages of the love he longed for and the revolution he dreamed of starting.

He got paid for creating music that was entirely different than the music he made for himself, but believed that he had to do what he had to do, and making the kind of commercially demanded music the record company wanted would give him the economic independence to do what he *really* wanted to do artistically.

"This whole business is about leverage, Grand," Freedom had said to his grandmother, and had then reluctantly allowed her to hear one of his recordings, a cut called "Buck Naked," that had become a number one hit for three months. His grandmother immediately went into a prayer.

"Lord, please save my child from hisself. He's walked into a place where he's not protected. Ain't no truth in it. Lead him back to wisdom, God. Call him by his name." When she was finished praying a prayer that was lengthy, even for her, Freedom told her that he had to do this kind of work until he was so popular that he would be able to do whatever he wanted.

"Grand," he'd said, "when you get a certain amount of money and power, people pay you what you want to balance the scales back toward them. It's complicated, but you'll under-stand later."

His grandmother stared at Freedom long enough to make him uncomfortable. "Son, you can't work for the Devil and ex-pect to get heavenly wages." With that she left the place where she'd been sitting, went to her room, and shut the door.

Now all the music Freedom produced went to the top of the charts, and he was the most popular hip-hop producer in the business. He'd won a Grammy for his category of music four years in a row and he was in demand. So much in demand that he was not free to produce anything *he* wanted to. He tried to share his own creations with a record executive once, but was shut down before he ever had the chance to play the demo.

"Yeah, yeah," the man told him. "We'll do that next time out. I've got three new artists I need you to handle."

At that time Freedom had figured that he just needed more leverage. Today, however, he remembered his grandmother's comments and got her message loud and clear. Maybe he was earning the Devil's wages after all.

As he drove over the bridge to the New Jersey studio, he tried to imagine his life in what he knew would be his new home in Harlem. When he couldn't conjure the image quickly, he let his mind wander and started thinking about the woman he'd been with the night before. She was wild and fine. The physical pleasure was the memory he wanted to revisit, but then the emotional thing hit him. She'd already called him five times, and it wasn't even noon. He remembered how good it felt to climax, only to have the pleasure disappear in a flash when the woman started telling him that she loved him and had to have him in her life. He'd tried to explain that it wouldn't work, but it only made her cry. He hated to make any woman cry. It always made him think of the nights when he'd heard his mother crying about the things his father had either done or not done.

Freedom had once vowed to never be the rolling stone that his father had been, yet he'd become just that.

This woman's crying had the opposite effect than the one she desired, but he couldn't tell her that. Instead, he said they'd take things slowly and see where they'd end up, but then he stupidly made love to her again.

As she slept, dreaming of the life he knew they'd never have together, he slipped out of her house. *I'll deal with that later,* he told himself.

His one-night stands always left him unfulfilled and feeling shameful. He knew his grandmother would have hated the way he treated women.

While his mother had been the hardworking disciplinarian who kept him on track, his grandmother made sure that he was properly spoiled. Grand was the love of his life. "Aw, gowan and git dat boy whatever he wants," she'd say to his mother right in front of him. No matter how much his mother argued and swore to never back down, he knew that his grandmother would win. She always did.

Despite his closeness with his grandmother, Freedom and his mother shared an undeniably strong bond, and not just because they were mother and son. They were a whole lot alike, and he respected all that she was. With his grandmother, it was something else, something he couldn't put a finger on. Maybe it was her age or the era she was from. She had a way of always knowing what he needed and what he was feeling and would meet those needs with just the right look or an old song. Freedom would frequently fall asleep with his head in her lap, even when he was way past the age when that was culturally or socially acceptable. And he would tell her everything—except the way he dealt with women.

He was sure she knew that part of him, though. He would see the look on her face after he'd had one of his nights. It was a look of pure disappointment. On one balmy autumn evening after she'd given Freedom one of those looks, his grandmother passed away.

Freedom's mind went back to that night. He could still smell the meal she had cooked. Pork chops and baked beans.

"That stuff will kill you, Grand," Freedom had said. "Pork ain't nothin' but death. Death given to us by The Man. You know you shouldn't be—"

When Freedom's grandmother raised her hand and said "Don't change the subject on me, boy," he knew he was about to be lectured. Grand was always able to look at Freedom and see clear through him.

"You need to do better by women, boy," was all she finally said.

"I treat you and Moms real good." Freedom smiled to erase the disappointment that was coming from her but his grandmother wasn't having it.

"You keep trying to be the center of attention when real joy is all in the corners."

Unsure of what she meant, Freedom continued with his own argument. "Like I said," Freedom continued, "I try to take the best care of you, but you gotta help me. For real, Grand. You need to cool it with the pork. Swine is death."

Freedom's grandmother finally smiled at her grandson. "I been eating pork for way longer than the twenty-eight years you been on this planet. When it's my time, it's my time. I'm ready. Are you?" Grand asked him.

"Uh-oh, is it time for my 'Jesus is coming back' speech? Love you, Grand, but I gotta go." With that, he did. He often played that moment over again in his mind. Grand died that night in her sleep. The cause was not diabetes or high blood pressure; her cholesterol was perfect. It had been, just as Grand said, "Her time."

3

Ngozi's capture

. . . And the wicked carried
us away to captivity.

—*Negro spiritual*

*N*gozi *felt others around him. Men and women were crying in languages some of which he'd heard before, but most he had not. His eyes were ready to see, but his heart was not. Ngozi was wedged in between and chained to strangers who were now linked together in a common suffering. Some were as young as he was and others younger, but all were crying and screaming. He would later learn that those who captured him would have no need for elders, but in his village the elders were the center of life. "Mama,"*

he cried. "Why did you not tell me? Where am I, and why am I here?"

Ngozi took in his surroundings and became sick from the foul stench of waste and sweat that was around him. His own sickness added to the thick air.

Someone behind him yelled over the screams. "Brother Ngozi, it is I, Stabo."

Ngozi's heart leapt at the sound of the familiar voice, but he felt no joy. He cried, "My brother, how is it that you too have been captured?"

Stabo, who was a part of Ngozi's village and the husband of his sister, cried loudly. Then he told the tale of his capture. He told of being beaten and dragged by men he'd never seen. Fierce warriors whose markings were not familiar had brought him to the water house where they now were. "We are moving, my brother," Stabo said. "We are far from home, and I am told we will never go back again."

Ngozi was silent. He thought of what his mother had told him. He had been preparing himself for death, but this was not the death he was prepared for.

This death was the death of separation. A separation from his true self and from those who were like him. Now he knew the power of the drum, and he fully understood why his mother told him to make it. It was to be a voice that would connect those who had been captured. For although they were from different villages, different tribes, they were one people, and now they were experiencing a similar death.

Ngozi wept for the loss of the village, the loss of his family, and he wept because he had no way to tell his family where he was or what was happening. He would never be able to tell those he left behind about his life in this strange place.

Ngozi wept until he had no more tears.

4

Ava takes care of business

> If you don't know where you're from,
> you can't know where you're going.
> —*Pastor Ralph Buchanan*

"What's up, my brother?" Ava said into the speakerphone. Her tone was businesslike and serious, but kind. She didn't much care for the real estate attorney on the other end of the receiver, but she respected his business savvy, and knew he would find out all he could about the house and maybe even get it for the right price.

"Mr. Campbell, I need your services, brother," Ava said to

Charles Campbell III, who had been Chucky, the neighborhood nerd, until he left for Princeton and came back white.

Charles smiled at his speakerphone and wished he could be as free as Ava. In truth he wished he could be with her. Instead, Charles had learned to act as if he liked more professional women, women who had perfectly combed hair, women who didn't laugh as loud as Ava, women who just weren't fun. But when he got right down to it, Charles wasn't much fun himself.

Whenever he'd run into someone from his old neighborhood, his mind would rush back to late-night games of hide-and-seek with a girl from down the street. Ava had a wide gap between her two front teeth, and whenever she smiled, which was almost always, Chucky wanted to take up residence right there in that gap. He could not have been more than eleven years old, but he'd observed his mother and her boyfriend, and thought he knew a little bit about love from watching them. Chucky had also heard the bigger boys talk about something called sex and how good it felt and figured if he could just kiss that girl with the gap, his life would be a whole lot better.

"Mr. Campbell," Ava said, interrupting his thoughts. "The house on the corner, across from the park. I need to know if it's available."

"Oh yeah, sorry," Charles said. "My secretary just came in. I'll get back to you in a moment," Charles said to the air. He had been so lost in thought that he heard none of what Ava had said past the initial request.

"Do you have an address?" he asked. Ava gave him the address and asked him to get back to her with the cost and other details as soon as possible.

"I heard that place is haunted, and that's why it's still empty," Ava said. Charles was now on the same page.

"You mean that house on Harriet Tubman Terrace just off the corner of One hundred thirty-eighth?" Charles asked.

"What do you think I've been rambling about?" Ava asked.

"I'm sure there is a reasonable explanation for all of those occurrences, most of which, by the way, are exaggerated," Charles informed her.

"Whatever." Ava sighed. "Get me some numbers. I may have a buyer, but it depends on the price."

"Really? When would you like to see it?" Charles asked.

"I'll get back to you," Ava told him. "Right now, I need that information for my client. Thanks," Ava said, and hung up.

Now it was Ava's turn to laugh. She would get the house for less than Charles would offer, and she'd get the city to pay for the renovations. But what really made her smile was the idea that she'd make Mr. Charles "Chucky" Campbell III remember where he was from.

5

•━◆━•

time is running out

How long before you think he gets here?" the voice asked.

"Don't know, but it better be soon," the second voice answered. "Time is running out for our people."

"Seems like it's taken him forever to find this place," the first voice offered.

"Yes, but this is how it's to be. Everything in its time."

As Freedom got closer to Manhattan, his cell phone rang. The music was kicking from his car stereo, and it was loud enough for others to hear, even with the windows of his Mercedes SUV completely shut. He was listening to Kathleen Battle's "So Many Stars." Freedom enjoyed every kind of music.

"If you want to make phat sounds, you gotta listen to everything," he was known to say. "You get a note from here, a hook from there, the beat from the sound of some drunk trying to find his way home. The music is everywhere, but you have to listen for it," he once told a magazine reporter. For the most part, Freedom liked to talk about *his* music, but he never told anyone about the rhythms of his childhood or the voices he used to hear.

"Peace," Freedom barked into the cell phone. "Whoever's on the other end, please turn that shit down."

Elum N Nation didn't have the same need for variety that Freedom had and was blaring some gangsta rap.

"What's up?" Freedom asked the rap artist who he'd taken to the top of the charts.

"What's up?" Nation yelled. "What's up is that you were supposed to be here an hour ago." Elum N Nation took a toke of whatever he was smoking.

"On my way now. What's the rush?" Freedom asked.

"The rush is we need you to start the session," Elum said.

"On my way. Stay up. Peace," he said as he ended the call.

Freedom did everything in his own time. He was always late and often missed appointments. "You're only late once," he'd say. "Five minutes or five days, late is late. People who get pissed about time will find something else to be pissed about when you're on time," he reasoned. His relationship with time was unreasonably strained, and he had his own theory. "We should control time and stop letting time control us," Freedom liked to say. "Time ain't real. It's a construct." Now that he was important, few people argued with him.

It was a known fact in the music industry that Freedom required little time to do what he did. Other producers might show up early, but they often ran over the allotted time. Freedom showed up late and left early. He usually got the sound he needed from an artist in one or two takes. If later on, while mixing the tracks, he felt that he needed more, he simply created the tracks electronically. Once he'd even mixed his own vocals over those of the artist's. The music executives loved the results and wanted to keep it. When the record was released, it immediately went to number one.

As Freedom pulled up to the studio, a young assistant came out to meet him.

"Hi, I'm Tangy," she said between cracking sounds she made with her chewing gum. "Pleased to meet you, Mr. Freedom," she said. Her clothes were at least two sizes too small, and there was little left to Freedom's imagination.

He preferred to have something to think about, but he didn't discriminate. "Check you later," he said.

Tangy had already taken his car keys and was moving into the driver's seat. She'd park the car and do anything else Freedom wanted. These "assistants" were now part of his package.

"Everyone's waiting inside. Is there anything I can get you?" she yelled back to Freedom.

"Not right now," he said, smiling.

Elum N Nation's lyrics were like pure darkness, but the beat was righteous. There was something alluring about the beat that could even make church ladies want to "back that thang up," but once they heard the lyrics, they'd be brought back to their senses. Elum N Nation's music was misogynistic, violent, and not at all pro-black. The uncensored version of Elum N Nation's songs were banned on most radio stations, which only made them much more popular. When a radio station did play his music, there was so much foul language to be bleeped out, his tunes were called the Bleeper Songs.

"Hey stank 'bleep,' come sit on my 'bleep.' You a dumb 'bleep' nig-'bleep,' but I want it now. When I say it, bring it here cause this boy ain't gonna wait. I wanna bring slavery back cause you my Black 'bleep.' "

"What up, baby?" Elum asked when he saw Freedom walk into the studio. Elum was high and happy and the gold and diamonds that adorned every one of his fingers caught the reflection of the low light as he reached out to embrace his producer. A huge diamond-studded medallion hung around Elum's neck and swung down below his waist.

"Alright. You ready?" Freedom asked.

"I was born ready," Elum barked back.

Freedom sat down at the sound deck and got to work. Within eight hours, he had laid not just all the tracks but also Tangy the assistant.

Feeling done but not satisfied, Freedom drove back to the house on Tubman Terrace and sat in front of the place that he was determined to make his own and took in all the details.

The house would need to be renovated, but it had good bones. The front steps had begun to crumble. The ironwork was rusted, and some of the windows had been broken. But he could also see the fine work that had gone into the place. Four different faces had been carved into the bricks of the archway. The railing, while rusted, spiraled into a braid and then curved into the head of a snake. A small apple protruded from the snake's mouth. As Freedom sat watching the house, he thought he spotted a light inside. The light flickered suddenly, and though he watched the same second-floor window, he didn't see it again. Suddenly Freedom was hearing rhythms. He looked down and noticed that he was the source of the sound. Unconsciously, he was beating out rhythms on the dashboard of his SUV.

Freedom stopped himself and decided to head home and get some sleep.

Inside the Harlem brownstone, it was neither late nor early. Time was simply drawing nearer.

6

a little sleep,
a little slumber

The difference between grown
folks and babies is a nap.
—*Mother Berry*

reedom only slept a few hours
and was restless, mentally and physically, so he went for a run.

"Boy, you need to sleep to hear what the ancestors are telling you," his grandmother used to say.

"Now, Grand," Freedom always responded, "sleep is for lazy people and old folks, except *you*." His grandmother would shake her head and mumble something about fools and babies, and then go back to the task at hand.

Freedom thought about his grandmother now as he ran. Running was how he got his energy and his ideas, so he would usually run five, or sometimes ten, miles a day.

Today Freedom hummed the tune he'd been sampling and reminded himself to pull another album by the same artist. He loved sampling short phrases from cats like Sinatra, Frankie Vallee, and the Allman Brothers. Whites had stolen their whole doo-wop from us, he reasoned, so it was past time for a little payback. While other producers and musicians sampled black artists, Freedom took pleasure in ripping off the rip-offs. It was his version of restitution, his forty acres and a mule.

After he ran eight miles, he took a long hot shower and was set. Then Freedom waded through the clutter of his bedroom. His mother used to come over and "organize" his things only to be told they were already organized.

But Freedom's crib, as he called it, was in total disarray. Albums and CDs were everywhere. Videotapes and video games were piled on the floor around the cart that was supposed to house them. Clothes were strewn everywhere and so was money. It was as if Freedom had no respect for the things he'd worked hard to get. Checks, cash, and coins of all denominations lay on his bed and dresser, as if he never intended to use them. The only items that seemed to be revered were his production equipment and the photos of his mother and grandmother. The latter hung on the wall just over the area where his equipment was placed. Once a female friend complained that she felt the photographs were watching her.

"They are," Freedom told her. Later that evening when he'd gone to the bathroom, he returned to find that the woman had taken the pictures down. Freedom said nothing. He simply tossed the woman her clothes and walked out to his car. After about twenty minutes, she realized Freedom wasn't coming back. She got dressed, went out, and found him sitting there. She got in and asked what happened. Freedom said nothing. He just blasted his music and drove the woman back to her apartment. She was yet another woman Freedom would never see or call again.

Freedom spent several hours listening to the tracks he'd laid down the night before. They were weak, but it wasn't his fault. "Can't get blood from a turnip," his grandmother would say. But what he considered weak, record executives and Elum N Nation would consider brilliant.

Freedom ejected the tape from the deck and popped in Phyllis Hyman. "Why did you have to die?" he asked out loud. "We could have made beautiful music," he said to the haunting melodies.

Freedom's cell phone rang, and after a few seconds, just before the call went into voice mail, he found the phone under the pillow he'd briefly slept on.

"Peace," he said.

"I knew you'd be up," his attorney said in her "I bet I was up before you were" voice.

"Hey," Freedom said to Ava.

"So, I been checking into this house thing," she said, changing the subject. "It's available, but it's been tied up in a trust. Fortunately, I happen to know the attorney who's handling it. Believe it or not," she said shyly, "we went to school together."

"Yeah?" Freedom said.

"Yes," she replied. "He's one of those 'I'm-not-really-from-the-hood-so-there's-no one-for-me-to-give-anything-back-to' brothers."

"Sounds like your type," Freedom teased. "But seriously, when do I move in?"

"From what my research tells me," she told him, "I'm going to have to do some fancy dancing. I'll do what I can to get you inside to see it quickly. And then you can see for yourself exactly *why* it's empty. I'm telling you, Freedom, the place is *haunted.*"

"Enough with that haunted madness."

"Alright, but when the ghosts come and get you, don't say I didn't warn you," she added.

"Girl, the only thing haunting me is the thought of *you* being with me."

"Right," Ava said, and hung up. She knew that her phone would immediately ring and that Freedom would be on the other end demanding that she end the conversation properly.

"You better tell me 'Peace' before I fire you," he would always say.

Today would not be any different.

7

a private matter

> History. Lived not written, is such a thing
> not to understand always, but to marvel.
>
> —*J. California Cooper*

M r. Campbell, please," Ava said on the phone to Charles's assistant.

"May I ask who's calling?" she asked.

Ava hated this question. She always wanted to say, "No, you may not." Either your boss is in or he's not. *Screen the call after you know who's on the other end,* she thought to herself. Instead, she answered politely. "Yes, you may. This is Ava Vercher. V-e-r-c-h-e-r." She spelled the name slowly. It was an odd name, but that's why she liked it. Ava knew that calls were returned and new appointments were kept because the name "Vercher" didn't sound like the name of a black attorney from Brooklyn. Vercher was her sister Myrna's last name. Myrna had raised Ava after their mother died when Ava was only five and just starting school. There was a thirteen-year gap between Ava and her sister, and although Myrna was young, she was a good mother to Ava. On the first day of school after their mother had died Ava saw the way the teacher looked at her and then at her very fair-skinned sister.

"Why is your child's last name different from yours?" Ava was named Brown after her black father. Myrna was a Vercher like her white father. In a very certain tone, Ava's sister told the teacher that it was a private matter. Young Ava loved the sound of that phrase "private matter."

"That means it's our business," Myrna would tell her little sister later. From then on, whenever anyone asked Ava something she didn't want to answer or something she didn't know the answer to, she would say, "It's a private matter." The answer worked well in her life, but she didn't want to be different from her sister, so along with her phrases and mannerisms, Ava took her sister's name.

"I'm calling Mr. Campbell about a property he's researching for me." Ava wanted to add her bra and panty size for the assistant, but decided against it.

"One moment please," the assistant replied.

He's either sleeping with her, or he used to, Ava said to herself once she heard the Muzak playing in her ear. Marvin Gaye's "What's Going On?" had been desecrated. *What is* really *going on?* Ava thought.

"Ava, good to hear from you," Charles said a few minutes

later, and a bit too happily for Ava. "I've done some preliminary work and found out that the house is available, but it's not as reasonable as I thought."

Ava wanted to say, "Look Chucky, you know I knew you when you were called Pee Pee boy," but again, she held her tongue. "Right," she said instead. "Look, I'm gonna be up-front with you because I know you'd do the same for me. My client wants the property, and I want him to have it. But I'm not going to let his wants outshine his needs. Before I even step foot in that haunted hellhole, I want figures—the *real* figures. When can we meet?"

Mr. Charles "Large and In-Charge" Campbell III was taken by surprise. "Um, um, well, I have to look at my calendar," he stammered.

"Calendar, my big butt," Ava said. "Now, you know I don't like to play hardball, because I *am* hardball, so I don't have to play. But for you, homeboy, I will. Meet me at, say, six o'clock, House of Tina. You remember the place?" Ava asked.

She knew that Charles was familiar with the neighborhood Chinese restaurant-nightclub that she'd forced him to meet her at before. Several years before, when they'd first reconnected, Charles said that he would prefer to do business over dinner, and he rather gallantly allowed her to pick the place. But he wasn't too thrilled when she chose a place in their old Brooklyn neighborhood. He'd planned on dazzling Ava with his new, improved self. Instead, he regressed into a grown-up version of Chucky. Now she was forcing that regression again.

"Can't we, I mean, is it possible for us to meet someplace else, someplace more—"

"White?" Ava interrupted. "No. I have to do some volunteer work at the shelter around the corner from there, so

HOT"—as she alone called House of Tina—"is the best I can do. You want to get rid of that albatross, don't you?"

"Fine," Charles said.

"Then, six o'clock it is," she added. "Oh, by the way, Charles, bring your dancing shoes. It's Ladies' Night."

Charles was fuming, but Ava was smiling, exposing the beautiful gap between her two front teeth that Charles Campbell III had fallen in love with long ago, when he was still called Chucky.

8

memories of long ago

> We wish to plead our own cause.
>
> —*Marcus Garvey*

The house on Tubman Terrace played back memories like a stereo programmed on repeat. The memories of its inhabitants rushed in like waves on a shore. Each one came in farther and farther until they had to recede and start over again. The memories were always the same, but sometimes, depending on the tide, they were more and more intense. At such times, the memories were close enough and loud enough to be felt by people outside the house, and anyone who happened to be near the house on Tubman Terrace would be carried away with those tides.

When they returned, they would not be themselves. Once people were touched by those tides they were changed forever.

Years before, in the twenties, a gangster had moved into the house. A month later he was found dead. The police, lacking any evidence of forced entry, ruled the death a suicide, but the folks who worked for him knew otherwise.

Tonight the memories played loudly.

Ngozi awoke hoping this all had been a dream. It was not. Cold water had been thrown at him with all the fervor of a sharpened spear. The water hit him like thousands of tiny knives meant to kill, but intending to do so slowly.

"Get up, you lazy dog," the voice of the pale man said.

Ngozi could not understand the words, but his spirit could interpret the hatred. He pulled himself upward and tried to shake off his pain. His body ached in places he hardly ever thought about. From the pit of his stomach to the lower part of his neck, he felt as if he'd been sliced in the same manner that one would open the prize of a difficult hunt. His wrist and ankles bled from the constant pulling they had received on board the ship, but the greatest pain was in his heart. He felt an emptiness he had experienced once long ago.

Years before, he'd fallen from a tree and hit the ground so hard his breath left his body. But very quickly his breath was restored, so he childishly climbed the tree again. Now it was as if he was falling and hitting the ground over and over again, so quickly that the life force could not come back, so quickly that he couldn't remember his life before this moment at all. He wished for death, but Ngozi knew that death could only come when he was ready, or at a point when he was doing his descendants more harm than they could ever overcome. This was the gracefulness of his God, to allow entrance into the next life when the spirit was prepared. He realized all that he had been: son, husband, brother, warrior. And he thought of everything that he no longer was.

Ngozi stood an entire foot and a half taller than the man who hated him, but the pale man's hatred loomed larger. Ngozi thought of the proverb his father spoke. "When you meet an envious man on the road and you pass him by, if the kindness in your heart is not as great as the hatred in his, you will become envious and full of hatred also. The man who is more committed to his feelings is the man who wins in the battle of spirits." Ngozi knew that the pale man was winning in the battle of spirits. And although Ngozi had reason to feel hatred toward the man, Ngozi had not been taught to hate; all he could feel for this man was pity. The pain in Ngozi's heart was not wild enough to push forth the poison of hate. It would be many generations before his children's children would be strong enough to walk among men who harbored enough hatred to enslave others. Once their hatred matched that of their captor, they would have forgotten the proverb that taught their ancestors that the only weapon that can do battle with hatred is the weapon of love and peace.

9

• ◆ •

between the beats

When you walk in purpose,
you collide with destiny.
—Pastor Ralph Buchanan

Freedom left his place in Brooklyn and drove to Manhattan. He had to meet a film producer who wanted some of his work for a movie. During the first part of his drive, Freedom felt like he should change his name. *I had more freedom when I was just Harry Hudson who cleaned banks after school when he was a kid,* he reflected.

He turned off at the next exit to go to the office where his appointment was. When he did, he saw that he was near the house on Tubman. He was already late, but chose to drive by the house and take in the fine architectural details. As he slowed to a stop, the same flicker of lights he'd seen last time danced in the upper window. *Must be my eyes,* Freedom thought to himself as he closed them. When he did, he heard the beating of a distant drum. Between the beats, Freedom could hear the sound of waves crashing into a shoreline. Had it not been for the sound of the water, Freedom would have assumed that the drum sounds were coming from one of his soon-to-be white neighbors, trying to connect with the spirit of Harlem. But Freedom was startled and somewhat frightened by the sound and when his eyes fluttered open, the sound disappeared and the dancing lights were gone. "Whoo," Freedom said out loud. "I need to stop listening to Ava's madness. She got me hearing *and* seeing things."

Freedom laughed uneasily and pulled away from the curb. Just as he did, a small boy, who looked to be no more than five years old, darted across the street in front of his car. Freedom swerved and slammed on his brakes, barely missing the boy. Freedom immediately looked for the child's parents so he could give them a good piece of his mind. But he didn't see anyone at all. He turned to yell at the kid, but couldn't find him either.

All of this had taken place in a matter of seconds, but the street was large enough to take longer than that to cross. Feeling cheated, Freedom cursed the air instead. If he had bothered to look in his rearview mirror, he would have seen the child, or rather, the spirit of the child in the backseat of his SUV. Johnny, as he had been known in life, had his hand over his mouth to muffle the sound of his laughter. Knowing that he could not go beyond this street until he'd made a connection, as Freedom pulled off, the little boy reluctantly left the car.

"See you later, alligator," Johnny said to the back of Freedom's head, and then was gone.

10

the office fling

va was filling out her last intake form at the women's shelter where she volunteered. Even though the place was full, compared to summer when this place would be overflowing, this was a slow period. Ava quickly learned the effects heat had on the human temper. In her first summer there she'd more than served her time as a volunteer. The shelter had been swamped—violence went up with the temperature. In between checking women in she gave legal counsel to women who couldn't afford it. Her friend Meredith, who was good at getting folks to volunteer, had convinced Ava to work at the shelter. Ava often wondered how she did it. Meredith was mild mannered and humble, but when it came to community work, she was a warrior.

When Ava began volunteering at the shelter, she was surprised to find out that very few battered women were ready to divorce their abusers. She was even more surprised by the number of women who went back to their men, only to return to the shelter a few months later.

Meredith told her, "This is why we need you."

"I'm a lawyer. I should be giving legal advice," she told her friend.

"What's even more important," Meredith said, "is that they see a strong sister who has made it and can take care of herself. They need to see that you exist."

Ava thought about this now as she sat in the closet that had been converted to an office. "Yeah, if the Harvard boys could see me now," she said to no one.

Although Ava did not regret her decision to work for herself and her people, she often wondered what her life would have been like had she chosen a different path. She wondered if she'd be married with kids, or simply lonely and chasing someone else's dreams. Ava couldn't admit to herself that she was lonely, so she decided that her single life was a choice. She was certain that she'd rather be miserable alone than wrapped up in some brother's madness.

But in quiet moments, Ava knew that her real fear was in surrendering herself to just the *idea* of love. She thought of love as an ocean in which you either get lost or drown. Ava, always the practical one, preferred solid ground, and the single life in which there was no possibility of abuse or arguments. No one to leave the toilet seat up or care that she had left it down. In her heart she wished for balanced love, but in her life she settled for what she knew she could control.

Ava looked at her watch and saw that it was already twenty minutes to six in the evening. She wanted to be at House of Tina before Charles. Ava filled out the rest of the forms in the stack that sat before her and dashed into the bathroom for a quick freshening up. She checked her reflection in the mirror and then dabbed a bit of frankincense and myrrh behind her ears, on her temples and wrists, and left for her appointment.

The weather was mild, so Ava walked the few blocks to House of Tina. Once there, Ava was greeted by Tina herself.

"You not been here long time," Tina said in her Chinese-Brooklyn accent. Ava stifled the desire to laugh that always came whenever she spoke to Tina.

"I know. I've been real busy," Ava replied.

"You too busy for your soul sister?" Tina asked. Tina was married to a brother that no one had ever seen in person. The story was that he lived somewhere down South and that Tina visited him on holidays. This was just one of the many mysteries surrounding Tina.

Tina sashayed her tiny body around Ava's and escorted her to what she thought of as the best seat in the house, placed at the center of the restaurant. Tables on the dinner side of the restaurant-nightclub were decorated with bright pink tablecloths topped off with red glass candles, which Tina lit for Ava. "You want order now, or you wait for some fine soul brother?" Tina asked.

"I'm waiting," Ava said, "but I don't know how fine he is."

Tina laughed. "You so funny, soul sister," she said as she moved on. "I send my best girl to wait on you," she shot back. Ava took in the familiar surroundings. She could see the dance floor from where she was. DJ Donny was already setting up.

"What's up, sis?" he asked between movements as he unloaded what was known to be the best record collection in all of Brooklyn.

"You got it, my brother," Ava answered.

"Gots to be a good night if you up in here," he said.

"And you know that," she added. Ava looked over the menu even though she knew what she would order. Tina's specialty was chicken and ribs, Chinese style, but she made a mean pot of greens, too. Ava always ordered the vegetable plate and vegetable fried rice. Ava looked around to see if Charles had managed to slip in, and instead she caught her reflection in the smoky block mirrors that covered the back wall. Against the wall was a big wicker chair where scantily clad women would later gather to have their picture taken. *You know you're ghetto if* . . . Ava said to herself and laughed. Bamboo fencing hung from the ceiling to give what Tina thought was an outdoor, island feeling. Ava knew Charles definitely thought this place was ghetto, and in truth, so did Ava. But she liked ghetto as much as Charles liked boring art openings. *To each his own,* Ava thought.

House of Tina was still somewhat empty, but folks were trickling in with hopes of getting a good spot. In a couple of more hours, the joint would be jumping. Ladies' Night started early, and folks who had worked hard honest jobs as well as those who had easy and not so honest jobs would pile in to get their groove on. Ava's cell phone rang, and she immediately suspected it was Charles.

"Yes?" she said into the phone as she looked at Charles's office number on her caller ID.

"Hello Ava, this is Charles," the absent attorney said.

Ava mouthed the word, "Duh," but said, "Hey, you're usually more prompt than this." She checked her watch. "It's— wow, my brother, you're an entire thirty minutes late. You keep this up, and people will be saying you operate on CP time. You're going to make it, aren't you?" she asked.

Charles sighed. "Yes, of course. I couldn't get out of my office on time, and now I'm stuck in traffic," he said, not realizing that Ava knew exactly where he was calling from. "It'll be another say thirty, forty minutes before I can get there," he added.

Ava thought before she responded. She didn't want to say anything that would make Charles play hard in their business negotiations, but she still wanted to let him know that her time was important. "Fine, I understand," she said calmly. "Can I order for you?"

Charles didn't respond right away, and just when Ava thought that maybe he wouldn't, he said, "Ah, yes, that would be nice. Surprise me."

"Dinner will be on the table when you get here. And by the way, Charles, tell your secretary I said hello," she said just before ending the call.

Charles cursed when he remembered that most cell phones were now equipped with caller ID. He adjusted his tie and ran from his office, barely saying goodnight to the secretary who hoped to be more than just an office fling.

11

the summons

What ain't done in this life,
has to get done in the next.
— *Caroline Freeman*

Ngozi *had been in this strange land long enough to understand some things. Although he could now grasp the meaning of the words these people spoke, he could not comprehend the motivation for their actions. He was not alone in this madness. There was Stabo, his sister's husband, and many, many others who looked like him but were born in this strange place. They spoke the same language as the pale people, but they had some of Ngozi's ways. Like the way they jumped the broom for marriage or hung palms over the door when* someone died. Still they looked upon him with suspicion. Ngozi could sense that they were ill at ease whenever he was present. He knew that their inability to connect had a great deal to do with the fact that there was no drum.

Everyone was worked hard. So hard that it made no sense to Ngozi. It was as if the pale people didn't care whether the people who looked like him lived or died. If they died, who would do their work? Back in his country, some of Ngozi's people had servants, but they were not treated in this manner.

Ngozi wondered how the warriors who had captured him would feel if they'd known the horror they had sold him into. Ngozi was certain that the blood of the lost would be on the heads of those traitors for generations to come. He saw in his spirit that they would be forced to war among themselves. No leader would ever find peace. One would be ousted for another in a bloody takeover, and the cycle would continue again. Plague and famine would rule their lands, and they would find little relief. This would be the price for selling their brothers into slavery, death with no release. But those who bought and worked the enslaved, they would pay an even greater price. They would do to one another what they had done to those they enslaved.

Ngozi noticed many differences between himself and the other blacks. His spirit was still in his homeland. Their spirit was (also) not here, and neither was the drum. Ngozi often wondered about this. The spiritless workers sang beautiful, sad songs as they toiled in the fields. Sometimes they played stringed instruments, and they even danced. The dances, though few and too far in between, were wild and passionate, but they were not the dances he remembered. His dances were not driven by melody. They were led by the raw sound of the beat.

Once, when they were allowed to play music and dance, Ngozi found a bucket and began to play the rhythms he'd grown up with. Suddenly, the dancing changed. It became more collective. Folks who'd been

dancing as couples became clusters. Groups formed, and the dancing became frenzied with more energy than Ngozi had ever seen experienced
by those who looked like him. He felt more connected than ever before.
But as quickly as that connection was made, it was put to an end.
Ngozi felt a sharp sting that he'd come to know as the lash. He turned
to see the plantation owner standing with a whip ready to come down on
him again.

"Boy, we don't 'low no Africa mess round here," he barked.

"He ain't know," one of the older men said. Tom, as he was called,
was respected by everyone that worked the fields. Even those who controlled the place had some respect for him.

"He may not know, but he will," the plantation owner said. He
beat him until his back was ripped open. Ngozi wondered what he'd
done to cause him to be punished as if he'd run away.

Later on, he was told that he'd done just that. After the older
women tended to his wounds and his feelings, the old man, Tom, came
to him with the wisdom of the fathers.

"He beat you for starting something," he said. "These drum beats
ain't allowed here or no place else. It cause folks to feel who they is, who
they really is. You know what I'm saying, boy?" the man asked.

Ngozi told him he was not sure of anything.

"That's what they want to beat the life out of you. They know that
the drum is special cause it can talk. It can say things they don't understand. That's why it ain't 'lowed. But if you listen close to our songs,
you'll hear something. We say one thing, we mean something more. I
been watching you," the old man told Ngozi. "Look to me, you think
we's bad as they is. But that ain't so. We just trying to live. We won't
ever be free, but our children's children, they will. So we have to save our-
selves for them. We take this life so they can live. Don't you forget that.
Play your drum, boy, but play it here," he said, pointing to his heart.
"Some day you'll have the drum, and you can pass it on to those who will

think they free, but ain't. You see boy, we know we ain't free, and we know we won't be. But inside, we are free, cause our children, they might be. Hold on for them, and someday you'll bring the drum back."

Ngozi no longer tried to make sense of his condition. He spent his days in remembrance of the words his mother had spoken to him. He felt the power in them. No one in this place had a drum. No rhythms were played for the birth of a child. Neither did they sound and tell of a death. Instead, his lost brethren sang melodies that were sad and somehow beautiful. Songs that made him weep no matter what the meaning. The songs were born of suffering and sorrow, but without the rhythm of the drum, they could not send the message home.

Ngozi wept for the drum he was to have made and for the son his wife would have but whom he would never see. He wept for his own capture. All these things were connected, for the loss of this drum and his life were a loss for his son and all of his people.

Ngozi vowed that day and every day that followed that he would find a way to bring back the drum.

Remembering this now as he stood in the house on Tubman Terrace, he was saddened because it had taken him centuries to carry out his vow. In his present state of existence, he could see that the drum was not just for his own life, it was also for those who came after. The drumbeat was needed to connect his people from today to those of the past. The separation had gone on for too long. Still he was encouraged. The rhythm of the drum was present, but it had to be put to the right use. Suddenly, Ngozi heard a whisper. "Ye oh Ye Ba Ba. I hear you, Papa." Ngozi knew that he was being summoned.

12

◆

the exploitation
of hip hop

Freedom walked down the corridor of the fancy office building and was greeted inside the double glass doors by what he would say were too many happy white people.

"Hey, how's the music master?" the famous filmmaker who'd requested the meeting asked.

"Yeah, Mr. Baker, I didn't plan to be late, but you know how it goes." Freedom had long ago stopped being sorry. He would occasionally apologize, but that was rare. And he never used the phrase, "I'm sorry." The black man has nothing to be sorry for, Freedom remembered he'd once heard a street-corner prophet say.

"What's up, Mr. Baker?" Freedom asked.

"Call me Scott, please. We're friends here," the filmmaker said. He led Freedom to a conference room filled with more happy white folks and one black man who upon seeing Freedom looked too uncomfortable to be happy.

"Let me introduce you to everyone," Scott said. Freedom's late arrival had bothered the filmmaker. He couldn't decide if the music producer was rude or just uncouth, but either way it didn't matter. Scott planned to use the man's music and discard him just as he had every other artist that had made him rich and famous. He introduced the conference table of "suits," which included representatives from the film division, financial office, creative department, legal affairs, promotions, publicity, and marketing. Everyone had an assistant present. Freedom felt that the only person missing was someone from the janitorial staff.

"We've all stayed late to accommodate you and to let you see how important this project is to us here," Scott said.

"Great," Freedom told them. "So like I said before, what's up?"

"Well, I like that, Freedom. I see you're a man who gets right down to business." The room was full of smiles and heads nodding in agreement. "I'm not sure if you're aware of this or not," Scott said, "but in the late sixties, early seventies, when this country was in a social uproar, a time when I was very much— what's the expression? 'Down for the cause,' yeah, that's it— most of the industry ignored the struggle, and they suffered for it."

Freedom had heard this pitch style before. He didn't like being in a room full of happy white folks any more than he liked being given a history lesson by one of them.

"MGM," Scott continued, "was about to sell Dorothy's shoes when Gordon Parks saved their lily white asses with *Shaft* and *Shaft's Big Score.*"

Freedom wanted to say, "Just get to the deal." He couldn't stand player hating, and here sat Mr. Clean himself, calling the folks who made *The Wizard of Oz*, which he loved, lily white. They were white, but so was Baker. And from what Freedom could see, he was way past white. In fact, he was transparent. Freedom had his own rating system for white folks. There was white, real white, almost white, which he used for uptight blacks, and transparent. The last category was where he placed people like Baker and William F. Buckley Jr.

"Yo, "Over the Rainbow" had mad lyrics," Freedom said.

"Right," Scott said, not following Freedom's thought. "What we're getting to is the fact that once again, we are in a period of change. Look at music. What kind of music sells more than any other?" Before waiting for anyone to answer, Scott continued, "Country and hip hop and Latin, or Hispanic, depending on which part of the country you're from," he said, evoking chuckles from all but Freedom. "The music of the people, the forgotten underclass, *la clase baja*. The voice of pain and sorrow. And the film industry has once again ignored the signs of change. That's where we come in," Scott said, about to make the point Freedom had been waiting for. Scott felt that he was truly connecting to Freedom. Freedom felt Scott was being condescending.

"We intend to do what Brother Parks did in the seventies," Scott continued.

"You mean Blaxploitation?" Freedom asked.

"Well, that's the label it's been given," Scott said, "but we don't intend to *exploit*, rather we want to *expose*." As if struck by some brilliant wand, he added, "Black Expos-ation."

The room began to buzz with support of the phrase that Freedom saw as just plain wack. "Right, whatever," he said. "What do you need me for? Am I the black part?" he said only half joking.

At first the room was silent. Then after Scott smiled, they all laughed.

"Great line. Can I use that?" the lone black man from the legal department asked.

"Sure, Money, just give me credit," Freedom said mockingly.

Scott allowed the laughter to build but then calmed the room. "We have a loose concept," he said, "but from what I hear, *you're* just the man we need to pull this baby together."

Freedom wanted to say, "Solid, Mack," but he held back.

"With your musical genius and contacts, we can make a lot of money together, and at the same time 'expose' the masses to the real side of your hip-hop world." When Scott said the word "expose," he raised his hands and used the tacky two-finger gesture to indicate that the word was in quotes.

Freedom wanted to hit the man, but he also wanted to make a movie. "So you want to make a movie around my music, but you don't have a script. And you don't have any actors, right?" he asked.

"Well, we're looking at Halle Berry as one of the lead rappers," someone from the creative department said.

Scott shot the man a look, and everyone sat silently. "We'd like you to lead the way on this," Scott said through clenched teeth.

"What do you have?" Freedom asked.

"We have the studio and the backing to make and distribute the film," Scott said smiling. "All the backing you need."

Freedom stood and grabbed one of the unopen bottles of Evian water that sat in front of him. "I'll think about it," he said as he started toward the door.

"Great," Scott said, dumbfounded. "So I'll hear from you when?" he asked.

Freedom turned and smiled and said, "When I call," and used the same in quotes gesture Scott had used earlier. Once again, all conference room held back their laughter until Scott indicated that he, too, thought Freedom had made a funny.

"Really," Freedom said, "let me talk with my attorney, and I'll call you, alright?" And then he left.

Scott looked around the room and nodded. "Well, I think that went real well, don't you?" Of course, everyone agreed.

Back in the house on Tubman Terrace, the spirit memory, Johnny, had been called back inside. The house had been inhabited by spirit memories for years and had become a holding place for memories waiting for the Gathering of Souls, a time when spirits could tell their story to connect with the living. The memories were difficult for them to relive, but they had to be experienced and told so that the living could find peace. It wasn't the spirit memories that were restless. It was the living, and because Harlem, New York, had been the port of entry as well as the dwelling place for millions of restless black folks, Harlem pulled the memories like few other places. This particular house was like lots of abandoned places, but because of its history, it had an even greater pull.

Johnny wanted to play kick ball, but the man with the drum and the funny name said that he had to come inside. "You're not my father," Johnny snapped.

"No," Ngozi said calmly. "Your father killed you, and I would not have done such a thing."

Johnny's attitude returned to sorrow. That was the reason he left the house in the first place. Johnny had been remembering his own death, and the memories were more intense than usual.

"Things will change soon," said Ngozi, the man with the drum.

"I hope so," Johnny whispered.

"They will. They have to for the sake of our souls and for his soul, too."

In the corner listening was the spirit memory of the woman that Freedom had called Grand. "Don't worry," she said. "He'll do the right thing. I know he will."

13

pain before pleasure

If you don't like my peaches,
don't shake my tree.
—Blues song

True to his word, Charles appeared within forty minutes, albeit somewhat flushed. He could barely look Ava in the eye. "Sorry I'm late," he mumbled.

"It's cool," Ava replied.

The waitress appeared with a tray full of food. There were ribs, chicken wings, shrimp fried rice and greens, along with Ava's vegetable plate. "The last time we were here you didn't eat, but I'm not letting you off tonight."

"Looks really good, and I'm famished." Charles was actually licking his lips.

"I figured you would be hungry," Ava said, grinning. Charles blushed but regained composure quickly. Ava knew that brothers like Charles didn't take too well to being caught in their mess, but he was too interested in the food to be bothered. At first he approached the ribs like he'd never seen them before, but quickly reacquainted himself with the kind of food he had tried to forget. After one bite, Charles was wondering why he ever liked sushi and tiny decorative plates of haute cuisine. He ate like a man on a mission. Ava wanted to laugh, but she was also thinking that there might be hope for Mr. Charles after all. She called the waitress over and asked for more ribs and chicken. Charles had barely looked up but managed to add, "More greens, too, please."

Now Ava laughed. "You might make it after all," she said, sharing her thoughts. By now DJ Donny was spinning his disks. He'd started slow for the supper crowd, playing jazz tunes and then eased into old school.

She noticed how happy Charles looked and made a mental note to hold more of her meetings at House of Tina. Charles finally looked up and wiped his hands. As if suddenly remembering why he was there, he said, "Oh yeah, about the house." His thought was interrupted when he saw that there was one more chicken wing left.

"Go for it, brother," Ava told him.

Without missing a beat, Charles grabbed the wing and continued his conversation. "The house is tied up in trust, but it will be pretty easy to handle. It's owned by a family that never lived in it. The house originally belonged to the grandfather, and he left it to the children of the son he referred to in his will as 'that no good son of mine.' The grandchildren took one look at the location and wanted to have nothing to do with it. They'd tried to sell it, but one of the siblings wanted a larger share of the inheritance and wouldn't allow the sale." Charles whispered this last bit of information as if it were his own family's secret.

"Yeah, we had that same problem," Ava said mockingly. "My grandfather left some bills, and now everybody is fighting over who's going to have to pay them."

Charles managed a weak laugh, though he didn't really see the connection. "They want a lot of money for the property even though it's in disrepair," he said. "Apparently, they've kept up on all of the recent development in the area so they figure that the house is worth twice what they were originally asking."

Ava eyed Charles curiously. "No doubt the white media and real estate brokers are keeping this greedy family appraised of all of the Harlem goings-on," Ava said.

"I see. As always, you've done your homework."

"Yes, and I know about the mall Disney is building and the fact that the parallel block is also now in transition. But none of that has anything to do with this particular house. What's really the deal with this house? Is it really haunted?" Ava asked, as if she was asking about something as common as taxes.

Charles responded in the same manner. "Well, I haven't seen anything myself, but to tell you the truth, that place gives me the willies. The family sees the rumor about the house being haunted as gossip generated by potential buyers, but they haven't even been inside."

"Do you have any history on the source of the haunting?" Ava asked.

"I've checked old newspapers, but I couldn't really find anything. Supposedly," Charles said, "there are several ghosts. Sort of like a poltergeist thing. Some say it's the original owners, but I don't think that's the case." Charles paused and looked as if he wanted to say more but had decided not to.

"There's something you're not telling me," Ava discerned.

"Well, I know this was improper, but I told my grand-mother about the place. She's sort of a, well . . . my grand-mother is different. When I told her I had a client who was interested in that house, she got spooked and told me not to deal with it."

"You know how old folks are," Ava said.

Ava remembered the woman, Miss Dora, who used to visit from somewhere down South every two or three years when they were still children. She was the first woman she'd ever seen who smoked a pipe. "She surely was strange," Ava muttered. Then she thought of how strange it was that two well-educated attorneys were having a normal conversation about what they believed to be a haunted house. *Maybe Charles is more in touch with the hood than he pretends to be,* she thought to herself. "Bottom line, Charles, what do they want?" Ava asked, getting right to the money.

"They're asking five hundred thousand," Charles said without blinking.

"Right," Ava said, laughing, "and I'm going to tell my client that he should pay just that."

Charles sat silently for a moment and finally said, "I'll try to get them down to four," as if it would be the most difficult thing he'd ever done.

"No, brother, we'll give the greedy tribe two fifty, but if they piss me off, it'll be two."

Now Charles laughed. "Look girl, we aren't playing hide-and-seek in the old neighborhood anymore."

Ava raised her eyebrows in surprise. Until now, she wasn't sure if Charles even remembered their childhood games.

"Yeah, and if we were," she said, "you'd be caught."

"Are you forgetting that I always found you?" Charles asked slyly.

Ava blushed. In fact, she had forgotten. Until now, she had also forgotten that Charles had had a crush on her that was so intense that it had almost been an obsession. She never liked it when her girlfriends teased her. "Pee Pee boy likes Gappy. Pee Pee boy likes Gappy," they'd say, calling them both by their nicknames. For the first time that evening, Ava was speechless.

But just as she was wondering what to say, she caught Lil' Man in the mirror strolling over in her direction. Rick James's "Fire and Desire" was playing, and Lil' Man was singing it loudly, using his beer bottle as a microphone. "And then I laid eyes on you. It was pain before plea-e-sure," he wailed. "Hey Miss Fine Thang, when you gonna break down and have dinner with me?" he said to Ava but staring at Charles and daring him to speak. Lil' Man was about six foot five and all of 450 pounds. He had beautiful, smooth, jet-black skin and a shoulder-length bob to match. Lil' Man always dressed monochromatically, right down to the shoes. Today he was outfitted in lime green, complete with matching alligator shoes. "You can at least give me a dance," he said, pulling at Ava, still staring at Charles like he was just a table decoration.

"Sure, Lil' Man, but not right now. I'm doing some business."

"Humph," Lil' Man snorted. "He don't look like he thinking 'bout no business to me."

Charles didn't bother to defend himself. He recognized Lil' Man as his childhood bully, but Lil' Man hadn't recognized him.

Ava was aware of this and decided to have some fun. "Lil' Man, you know Charles. We used to call him Chucky. He lived upstairs from you."

Lil' Man leaned back to get a better view. "That's you, Pee Pee boy?" he asked in disbelief. "Damn, man, you actually grew up. I thought you'd a drowned in your own pee. I used to hear your mama whipping your ass for peeing." Lil' Man raised an imaginary belt and swung with each syllable. "If-I-told-you-once-I-told-you-twice. Stop-pee-ing-on-my-fur-ni-ture." Lil' Man howled with laughter.

Ava's plan had gone too far. She was embarrassed for Charles. She suddenly realized that she needn't be.

Charles stared Lil' Man right in the eyes. "I see you grew up too, Lil' Man, or should I say blew up?"

Ava had been sipping her water trying to figure out a way to get rid of Lil' Man. Drinking water at that moment had not been a good idea. She laughed and watched as the contents of her mouth sprayed Lil' Man's green silk suit. "Ooo, I'm so sorry, Lil' Man," she said between snickers.

"It's not your fault," Charles told her. "You couldn't have missed the Jolly Green Giant if you'd tried."

Lil' Man, who had previously been all mouth, was now

reduced to silence. "I was just messing with you, Chucky. You ain't gotta be so mean," Lil' Man moaned.

"Then don't start nothing you can't finish, big boy, or Lil' Man, or whatever it is you go by. And by the way," Charles added, "isn't your real name Herbert Black? I remember *you* used to cry when the teachers called us by our last name first. Black Herbert."

This was all Lil' Man could take. "Look, man, I came in here to have a nice time. I wasn't trying to start no trouble. I know when I'm beat."

Charles was on a roll and was enjoying the fact that he was finally bullying his bully. "How would you know when you're beat? How could you feel it through all of that fat and green? Here, you left your microphone," he said, raising the beer bottle Lil' Man had set down.

Lil' Man was already at the door when Ava finally managed to say, "Alright, Charles. Alright, that's enough."

"Well, you know what they say," he said. "Don't start nothing, won't be nothing."

"And just when did *you* learn to play the dozens?" Ava asked.

"You know, I picked up a lil' something here and there. I'm on a roll," he said loudly.

"Great, then roll yourself over to your office and get the key to that house. I want to see what I'm bidding on."

"I thought you told me to put on my dancing shoes."

"Look, Charles, don't let the greens get to your head. Next thing I know, you'll be growing an afro. Do you have the key or not?" she persisted.

Charles was all teeth as he reached into his front jacket pocket and pulled out a key.

"Girl, I got it right here. It's getting late, but if you want to chance it, I'm game."

Now Ava smiled. When she did, Charles asked, "How 'bout a game of hide-and-seek?"

"Come on, boy, you've had too much to eat" was all she could manage.

14

things that go bump

During the ride up to Tubman Terrace, Charles and Ava barely spoke. The playfulness they had enjoyed back at House of Tina's was replaced by a feeling of apprehension. Both wondered why they were going to the house after dark. From what they had heard, daylight wasn't any less threatening, but at least they'd be able to *see* the things they feared.

"Is the electrical power on?" Ava finally asked.

"Uh, yes, I'm sure it is. It's required by the new neighbor-hood association in case of an emergency. I think it just makes the neighbors feel safer," Charles said.

"Good," Ava said. "I don't want to fall through some damn hole in the floor because your people haven't taken care of their business."

"Do you kiss your mother with that mouth?" Charles asked.

"As a matter of fact, I do. If you recall," Ava said, "I got this mouth from Myrna."

Charles smiled and remembered the cussing he would hear when Ava's sister, Myrna, had to come and get her after the streetlights were on. "Those were the days when authority fig-ures ruled," Charles said.

As they pulled up to the curb in front of the house on One hundred thirty-eighth Street and Tubman Terrace, Ava became more and more nervous. Charles parked the car, turned to her, and asked, "Remind me: Why are we doing this?"

"Because I want to, uh, need to," she corrected, "see what I'm bidding on. It's my responsibility to my client. This piece of shit may not be worth fifty cents."

"Yes," Charles agreed, "but why can't we do this tomorrow?"

"Well," Ava said, "we could go back to Tina's and get our groove on. I'm sure by now Lil' Man is tore up from the floor up and probably drunk enough to call you some real names."

"That sounds good," Charles said sarcastically, "but I'll take a rain check. How about tomorrow? I haven't eaten that well in a long time. Truth is," he added, "I'm wondering why it took you to bring me back to my old hood."

Ava ignored the direction the conversation was moving in.

"Tomorrow sounds fine," she said. "I'll just have to check my calendar."

Charles laughed. "Well, are we or aren't we?" Charles asked.

"Yes, dinner sounds fine," Ava told him.

"No, Gappy," he said, using the nickname Ava hadn't heard since she was a teenager, "are we going in or not?"

There was a part of Ava that wanted to scream, "No," but she fought the urge and allowed her curiosity to win out.

It was a decision she would come to regret.

15

the Gathering

When one is on the
soil of one's ancestors,
most anything can come.

—*Jean Toomer*

*T*hey're coming," Johnny said excitedly so all could hear.

"*But he's not with them,*" *a voice said.*

"*He'll soon come,*" *a third voice added.*

"*They are still our people,*" *someone chimed.*

"*Speak for yourself,*" *the memory of a woman hissed.* "*I had no
people,*" *she said.*

"*Whose fault is it that you were just a broke-down whore?*" *young*

Johnny said. Seeing his sweet image, it was hard to believe that the words had come from his five-year-old mouth. His spirit, however, was much, much older.

"I was never broke down," the woman responded.

"That will be enough," Ngozi said, standing on the huge staircase in front of the others. "This is the beginning of what was to be. We gather for those who are forgotten, those who are lost at sea, and those who are lost to their own children. We gather to tell our stories with the hopes that one day they will be heard. The sea is full, the tide is high. Johnny," the man said, "tonight we will hear your tale."

Johnny smiled and pushed through the crowd of spirit memories. He was about to speak when they heard a key push through the chambers of the lock. They stood on one side of the door in anticipation and Charles and Ava stood the same way on the other.

"After you," Charles said once the lock had been disengaged.

"Naw, after you," Ava returned. "Haven't you heard in African culture, the man goes first to check for danger? Besides, age before beauty."

Charles laughed, but he was not feeling giddy at all. He pushed open the door and felt the wall for the light switch.

"Can't your clients afford to keep one light on?" Ava whispered.

"Woman, why are you whispering?" Charles asked. "You afraid you might wake the dead?"

"Something like that," she said just a bit louder.

"Ah, here we are," Charles said, feeling the switch. He flipped it into the up position. A light so bright flashed that he was temporarily blinded. He adjusted his eyes and looked at Ava. "What the—?" Before he could finish, a huge mahogany staircase became visible. There standing in front of them was the Gathering. The spirit memories of beings long gone were gathered together. They had come together out of the necessity to communicate with the next generation. Some were old when they made their transition, others were young. Some were dressed in clothing that dated back to the 1800s. Some had afros. One even looked like a pimp from a bad movie. There was a woman with a bloody newborn. No one made a sound. All of them were black. All had a message to convey.

There in the front of the group stood a very dark man holding a drum. Next to him stood the young boy. He looked as if he were about to speak, but before he did, Ava let out a scream that caused Charles to scream, too. The lights flashed again, and the staircase was empty.

What happened next was like the punch line of the black comedian's joke about the difference between blacks and whites in a haunted house. "White folk go into a big, abandoned house, the chandelier falls, and they say, 'Honey, let's look at the bedroom.' Black folks, in the same situation say, 'Baby, let's get the hell out of here.' " Ava no longer questioned how black Charles was. He reached the door before she did, and in no time they were back outside and in the car he had opened by remote.

16

visitation of spirits

When indigenous people talk about spirit,
they are basically referring to the
life force in everything.
—*Sobonfu Somé*

*F*reedom walked into House of Tina, his attorney's favorite spot, and tried to figure out why she liked it. *There's more jheri curls in here than all of Detroit and L.A. combined,* he said to himself. Freedom recognized the DJ and made his way over to say hello. Before he could, Donny was announcing his presence over the mike.

"We got big Freedom in the house, the phattest producer of

hip-hop music in the WO-RLD. Big Freedom, big Freedom. Say yo, yo, yo big Freedom."

Women looked at Freedom through weaves and extensions. Brothers gave him high fives and acted like he was an old friend. "So much for keeping a low profile," he said as he reached the DJ.

"What's up, baby?" Donny said.

"You seen Ava?" Freedom said, getting right to the point. Freedom had known and admired Donny for years. In the DJ world Donny was something of a legend. In the eighties, he could have played in the big hot clubs, but he chose to stay in the hood. "I have what I need. I like my job and the people I work with. I make folks happy. So what more do I need?" he'd say. What he never said, and what no one knew, was that he was House of Tina's mystery man. Donny was Tina's husband.

"Hey, you ain't got time to at least say hello, Harry?" Donny said, forcing Freedom to be respectful.

"Sorry, man, I got too much on my mind, you know how it is."

"Yeah, and I know how it should be, too," Donny responded. "Ava was here for dinner. You know you can't miss that fine queen."

"Yeah, yeah. You know how long ago she left?" Freedom always liked to have as much information as possible so he could challenge Ava later concerning her whereabouts.

"She left about an hour ago maybe."

"Thanks, man," Freedom said. "Yo, I'll catch you."

"Hold up, Freedom," Donny yelled. "Check this tape and tell me what you think."

"Alright," Freedom relented.

"Don't let me hear it on none of that rap shit either," Donny yelled. Freedom held up a black power salute and pushed through the crowded dance floor. He got to his car and dialed his attorney's number. He knew if he didn't do what he'd come to do and leave, he would have about twenty homemade tapes, most from wannabe performers. They were usually bad, but if he didn't take them, he'd be accused of selling out. If he did take them, he ran the risk of being accused of stealing or sucking someone's flavor. Freedom just wanted to find Ava.

Ava and Charles were both trying to determine what it was they had seen, but neither said a word. They were startled by the sound of Ava's cell phone ringing and it was as if they'd been brought back from a time before telephones existed. Ava looked at the phone, as if trying to remember how to use it. Finally, she hit the appropriate button and put her ear to the receiver.

"Peace, girl," Freedom said before Ava could answer.

"Freedom," she said, "thank God. I need to talk to you."

"Well, I got to talk to you first," Freedom said excitedly. "Guess who I had a meeting with?" he said. Before she could answer, Freedom blurted out "Scott Baker, the film-maker. Hey, I rhymed," he said childishly. "He wants to do a movie based on my music. They say they'll give me whatever I need."

Ava understood the importance of what Freedom was

saying and transitioned into attorney mode. "You had an important meeting, and you didn't call me? Who was there? Did you agree to anything? Did you take notes? Boy, you know what happened the last time you went to a meeting without me!"

Freedom did remember, but he didn't want to. He ended up in a verbal contract that caused Ava to have to pull every trick she'd learned in law school and some she'd learned growing up to free him from the deal.

Freedom sucked his teeth. "Chill, woman. They put on the whole dog and pony show. I didn't agree to anything. As a matter of fact, I told them I had to call you first, and you know I don't take notes, but I got it all up here," he said, pointing to his head as if Ava could see him.

"Well, I want to know all of the details," she said.

"Yo, I'll be paying for that house in cash," Freedom told her.

Ava immediately remembered what had just happened. "That's what I need to talk to you about, Freedom. I just left there, and well . . . that place ain't right. We'll find you something else."

"Girl, get out of here with that madness. So you went over there with the Brooks Brother, huh?"

"How did you—"

Before Ava could finish, Freedom added, "Yeah, took that Negro to eat in the hood, and he took you to my house. You ain't supposed to be up in there with nobody but me," he said only half teasing.

"You went by House of Tina?" Ava said. "Boy, you can't do nothing in the hood without everybody knowing about it."

"True that," Freedom said. "So what's he got that I ain't got?"

Ava almost laughed, but she was still shaken from her experience inside the house. "For one thing, he has that age advantage, and for another, he doesn't order me around and tell me how to do my job."

"Right," Freedom said. "If I was that easy, you wouldn't like me so much."

"Listen, little boy," Ava said smiling, "what time can we meet tomorrow?"

"I want to see the house," Freedom said.

"And I told you to forget it. I'm not playing. This is for real," she told him.

"Look, girl, no house, no movie. And I'm not playing. Every time I go by there, it's like the place is calling me home."

Ava stopped smiling. "I know what you mean, Freedom, but believe me, in this case home is not where the heart is. Listen, Harry," she said, calling him by his given name, "let's talk about this tomorrow."

Freedom only allowed his true elders, those with real age advantage, to call him Harry, and only when they were alone. Ava knew this, so he figured she was upset about something and decided to let it slide. "I'll talk with you tomorrow. By then, I hope you have some sense," he said before he barked, "Peace," and hung up.

"Second time in one night someone called me by my birth name," Freedom said aloud. He thought about it only briefly. Freedom hadn't yet accepted what his grandmother used to tell him. She'd say, "Boy, in life there are no coincidences."

Charles had listened to Ava's conversation and now knew who her client was. He wondered if her client was more than just a client and if their relationship was anything like the one he had with his secretary. Thinking about his secretary reminded him of the images he had seen earlier on the steps of the house, particularly the woman who held the bloody newborn. For now, Charles decided he wanted to go home. He would call his grandmother and find out just what was going on.

Ava had Charles drop her off at her apartment. Since she'd walked to Tina's from the women's shelter earlier that evening, she could pick up her car from the shelter the next day. Once she was home Ava felt a little more at ease. But like a teenager in a bad slash-and-gore movie, she checked her closets and under her bed before she got in it. She thought about a nice hot shower but was immediately reminded of *Psycho*. "Naw, I'll just go to bed dirty," she said out loud. She turned on her television and noticed that almost every network was playing a horror flick. So instead, she turned on the radio and jumped into bed.

The light jazz station was just what she needed to fall into the comfort of sleep, and Gerald Albright's sexy saxophone had her dreaming before she knew it. She always dreamt multiple dreams in rapid succession and Ava had taught herself to remember her dreams, because in that state she was able to work out her incomplete tasks of the day. She'd been doing this for years before she stumbled on an article about lucid dreaming. "So this is what it's called." She had laughed. "Why do people have to make a career out of the stuff that should just come natural?" She allowed herself to slide into a deep state of unconsciousness, not quite asleep, but certainly not awake, and she began to dream.

In the first dream she had successfully convinced a woman to stay at the women's shelter with her three children. In the next, she was present at Freedom's meeting. There she structured a deal that made both of them wealthy. Her third dream was more personal and satisfying. In that dream Lil' Man had proposed marriage while Charles interrupted and told him she was spoken for. When he did, the singer Seal glided into House of Tina and told them both to forget it. "She's mine," he told them in his melodious Afro-British accent.

But it was the last dream that spiraled into a nightmare. In this dream the young spirit memory she had seen at the house earlier took her by the hand and said, "Follow me." It was a request that felt more like a command. The feeling was so disturbing that Ava had to force herself to wake up. It was difficult to do and made her think of the old folks' saying, "A witch is riding your back." That's what they said when you were caught in a dream and couldn't get out. Ava had had this feeling many times and luckily knew what to do. She flexed her toes until she was able to blink her eyes. With eyes fully open, she wished she'd left them closed. For at the foot of her bed sat the young spirit child, Johnny. He was tossing an old can in the air and catching it.

Johnny looked directly at Ava and said, "I thought you'd never get here."

Ava blinked her eyes again, thinking that she was still asleep. "Cut that out, girl," the fifty-year-old spirit that appeared in the form of a five-year-old's body said. "I'm real. What you should be asking yourself is whether or not *you* are." Then, he laughed so wickedly that Ava actually cried. "They'll be no sleep for you tonight. Hasn't anyone ever told you not to walk out on your hosts? It's time for you to hear my story."

17

Grandma's hands

The souls of old folks have
a way of seein' things.
—*Jean Toomer*

harles walked into his apartment and dialed the familiar number. Charles's grandmother was always up. If he hadn't seen her take naps with his own eyes, he would assume she never slept. His grandmother usually answered her telephone within two or three rings. After the fifth, Charles wondered if maybe she'd started to sleep more since she was getting older. By the seventh ring, he grew anxious and wondered if she was okay.

"Hello," a grumpy voice answered. "This better be good."

"Goober," Charles asked in disbelief, "that you?"

His cousin Tony, a.k.a. Goober because of his peanut-shaped head, had been helping out around his grandmother's house as long as Charles could remember. Goober was a little slow in school, but his grandmother had a tender place for him in her heart, and he was good with his hands.

"Where's Grandma, Goober?" Charles asked.

"Hello, cuz. How are you? Hope everything is good down South. Maybe you can come visit sometime?" Goober said with all the sarcasm Charles had ever heard anybody use. Charles never thought Goober was slow. As a kid, he figured it was an act Goober put on so he could get away with all kinds of stuff.

"Sorry, man, how are you? I was just worried when Grandma didn't answer."

"Maybe you should check your messages before you call people in the middle of the night," Goober said.

Charles looked down and saw that there were messages on his machine, but that was always the case. "Grandma called me?" Charles asked.

"Hello, am I speaking English? They say I'm slow, and you're a genius?!" Goober mocked.

"Okay, let's start again," Charles said slowly. "Where's Grandma?"

"She's not here, or I wouldn't be answering the phone."

"Okay, Goober. Calm down," Charles said. "Where is she?"

"I'm calm," Goober said, " 'cause I know where she is. You the one in trouble messing in things that ain't got nothing to do with you. She told you to stay away from that place, but did you listen? Nooo," he said loudly.

Now Charles was truly spooked. "What did . . . how did you know?" Charles asked as his door buzzer sounded.

"If you want to know where Grandma is, go answer your door," Goober told him and hung up.

It was a good thing he'd been warned; otherwise Charles would have had his second fright of the day. There standing in his doorway was his grandmother, holding the handle of a suitcase on wheels and carrying a bag that smelled like the herbs and roots that filled her house.

"Don't stand there, boy. Get this stuff and tell me everything. Don't leave nothing out. I'm already mad at you for doing what I told you not to."

18

rhythm of the night

> You done taken my blues and gone.
>
> —*Langston Hughes*

reedom drove back to the house on Tubman Terrace. Very few would call this place peaceful, but to Freedom the brownstone offered him a measure of peace. He got out of the car, sat on the steps, and eventually fell asleep. He'd only been asleep for about twenty minutes when a homeless man brought him out of his bliss.

"Not the place to crash, chief. Haven't you heard? This house is haunted," the man said to him.

"It's cool," he said to the man. "I'm buying this place."

The man raised his eyebrows, laughed, and said, "Save your money," and walked off. He didn't even bother to ask Freedom for a dollar.

Freedom shook his head and smiled. "Maybe this place is haunted. Anytime the homeless folk don't ask for money, something ain't right."

But Freedom felt more peaceful than he'd felt in a long, long time and knew beyond doubt that this would be his home. "I don't care what foolishness Ava is trying to pull. This is the spot," he said before getting back into his SUV and driving off to decide which honey would get the pleasure of his company tonight.

"Johnny made contact with that woman," a voice said.

"Walked right through her, and she didn't notice," someone else added.

"They were too busy running out of here," a voice said, laughing.

"I almost got him," the woman with the bloody newborn said.

Ngozi sat down with his drum and played a melody with a rhythm that was truly an honor to his people.

Freedom was somewhere else submerged in the ecstasy of a body whose heart he didn't love. Somewhere in the rhythm of his movements, though, he heard the rhythm of a drum. The woman whose body he rode sounded out her pleasure. Freedom was done, but he could still hear the drum song. He would hardly remember this woman's name, but those rhythms would remain with him forever.

part

two

19

restless lives, restless spirits

> The wicked shall cease from troubling.
> The weary shall be at rest.
>
> —*Job 3:17*

Ava was in a panic unlike any she'd remembered. She'd been through quite a bit in life; her mother had died when Ava was just a small girl. The racism in her upstate New York college town had been almost too much to bear, and law school hadn't been much easier, but by then she'd learned to hold her own. But none of the real-life dangers that she'd been exposed to had ever caused her as much fear as she felt now.

"My name is Johnny Freeman, which is kind of dumb given that I ain't really free," the spirit memory said.

Ava just looked at him.

"To which you say, 'Pleased to meet you, Johnny,'" he said.

Ava parted her lips to speak but found that she couldn't.

"Nice place," he said. "Why you ain't got no kids? You like 'em, don't you?"

Still, she couldn't speak.

"Sure you do, you just . . ." He paused, looking for the right words. ". . . Haven't had the time or the right man," he said in a voice that Ava would have sworn came from her. It was her own voice, her own thoughts, but he had spoken them as if they were his.

"How did you do that?" was all that she managed.

"Parlor trick," Johnny said nonchalantly. "I got loads of 'em, but I ain't got that much time. I have to tell you my story 'fore the night is over so somebody will remember me and know that my life counted for something. Otherwise," he continued, "I'm just here, incomplete."

"Why me?" Ava asked.

"'Cause you restless, and 'cause you here listening."

Ava was confused but couldn't say so.

"It's not hard to understand," Johnny told her. "You have no children, and you've been restless about it. Your anxiety can cause your mind to create all kinds of things," he said and winked. "I need to tell my story so folks like you can learn from the past. You listening. That's real good. Some listen. Most don't. When you listen, my memory can rest and you can look for peace."

And with that, he began his tale.

"I was born in a colored hospital in a colored town. They both

long gone, but they were real. You can check. Town called Whitesville, Alabama. All the blacks lived in Whitesville, but the white folks
lived in Browntown. That was somebody's idea of a joke. Ain't funny,
is it?"

Ava slowly shook her head, though she knew she hadn't done it
herself.

"I didn't think so either. Anyway, my mama died when I was born.
My daddy say I kill her. But he say a lot of mean things. I lived with
him and my sister. I don't know what kind of man he was 'fore my
mama died. Maybe he was nice then. If he was, wasn't none of that left
in him. I was what you smart folks call a precocious child. Always getting into things. I like to see how things work. I was like that from when
I first start walking, and that was early, too. They have fancy schools
for kids like me now. They say kids like that can grow up and invent
all kinds of things. Maybe I would've done that, too."

Johnny paused and stared at nothing in particular. "Anyway, my
sister, Ruth was her name, she used to read to me and talk to me like
my daddy should've. I started reading when I was just three. It got so I
was reading to Ruth. She say I'm special, and I'm a do great things. I
understand all that she saying, even though I'm young. She get books
from her teacher and say that they for her. Her teacher happy to have a
bright student. She think Ruth is bright 'cause I read the books to her,
and I tell her what they say. Ruth is smart, but not like me. She bring
me books on the stars and planets, books about places all over the world,
and she even get a big book on medicine and the human body. One day
she get a book on inventors. That there was my favorite of all. It had
all kind of mechanical things in it. One day I get into my daddy's shed.
He had some tools and farm equipment. I take a bunch of stuff apart
and put it back together. I was only five. My daddy walk up and see me
doing this, and he say I'm sure enough the Devil. He stay away from
me then. He wouldn't sleep in the house with me, and after a while, he

stop sleeping altogether. He stop eating, too. He gets to acting meaner than he was, and Ruth try to protect me. But she can't."

Johnny's delivery hastened and his breathing became rapid. "One day when my sister was at school and I was at home with my daddy, he get to mumbling, 'I'm gonna get you. I'm gonna get you. I'm gonna do it. I'm gonna do it.' He say that for three days 'til I guess he can't stand the sight of me no more. My daddy grab me by my throat, and he choke the life out of me. Seem like it take a long time for me to die. I saw it happen, still do. I still see his face, I smell his breath. Especially when the Gathering is here. Bet it never seemed to you that spirits can be haunted, too. But they can. Anyway, he bury my body. When my sister come home, she asked for me. At first, he lie, but she know that he done something to me. He make her scared and tell her she better not talk about nothing to nobody. My sister run off and leave. She have a life of her own, though it ain't a good one. She afraid to love 'cause she afraid to lose. But I guess you know about that, huh, Miss Ava?"

Ava shuddered, and Johnny continued his story. "My sister ain't cross over yet. She still alive, living down South, alone. Somewhere in Mississippi. She real sad. If she had some children, I could've told my story to them. I could've passed my ideas over to her kids, and they could've done all that I would have."

Johnny sat looking at Ava for what seemed to be a very long time. In fact, only a few minutes had passed. "So what you think?" he said. Ava began to cry. She cried for Johnny's life and for all the lost children whose stories had not been heard. Then she cried for her own childlessness and fell asleep.

20

the elders speak

s Charles brought his grandmother's bags in, he had so many questions for her that he wasn't sure where to start.

"I thought you lawyers were supposed to know how to talk," his grandmother teased. "I got to use the bathroom, son. You know I can't use the one on the plane, not even in first class. Too many nasty people been in there. I been holding it for some time. While I'm in the bathroom doing my business, why don't you listen to your messages and take care of your business. We'll talk when I'm done," she told him and made her way to the bathroom.

Charles just sat, still too stunned to do anything but what he was told. He walked over to the answering machine and hit the play button. He had ten new messages. The first five were all work related. By the sixth message, he heard his grandmother's voice. "Charles, you there? Course you ain't. You over there with that woman who works for you. Boy, you need to watch where you put yourself. Anyway, I had a dream about you."

Charles was thinking about how she hardly ever slept and wondered when she had time to dream.

"Don't worry about when I sleep," his grandmother's voice on the machine said. "And don't worry about how I know what I know. You been away from yourself and your people for too long, but that's another conversation. Anyway, in the dream I saw you going into that house that I told you to stay clear of. Shucks, boy, do you listen to your elders? Anyway, you stepped into something that's bigger than you. Shoot, it's bigger than me, too. By the time you hear this, I'll already be there. Oh, by the way, this is me, Grandma," the voice said just before time ran out.

The next four messages were all from Charles's secretary. The first was simple enough. "Hey, Charles, this is me. Call me when you get in." The ones that followed became more and more desperate. "Charles, I know you're out with that bitch," the last message started. "You need to call me. And oh, by the way, there was something I didn't tell you today. It was kinda hard cause we were real busy, remember?" she said sarcastically. "Anyway, you need to call me, Charles. I'm pregnant." Beep.

Charles thought of the spirit memory who held the bloody newborn and his head started spinning. Just then, his grand-mother emerged from his bathroom.

"Well, son, handle your business," she said as she handed him the phone.

Charles called his secretary but dreaded the conversation. The phone rang six times and then went to voice mail. He left a sorry-sounding message. "Hey, Sandra, this is me. Got your messages. Give me a call."

His grandmother looked at him and rolled her eyes. "Some things I'm going to have to let you work out on your own. Besides," she told him, "I'm not here to deal with your love life or better yet, your sex life."

His grandmother had changed into what she called a shift—a simple housedress that looked as if she'd had it for years. The color was faded, and the fabric was worn. But it was comfortable. She had removed her wig and had tied a scarf over her long, thick, gray braids. "Well, I'm waiting," she said to Charles, who was still too shaken to do much of anything. "What happened in that house tonight? Tell me from the start."

Charles sat down as his grandmother moved behind the counter of his high-tech, stainless steel kitchen. She boiled water but removed tea from her own purse.

"I'm waiting," she said over the counter.

Charles started to tell the evening's tale. His grandmother was as good a listener as she was a talker. She interrupted him just when Charles had gotten to the point about the property and handed him the tea she had brewed. "Drink this, son," she said. It was strong but helped to calm his nerves.

Charles had to struggle to stay awake, but he did so just long enough to get up to what happened that made him run out of the house. The last thing he heard was his grandmother saying, "That's okay, son, you sleep now."

It was all the encouragement he needed. Charles did sleep, and it was a good thing, because he would need all the rest he could get.

21

acquire wisdom

> In all your ways acknowledge God
> and God will direct your path.
>
> —*Proverbs 3:6*

va awoke to the sound of her alarm. She took her time getting up. Daylight gave her a sense of security, but she wasn't sure just how safe she should feel. At first, it seemed as if everything had been a dream, but all doubts left when she saw something next to the foot of her sleigh bed. It was the can that the young boy had been playing with. She closed her eyes with the hope that it would disappear but knew that it wouldn't. "Alright, Ava, get up," she demanded of herself. Just as she pulled her leg out of her bed, her fear forced her to pull it back. Instead of getting out of the bed, she swung her upper body over far enough to look under it first. A wave of relief washed over her when she saw that there was nothing under her bed but her fuzzy slippers.

Ava got up and timidly checked her apartment. She took in a deep breath and realized that in spite of all that had happened, she felt amazingly energized. She showered and made herself some raspberry tea. She drank it and read her daily scriptures from Proverbs. From the time she was a child, she had made a practice of reading a chapter each day. "A chapter a day keeps the Devil away," her Sunday school teacher used to say. Today Ava felt like she needed to read the entire Bible. She finished and pulled out a pen and pad of paper. "The beginning of wisdom is to acquire wisdom, and with all your acquiring, acquire an understanding," she wrote the passage from Proverbs 4:7. "How appropriate," she said out loud. Always the good student, Ava began to outline what would be her course of action.

    I. Find out what's going on with the house
        A. Sources
            1. Schomburg Library
            2. Newspaper clippings
            3. Woman at herb store
            4. Owner of the house—maybe
            5. Any old folk still in neighborhood—unlikely
        B. Any similar occurrences in the area
            1. Neighbors
            2. Newspaper clippings

3. Historian in area

4. Newspaper morgue

II. Why me?

III. Find Ruth, Johnny's sister

Although it was the easiest to do, the last section of her outline would have to wait. She knew that wisdom and understanding must go hand in hand. Before she talked with Ruth,
she would have to know what to say to her.

Freedom got up at nine A.M., which was much earlier
than usual. He checked his voice mail and was rewarded with a
call from Scott Baker.

"Hey, babe," Scott said, doing the Hollywood thing, "everybody was psyched to meet you. We want to move as quickly as
possible on this project. Like I said yesterday, the time is right.
Let's do it. Give me a call so we can set up a meeting with you
and your attorney. Let's make a movie," Scott almost screamed
into the phone.

Freedom was smiling and dancing as he checked the rest of
his messages. They were mostly from women wondering why
Freedom hadn't called and musicians who wanted him on their
projects. There was one call from his mother, wondering why
he hadn't visited with his cousins who were in town. " 'Cause I
don't like them," he said to the message. Freedom then called

his mother's voice mail and left her a message saying just that. He then took a quick shower and called his attorney. *I can run later,* he told himself. *Today I'm gonna make money.* He grabbed his phone and punched in a number.

Ava answered immediately.

"Peace. Guess who called already?" Freedom asked.

"Let me guess, your new best friend, Scott Baker?" she said.

"You got it. He wants a meeting with us right away," Freedom informed her.

"Fine," Ava said, "but you and I need to meet first. It's ten o'clock now. How about noon at my office? Then we can make the meeting with Scott at two."

"Cool," Freedom said, but he could hear from his attorney's tone that everything wasn't cool.

"Alright, I'll see you then," she said.

Sounded like she was somewhere else, Freedom thought. He rationalized her lack of interest was due to the fact that she was already researching Scott's company and what kind of deal they should make. Freedom was only partially right. She was busy doing research, and it was for him. But it had nothing to do with his film project and everything to do with what he was already calling home.

22

precious memories

Ngozi was trying hard to remember his story. The details were beginning to fade. The tide had moved out and the memories were shallow. His memory often faded at high tide after the soul stirring had mellowed. His ability to remember his own life was starting to fade. Time was running out. But not just for him. It was running out for Freedom and the restless young men like him. He could feel it in the air. He could see it in how they were treating one another, and he felt it in their desperation to become enslaved again. And he could hear it in their music. They were unaware of the enslavement. The economic enslavement. The ones who thought that having things made them more important. They didn't understand that they didn't own things, rather the things owned them. Ngozi knew that voluntary slavery was the greatest form of sin. It was committed against God, against nature, and against one's own self. Time was running out, but he still had the drum. He could still do something about it.

"Yo," Freedom said as he walked into his attorney's office a little after noon. "I got this mad rhythm in my head, and I can't get it out. I think I want to open my film with it. Woo, no offense," he said, actually looking at Ava for the first time, "you look like . . . bad. You look bad. See, you need to get you some young stuff 'cause that old stuff didn't do nothing for you."

"Sit down," Ava told Freedom. "I need to talk to you, and you need to listen."

Freedom was not accustomed to being spoken to like this, but neither had he ever seen Ava in this kind of mood.

"What's wrong?" he asked as he sat down.

"It's about the house."

"Yo, Ava, I'm not trying to play your dumb games. Where's the camera?" he said, looking around.

"This is not a game," Ava said slowly.

Freedom heard the seriousness in Ava's tone, so he listened without further protest. Ava slowly, but firmly, told Freedom of the events that transpired the night before. Then she told him about what happened in her own apartment. When she was done, Freedom wasn't sure how he should respond.

"Look, Ava, I'm not good with anything too mysterious. Life is a mystery. We don't need to add no spooky stuff to it, you know what I'm saying? I'm not down with no ghosts and goblins. I believe something happened 'cause it's you telling me, but there is a logical explanation for this. And you, being the queen of logic, I know you'll find it." Ava said nothing in response to Freedom's pat explanation. "Tell you what," he said, "when we're through with Baker, we can go over there and check the house out. I'm dying to see the inside anyway."

Ava shook her head. "I'm not going back in there. I already brought something out. I'm not bringing anything else."

"Fine, then I'll go," Freedom told her. "Ava," he said reassuring her, "there is a logical explanation. We just have to find it." Freedom smiled and made a face.

When Ava didn't respond, he took another approach.

"Come on, girl, smile. I'll give you some." He raised an eyebrow and tried to look sexy. With that, Ava did more than smile; she laughed a real laugh.

"Negro, please," she told him, "give me some time to pull myself all together. Meet me back here in an hour."

Charles woke from a deep sleep. He was more refreshed than he knew he deserved to be. It was a surprise to him that he was more concerned about Sandra's call than he was by what had occurred in the house. He got out of bed and found his grandmother already awake.

"Good morning, Charles."

"Morning, Grandma," he said sheepishly.

She was cooking breakfast. "You ain't got nothing in this kitchen. That's okay, you can pick up some stuff later."

Charles prided himself on having a well-equipped kitchen. It was one of the things he dazzled women with. His culinary abilities were well admired.

"Yeah, but you ain't got nothing in here for any real cooking," his grandmother said, reading his thoughts.

"How *do* you do that?" Charles asked. His entire life, Charles had marveled at how his grandmother knew about major events before they happened. On the day his father left them, his mother had already packed his suitcase and a meal. His grandmother had told her to do so. Another time, when his grandmother was visiting, Charles had broken his arm. His mother and grandmother were in the car with the engine running, waiting to take him to the hospital, when he came screaming around the corner. "Get in," his grandmother had barked. Her "knowing" was something the family just took for granted. Now Charles wanted to know how she knew. "How *do* you do that?" he repeated.

"It's simple, Charles. I listen. Stuff is all in the air," she continued. "Most folks don't listen. Sometimes," she said, looking at him sternly, "folks who have a natural ability to hear learn to shut things out. This life is too much for most folks, so they choose to not hear."

"But it must be hard, always knowing what's on folks' minds," Charles said.

"Sometimes yes. Most times no," she told him. "If I

couldn't listen, it would be like not being able to see, hear, feel, taste, touch, all together. Getting rid of this be like getting rid of myself. You oughta try to listen more," she told him. "You'll find yourself in less trouble."

Charles ate a breakfast that beat anything he could make and got ready for work.

"You get done early," his grandmother said. "I need to get in that house."

Charles was about to leave when he stopped where he was standing. "Grandma, I'm not going back in there, and I'm not letting you go either."

"Baby," she said, "I don't know if you got the memo, 'cause most times you don't act like it, but slavery is over. Everything that's gonna happen has already started. It can't be stopped. That house is the seat of a message we need to hear, but there's something else, too. Something I'm not yet sure of how to deal with. You gonna find that no matter where you are, you will be bothered by what happened in that house. You right to be scared, but you should've been scared long before now. Pick me up at one-thirty. Now you go handle your business. It's not as bad as you think. You getting off easy this time, but the next time you act like life is a game, you gonna find out what it's like to be played with."

Charles was listening. And without her saying so, he knew that his grandmother was referring to his secretary. She smiled at him and said, "Now go on and have a Godly day."

Charles mumbled a thanks, kissed his grandmother on the cheek, and left for his office. *Thank God for this crazy woman,* he thought on the way out.

To which he heard his grandmother yell, "I heard that."

All Charles could do was smile.

Ngozi was dreaming of the homeland he couldn't get back to. He saw the beauty, the richness. He saw the shoreline. The waters had receded and the sand was within reach. Ngozi felt as if he could walk there from where he was, but he knew otherwise. He was far from home. Generations away. He looked at the lush greenery and could hear the ocean lapping onto the shore. The rippling of the water at one end and the rustling from the other. One sound danced and sang while another sloshed and pulled. It was rhythm and melody together, as it was meant to be. It was the sound that called him home. These sounds had been separated for too long. The separation hadn't just happened in this place that they called new, this America. It had spread to the shores of all of his people. He looked into the sky and saw birds that had no song. And he wept.

23

Freedom's here

> We were afraid of the dead because
> we never could tell when they
> might show up again.
> —*Jamaica Kincaid*

va was a whiz with research, and often lost herself in the process. Today, however, she was even more focused. Ava logged on to her computer and researched only as many entries on Scott Baker and his film company as she had time for. Most of what she found she'd expected. Scott Baker had been credited for writing, producing, and/or directing a total of fifteen movies in the past ten years. The last four had been box office hits, but not worthy of critical acclaim, while his previous works yielded eight Oscar nominations and several Golden Globe awards. One article pointed out the fact that when Scott made a box office hit and brought in lots of money, the artistic quality of the movie was low, but when he made a brilliant film, he couldn't sell any tickets. Ava knew that Freedom's involvement in a movie project would certainly draw mass appeal. Creating something that would also be brilliant would be Ava's task. Scott Baker wouldn't agree with her involvement, and for now, he didn't have to. This time her collaboration with Freedom would go way beyond legal advice.

At 1:00 Ava's assistant, Jennifer, buzzed and told her that Freedom had returned. "Freedom's here," she said, laughing. "Girl, every time I say that, I feel like it's Juneteenth or something. 'Freedom's here, people, slavery is over.'"

"Send him in," Ava said.

"You know Freedom can't wait," Jennifer said and burst into laughter. "I'm on a roll," she said and hung up. Before Ava could do the same, Freedom was standing in the doorway.

"What's up, girl?" Freedom said, grinning.

"I'd smack you for calling me girl again, but I'm too shocked to see you here on time," Ava said.

"I'm always on time," Freedom informed.

Ava rolled her eyes and laughed. "You have never been on time a day in your life," she told him.

"Oh yes I have. 'Cause when I arrive, that's the right time."

"Whatever," Ava told Freedom. "Sit down, I want you to see something," she said, handing Freedom the article she had printed out.

Freedom read it quickly. "So he does a lot of movies. I know that."

"Yes," Ava said. "But do you see the point the critic is making?" she asked.

"Yeah, that he can't do quality and box office in the same movie," Freedom told her.

"Right." Ava was smiling. "Now tell me everything that happened in that meeting, and don't leave anything out."

Freedom sucked his teeth and relayed every detail from start to finish. Ava took notes and nodded but didn't interrupt. She wrote out the questions she would ask and made marks next to the ones that would require further research. When Freedom was finished, Ava was still writing.

"Okay, professor," Freedom said, "what's up?"

Ava held up her hand and wrote a final sentence. She looked up and smiled again. "Are you ready to be larger than life?" she asked.

Freedom smiled. "Been ready," he told her.

"Then, let's go," Ava said.

"I take it you'll fill me in on the way," Freedom said.

"Maybe," she told him, grinning.

"You'll fill me in, and I'll fill you up." Freedom was reaching for the door and moving in way too close for his attorney's comfort.

"Touch me and die, little boy," Ava said playfully.

Freedom laughed. "You let me touch you, and *you* will die," he said. Freedom ran ahead to retrieve his car from the parking garage.

The work and the light mood had calmed Ava's nerves. If it hadn't been for a little boy in the lobby of her office building, she would have almost forgotten about Johnny and the events that occurred the night before. This child was not Johnny. He didn't even look like him, but he smiled and waved, and Ava smiled back.

As Ava began to walk away, the boy called to her. "Hey lady," he said, "Johnny says to tell you 'hello.' "

24

save the drama

harles Campbell III was taking his time getting to his office. He had to prepare himself mentally for the drama that he knew would unfold. But something his grandmother said helped to ease his anxiety. Charles hadn't planned to, but found himself on Tubman Terrace in front of the house. He knew he couldn't go inside. Instead, he sat on a park bench across from the house and stared at it. It was a beautiful building, and right now, the house looked peaceful and innocent. If he hadn't seen the odd images on the staircase himself, he would never have believed such a thing was possible. Sitting here in the early morning light the house actually seemed inviting. He felt drawn to it, and he began to walk toward the house. He reached the front stairs and searched for the key he'd placed in his briefcase. He couldn't locate the key, but it didn't matter: The door slowly opened, and the feeling of warmth and comfort grew stronger. Just as he was about to step into the darkness, his cell phone startled him back to his senses. Charles grabbed his phone and before he could remember to say the word, "Hello," he could hear the familiar voice.

"Don't even think about it," his grandmother said. "Go directly to your office. Handle your business, then pick me up." She didn't wait for a response and hung up. He shook his head and almost laughed.

If he could see what his grandmother had sensed, he would have completely forgotten how to laugh.

"I almost had him," the spirit memory with the bloody newborn said. "That old bitch stopped him, but he would have been mine."

Ngozi moved toward the memory. He felt sorry for her, just as he had for so many in life. "Woman, you cannot exist as you did before. You want to keep a man, just as your ancestors had been kept. You must share yourself with him. You must tell him your story and nothing more."

Ngozi moved away from the memory of the woman. When he did, she laughed a wicked laugh. "I will have him," she said to the bloody bundle in her arms. "And you will finally have a father. We'll be a family. All of us. Me, you, and your daddy.

As Charles drove to his office, he tried to imagine the conversation he'd have with Sandra. He didn't have the words. He was not ready to be a father and certainly didn't want to be a husband. Sandra was very satisfying sexually but not stimulating mentally or emotionally. It suddenly dawned on him that he hadn't been these things for her either. He couldn't be a family man, not with Sandra. Instead, he'd give her a nice severance check and talk her into getting an abortion. As soon as he voiced these plans out loud to himself, his mind went back to the house and the woman with the bloody newborn. Then he thought of Vanessa. He hadn't thought of her in years. She was a one-night stand. He'd met her at a club and wanted her from the first moment he saw her. She approached him first.

"Hello, beautiful," Vanessa had said. She was tall, voluptuous, and white.

When he met her, he remembered what one of the brothers once said. "White women are wild in bed, but don't try to bring one home. Your grandma will kill you. Besides," the brother told him, "white women will give a black man whatever he wants, but a black woman will give him what he needs."

Charles enjoyed the passion of Vanessa for that one night only. She called him two months later to say that she was pregnant. She had already decided to get an abortion but thought it fair to let him know. Charles paid for it and acted like he cared.

Now his problems were closer to home. Sandra wasn't some one-night stand. She was his assistant, and while it was difficult for him to admit, he did care for her. She had been what he would call "accommodating" in every way. She was available whenever he wanted her to be and made no demands. True, she would whine about him not taking her out to business parties, but she got over it. Sandra knew what he liked and gave it to him. Still, it was not enough for Charles. He was searching for the perfect woman, even though he was nowhere near perfection himself.

Charles reached his office, took in a deep breath, and went inside. Sandra's desk was on just the other side of the door in the reception area. She wasn't there. Instead there was an envelope with his name on it. Charles pulled out the letter that read, "Charles,"

I'm sorry for the drama last night. I'm not good at this so I'll get to the point. I'm not pregnant, but I wish I were. Maybe then you'd see how much I love and need you. I'm quitting because I must. Last night I almost ended my own life. That's when I realized that I'm the problem. You never told me you loved me. You never even said that you cared about me. I pursued you because I thought you'd be the perfect husband. I was wrong. I say this not to get back at you, but for my own hearing. You only care about yourself. If I had somehow won you over, I would've been miserable. Charles, you are not loving. You are not giving. The very fact that you would watch me hurt and feel nothing, even when you are so intimately close to me, tells me that I have truly wasted my time. I don't know what has given me the strength to do this, but I quit. Send my last check to my home address. Please messenger it today, as I am leaving New York tomorrow.

Good luck in your life. You will reap what you have sown.

Sandra

Charles wanted to crush the letter and burn it. How dare she tell him who he was? "That's why I didn't take your crazy behind nowhere," he said out loud. "Clinging vine is what you are." In his heart Charles knew that Sandra was right, but his heart couldn't admit it to his head. Not just yet. For now, he would feel relief and move on as if nothing had happened. Charles wrote the check and attached a note that said, "Best of luck in the future." He called a messenger service, something he hadn't done for himself in a long time, and then he called a temp employment agency for a quick replacement. "I want an older woman," he told them. "Real old."

25

the gift

I believe in prayer. It's the
best way we have to draw
strength from heaven.
—Josephine Baker

W hile Charles was poking around
at the house on Tubman, his grandmother, Dora, had been
reading the Bible. She could spiritually see that he was about to
enter. She said a quick prayer before calling him. "Please Lord,
let this ignorant boy listen."

Her grandmother had the "gift," as it was called, and Dora
had been gifted for as long as she could remember. But when
she was still a girl, she wasn't able to think of it as a gift. It was

more like a curse. She would tell people things that she felt had happened and then tell them what she thought would happen. Folks didn't take kindly to her knowledge. "In a small town people are dumb enough to believe that they can do whatever they want with nobody finding out," her grandmother had said. "You can find things out without the gift in a place this small," she said of the little town outside of Savannah. "Don't you worry 'bout what folks say. God is in control. Just don't let none of their mean talk spoil you or cause you to use this gift for harm." Her grandmother was more like a mother to her than her biological one. Dora was too much for her mother to handle, or so she was told. Her grandmother taught her how to cook, sew, clean, fix almost anything. But mainly she taught her the importance of her gift and the use of herbs and other plants. "Ain't nothing spooky about who we are," she often said. "God measures out to everyone spiritual gifts. Most folks just too earthly to find 'em." Dora's grandmother raised her to feel completely normal. But others still found it hard to be around her, especially when she and her grandmother were in the same room.

Once, when Dora was a teenager, an uncle she had never met came to visit. He had been away for years and had finally returned home. Dora knew he was coming even before her grandmother. "Who's the man with the limp, Big Mama?" she asked. "He's on his way home, said he needs to be with his people. I don't think he'll be here long though 'cause he's real sickly."

Dora's grandmother began to cry. She cried all day.

That evening, her oldest boy, Sonny, drove up in a big Cadillac. "Been gone from you all for too long," he said to his mother.

"You didn't have to wait 'til you were dying" was all she said. She held her son and cried with him.

Uncle Sonny lived another three years even though his doctor had only given him three months. People said it was a combination of loving, healing, and knowing that gave him the extra time. It was time well spent.

Uncle Sonny had left when he was young to seek his fortune and to get away from what he called "pure backwardness." In truth, he feared his mother's abilities. Later on, the thing he feared became the very thing he missed most. He had made a lot of money as a car dealer, but he missed the comfort of the same backward folks that he'd tried to run from.

During his final three years, he never left his hometown. He soaked up all the love he needed and gave love and advice freely to anyone who wanted it. He and Dora had become fishing buddies. In a way he was the father she didn't know. Sonny, who's real name was Charles, had been her grandson's namesake. Dora knew that the similarities went way beyond the name. Her own brother, Charles, had also tried to run from his roots and from his true nature.

Dora put the Bible down on Charles's coffee table, where she hoped he would be forced to find it, and gathered the things she would need for her trip to the house. She had envisioned the woman with the newborn child. This was a familiar spirit. A spirit that was of the Devil. When people dabble with the occult, they often conjured these spirits. Unlike spirit memories that provide peace for the living, familiar spirits cause people to fret. Her grandson was in danger. The greatest danger for Charles, however, would come from within himself.

Dora had come close to the things inside the house before, but it hadn't been the proper time. Years before, when Charles was still a boy and Dora was on one of her annual summer visits, Dora had gone to see a friend who worked at a house on the same street. As she walked past the corner house, she sensed something unnatural. She was accustomed to spirit memories. Her grandmother had taught her all about them.

"There are no ghosts and goblins," she had said to Dora. "When a person passes over, we still hold memories of them, but because the living have not made peace with the deceased, they often create a presence in their own mind. That presence may or may not manifest itself. The spirit memory exists until the living are able to be at peace with those who are passed on."

Dora was confused by this. "So the real ghosts are the people who are alive?" she asked.

"Sort of," her grandmother explained. "The living are unresolved. In the spirit realm, you know everything and have the power to forgive. The living make a spirit memory. It's the part of what hasn't been dealt with."

"So what do I do when I see one?" Dora wondered.

"All you have to do is listen. They trying to tell their story to anybody who'll listen. You listen, and your life won't be so confused."

When Dora encountered the memories in the house years before, she knew that it was a place of gathering for many untold stories. It hadn't been her time to listen then, but the time was drawing near. There was now a purpose in the house. There was a memory that had to be heard and another that had to be dealt with. She prayed that when the time came, she would know the difference.

26

getting to know you

Ava and Freedom arrived for the meeting. They were met by the same fanfare that Freedom had seen the day before. This time, though, there were printed proposals in front of each department head. Scott Baker was always proud of his ability to impress, but today he would go even farther. He knew a lot about Ms. Ava Vercher. She would not be won over as easily as most lawyers whose greed outweighed what was good for their client. Scott would win her and her client's confidence as well.

"So, I hear you want to make a movie using Freedom's music," Ava began.

Scott laid out his idea, as if for the first time. This time, though, he brought along visual aids in the form of charts and graphs. He had charted the ratio of blacks to whites who go to the movies, then his movies. He broke it down by regions and income. He then presented the numbers of folks who buy Freedom's music, where they lived, what video and computer equipment they had, and how many people from age eighteen to forty lived in their households. He'd done his homework. Still, Scott Baker was not ready for Ava Vercher.

"Impressive," she admitted to the room. "So where do we go from here?" she asked.

"Well, we'd like to start developing a script based on several of Freedom's signature songs. Then we hash out the 'who gets cast as who' details. Then we shoot," Scott said.

Ava smiled. "You think you can do this and still have it released in time for Oscar consideration?"

Baker, who had also been smiling, stopped. "We just want to make a good movie that depicts the life of the underclass," Baker said.

"According to whom?" Ava asked him. "Naw, brother, you want to exploit, or excuse me 'expose,'" she said, using the gesture she heard he'd used the day before. "We don't intend to participate in any further exploitation of the 'underclass.' Thanks for your time and for planting the idea. I think I know who would be willing to roll with this right away."

Ava had packed up her notes, dropped the proposal in the

trash, and was on her way out of the conference room when Scott stood up and stammered, "There's no need to be hasty."

"I'm not hasty. I'm in a hurry. We need to make our announcement before you do."

"Okay, okay," Scott said. "What's the problem with our proposal, and what do you want?"

Freedom had the good sense to be right behind Ava, and while Ava paused to give Baker another chance, Freedom was already outside of the double glass doors. Ava made a mental note to thank him for adding to the effect. She called Freedom back inside and told Baker how things would need to proceed. "We will give you a script. We will go over it with you after it's completed in, say, two weeks," she said. "Maybe three, tops. We'll give you a list of principals, and you can play with it. Freedom will of course be in control of the soundtrack and will retain a writing and producing credit. He gets foreign distribution and a cut of the film. We'll hash out dollars later, but we need to meet in a smaller room to talk about percentage points. You direct and produce the film. We write it and help cast it. By the way, Freedom will also appear in the movie. We also need to find out what you intend to do for publicity." Ava paused, but she wasn't done. Someone from the creative department was about to speak, but Scott held up his hand. "You, Mr. Scott Baker, can take it or leave it, but we intend to give you mass appeal and critical acclaim all in one movie. In other words we shall 'expose,'" she said with the gesture, "your true capability to the world. Power to the people," she added.

Scott tried to look impressed. Instead, he appeared whipped. "Can I get back to you in the morning?" he asked.

"Sure, but when you do, make sure you've read the gossip

column in the *New York Post*. We don't have time to wait. It will cost you more by tomorrow."

Ava was asking for more involvement than Scott had ever allowed. But she also knew which buttons to push.

"Fine," he said. "We'll agree to those things and work out the numbers later, but not much later," he added. "You play a little too hard for me. Do you need this in writing?" Scott asked.

"Sure, but I'll write it up and send it over for your signature," Ava told him.

"I'm glad we'll be on the same team," Scott said.

Freedom smiled, and when he did, everyone else did, too.

When the small-talk-to-make-nice was complete and Ava and Freedom had left, Scott Baker broke the silence that had fallen over the conference room. "I'm so glad they're doing the script," he said. "I have no idea what those people are saying or thinking."

Everyone laughed because they had no idea that the people they didn't understand knew them very well. Ava had learned to capitalize on that knowledge.

27

◆

the fall

Circumstances not only alter
causes; they alter character.
—*Kelly Miller*

At 1:30 Charles picked up his grandmother, who was already standing outside when he arrived. She had a large bag that smelled like all the herbs he ever heard of.

"You sure are ready huh, Grandma?" Charles asked.

"Boy, don't be sassing me. Just drive."

Charles did so, as his grandmother hummed old church songs. Every now and then she would sing songs Charles hadn't heard since he was a boy. "Come by here, Lord. Come by here. Come by here, Lord. Come by here. Somebody needs you, Lord. Come by here."

Charles loved his grandmother's singing. When she sang, she was almost a normal grandmother, old and comfortable. Charles was about to turn the corner to Tubman Terrace when his grandmother stopped singing. Her eyes became watery, and she began to cry. "So many lonely memories," she said.

"You okay, Grandma?" Charles asked.

"Yes, son, I am," she said.

Charles pulled up to the curb and was about to point out the house to his grandmother. He realized it wasn't necessary and sat silently instead. His grandmother got out of the car, lugging her bag alongside her. She slowly walked up the steps.

Things happened too quickly for Charles to take it all in. He had only turned his head for a second, and before he knew it, his grandmother, her bag, and all of its contents were laid out on the sidewalk. "Don't be pushing me" she was yelling. Charles ran toward her, cell phone in hand. He was already dialing 911. He reached his grandmother in no time and was holding her.

"You okay? What happened?" he managed.

"Boy, I sure wish you would use the gifts God gave you. Then you wouldn't have to ask so many dumb questions," she said. "Something pushed me down those stairs, and I think I broke something." She tried to move, but when she did so, she let out a loud moan. Charles had never seen his grandmother ill. He couldn't even remember her ever having a cold. Seeing her helpless made him feel helpless, too.

"Grandma, what should I do?" he asked.

His grandmother pointed to her purse, which was among

the herbs and plants that had been thrown about. "Get me my bag, boy." Charles did so, and his grandmother pulled out a plastic baggie that contained something that looked akin to marijuana.

"Grandma, what—" Before he could finish, she told him to stop thinking foolishness.

"This kills the pain, not my brain." She began to chew on it. In the distance Charles could hear an ambulance approaching. "What you go calling them for? You know I don't like no hospistals," she said, mispronouncing the word.

"You said it yourself, Grandma. Something is broken. We have to get it taken care of. You too old to just let things go."

Charles wanted to smack himself for that remark. His grandmother just laughed. The emergency attendants loaded Charles's grandmother into the vehicle, and Charles followed. The last twenty-four hours had truly been hard, but his grandmother braced herself, for she knew that the next twenty-four would be even harder.

28

yo Tayembé

> We feared the heartlessness of human
> beings. All of whom are born blind.
> Few of whom ever learn to see.
>
> —*Ben Okri,*
> The Famished Road

Ngozi thought of the son he'd never seen in life. Ngozi saw his son's life. He knew that he had been a wonderful son to his mother and a kind husband and father. Knowing never made Ngozi's existence any easier. There were times when he felt what the living would call pride, but those moments were short lived. His existence was connected to the completion of his task.

He had watched his descendants one by one, hoping that someone would hear his story. Until now, it hadn't happened. He would soon have the opportunity. Telling his story and passing on the drum was his reason for existing. He hoped that this boy, Freedom, would hear more than the beat. What he needed him to do was hear and tell the story. It was Freedom and all of his fathers before him that willed Ngozi to be. Ngozi's presence was the result of the unresolved issues between boys who didn't know their fathers. The boys who had no voice, no connection, no beat of their own. "Yo Tayembé. I'm calling you, Son," Ngozi chanted.

There would be one chance, and one chance only. Ngozi was running out of time. The survival of his people depended on him. The old woman, Dora, would have been able to help, but Bella, the woman with the child, had interfered. Her will, as misguided as it was, was growing stronger. Soon it would be stronger than his. He would have to act quickly. Ngozi sat down and began to play the drum. He played slowly and sweetly at first. The rhythm became stronger and more and more syncopated. The beat was now fast and furious. "Do you know who you are? Do you see what you once were? Do you feel all that you could be again?" Ngozi yelled these words over and over as he played. The playing continued. As it did, the spirit memories gathered. No stories would be told on this night. The tide was not high. The moon was not full. It wasn't time for the Gathering. Instead they would wait, like a pregnant woman who's reached full term, yet still cannot deliver. Her pains were their pains. They rocked and travailed in time with the drum rhythms, picking up the chant. "Do you know who you are? Do you see what you once were? Do you feel all that you could be again?"

This song was for the living. But somewhere in the lower part of the house, the familiar spirit that belonged to Bella sang the song for herself. "Yes, I know what I will be, what we will be again," she said to the bloody newborn. She laughed a wicked laugh and said, "Nathan, this can be our home again."

29

ye oh ye ba ba

Don't trouble trouble til trouble troubles you.

—African American proverb

If I told you once, I told you twice. I don't want to stay here." Charles's grandmother was putting up a good fight. Once the X rays were completed and everyone knew that she had in fact broken something, her arm and a rib to be exact, there was no calming her down.

"I think it was Gilda Radner who said, 'Doctors don't know anything because they practice on the dead.'"

Charles laughed. "Grandma, how is it that you know what Gilda Radner said about doctors?" he asked.

"I can read, can't I?" His grandmother was protesting, but she knew that she would have to stay put. There was one fear that she could not shake; that was the fear of falling. At her age, which she never mentioned, falling could be the beginning of the end. Many of her friends and old schoolmates had died by the way of a fall. It was true that she had more energy and ability than folks half her age, but there was little she'd be able to do after a terrible fall. Now her fear had been realized. In a way Dora was relieved. Her worst fear hadn't been so bad. She'd mend well, the doctors had told her, but they wanted to have her stay long enough to make sure that everything was okay.

"I'm healthier than you, young man. Don't make no sense for somebody as young as you to have high blood pressure."

The doctor went pale and asked Dora how she knew about his high blood pressure.

"It's in your color," she told him.

"Well, we'd like to do some observations on you anyway," he said.

Dora did want to make sure that everything would mend properly. "I'm old, but I ain't no fool," she said. She just didn't want to be held up in a hospital or anywhere else for that matter. What she needed to do was get inside that house. She felt the pull. She also knew she'd been pushed. *Something in that place needs me*, she said to herself. *But something else don't want me near.*

"You say something, Grandma?" Charles had dozed off in the chair beside his grandmother's bed.

"Boy, I ain't talking to you, but if I had been, you would not have heard me."

"You okay, Grandma? Can I get you anything?"

"Yes," she said. "You can stay away from that house until I tell you what to do."

"That's gonna be hard to do right now," he said. "I got a call from the people who started this. I was supposed to let them in to see the place."

Charles's grandmother studied his face. To him it looked as if she were miles away, but it was only her ability to see that had left the room. Dora was trying to read the thoughts of the woman who made the call. She could see Ava clearly. Dora smiled. "Now, she would have made you into a good man, Chucky. I tried to tell you that when you were little."

"Grandma," Charles said loudly. "You okay?" His grandmother, who'd always been odd, was acting even more strange.

"They gave me something that didn't mix well with my herbs," Dora mumbled. "I think I better sleep now," she said. By the time she finished her sentence, she was already asleep.

Charles kissed his grandmother on the forehead. It was something he hadn't done in a long time. He smiled and allowed the feeling to envelop him. As he left the hospital and got to his car, he thought of Ava and his childhood desire to live between the gap in her two front teeth. His cell phone went off. "Hey," he heard from the other end.

"Hey, yourself. I was just thinking about you."

"Yeah, well," Ava said as she and Freedom sped down the highway. "This client of mine wants to go into the house, and well, I think I'm okay with it," she said. Charles didn't know what to say, but he knew what Ava was feeling. He too had felt that pull.

"Are you there now?" he asked.

"Yes, and my client is with me." Feeling great after the

meeting with Scott Baker and associates, Freedom had almost demanded that they go to the house. Before calling Charles, Ava tried again to tell Freedom what happened the night before. He only half believed her.

"Yo, you only had a bad experience 'cause you went in there with that old bourgeois Negro."

"If you think he's old, what does that make me?" Ava asked. "I told you we grew up together."

"It makes you seasoned," Freedom said slyly.

Ava was accustomed to Freedom's flirting, but lately he'd made an attempt at being charming. It made her uncomfortable and a bit giddy all at once. "Look, little boy," Ava began.

"Don't 'little boy' me," Freedom told her. "Age ain't nothing but a number. Besides, you're not that much older than I am."

Ava laughed, but she was trying to compose herself. She didn't like being hit on by clients, but she regarded Freedom as more than a client. He'd often been her sounding board. She respected his opinion and liked his aloof style. The name Freedom suited him. Whenever a deal was made with record executives, Freedom let her do her thing. He stood back, trusting her to get him whatever he needed. Most of her clients didn't have the same confidence. They all felt it necessary to tell her just how to go about doing the deal. Freedom turned to Ava who was trying to focus on the road, the house, the movie deal, and anything but Freedom.

"Look, woman," he said, "I know who you are, and I like it." Freedom didn't say another word. This was the closest he'd ever come to showing any emotion toward a woman. Ever since his childhood experience with Stacey Brown, he never allowed himself to care. It was true that he'd said whatever it took to get a woman into bed. Once or twice when he was younger, he'd even used the "L" word. He didn't go that far anymore, but he didn't need to. He knew he wasn't trying to get Ava into bed. He would have liked to, but for some reason, he was feeling like he wanted much more. His feelings had something to do with the way she handled Scott Baker. Freedom had seen Ava in action, but today she was in rare form. What moved him the most was the fact that she believed in his ability to deliver something he'd never done. Freedom was beginning to sense a lot of what he'd been missing, and he suddenly felt a tinge of loneliness. He would not admit this to anyone, but if his grandmother were still alive, he knew he wouldn't have to. Just as he was having this thought, Ava pulled up to the curb in front of the house on Tubman Terrace.

Freedom looked at the house and then back to Ava. "Yo, I know this is my home," he said to her. "After that deal you pulled today, I might even let you spend the night."

Ava laughed and so did Freedom. It was the comic relief they both needed. The mood in the car was thick enough to cut, but it was nothing compared to the mood or moods inside the house. Inside, the beginnings of a battle were just starting. Ava was still talking to Charles while Freedom was watching his house. He thought he got a glimpse of the lights he'd seen before, then he saw nothing. The whole Johnny thing that Ava told him about was messing with him. When Ava told him about the boy, he hadn't made a connection. But now, he remembered the odd kid that had run in front of his car. "Naw, now she got me tripping," he said to the air.

Ava was still talking with the attorney, but her tone had changed. "No, you're kidding. Is she okay?" she was saying. "How long before she'll be able to go home?" Ava was asking.

Freedom was only half listening to the conversation when he looked up to the second-story window. What he saw caused a scream to stir from somewhere within him. He would have let out the scream, but his grandmother had told him to be silent. There in that window the woman Freedom had called Grand, or something that looked and somehow felt like her, had raised a finger to its lips and was telling him to be still. He did as he was told. He was still nodding his head when Ava finished her call.

"You won't believe this," she was saying. She continued to talk about Charles's grandmother. It had something to do with her coming to the house and either falling down or being pushed. She said the woman didn't want them to go into the house.

"Okay, yeah," Freedom said. He was still nodding.

Ava saw that he was not paying attention to what she was saying. Instead, he was staring at the house. She looked to the window he was fixed on and saw nothing. "You okay?" she asked.

"I'm good," he responded.

"Did you hear what I said? We can't go in."

"Okay," Freedom said, "then we won't."

She wasn't sure, but Ava thought that there had been an emphasis on the word we. "I'm not playing, Freedom. You don't know what you're dealing with, and neither do I. Let's wait until we hear what happened from Charles's grandmother."

Freedom nodded his agreement, but he knew he'd do otherwise. He heard what Ava said about Charles's grandmother, but now he was listening to his own grandmother. She had never led him wrong. He missed her more than he'd realized. Now she was back. Freedom thought that he had never believed in anything spooky. He believed in God and had accepted him as his savior when he was a boy, but formal religion, especially in the black church, was too spooky for him. He didn't need any craziness in his life. He had forgotten about the childhood voices. He'd forgotten about the drum song. It was slowly coming back to him. "Ye oh Ye Ba Ba," he said to himself.

"Okay, okay," Freedom said, snapping out of what appeared to Ava to have been a trance. "I heard you, and if you believe there's something there, then I believe it." Freedom's tone had changed, and he appeared to be back to himself. But there was still something odd about his manner.

"I'd love to go get something to eat now, but we have only two weeks to knock out that script," Ava was saying. "I'm going to have to go home to work, and you should do the same. I need you to pull out the good stuff on this. None of those same tired tunes that you keep reproducing, okay?" she said.

"Yeah, I got you," Freedom was saying. Ava dropped Freedom off at her office, where they had left his car earlier. She didn't stay. She would go home and begin work on an outline that would blow Scott Baker away. Freedom was also about to begin his work. It was the work that he was here to do. The question that folks would ask for a long time afterward was why he had done it in this manner.

30

echoes

Rap is an authentic descendant
of a people with ancient
African oral traditions.

—*Mumia Abu-Jamal*

he music in the house played over and over. There was no Gathering, and therefore, there was no balance. The beat was incredible, but without the words that echoed truth, it was pure emotion. Raw passion that was poisonous. Beat with no truth was not the form that was meant to be heard. This form of music, this hollow beat, fast, furious, passionate, had been all that the descendants of the drum had connected with. Ngozi had been successful in bringing back the beat, but also had to infuse it with truth. To do that, much was required.

Some artists heard the beat that echoed from Harlem to Atlanta to California to the Midwest through swaying bodies of the young, to black Brits and over to Japan to the islands and back home to Africa. The beat was back in the rhythm of words. Words that rarely echoed truth. And when they did, it was short lived. When Tupac was moving close to truth, close to melody, close to harmony, his life was cut off. Biggie had only begun to barely see; he, too, was gone. Others were finding truth and *life*, but their music was rarely produced. The labels didn't want this new sound to survive, so without support, they either went back to the old or fell out of the scene completely. The truth was trying to come forth, but there would be a great struggle.

The beat, the rhythm, the words of hip-hop music rarely spoke the truth of the drum, but because they were chanted inside of the same syncopation, they had the ability to capture the listener in a way that had never been heard. Rap, hip hop, the beat had taken the world by storm. It was played by rebels from Nicaragua to Kosovo. The beat was copied, watered down, and sold in suburban record stores to young whites who loved being connected to something and whose parents didn't understand that connection. The music most often spoke of violence and sex in the same breath. Sometimes, but not too often, the music spoke of love and truth, but these songs were rarely popular. The righteous artists, like Amon Rashidi, The Roots, and Black Thought, who dared to use the music in this manner, were few and far between. They were not mass produced and carbon copied. It was the raw form that was duplicated and exported for the world to hear. Tonight the music from the house played loudly. Artists like Elum N Nation would awake the next day swearing they'd written their best work ever. Some of them would hear the same tune. None of them would have the ability to comprehend that this was a universal tune, a beat that belonged to all African people, a beat that would link the younger generation to the ancestors and free them from the bondage of negativity. That it was a work in progress. It was raw. "Yeah, whoever puts it on wax first" was the old saying. But first was not always best.

Freedom drove back up to the house. He, too, heard the music. He went to the side of the house as his grandmother had instructed him to do. Using a tire iron, he bent the bars to the basement window. Jimmying the lock was easy. Getting inside was easier still.

31

time for all things

> Time is swiftly running out, and a new
> dialogue is indispensable. It is so long
> overdue, it is already half past midnight.
> —*John O. Killens,*
> *"The Black Psyche"*

Somewhere in a hospital, Charles's grandmother was tossing in her sleep. Ava was at home working furiously on the outline of the script idea. Charles was reading the Bible that had been left open by his grandmother. She had left markers in two places. The book of Luke, chapter 16, verses 19 to 31, was highlighted in yellow marker. It told the story of a rich man and a poor man. The poor man had a miserable life due to poverty and illness. The rich man lived in splendor, feeding his passions daily. Both died. The poor man went to heaven; the rich man went to hell. The rich man cried out for mercy and begged for the poor man to simply dip his finger in water and cool his tongue. His request was denied. He then begged that the man be able to go back and warn his brothers. But he was again denied and told that his brothers had Moses and the prophets; let them hear them. The rich man continued to plead. "But if someone from the dead could go to them, then surely they would repent," he urged. But again, he was denied. "If they do not listen to Moses and the prophets, neither will they be persuaded of someone who rises from the dead."

After reading the short passage, Charles made notes. "Why this scripture?" he wrote. Then he wrote the question that would've made his grandmother proud. "If no one comes back, who's in that house?" Charles flipped to the other marked section. It was the book of Ecclesiastes. This time the entire book had been highlighted. He read it and came to the familiar passage that had even been made into a song. "There is a season for everything, and there is time for every event under the sun. There is a season turn, turn, turn." Charles hummed the popular sixties tune. He continued to read. He read about the evils of oppression, the folly of riches, and the futility of life. The more he read, the more confused he became. Then he remembered the scripture he'd been taught as a child. "Wisdom is the principal thing, therefore, get wisdom, but in all thy getting, get an understanding."

"I wish I could understand anything this crazy woman does," he said to himself. Charles looked at the large art deco clock and saw that he'd been trying to get an understanding for almost three hours. He must have dozed off or read more than he realized. Just as he was about to call it a night, or better yet a morning, his cell phone rang. Charles had to follow the ringing to find it. It lay under the jacket he wore the day before, and he reached it just in time. "This had better be good," he said into the phone.

"Charles. Oh Charles." It was Ava, and she was crying.

"What is it? Where are you? Are you okay?" Charles rattled off a string of questions. All he knew was that Ava was in trouble. "Talk to me," he managed.

"He's . . . he's . . . ." Ava stammered to find the words. "Freedom's dead."

32

the transition

> But this time, somewhere in the
> interspace between the spirit world
> and the living, I chose to stay.
> —*Ben Okri*

Charles wasn't sure who or what Ava was talking about. "What?" Charles asked in disbelief.

Ava somehow discerned this. "Freedom, the client who wanted the house, he's dead. I'm there now. I'm at the house. Please come."

Charles wasn't able to respond in words, but he was in his shoes and his car before Ava had even begun to tell him what was happening. "Ten minutes. Give me ten minutes," he told her.

Ava put down the phone and wept. Police and emergency workers were all over the place. Someone had alerted the media, and camera crews were now arriving. Onlookers had surrounded the house. Not just the white neighbors who had heard the screams, but also the black Harlemites who'd always crossed the street whenever they passed the house. An old blind man with a cane was shaking his head. "Can anything good come out of this place?" he said to no one in particular.

The officer who contacted Ava earlier walked over to her. "We need to ask you more questions. Can you come inside?"

She gathered her wits to do as she had been asked, but before she could move toward the place, she felt herself falling.

"She's fainted," one officer said to another.

"It's gonna be a long night," the other responded.

33

knowing

I just say, "Never mine, never mine, long as I
can spell G-O-D I got somebody along."
—*Alice Walker,* The Color Purple

Charles's grandmother slipped in
and out of consciousness. As she'd predicted, the medicine the
doctors had given her did not mix well with the herbs she had
prescribed for herself. She was in a semi-private room. Dora
didn't like the term "semi." In her mind, either something was
or it wasn't. She didn't want anything semi or demi or halfway.
Right now she wished for complete privacy. She would need it

when she came to herself. Her roommate's television was on, and even though it was semi-loud, it was disturbing her sleep completely. Dora could hear a news announcer saying something about the death of Freedom. "So what else is old?" Dora asked. "Freedom been dead." She looked past the thin curtain that was supposed to provide privacy. She reached and pulled it back to get a better view of the television set. For a brief second, she thought she saw Charles escorting a woman she was sure had been little Ava, who had lived around the corner from her daughter and grandchild years before. Suddenly, a picture of the house on Tubman Terrace flashed across the television screen. Charles was in deeper than she thought. Dora tried to raise up from the bed and found that she couldn't. A searing pain ripped across her chest. Even in her foggy state of mind, Dora knew not to interfere with her healing process.

It took some effort, but she lay back and tried to think. The thinking caused a rush of pain to her head so Dora unwittingly gave up the fight and fell into an even deeper sleep. Once there, she would see more clearly. She would hear more truths—the truths that would be too profound to deal with in a conscious state. In her sleep Dora would be able to face whatever resided inside the house.

Charles had arrived just in time to help Ava up but too late to catch her. From his car he could see her falling. Her color was bad. It was the color black folks took on when their life was about to leave them. Charles knew this from the stories he'd heard his grandmother tell. He hated overhearing what he called her "ghost stories." When he was a child and trying to hear the grown folks talk, he'd sit on the steps that led to the cellar. No one saw him there, but later on he suspected that his grandmother knew and that she told these stories to frighten him. One night it almost killed him. His relatives had gathered to talk about who was seen with whom. The conversation was getting real grown when his grandmother said how she saw the spirit memory, as she called it, of a dead relative. Someone who had appeared to instruct her on how to deal with an impending danger.

"Speaking of Louise and Jim," she'd begun. "Guess who came right up to my bed last night?" The listening relatives never asked, "Who?" Dora would tell them in time. Besides, they were afraid to ask. "Jim's Uncle Gus," she said matter-of-factly. "Come right up to my bed. Didn't say a word. Just stood there with that gaping hole in his head, like it wasn't there. He was grinning like we liked each other or something. That there's a sight to see, a man with a hole in his head, just smiling at you." Dora would go on to say that she knew he was trying to tell her something and that he wouldn't leave until she figured it out. "Ain't no use me trying to sleep. I can see you ain't gonna let me," she'd told the spirit memory. She got the pad of paper and pen that she kept next to her bed and began to write as she'd done on many nights like this.

She started by writing Uncle Gus's full name and the names of his living relatives. When she finally got to the name that Uncle Gus had come about, his grin became broader, she had said. "I wrote Jim's name on that paper, and that man got to smiling like a cat." Then she would write about Jim's life and his family. Uncle Gus had indicated that trouble was brewing in Jim's love life, and it had nothing to do with his wife of twenty years. The fact that Uncle Gus, and not some other relative, had come, told Dora that if Jim didn't stop fooling around, he would end up with a big hole in his body. Charles's grandmother told the story like she was reciting a list of sale items downtown. Those who had been listening were accustomed to these stories. Charles was not. He fell down the steps onto the hard cellar floor and turned what his grandmother later called a death color. He awoke to her tapping him on the head and saying, "Come on back, boy. It ain't hardly your time. You got work to do." He remembered being sad that all she could think of was his chores. Now seeing Ava with the same near-death color, he somehow knew what she meant about having work to do. He felt that Ava, the house, and all that had recently occurred was part of that work.

When he first got to Tubman Terrace, Charles had pulled his SUV up on the curb of the park side of the street. As he got out of the car, Charles remembered to grab the business card he always left on his dashboard and then ran to where Ava had fallen. He had to cross the barricade line the police had put up between Ava and the house. Just as he reached Ava, a uniformed officer reached him.

"You can't be over here. Get back," he barked.

"She called me," Charles said while producing the business card in one smooth move. Whenever he walked, he kept one in the palm of his hand. As an upwardly mobile black man,

Charles was accustomed to being stopped by police officers. He was used to explaining his presence in the so-called good neighborhoods and had learned how to deal with the police gently. He kept a white card outside of his wallet for such occasions. Reaching for a wallet had been enough for a jury to decide that Amadou Diallo's death was not a product of racism, but accidental. It was reason enough for four police officers to shoot forty-one times. Charles, and most black men like him, lived prepared for a moment that his white peers never even thought about. His business card, which indicated that he was an attorney, along with his whitewashed manner, were usually enough to deter even the most brash officers. The card was produced so quickly that the officer looked dumbfounded.

"There's no suspect that I know of. Who are you representing?" he asked.

Ava was just coming to, and Charles moved to reach her. "She's my friend. She called," he managed.

Ava's eyes fluttered, and she could see Charles. He was talking to a police officer. "I'm here," she wanted to say but couldn't. Charles was moving away from the officer and over to her. "Help me. I saw him. He's there with the others," she said.

"What others?" Charles was asking, but she couldn't respond.

Because the media had already arrived, and because this was white row, the paramedics responded quickly. They were lifting Ava before Charles had time to figure out what he should be doing. "Step back, sir. She's in shock," the short, stocky paramedic said.

Charles did so, but in his mind he was tapping Ava on the

head and repeating the words he'd heard years before. "Come back. It's not your time. You've got work to do."

If Charles had grown up with his grandmother Dora's "knowing," he would have been able to see Freedom standing next to Ava, saying almost the same thing.

34

• ◆ •

clarity

Pour oh pour, that
parting soul in song.
—*Jean Toomer*

Freedom didn't really know what had happened, but he knew why it had. He knew all kinds of things now. He knew that his previous life had been almost a waste, but he thanked God for it anyway. He wished for his life back so he could relive it with the clarity he now had. He knew it would be futile to go back. He had to go forward.

Freedom waited for Ava, his friend, his love, his purpose, to come to. Once she did, he went back to the house that he would, for now, call home.

35

fade to black

What key are you struggling in?

—*Fats Waller*

Ava regained consciousness but not much clarity. "What's going on?" she wondered out loud. As soon as she saw Charles, everything came rushing back. She'd received a call she thought was a prank. It was two A.M. when the phone rang. She was already deep into writing the outline that would blow Scott Baker's mind. The phone startled her. Freedom's cell number showed up on her caller ID. She expected to hear the familiar "Peace," but instead was greeted with what had to be Freedom's best work. She waited for him to put the receiver to his mouth and start bragging. She was ready to accept all of it because the music was marvelous. It had an African feel with black soul flowing on top. It grabbed at her heart and made her want to sing and dance all at the same time. There were no lyrics, but Freedom was a master lyricist, and she knew that part would be easy for him. She marveled at how well the music fit the outline she'd been working on. Ava was listening for some time before she even thought about the conversation she should be having with Freedom. She called his name, but he did not answer. The music was blaring. She called again, expecting him to remember or even realize he'd placed a call. This kind of thing had happened several times before. Freedom had accidentally pushed the send button on his cell phone. Because Ava had been the last number he'd dialed, she became privy to more of her client's life than she cared to be. This time was probably the same thing, she reasoned. Ava figured that he was caught up in his work and had leaned on his phone, which he often kept in his front pants pocket. She was glad that he had. The music was both an inspiration and a confirmation for the outline she was preparing. It allowed her to complete her work and fall into a deep sleep. So deep that she forgot about little Johnny. So deep she even forgot about the house. Three hours later, her phone rang again. She slid from under the deep of her sleep, half expecting to hear that beautiful music. Instead, she heard the gruff voice of one of New York's finest. "Ms. Ava Vercher?" the voice commanded.

"This better be good," she replied. With athletes and musicians for clients, Ava was often awakened in the middle of the night.

"Ms. Vercher, this is Detective Don Donaldson." For a second, Ava thought this was someone's idea of a joke.

Who gave their child the same name twice? she thought. "Yeah, you got her," she said, feigning interest.

"Ma'am, there appears to have been some sort of accident, and well, we got your number from the de—." Detective Donaldson stumbled over the part of his job that always made him sweat. "Ma'am," he said, "we need you to come over to One hundred thirty-eighth and Tubman Terrace. There's been an accident, and we were instructed . . . well, we knew, to call you," he stammered.

Ava was remembering all of this now. She'd rushed to the house, hoping simply to find Freedom mildly hurt by a neighbor who mistook him for a prowler. She had even halfheartedly prepared to cuss him out for doing what she told him not to do. In her heart, though, she'd already begun to mourn. The detective wouldn't answer any of her questions on the phone, nor would he allow her to speak to Freedom. An even surer sign was the feeling she had in her gut. The peace she experienced earlier had been replaced by one of dread. When she got to the house, she was escorted inside and informed of what she already felt. Freedom was dead. She needed to cry, but couldn't. Freedom had grown from overinvolved client to friend and confidant. She'd evolved from independent attorney to a woman who could now listen to a friend. She acknowledged the growth and missed it all in the same moment. She needed solitude and sadness, but it was outweighed by her need for answers.

She ran to where the police were working, and she saw him. Detective Donaldson was trying to hold her back, but she would not be restrained. Ava made her way through the

officers, medical examiners, and investigators. They were turning to her and looking as if she knew more than they did. She
reached Freedom but immediately wished she hadn't. His body
was at the foot of the stairs, the same stairs that had held the
group whose presence had caused her to flee several nights before. Freedom's body was bent in an unnatural position. His
head was angled and tilted, as if it had been pulled completely
around. From his mouth had poured a pool of blood. Had it
not been for the blood, Freedom would have appeared to be
smiling.

Ava stood frozen, unable to think or speak. She shook her
head, and her tears began to flow. They started as tiny droplets
from the corners of her eyes, but soon became a flood accompanied by a wail. "No," she screamed. "No" over and over, until someone had the sense, decency, or both, to escort her
outside. Television crews had arrived, and so had some of the
neighbors. Ava felt as if she were in a white person's dream.
With the exception of Detective Donaldson, who was black,
and a Latino officer, everyone else was white. The bright lights
and bright faces didn't do much to calm her emotions.

"Is there anyone we can call?" Donaldson asked. Ava immediately thought of Charles and called him. Then, she remembered, she felt dizzy. *Good,* she thought to herself, *it's
nighttime, and this is a dream.* And then everything around her
went blank.

When she came to, she saw that it wasn't a dream. She'd
been loaded onto a stretcher, and there was something over her
nose and mouth. Charles was there, but he looked strange
through the plastic mouthpiece. She moved the oxygen mask
and tried to get up.

"Whoa there, Nellie," a stocky woman was saying. "Down, girl. You ain't got nowhere to be just yet."

"I'm fine," Ava told her. "I need to get back to Freedom."

"He's gone, honey," the woman said. "But you know that. You just need to rest and accept it."

Charles stepped in and asked Ava to give herself a moment. "This is more than even you can handle. I'm here, and I'll do what I can to help," he said calmly.

"Don't patronize me," she said. "Freedom's dead."

Charles was still stunned and confused. It was more like a proclamation. Freedom's dead. Then everything was clear. "Your client went into the house. God no, please no," he said.

Ava's coloring, which had begun to come back, was again drained. "Freedom is at the bottom of the stairs where—" she paused, thinking of what Charles had told her about Dora, and remembering the spirit memories she and Charles had seen together. She didn't want to believe. She was an attorney, a logical woman. One of the brightest in her bright class. But these past few days had confirmed something that most old folks already knew, that there was more to life than what we could see, touch, hear, or feel. "He was where we saw them," Ava managed. "Oh, I have to call his mother," she said suddenly, realizing that she still had responsibilities to fulfill for her client.

When Freedom's grandmother died, his mother had moved back to the South. "You on your own, big man," she'd said lovingly to her son. "It's time for me to get back to my roots." Freedom's mother told Ava that he talked to her "on the regular," so getting her number would be easy. It was probably even programmed into Freedom's cell phone. Ava knew she needed to make the call quickly. The camera crew was already in full swing. Freedom tried to be low key, but was well known and popular with all of the hip-hop industry. The news would spread like fire in a field.

She counted to ten as she had done her entire life. "Don't rush into the day or nothing important," her old Uncle Brother had said. "Life will be there, but how you approach it is more important than what you approach." Ava had taken this advice seriously. Old Uncle Brother was still alive and driving, and he had to be close to one hundred years old by now. Each morning when Ava got up, she'd count to ten first. If she had to go into a big meeting or anything important, she did the ten count. She wished that she could do it now and have everything go away. She knew it wouldn't, so she would do what needed to be done.

"You need to rest a bit longer," the paramedic said.

"I've got work to do," Ava shot back. The paramedic was still trying to do her job, but Ava ignored her concern.

"Thanks for coming, Charles," she said. Charles helped Ava up.

"Thanks," she said. He led her back toward the house that had caused fear and now grief. Back to the house where their troubles had started. Back to the house that held not only answers, but Freedom, in body and spirit.

36

❖

the more things change . . .

> I believe in praising the
> bridge that carries me over.
> —*African American proverb*

ora was asleep but working harder than she had for years. She remembered the last time she had to go to sleep to work things out like this. It had been years, and although she hadn't forgotten the incident, she no longer carried the pain. "Pain is the thing that won't let you forgive," she often told women who came to her for advice on similar matters. "Let the pain go, or you won't be able to move on in your own life," she told them.

The last time she had to work this hard was when she was still "youngish" as she called it. Her husband had been cheating on her and drinking harder than ever.

"You spooky woman," he told her. "If I had known that you were crazy, I'd a never married you. Besides, I only did it cause my daddy paid me to," he said. "We made money off a you." He laughed wickedly and told her to take her clothes off. When Dora refused, he beat her and took them off himself. He raped her, but it wasn't called that back then. Then, it was referred to as a man taking matters into his own hands. He was her husband. He could do as he pleased, and he told her so. His drinking and his beatings got worse.

Dora's grandmother had passed on. Dora didn't know as much about her abilities then. She would try to remember every detail of what her grandmother had taught her. One day it came to her to contact her grandmother in her sleep. It took her a week to make contact, but she did. Once there, her grandmother told her everything the beatings had caused her to forget. She also understood the importance of control. Dora used the wisdom to get an understanding of why her husband did what he'd been doing. Once she did, she would make him pay. Dora started reading the signs around him. She learned that her husband was the product of a loveless marriage. On the surface, things seemed fine between his parents, but when she looked closer, she could read the sadness and regret. She could also see that her husband, a grown man who was still referred to as Junior, was a disappointment to his parents. He couldn't hold down a job, even though his parents were his employers. His father's displeasure was not hard to detect, so it became apparent to Dora that she was a punching bag for a battle that went beyond her presence. When she looked closer still, she saw that the patterns of life for Junior had been generational and changed very little from father to son, and so on. Junior's mother had also been abused, but had masked her pain with fine clothes and young men from other counties.

Dora had been instructed by her grandmother to work in her sleep and to go to the root of the problem. "Ain't no need to cut down a branch and leave the tree to stand. You gotta take out the poison that's in the roots," she said. In the daytime Dora took the abuse, but at night she worked her way back to the beginning. The daily beatings had become less and less severe until one day her husband decided he could take no more of this woman or his life, and so he took his own. Dora found him and the note he left.

Dora,

Somewhere in me I love you. But I just ain't had no love for myself. My daddy would kill me for telling you this, cause he got a heap of false pride. He got his money and his ways from his daddy, and all they ever care about is finding ways to get more. My daddy's daddy was the son of a slave owner. You can tell by looking at us that we got a lot of white blood. Until I marry you, we try to keep it that way. My daddy said that by marrying you we could get things straight. I just find out that that ain't so. He tell me that your people were related to somebody one of his folks loved, and that by us coming together, things would be made right. I didn't want to marry you on account of you so black, so he paid me. Something in me really wanted to love you. Well, I guess I messed that up, too. I'm sorry for how I been treating you. I am. I told you, we tried to keep high color in the family. Sometimes our relatives marry one another to make that happen. You know what happen when folks keep marrying they own. They end up with a mess. Life ain't supposed to mix that way. I know you carrying a child, and I hope it's alright. I tried to beat it out of you. But now I want it to have some hope and that maybe our seed can have the peace I never let you have. My daddy tell me what don't work out for you in this life will have to work out in someone else's. I hope that was true 'cause not much else of the way he live is. But I guess he got it from his daddy before him. I can't hate him no more, but I can't stay neither. I'm afraid that I'm just gonna keep doing you harm. Being with you make me think about myself. I don't like what you making me see. So I'm a end it. If I don't, I know I'll end you and my seed. If I do that, my line won't have no future. Good-bye, Dora, I hope your life comes back to you the way it's supposed to.

James

Dora tried to cry but knew she couldn't. Her husband had spoken the truth about who and why he was. He had also released her from the agony that had become her life. She copied the note, packed her bags, and left her husband and his original letter for his family to deal with. Dora didn't want their anguish to be a new source of pain for herself or her child. She moved to the next county and raised her child on her own.

Dora thought of all of this in her sleep. There was a connection, she was sure. Working out life's problems usually brings you back to the circles and circumstances of the past.

She went deeper into her sleep where she could see more clearly. When she did, a young man ran up to introduce himself.

"How in the world did a cool woman like you get such a zero for a grandson? Oh, excuse me," he said, stretching forth his hand. *"My name is Freedom, and I'm honored to meet you."*

37

Ngozi's story

How come mister you think you
can tell me about that old song,
when it was born in my mouth?
—*Mahalia Jackson*

*N*gozi was remembering the life he was forced into. He saw the children he had fathered, but was not allowed to hold.

"*Please master, let me keep this one,*" he said to no one. "*That's when I met her. Sara was her name. She was lame, but she was beautiful. Beautiful because no one touched her. The place that had been entered by so many in other women was left alone for Sara. She had never been raped. She had been scarred by an attack of the master's wife,*

who'd flown into a rage when Sara was still a child. Her mother was being sold, and Sara tried to hold on. She refused to let go, so the woman
ordered Sara to be tied to the cart that her mother was carried away in.
She was dragged for miles before the driver couldn't take the wails of her
mother any longer, and cut Sara loose. Her mother, who took her child
for dead, grabbed the knife from the driver and plunged it into her own
heart.

" 'Dumb-ass wench,' the driver said. 'Why she getting so upset over
one pickaninny when she could've had plenty more?'

"Sara was left there on the road, but found later by a black man
who was running errands for his master. He took her back to his plantation. The master, who was better than most but still a slave owner,
protested. 'We don't need no piece of girl to have to feed.'

"The man, Jason, pleaded and said, 'The women will care for her,
and she'll be able to work like everyone else.' Free labor was reason
enough for the master to go along. Sara lived, but her scars were deep.
She was deformed to white folks, but the black folks just saw her as one
who wore her scars on the outside. When I met her, I knew she was my
hope, our hope. I loved her in secret because my seed, I was told, was only
to be used for certain women. Master say he need to breed strong bucks
from my seed. To have come from a land where love and children were
honored, and forced to produce as a bull, has brought me much shame.

"When I found Sara, I knew that I could have some small joy. She
saw me looking at her and smiled. Well, it was almost a smile. That
sad, crooked face told me of the pain she had been through and of the
emptiness in her heart. I took her that same night. We cried together
when our baby's life was conceived.

"I met her only two more times, but I watch my child grow 'til they
take her away. Before they did, I teached Sara the things I learned from
my mother, and Sara teach them to my daughter. It was not until I
passed from that life that I could see my baby, Miella. She was bought

by a man who died the day he got her. The slaves just walk off and take little Miella with them. Her daddy and mama were free, but not for long. Miella's life was as bad as her mama Sara's. But Miella pass on the love she got to a lil' motherless child named Iona. Iona's line was troubled, but they getting to their truth. I see all of that now. I also see the reason to watch over children who don't come through you. Things pass down through more than blood.

"So I'm passing on this drum to the one who has called me. The one who calls himself Freedom, even though he is not free.

"It was not possible for me to make the drum in life. It was not until I made my transition that I was able to do all that I was created for. The sounds that I've played have been heard by others who are also unconnected. They do not know who they are, and yet they attempt to make music that tells our story. The beat is powerful, but their message is hollow. I know this feeling of emptiness. It comes from our inability to connect to one another in spirit and in life, from past to present. Freedom will tie the present to the past. He is the son who has called for a father. We have been listening and now we have answered."

When Ngozi finished his story, he could see that many of the souls had gathered. It was not yet time for the Gathering. But Ngozi had learned long ago that the clarity he had on this side was still incomplete, and that there was only one who knew all. The souls around him began the circle of life. They created a spirit chain around him and made the music that had been lost when he did not make the drum. The music was hollow without the fullness of understanding.

At the top of the stairs stood Bella, the woman with the bloody newborn. "No," she screamed. "It's time for my story to be heard."

That's when Freedom appeared, caught up in the music. He'd walked to the top of the stairs to find where the music had come from. "Ye oh Ye Ba Ba. I hear you, Papa," he said. And then he saw her. She stood taller than him by at least six inches, or she appeared to.

"*Take your child,*" she said, thrusting the lifeless baby into his arms. Freedom could not respond because he saw what he hadn't wanted to believe. Freedom stepped back from the woman. As he did, he saw what he thought was his grandmother.

"*Hello, baby, it's your time. And I told you, when it's time, it's time,*" his grandmother's memory said. He was sure of it. He didn't speak this, but his grandmother nodded in agreement.

The woman with the child moved closer. "*Don't you want him?*" she screamed. "*You told me you did.*" Freedom stepped back too far too quickly. He tried to grab the banister but reached out in vain. It was his time. He hit the floor below, the impact engaging the send button on his cell phone, calling Ava. The music was still being made, but now it had changed. The hollow space in his life was being filled with the life and music of Freedom's pain, joy, and confusion. He couldn't hear Ava yelling his name. He sensed it, but couldn't do anything about that just now. He was experiencing and enjoying the music. Why shouldn't he? It had cost him his life.

The others welcomed him as they had done for one another in the past. The woman with the baby was not thrilled. "*You ain't nobody. I thought you was . . .*" she said and walked away.

38

the reasons

> We must accept finite disappointment,
> but we must never lose infinite hope.
> —*Dr. Martin Luther King, Jr.*

va walked inside the house. The fear that had gripped her earlier was replaced by sadness. "You've had a good shock and should be resting," Detective Donaldson told her.

"No, I have to contact his mother. I don't want her to find out from the news or some reporter. I have her number in my office, but I can get to her quicker if you'll let me have his cell phone," Ava said. "He keeps it, *kept* it," she corrected herself and thought of the other language adjustments that had to be made whenever a loved one passed away. "He kept it in his pocket."

"We know," Donaldson smiled. "That's how we contacted you. The phone must have fallen out of his pocket. It was on his chest when we found him. The last call he made was to you. When did you speak to him?" Donaldson asked.

"I didn't. A call came in around two, but I only heard his music. I thought he was working. Who found him?" Ava asked.

"Well," Donaldson started, "this is a little strange. One of the neighbors was coming home when he thought he'd heard music from inside. He'd seen several vehicles in front of the house in the last couple of days and thought someone had broken in and was using the place for an illegal party. He called the police and Officer Rivera found him. He's the one who noticed your number on the ID. Rivera keeps up with the music scene. He does some DJing on the side. He knew who Freedom was and knew of your reputation as well. I guess it pays to have diversity on the force, huh?"

Ava made a mental note to send a thank you letter to Rivera and a copy to his captain. "The phone," she said. "I need to use it."

"I'll do what I can, but we haven't ruled out foul play. The phone has to be dusted for prints."

Officer Rivera was sent to check the progress of the fingerprinting and came back to say that Ava could use it. Vincent Rivera was young and handsome. Too young, Ava thought, to find a dead hip-hop producer, particularly one whose career he'd followed. He escorted Ava to a side room that had probably been a parlor room back in a time when the house was grand, back before it was haunted.

"I'm sorry for your loss," the young officer said. "He had the juice, you know. He was the baddest producer who ever—" Rivera paused, feeling that he was saying too much.

"He was wonderful," Ava said.

"You have to put on these gloves," Rivera said, handing Ava a pair of latex gloves with one hand and holding the phone in his own protected palm. "They love to go over things again, and well, we just don't want to make any mistakes, especially since I told them who he is." Rivera's voice dropped to a whisper. "I'm glad I got here first. They would've treated him like he was nobody."

Ava nodded at the facts this new officer shared. Ava scrolled through Freedom's phone book list but didn't have to go far. She smiled at the fact that her number was first, and that Freedom's mother's number was right behind it. They had become more like colleagues than anything else. Making this call would be the hardest job he'd ever given her. The number had an area code that Ava didn't know. All she remembered Freedom saying was that his mom lived down South. Ava pushed the send button, and the phone was answered immediately.

"Mrs. Hudson?" Ava said slowly.

"No, she's not taking any more calls," the voice said.

"I'm her son's attorney, Ava Vercher."

"Y'all don't waste no time, now, do you, Ms. Vercher?" the woman was saying.

"What?" she said to someone in the background. "Hold on," she said to the receiver, "she'll talk to you. Sorry." The woman was curt, but trying to correct a mistake without relinquishing her right to make it.

"Hello, Ava," Freedom's mother said. "Harry told me all about you. You probably called to tell me. Some damned reporter beat you, but I thank you just the same. Truth be told," the woman said, "I had a feeling something was wrong. My boy called me last night. Told me he loved me and that he missed me. Said he was getting a place and wanted me to live with him. Ava," she said, pausing for the first time, "I knew then that I wouldn't see my baby no more." Freedom's mother could no longer contain her grief and didn't bother to try. She sobbed loudly, and Ava wept with her.

"I'm sorry," she was trying to say, but before she could finish, the woman who had answered the phone was taking the phone from her.

"It's alright girl, go on and cry. Hello," she said into the receiver, "you can call back later. We need to figure things out. We'll hold a memorial there, but the services will be down here. The reporter said he fell, but homicide wasn't ruled out. Do you know anything more?" she asked.

Ava admitted she didn't. She spared the details of the way Freedom had been found and where. She thought that all that could wait. "I'll find out all I can, and I'll contact you as soon as I do. If you want," Ava said, "I can take care of the details for the memorial on this end."

"Thank you, Miss," the woman said.

"One more thing," Ava remembered to ask. "What's your name and the name of the town I'm calling?"

"Oh, I guess that would help," she said. "This is Port Gibson, Mississippi. I'm Harry's mama's neighbor. My name is Ruth, Ruth Freeman. I'll talk to you later."

Ava was about to say something about how she'd be praying for the family, but Ruth had already hung up. As soon as she did, she remembered that she'd heard the name Ruth Freeman before. Once the thought came to her, she knew exactly where.

If she had been looking behind her, she would have seen Johnny smiling, smiling because his story had been heard, smiling because his life could be connected to something greater than his short years on earth had allowed. He was smiling because Ava and the woman who'd given birth to the new spirit called Freedom had found his sister, Ruth. Mainly, though, he smiled because his work was through.

◆

can I get a witness?

Dora pushed farther into her sleep than she'd ever had to. The memory of Freedom was guiding her back to the house. As soon as she was inside, she felt the presence of those who had gone on and those who were still here.

Freedom came to the stairs where his body lay and looked down at himself. There was always a fascination with seeing oneself without the interference of the opinions of others.

Freedom smiled at his own form, and then stepped right over his own body.

Dora followed, as this was the path that was allowed. She saw Ava and her own grandson, but she could talk with them later. What she fought hard to get to was the center of the Gathering. There she would experience the stories of the memories that needed her to be a witness to their lives.

Freedom expressed his ideas to her, but never said a word. She heard it in the music he presented to her. "It's deep," his memory was telling her. She listened, or rather felt, the full force of the music and knew what needed to be done. She allowed her consciousness to slip back to the surface, but not to awaken. Her body still needed its rest. It was days before she would come to and find out that the doctors thought they had lost her when she told them she was never theirs to lose.

40

lessons of life

> The young get the energy;
> the old get the wisdom.
> — *Caroline Freeman*

reedom's death had been ruled an accident. There were no footprints going into the house other than his, so there was no one to blame. The only other recent fingerprints that were found were Charles's on the light switch from several days earlier. The "brilliant" detectives had deduced that the music was coming from some other house and that it had been the car of the young black man that aroused the suspicion.

Ava was talking to Freedom's mother regularly to work out the details of the memorial service. The tabloid media had a field day with the loss of another one of rap music's giants. There were Web pages that pointed to conspiracy theories and speculated about whether or not Freedom was really dead.

Scott Baker announced the deal that had been made and also said that he was going on with the project. "Freedom would have wanted it this way," he surmised. He hadn't even bothered to call Ava or Freedom's mother. The labels that Freedom had worked with also cashed in on his death. An extra-added bonus to Ava's workload was the women who called Ava's office, claiming to carry Freedom's love child. Most of them were warned off easily. "When will you be available for DNA testing?" her assistant would ask. And the phone usually went dead.

The New York service was held just five days after his death. The church hall gathering looked more like the Soul Train or Grammy Awards than a memorial service. Everybody who was anybody, or who thought they were, had shown up. Freedom's family and closest friends had all avoided the New York show and had opted for the private gathering that would be held down South two days later. Charles aided Ava through the entire thing. He was connected to this situation whether he wanted to be or not. Charles, who had tried to run from his grandmother's craziness and from anything too black, had been thrust back into a life that was filled with the unknown. And to her surprise, Ava found comfort in Charles and their bond.

One day, on the way to visit Charles's grandmother in the hospital, they laughed together for the first time since the initial visit to the house. One of Freedom's songs was playing on the radio. The announcer proclaimed, "That's Brother Freedom. He's gone, but I know he's somewhere making phat music."

Shortly after the memorial service ended, Charles received a call that his grandmother had regained consciousness. During the days that had preceded, the doctors had called, saying that he'd better get there quick and that his grandmother wouldn't make it. But Dora was stronger than the doctors' predictions. Each time, her heartbeat came back stronger than ever. When the hospital call appeared on his cell ID, he braced himself for another jolt. He was jolted, but not in the way he expected.

"Where you at, boy?" Dora said into the phone. "The least you can do is come and see me after you done put me in this semi-hell of a place." Charles couldn't find the words to express the joy he felt at hearing the voice of the woman who had frightened him as a child and embarrassed him as an adult. "I know you glad I'm here, but if you listened to the voice within you, you'd of known that I wasn't going nowhere. Now get over here," she said and hung up.

Charles's and Ava's spirits were higher than they'd been since the night they met at House of Tina. "How come you stopped liking me?" he asked her during the drive.

"I never liked you," Ava said, blushing.

"You did too," Charles reminded her. Sitting next to Charles, having a normal moment allowed him to think back to easier times, times that he thought were rough but could now see in their proper perspective.

"I was a girl, and you were weird. I liked your weirdness, but I didn't want anybody to know it. Anyway, we were kids," she said and left it at that. The rest of the ride was silent and peaceful, and both felt it was good to not have to talk or listen.

Dora was sitting up in her hospital bed, drinking juice and talking to a group of young interns. "Don't let the work of this place move you from your purpose. There's a reason medicine is called an art. Be creative and remember, you are modern-day healers. Oh, here he is. Handsome, ain't he?" she said and winked at a nurse who was eyeing Charles. "Sorry honey, he's taken," she said. "You must be Ava. I've heard so much about you. Plus I sort of remember you when you were just a little girl. Gappy, they called you. You were so good for this boy. But he was strange. I don't blame you for running from him. Besides, God is in control, and look, you two done found each other again."

Neither Ava nor Charles was able to say anything. They looked at each other and laughed. Had it not been for all that had transpired, they would've thought the old woman was losing it. But now they could see just how much sense she made. "Ya'll got to get out of here. I got work to do. Go look for some other miracle lady," she said to the young interns. "The woman two doors down should be pulling out soon. Out of the coma," she added, "not life." The interns hurriedly moved to do as they were instructed. "Lord, have mercy on the young," she said. "When I get to see Jesus, I'm gonna ask why the young get the energy while the old get the wisdom. Just ain't right. By the time you know how to spend your years, you find that you done already wasted them."

Ava walked over to Dora and touched her hand. "Hello," she said simply.

"You sure are cute," Dora said to Ava. She said it as if she were letting Ava know for sure. Ava had been wondering about her looks lately. She felt that Charles had probably been attracted to more professional-looking women, whatever that meant. Sometimes she felt like she didn't have the polish that would make him ask for seconds. Charles's grandmother was grinning and laughing.

"Don't you worry none, child. When things calm down, he'll be on you like white on rice."

Ava was embarrassed and relieved at the same time.

"Now," Dora said, clearing the way for things to get serious, "y'all got work to do. I won't be able to get out of here, and don't think I haven't tried. Besides, I do my best travel at night when I sleep anyway. You all been working, but you need to set things in proper order. Pull up your chair, and get some paper out."

They had no idea they were about to receive a lesson that would beat any either had experienced in a classroom. Dora would prove to be brilliant, spiritual, and loving. She was the perfect teacher.

41

• ◆ •

his story

Seemed to me that drumming was
the best way to get close to God.

—*Lionel Hampton*

*Ngozi was sharing what was left of
his memory self with Freedom and those who had gathered. His work
was near completion, so he could pass on what he had seen. "I only knew
joy when I was in my homeland. Joy extends beyond happiness. Happy
is what you have here. It is short lived. Joy is strength that comes from
knowing that things work together. Even when trouble comes, you can
see it as joy, for you are strong. I told you of Sara, the woman I loved
in secret. Our kind of love is the pattern many follow now. They steal*

away for moments of pleasure out of fear that if this love is seen, it will be destroyed. We had to live like this. Our descendants have chosen to do so. This undercover love is more dangerous than what we lived because it is chosen. Iona, the life daughter of my child, told of her love. She was not of my blood, but she was of my spirit. She found a way to perform another kind of gathering. She wrote her story and left it for others to find. It has already begun to work its wisdom. This wisdom is seen by those who think and learn from written words, but there are those who will not hear in this manner. More of our children have been lost and enslaved to the hollow music that gives no strength; it gives no joy. Freedom's music will find its way to them, and they will listen. Still others will need more, so your stories must be told. They will find a vessel in one who listens and passes on our truths. Balance, the harmony, the beat, the words will come together. The music must tell them the truth. To love, forgive, and never forget. Tell them to search for peace and to honor wisdom. They must allow the elders to be a part of their lives. This has been missing. They must value the gifts they have been given and never use them for destruction. Speak truth to power. Come back to God and yearn for all that is good. When they do, we will have redemption.

Ngozi disappeared, but to those who had looked to him and listened to his wisdom, he could never really be apart from them. They understood the principle behind the scientific parable that says matter is neither created nor destroyed; it just changes its form. Ngozi, the blessing, was with them and everyone else.

Bella, the familiar spirit that held on to the dead baby heard all of this and began to cry. Ngozi had told her that she loved in death the same way she had in life. What she called love was not. Her spirit was possessive and unforgiving. Love and unforgiveness could not dwell in the same place.

She could not let go of the things that had caused her pain. Because of this, she could only inflict that pain on others. Freedom was not the one she searched for, but he had been similar to the man she longed to find. She could tell. He had been the kind of man who promised love just to get his physical needs met. It didn't matter to him that he left behind a broken spirit and sometimes, as it was in her case, the broken body of a child. They took what they wanted and left. But what she did not know was that by failing to forgive the man who caused her this pain, she had become like him.

Ngozi was right about this, but it didn't matter now. He was gone. Freedom's presence was powerful, but it was new. She had been this way for many years. She decided that she would control him, and in doing so, she would stop the work that needed to be done.

42

Sister Space

> Take off your shoes,
> you're on holy ground.
>
> —*Exodus 3:5*

Ava and Charles had been given their instructions. Dora had rambled on for some time, demanding that they take notes. At first, nothing made any sense, but as the hours progressed, so did their clarity. The first task was to get to Sister Space Books. There, Ava was to talk with the two owners. Ava had been there once before but found Valentine, the taller of the two, to be the opposite of her name. Miss Althea was nicer, but only by a little bit. This second visit enabled Ava to see she had been wrong. This time, Ava watched the way the owners directed customers to books they didn't know existed.

"You don't want that book, girl. This is what you need. Just buy it, and read it," Valentine told an indecisive customer. Now she knew why Miss Dora wanted her to see Sister Space.

"Those two have clarity and a spiritual base," she had said. "Don't let them fool you. They're softies, but in their business, they can't afford to show it. They're not just about the business of selling books," Dora had replied to an unspoken query. "They're about the business of teaching women how to heal and then serve one another. They look like booksellers, but they are warriors, child. Don't be fooled."

When she approached Valentine and Althea, Ava bowed her head slightly in deference. "Good afternoon," she said. "Miss Dora sent me." A young assistant was called to take over the counter, and Ava was escorted to a room in the back. The room was set up like a large classroom. Author readings and instructional courses, among other events, were held there. At the front of the room an altar had been made. It held objects of the earth and objects of art. The air was filled with an aroma that was sweet like an oil. Ava couldn't put her finger on the scent. At first she thought it was frankincense. Then, she thought she smelled sage. The aroma shifted again and became myrrh and patchouli. "What is that wonderful smell?" she asked.

"Little bit of this, little bit of that," the women said, laughing.

"Miss Dora sent me here and said that you would have something for me. That you would know what to do." Ava felt like a schoolgirl sent to run errands for some of the older neighbors. Because she'd been bright and good with math as a child, she was often called on to play the numbers for them. Being in the bookstore had brought this memory back.

The women were studying her face, looking to see if what she was saying was true. Once they determined that it was, Valentine got up and went into a room that was behind the one she now sat in.

No telling what's back there, Ava thought to herself.

Valentine returned with what appeared to be a manuscript. "This is what you need, this and a prayer," Althea said. They stood and gathered hands and prayed. "Lord, make us true and thankful. Keep us mindful and focused on your perfect will. Surround us with the love that protects from all danger. Amen."

"We got this from another one of our sisters. Perhaps you've heard of her? Her name," Valentine said, "is Cosina Brown." Ava looked down and saw that what Valentine had retrieved was in fact a manuscript. It was the original manuscript of *Redemption Song,* the book that had been like a *Celestine Prophecy* or *Alchemist* for black folks. Ava had read *Redemption Song* and enjoyed the way it weaved the story of love between an enslaved man and woman with the love of their modern-day descendants. It was a fun read and had become a popular and almost cult-like phenomenon. Valentine stared into Ava's eyes and proclaimed, "This wasn't just a fun read, Missy. Every bit of it was true. Now that you've witnessed the Gathering, you should know that."

"I need to read it again, don't I?" she asked.

"Whoo, girl, you brilliant. You should be an attorney or something," Valentine teased. This time, though, she smiled, and before Ava could return the gesture, she was being led out of the store. "Time to do your work, and we got ours to do. We can't hang with you all day, no matter how important you are, huh, Althea?" Valentine said.

"That's right. Don't lose that manuscript. Don't worry, sister. Dora said it will be fine," Althea told her.

Ava didn't know what they were talking about, but she found herself believing them.

43

testing the spirits

Be concerned, but don't worry.
—*Pastor Ralph Buchanan*

Charles's task had not been as easy as the one Ava was sent to perform. He had to go back into the house. He'd been sent there to leave something. Now he was praying that nothing came out with him. Dora instructed him to set up candles and burn sage in the northern most corner of each room. He was to pray and read a passage of scripture before he left. He had no idea that the candles and sage burning were for him. Dora would tell him this later. For now, she'd allow him to think that he could actually ward a spirit off. The sage was burned to give him comfort. The candles were lit to represent the illumination of his own light. It was the scripture, the word, that would do more than any other ritual could.

Charles had been put at ease. On his way out, he opened the Bible to 1 John 4: "Beloved, do not believe every spirit, but test the spirits to see whether they are from God because many false prophets have gone out into this world. By this, you know the Spirit of God. Every spirit that confesses that Jesus Christ had come in the flesh is from God. And every spirit that does not confess Jesus is not from God. And this is the spirit of the anti-Christ of which you have heard is coming and now is already in the world. You are from God, little children, and have overcome them because greater is he who is in you, than he who is in the world."

Charles had read the scripture before coming here. His New Age worldview didn't want to accept a distinction that was so narrow, one that only spoke of Jesus Christ. But by his third reading, he could see that the thing that needed to be tested was spirit. If the *spirit* rejected Christ, it was not from God. He saw the importance in this clarification, since the spirit realm held a much broader perspective on what was real. He felt the power he received from this reading and wanted to challenge the inhabitants of the house right then. But he'd already been instructed to read and then leave. He did as he was told. Dora was glad for this. If Charles had seen what he had stirred, he would have been glad, too.

44

going home

> Life is all in the play.
> How you play is how you stay.
> —*Freedom*

With the assignments completed, Charles and Ava were free to travel to Port Gibson, Mississippi, for Freedom's home-going service. They were amazed to see the beautiful woman who was his mother. Earlene was fifty-five, she said, but could have easily passed for thirty. She had the same intense gaze that Ava thought Freedom had created on his own. She now saw the source of the look.

"Thanks for everything," she told Ava. "Come on in and meet the rest of your family." She was holding Ava's arm on one side and Charles's hand on the other.

Once inside and introductions were made, Ava and Charles settled into the flow of the conversations.

Relatives shared stories of Freedom's childhood and transition into manhood. "That boy knew how to make an entrance," they said, laughing after hearing the story of his birth.

His mother was laughing, too. Her laughter slowed, and as it did, she moved closer to Ava. "Alright, child, we know the story of how he got here, and we talked about what he did while he was here. You the witness to his passing. You gotta tell us what you know." Before Ava could protest, Earlene stared at her with the Freedom intensity and said, "This time, don't leave nothing out."

Ava thought over all she knew and realized the ritual she was seeing was similar to what had gone on in the house. It was a gathering of the living. A ritual that was performed to enable the life of the deceased to be remembered. This link between the living and the dead played a crucial role in the transition. It was why black folks spoke of the dead as if they were still alive. She looked into the faces of those who had gathered. They were folks who would not have been invited into the New York service. They would not have been thought to be important enough. Only weeks before, she herself would not have been able to see just how important they were. Now she knew that these simple country folks were wiser and lived better than she herself did. They understood that prosperity was not in material wealth and could not be measured. For them, prosperity was peace.

Ava began her story. "When Freedom, I mean Harry—"

"That's alright, girl, call him by the name you knew."

Ava smiled. "When Freedom wanted something, there was nothing that could keep him from getting it."

"Um-hmm, that there's the truth," they proclaimed. "That boy set his feet to something and did it."

"Sure did. Remember the time he wanted to catch a fish, but couldn't?" a relative said. Everyone started laughing.

"Ava," someone else said, "that boy had been out all day. When he couldn't catch nothing, he jumped into the river and tried to find a fish and bring him back in." The room rocked with laughter.

The clamor died down, allowing Ava to get back to the tale. She told the whole truth, but not in the order that it happened. She waited to the end to tell the story of Johnny. When she did so, she turned to Ruth and said, "Miss Ruth, your brother Johnny is free now, too. He wanted me to let you know." Ruth, who hadn't shared her childhood with anyone in the room, was crying. She stood up, trying to leave. Earlene went to her and held her.

"Go on, child, tell the whole thing."

She told them about Johnny, the fifty-year-old spirit memory that appeared to her as a body of the young child. "He was there to help guide us and bring me to you. I see now how connected we all are, how my family and yours come together now to complete the unfulfilled longing of the ancestors. I've been hearing things that only touch the surface of where we need to be. I'm just grateful to be a part of it."

To Charles's surprise, not one person in that room found

this tale to be unbelievable. It was true because Ava said it was. But also because they all had their encounters with memories of others. These memories were carried with us. Sometimes they haunted us. This Ava learned due to our inability to forgive and let go. Memories, she learned from Miss Dora, are stored in our minds. Spirit memories are a manifestation of what we have stored. When we have unresolved issues with the dead, we cause them to appear as spirits. Ava had been amazed when she first learned this. She had always heard that the spirit had the unresolved issues.

Miss Dora had said, "If you in the spirit realm, why couldn't you know how to forgive the living? You're either in a much better place or wishing you were," she said, referring to heaven and hell. It all made sense now. "Ain't spooky at all," she said. Now Ava could see that death was a normal part of life. She was able to have peace.

The service was not long, but it was eventful. Others, who had not been at the house but were fans from neighboring cities or just folks who like to show respect, had crowded into the church along with the family Ava had met before. Some of them cried openly. Earlene was fanning herself and looking sternly at those who she'd later proclaim were trying to "create drama." "Those folks create drama just so they can star in it," she said. The minister's sermon was short but powerful, professing the love and comfort of Christ to all who were connected.

As they drove to the burial site, Ava marveled at the way passing cars all pulled over in respect for the family. "This doesn't happen in New York," she told those she shared a ride with.

"That's why we live here," someone responded.

After the burial, a woman sang a gospel rendition of one of Freedom's songs.

> Life is all in the play.
> How you play is how you stay.
> Stay long enough you leave enough to be enough.

In Freedom's version, the meaning was not this clear. Ava cried for her own loss and smiled for the love she had for Freedom.

Ava and Charles stayed an extra day and took time to relax. This was another one of Dora's instructions. On the day they were leaving, they drove to Freedom's mother's house to say "thanks" and to receive huge packages of food. They were surprised to see Ruth and Earlene's bags waiting for them on the porch. They were smiling when Ava knocked on the screen door.

"Hey, ya'll ready?" Ruth asked.

"Ready?" Charles said, somewhat baffled.

"Yeah, we going with you. There's a presence in that house that must be confronted. You think we're gonna let you do it alone? You're crazy. Besides," Ruth said, "my brother was there for a reason. I have not told anyone about his life. I was wrong. By telling the story of him and all he knew, I could have given him rest. He wanted to pass on his memory to others. Instead, I caused all the energy to remain locked up. Let's go," she said.

Ava and Charles would not argue with these two. They reached the airport to find that the women had already purchased their own tickets.

"When did you have time to do that?" Charles asked. "We

did it online," Earlene said, laughing. "Y'all think New York is the only place where they got computers?"

Charles laughed. "Touché," he said.

"Oh Lord, here go black people trying to be French," Earlene quipped.

45

the voice within

*T*onight my story will be told," said Bella, *the familiar spirit of the woman with the dead baby. "And when it is, your father will come back, and he will love us. And if he doesn't, he will die a death more horrible than my own."*

The group arrived in New York at eight o'clock in the evening. They went right to the hospital, only to find that Dora had checked herself out. Charles called his house and got no answer. He called his cousin, Goober, at his grandmother's house and was told to go handle his business. "You should listen to the voice within you, and you would know not to worry," Goober said and hung up.

In his spirit Charles knew where his grandmother was. He didn't want to hear. He had no desire to listen to the voice from within. It was telling him that Dora had fought the good fight.

46

when purpose collides
with destiny

They drove to the house in silence. Charles was holding back tears. Ava held his hand the entire ride. She sensed something was wrong, too, so she drove. When they reached the house at 138th Street, Ava looked to him and said, "Everything will be okay."

"I know that," Charles said. "I just don't like it right now."

They used the key to enter and found that the house was amazingly still. The unlit candles and sage were in all of the corners where Charles had left them, and the four went around and lit them. "This lighting is better," Charles said. He was taking charge in a way he hadn't been accustomed. He climbed the stairs slowly. He had not called out to his grandmother and knew there was no need to. She had made her transition. Before, he would have said she was dead. Now he knew better. He walked to the top of the landing and found his grandmother's body. She was lying peacefully on her side. From behind, she looked like she had been sleeping. Charles walked around to face her. He wanted to thank the body that had been his grandmother. He knelt down to pray. He looked into the face of the corpse. What he saw was the embodiment of sheer horror. His grandmother's face was contorted into an expression she had never shown in life. It was that of one who'd been terrified.

Charles didn't have time to react to what he saw. Someone was caressing and kissing the back of his neck. He knew immediately that the touch was not human. He spun around and saw what Freedom and his grandmother had seen. It was the woman with the dead child. This time, though, she was not alone. Beside her and around her were a host of other lost souls. Souls whose death brought no more peace than their lives had. How they died was how they remained: bloody and hideous.

Charles couldn't scream, but there was a pull of energy in the house that caused Ava, Ruth, and Earlene to leave the rooms they were in and run to Charles. They tried to reach him but found that they couldn't. They were tossed back down the stairs as if they were nothing.

"Leave," the woman hissed. "He belongs to me." Ruth, the sister of one who had resided here, stood to correct her own errors. "Tell your

story," Ruth commanded the woman. "We have come to hear you." Gathering now on the lower landing were those who accepted God's truth and knew that God was in control. These memories were the witness to Christ's resurrection. They were many. Among them was Freedom, and now Dora. Both were smiling. Ruth did her best to ignore them. This was a battle for the living. The years of grief had taught her this. "Tell your story," she commanded again.

The woman smiled, "Alright, and then he comes with me. I was always beautiful," she began, "but when I started singing, I was something else. My folks raised me to know that I was better than all the other black girls. I was, too. I could have anybody in my town if I wanted, but none of them were good enough. My daddy told me so. He loved me and showed me the secret love that a daddy has for his daughter. He said that I could do things for him that my momma couldn't. Anyway, when my daddy died, wasn't no more reason to stay in that deadbeat town. I left for New York 'cause I could sing. I got a job right away. With my looks and my voice and my daddy's money—he had left me plenty—I could do what most black women never dreamed of. I hired my own band 'cause I wanted them to complement me, and not me complement them. I got jobs at all the best places. That's when I met you, Nathan." She was saying this to Charles. "You were one of the biggest racketeers in New York."

She let out a cackled sound that was supposed to be laughter. "He owned a big ol' nightclub. Had something to do with that racket money. I sang there lots of times. White folks came from all over to hear the Black Angel. That's what they called me. Folks only talk about Billie Holiday, but I gave her a run for her money. I'm a tell you that. Anyway, Nathan and me started looking at each other, and he started whispering to me between sets. Before I knew it, we were doing that thing. Nathan was good to me. Told me I deserved the best. I loved him more than any man I know. Even my daddy, 'cause Nathan, you can see, is *white, and wasn't too many white men who would show their black woman off back then."*

Ava was as confused as the others were, but she hadn't expected this night to make any sense.

"We did our thing every night, right there in the back of the club. One thing led to the next, and I got pregnant. I was so happy. I knew my man would be happy, too. I told him, and he punched me so hard, he broke my face. I said, 'What's wrong, Daddy? Ain't you happy? We can be a family now.'

" 'Black whore,' he said. Told me I was stupid for ever thinking he would want me. He dragged me out back and put me in a car. His driver came out and took me to some man who said he was a doctor. The man was crazy. He feel me up and tell me to take off my clothes. I didn't know what he was gonna do, but I thought that this was the doctor who was gonna make sure my baby was alright. I figure Nathan had a change of heart. He didn't, not until now, huh, Daddy?" she said to Charles.

"That man who say he was a doctor still rubbing my legs. Then he put a metal thing inside me. I'm screaming, but he just smiling. He say when he done, maybe we can go someplace. I hear something inside me snap, and he must a hear it, too. All he saying is 'Uh-oh. You farther along than I thought.'

"My baby came sliding out of me, but he don't say nothing. He don't say nothing. I felt the blood and life running out of me. I see that doctor calling Nathan. He tell him to come and get me, that I'm dying.

"But Nathan say, 'That black whore's your problem, not mine. You the doctor.' None of that matter 'cause I'm already dead. But I knew if I waited, you would come around. Took you a long time, but you came back to me, Nathan.

"Here," she said to Charles, "come hold your baby boy."

For a second, no one spoke. Charles was trying to move away from her just as Freedom had. He had managed to stand, but the lost souls had created a circle around him. He looked down to his grandmother's memory and realized that she was letting him listen to the voice within. In his mind he played back all that had occurred. He remembered the scripture he'd read and the confusion he felt after reading Ecclesiastes. Now he saw its importance. In the end, the only thing that mattered in life was that we honored God in all that we did. In that we were to also honor those who had gone before us. "You are a memory of something lost, nothing more," he said to the dead woman.

As he did, the woman turned as if to walk away, then suddenly she raised the bloody thing that had been her child and struck down hard. "Take your child," she was screaming. Ava ran to help, but again was thrown back. Freedom stepped forward.

"Yo," he said, "I was made in the night, but it wasn't last night." He opened his mouth and released a sound that was beautiful and powerful. It was the music he'd been sent to make. It was righteousness rolled into sound. The beat and the melody had merged. For Freedom, purpose had collided with destiny. He had taken all that Ngozi had given him and infused it with the memory of his only life. The fathers had now joined with the sons, and the path of those lives was completed. The woman turned and watched as those who had joined her now left her side. They moved toward the music.

Freedom's mother, Earlene, cried for only the second time since Freedom's death. He looked at her, and she knew that all was well with his soul. His life had been a mess, but he had accepted the Belief as a child. He walked in that Belief even when his actions did not reflect it. Now she knew that nothing we did could win or lose redemption because redemption has been won for us.

The spirit woman was on her own, and now it was Ava's turn. "You have a choice," she said, approaching the memory. "You can choose to forgive or continue to suffer."

"I can't," she said.

"Learn to love, strive to love 'cause we ain't got time for nothing else." Ava recited the line she read in Redemption Song, the line that Valentine and Althea knew would be empowering. "I love you," Ava said to the woman. "And I love you," she admitted to Charles.

He was unconscious but in a state where he could perceive what was occurring. He wanted to tell Ava that he deeply received her love, her forgiveness. He needed forgiveness for all the hurt he had caused to others. But he wanted peace from Ava.

"You're already forgiven," Ava said.

Bella, the spirit woman, looked at Ava. She was tired. She had held on to her death long enough. She had also been responsible for the deaths of others. She treated every man who came to the house on Tubman Terrace as if he were Nathan. Only when they had finally crossed over could she see them for who they really were. Now it was time for Bella to settle into her spirit and be her true self. It was time to forgive. "Time to be free," Bella said. "I forgive you," she said to Charles. "Sleep, baby," she said to her child. "Go on and sleep. Mama needs to rest." When she did, she was released and so were the others.

Freedom left, but he left behind the righteous music. Ava was physically tired, but her spirit was revived. She had to deal with the matter of Dora's death and explain their presence there, so she called the police.

By the time the police arrived, Charles had come to. They decided to report that his grandmother had come back to the house because she was delirious and looking for Freedom. This was a tale that he would have been whipped for, but Charles knew the police would buy this and not what really happened.

When the paramedics lifted Dora's body and placed it on the stretcher, a tape recorder fell from her hands. They all looked at each other, wondering what part of the evening's truth had been recorded. An *officer rewound and played the tape. The only thing on it was the phat, righteous music that Freedom had made.*

"Your grandma sure liked good music," the officer said, handing Charles the machine.

"Yeah, she sure did. She surely did."

epilogue

va and Charles were now locked in purpose. They would work together and grow into love. They proceeded to do with this music what had been done with *Redemption Song*. The tape was released as Freedom's last work. But after Earlene went through Freedom's things, she found a collection that would put Prince's vault collection to shame. The music opened up a new wave of opportunity in the

recording industry. Labels now looked for artists who could du-
plicate the sound.

Ava was about to strike up a deal with Scott Baker to make
a movie, but she found out she had the backing to do it independently. With Earlene as a backer, she had all the finances she
needed. Some of his friends from the hip-hop world worked
for less than scale, while others donated their time and talent
free of charge. The movie was the story of Freedom's life, his
music, and his transition. Charles and Ava told the whole story,
including the occurrences at Tubman Terrace. It was received
with rave reviews. One critic called it the perfect marriage of
real life and fiction. Someone else called it a ghost story with a
righteous beat. The film broke box office records and won numerous awards, including several Oscars.

Ruth and Earlene funded other independent projects under
the name of "Freedom Lives Productions." Their offices were,
of course, in the house on Tubman Terrace.

acknowledgments

There is a feeling of reward that one gets when writing acknowledgments. It represents many things. It is a sign of the completion of a project and more importantly, it reminds one that without the help and support of others the project could not have been realized. That is the reasoning behind my dedication. It is given to those whose purpose is found in supporting others. The list of names of supportive people would be longer than this book. The majority of people who actually get things done, who are the real movers and shakers, the proverbial wind-beneath-our-wings, hardly ever see their names. I would like to acknowledge some of them now.

*T*he concept of the book came to me when a longtime friend and hip hop producer, True Master, took me to a brownstone he wanted to buy. True is a night creature and when we got to the house there was no electricity, and the place was downright spooky. Additionally, at that hour, with just a small flashlight to guide us, the floor didn't look safe. Still, I could tell as he showed me around that he was excited about the prospect of moving in. I, however, was looking for something to jump out of a corner. That's when I got the idea for this book. I am grateful to True Master for sharing with me the haunting experience of his now wonderful home (not to mention the gift of his incredible music).

Shortly after I began writing, my brilliant editor Janet Hill introduced me to Harry Davis, an insightful, and creative young filmmaker who has a presence that won't go away. He embodies the spirit of Harry/Freedom in his need to create work that is truly reflective of our struggle. Thanks, Harry.

In *Redemption Song*, we met Miss Cozy, who was based on Emma Rogers of Black Images in Dallas, Texas. Emma has a partner, Ashira Tashany, who also has spoken into my life. Thank you, Emma and Ashira for your guidance.

*D*uring the book tour for *Redemption Song*, I came into contact with other wonderful booksellers. These folks are gems to their community and to the world of literature. Fay and Cassandra of Sister Space in Washington, D.C., are included in this book. Thanks for the healing. The place is deep. Blanche Richardson of Marcus Books in Oakland is a real descendant of Marcus Garvey. There are many others I will introduce in my next book.

*T*hanks also to publicist Gail Brussell, interior designer Dana Treglia; editor-in-chief Bill Thomas (thanks for getting it); my agent and editor (to whom I dedicate this book); and to Melissa Rivera's husband, Dino Martínez, who helps us with this movement. My mother, Beatrice, and my children, William, Jabril, and Fatima who are amazingly supportive of all that I try to accomplish. My sisters who put up with my ramblings: Ava Beard; Christine Berry, Tanya Berry, Dr. Bernita Berry, Ollie Calvin, Dawn Cone, Marcia Dyson, Starla Lewis, Dr. Barbara King, Johnnie Mae Chandler, Callie Spillman, Suzanne Burnell, Lavetta Buchanan, Tia Thompson, Cheryl Hardwood, Jennifer Porter, Bethany Pickens, Vikki Hardy, Dora Taylor, Dalonda Groomer, Novia Taylor, Terry Davis, Ruth Watson, Kalada Salaam, and Rocki Rockingham. My brothers Kevin and Brent Berry, Mumia Abu-Jamal (you will be free), Kevin "what are you doing" Sanders, Wantaregh, Brother Haki Salaam, Kasimu Harley, Terry Evenson (wouldn't be here without you), Jim Keinz, Winston Scully, Michael Asbury, Stan Spillman, Vince Stokes, Will Downing, my spiritual teacher and pastor, the Pastor Ralph Buchanan.

*T*hanks also to the readers who e-mail, call, write and stop me in the airport, encouraging me to keep writing . . . don't stop telling me.

*T*hanks to everyone who reads. The brothers and sisters behind bars who, through certain circumstances, are still finding their purpose . . . believe in yourselves and don't lose hope. It's not too late. To the ancestors who are still fighting for our freedom. By the way, like Black Images in Dallas, Sister Space Books actually exists in D.C. Go, call, or e-mail. But be ready to hear the truth. Much Peace. Much Grace.

*H*ere's a special preview of *Jim and Louella's Homemade Heart-Fix Remedy,* a sizzling, smart, and utterly engaging novel about sex, love, folklore, and family history from Bertice Berry.

A Doubleday hardcover on sale in August 2002.

CHAPTER ONE

Discovery

"Possibilities are like promises:
they only work if you work them."

*I*t all started when Jim couldn't get it up. I guess I should find another way to say it, but we just country folks, so that's how we put it. That was two months ago, and he been 'fraid to try ever since. Anyway, we'd been married for twenty-six years and have had more than our share of it in the love department. We youngish still, me somewhere at the end of my fifties and Jim starting in his sixties. We got a lot of love left. I told Jim just that, but it didn't help none. In all our years of marriage and the three before, I've never seen him so upset. Jim has lots of pride and he don't like the idea of not being able to do his business, so I stopped trying to talk sense into him and did the next best thing.

Now, I've learned years before not to take stock in none of those women's magazines. Their sex tips usually include food or Saran Wrap, and Jim didn't like nothing too messy. He say the only thing he wants wet is me. Anyway, whenever things were tough with me and Jim, I pray that God will give me strength, make me humble, and show me where I'm wrong. Then, I talk to the ancestors. I talk to them like they still alive too, but I do it in my sleep and they always know the answers. This time I call on the women: my mama, Aunt T, and Grandma Sadie. They a hoot.

Mama say, "Hey, girl, don't say a word. We know just why we here."

"Uh-huh," Aunt T say. "Jim can't do the do."

Grandma Sadie tell her to hush. She say, "Your man weren't too good *no* time." She say it's better to have a man who have it but lose it all the way once, than to have one who never lose it, but only halfway does it the rest of the time.

Now, I laugh. Grandma Sadie tell me that our problem is that Jim and me done got way too comfortable with each other. She notice we hit it every Wednesday and sometimes on Sunday (depending on how good my fried chicken is). Until then, I didn't know about that connection, but I vow to take more time with Sunday dinner from that point on.

Mama say, "Girl, you need to spice things up a bit. Fix your hair and put on a little makeup."

Mama know that I ain't into nothing too fancy, but I remind her anyway. Aunt T say I need to learn some other positions. She say I got the wife and the mother part down pat, but I need to be a bit more whorish in the bedroom.

Grandma Sadie say, "Hush up, good loving ain't in no makeup, and it certainly ain't in no slutty ways. If the man want a whore, he'd pay one."

Grandma Sadie say the loving in the bedroom is in all the things you do before you get there. She also say me and Jim are real good to each other, better than most, but we need to find one another all over again.

I ask her what she mean, and she say, "Girl, when the last time you rubbed that man's behind?" Before I can act shocked or tell her "never," she say, "Uh-huh, that's what I'm talking about. Jim knows what he got, and he thinks he knows how he likes it. What makes a man hot is making his woman hot. He thinks he knows just what to touch and how to touch it. In all the years you've been married and all the time you were sneaking around before, Jim ain't had to figure out too much. He made you happy in bed because he made you happy in life, but girl, there's a lot more you should be doing."

At that point I want to ask what, but I hear Jim getting up, so I do too. I roll over and see Jim lying on his stomach. I can tell that he's feeling badly because it's Wednesday, and in the morning he's usually feeling like he want it. Most times, but not always, he gets it too. Usually, I wait for him to come to me, but this time I go to him. I rub Jim's behind slow and soft at first. I hear him moaning real low.

"Mmm baby, that feels good," he say.

I rub it some more, and he turn over. And I see what I

hadn't seen in a long time. Mr. Jim, that's what I call him, is standing at full attention. Jim so excited he can't wait to say hello to Miss Lou. That's what he call me down there, on account of my name is Louella. Jim open my legs quicker than he usually do. He ain't wait to see if I'm ready, but I didn't care, seeing his joy make me too happy to say anything. As soon as Jim try to get in Miss Lou, he loses himself.

"Dammit, God dammit," he say.

"Take your time, baby," I tell him. My man ain't big on cussing, so I know he upset.

I start rubbing his behind some more, but Jim too shamed to try again. He mumble "sorry" and get dressed and go off to the job he had for as long we been married. I pray that he don't lose that too.

After he left, I went back to sleep so I can ask Grandma Sadie what I need to do. They were waiting for me.

"Girl, I told you. You need to be more seductive," Aunt T was saying.

"Hush up, girl," my mama told her. "Can't you see she feels badly enough?"

"Look like to me she ain't feeling nothing at all," Aunt T said, laughing.

"Be quiet, y'all," Grandma Sadie told them. "Baby, listen, and listen good. I'm gonna give you the magic you need, but you got to add the spice to it. Like I said before, you've been doing the same thing the same way for years. You need to get to know every inch of that man's body and what really makes him feel good."

I tell her I thought I did. She say Jim and me don't know what we like. I figure she on the other side, so she got to know more than I do.

She say, "Baby, what I'm gonna tell you take patience and your 'bility to follow through. You got to do just what I tell you. How you do it is up to you, though."

"Tonight," she say, looking me right in the eyes, "you and Jim sit on this bed and talk about everything you think you want to do, or have done to you. It's gonna be hard, but all you can do is talk. Don't touch him no matter how hard he get. Tomorrow night you can touch each other, but you can't touch it. Then, the next night you can touch it, but don't taste. The night after, taste but don't enter. Then, on the last night, get ready to go on in."

That night, Jim came home tired as always. I cooked him his Sunday chicken dinner, and it ain't even Sunday. Jim smile at me real sweet, but say, "Baby, I don't want to try . . . let's give it some time."

I tell him, "Fine. I don't want to, but I do want to talk."

I take Jim into the bedroom, which I had cleaned real good. I had changed the bed linens and even sprinkled my best perfume on it.

"Sit down, baby. Now, Jim," I say, "for years we've been doing things the same, but we gonna try something new."

Jim start to tell me how tired he is, but I tell him to listen. He ain't really seen me act like that, but I know he like it. I sit him on the bed and undress him real slow. I never did that before either. When I take off his pants, I let my fingers touch him real light, but then I remember what my grandma say, so I stop myself. Then I undress. Now, you got to believe me when I say this . . . I don't remember the last time I got naked in front of my man with the lights on, so all this is making him crazy. I'm not as fine as I used to be, but I still look pretty good. I sit down slowly on the other side of the bed, and Jim thinks I'm asking for some.

I tell him, "Tonight, baby, we just gonna talk. Tell me what you like, and then I'll tell you. Tomorrow, you get to touch me, but you can't touch me tonight. Friday you can touch and Saturday you can touch it and taste it. Sunday, after church, if you still want to, I'll let you in."

With that, Mr. Jim came right to attention, and I was so wet I could have slid right off my bed. Just that little bit of talk done got us hot and ready, but I know that I gotta do just what Grandma Sadie say. So I start.

"Jim," I tell him, "I love the way you moan. It's telling me that it's good. I love the way you pull my knees apart, but I wish you would stroke my thighs and play with my breasts more and my nipples. I know they ain't like they used to be, but I still got feelings. I love your kisses too, but I wish . . ."

This takes me a while to say, but Jim jump up and say, "What, baby? Just tell me."

Finally, I get to it. "I wish you would kiss Miss Lou. I want you to put those big lips of yours right down there. I want you to kiss it and put your tongue on it."

I was shamed to say all that, but Jim say, "Alright, baby." He was about to do it right then, but I tell him it gotta wait.

Then, I say, "Jim, I need you to touch me more. I want you to put your hand on my head like you used to, and Jim, years ago, you used to smack me on the behind a little. I won't mind if you do that too."

Jim sure enough was grinning now. So was I. Talking about it made me want to climb on top of him and ride him to kingdom come.

"Jim," I say, "it's your turn."

Jim ain't say nothing, but I open my eyes to see his hand is holding Mr. Jim and giving himself some good love.

"Jim!" I say. "You gotta wait." I declare. I had to call him three times before he came to.

"Oh yeah. Okay. Sorry, babe. Seem like I kind of got lost."

"It's your turn," I say.

Jim say okay and tell me things that make me want to lose my mind. "Baby," he say in his deep voice, "I want you to act like you can't wait to get it."

"I can't," I almost yell.

"Well, sometimes it seems like you just doing your duty."

I don't say nothing 'cause I know I got something to learn.

"I want you to talk back too," he say. "Tell me what you want. Say it right in my ear. I want you to tell me it's good, that it's always good. I want you to put your mouth all over me."

I'm blushing now, but I try not to show it.

"Everywhere, my chest. I got nipples too, and I want your

mouth on them. Baby, I want you to put Mr. Jim in your mouth too. I want you to suck him and lick him good. I been scared to ask you for it, but we talking, ain't we?"

Jim stood up and started fondling himself again.

"We gotta wait, baby," I say.

"I know. I just want to show you how I want it. Is that okay?" Jim ask. He hold Mr. Jim up with one hand and start stroking slowly with the other. "Take your mouth up and down like this, baby," he say. "Start slow and the suck harder and faster. You can touch my balls too."

That make me want to laugh, but something tell me not to. Jim tell me to suck it 'til he say he want to come. Then he want me to stand up and bend over. He say he loves taking me from behind, but he don't do it too often because it seem like I don't like it. Now I know my grandma was right because I only remember Jim doing it twice, and both times it was so good I commence to crying. Jim must've thought I was sad, and I was too old-fashioned to tell him otherwise. I'm thinking all of this and look over to find Jim done come all over himself.

"Jim, we s'posed to wait," I say. Jim kiss me like he ain't never kiss me before and went to sleep right there in my arms.

The next day Jim wake up singing, and so do I. He called me three times from work, something he used to do back when we just got married.

"Can't wait to touch you," he say.

"Me neither," I whisper.

That night, I undress Jim again, but this time I lay him

on his stomach. I open up some of one of my grand's baby oil I found in the back of my cupboard and pour it all over his back.

"Mmm, that's nice," he say.

I rub his shoulders and back and down to his waist. I knead his strong back like I'm making bread.

"Yes, woman," he says between strokes.

Then, I pour baby oil on his behind and down between his legs. I rubbed his behind and slip my oily fingers between his cheeks. It must feel good because he snatched my hands and tried to take me right then.

"Not yet," I whisper in his ear.

"Oh, woman, you driving me crazy," he say.

"You don't know the half," I whisper back.

"Who are you, and what have you done with my wife?" he say, laughing.

"Lay down, man, and let me finish my business."

I oil his legs and rub them hard, front and back. I touch everything but Mr. Jim. Jim trying to get me to, but he know we gotta wait.

"Alright, woman," he say, "your turn."

He lay me down and pour oil right in the crack of my behind. He rubbed my behind until I thought I could see Jesus. I moaned, and Jim moaned with me. He rubbed everything but Miss Lou. I gotta tell the truth and shame the devil, Jim rubbed my feet so good, I thought I would die. I didn't know feet could get you so wet. He start at my feet and worked his way back up. When he got to my breasts, he could have asked me to run down the street buck-naked, and I might have done it! He rubbed my breasts in a way that let me know he had done it before, but not with me. I forgave him right when the thought came to me. I know that he wasn't getting this from me, and part of that is my fault. Besides, we been too far not to know how to forgive. Jim must've somehow felt my thoughts because he started to cry. I told him it was okay and held him. We rocked each other 'til we fell asleep, oily and wet.

The next day was my grocery shopping day. I got up and took a long, hot shower, fixed my hair, and put on a little makeup. Dora, who works down at the market say, "Girl, you look like you been getting some on the side." I want to tell her to hush and that she needs salvation, but I just grin. I couldn't help it, but something about what she said make me feel kinda proud. I push my pride back 'cause the Bible say pride comes before a fall and say, "Thank you." That got other folks whispering, and I let them. We live in a small town. I know folks gonna think and say whatever they want anyway.

That night, Jim came in smiling. He brought me a cupcake from the little bakery, and it ain't even my birthday. This our night to touch Mr. Jim and Miss Lou, and neither one of us can wait. Now, I have always had my husband's dinner on the table for him when he gets home. With the exception of the birth of two of our five children and a time when I wasn't really myself, his meal has always been waiting. Back then, I learned a lot about real love, but I'll fill you in on that later. This time, though, I meet him on the porch. I give him some cold, tart lemonade and kiss him right on the mouth. Miss Brown from across the street is looking. I don't care, but Jim do.

"We better go in," he say.

"Let her go in if she don't like what she see."

Miss Brown must've heard me 'cause she did go in, but I saw her curtain pull back and her eye peeping through. Jim sit next to me on the porch step.

"I get to touch it tonight, don't I?" he say right up next to my ear.

His hot, sticky breath on my neck make my nipples stand out at attention, and my behind got real hot. Before I could answer, Jim shock me by slipping his hand up under my dress. Now it was already dark, so I know Miss Brown couldn't see nothing, but all of this is new to me. I was sure surprised, but I had one for Mr. Jim too. He reach under my dress and find me naked as the day I was born. I didn't have on a stitch of underwear.

"Louella Givens," he say, calling me by my maiden name.

I grin, and Jim commence to laugh like I ain't heard in years. He pull me by the hand and take me in. We didn't make it to the bedroom though. Good thing the children are grown and moved out of town, 'cause otherwise they'd seen more than they ever wanted to know. Jim lay me down right on the living room carpet and pull my dress up over my head. He start to kiss my breasts, and I remind him that he couldn't use his mouth 'til the next day. He shook his head but said he wasn't going to argue. He grab my breast with one hand and start playing with my nipple with the other. It feel too good to be true. I didn't know my nipple had that much life left in it. Then, I take one of his hands and put it down on Miss Lou.

"You full of all kinds of surprises, ain't you, woman?" Jim say.

He rub across my thighs real light for what seemed like hours. I want to scream, "Touch it, man," but I was learning the importance of patience. By the time Jim stroke the hairs on Miss Lou, I want to skip over the next few days and get right to it. Jim stroked the inside and whispered in my ear, "I love this pussy. This my pussy."

My husband had never talked like this to me before. Three days before I would have been shamed to hear this kind of talk coming from him, but that night I couldn't get enough. He stroked the inside of my kitty until it was hard as him. I was moaning and hollering like I was crazy. Then, when Jim stroked my spot, which by the way I wasn't aware of before then, I squirted all over the place like a man. I was shaking so hard, Jim came right through his pants.

"Woman," he said, "what have we been missing?"

I was panting hard and smiling like a mad woman. Jim carried me to bed. I felt too weak to touch anything he had, but it was okay. I slept until twelve midnight exactly and awoke to find Jim sleeping like a baby. I waited until one minute past and pulled Mr. Jim out of the slit of his pj's and commenced to sucking him the way Jim showed me. Jim must've done thought he was dreaming 'cause he was moaning something 'bout "No, I'm married. Please don't."

He opened his eyes and saw my mouth on him. I was

looking right in his eyes. His head rolled back, and he let out a moan that probably made Miss Brown across the street come to attention.

"I'm coming, baby." When he said that, I climbed on top of him and rocked slowly, allowing him to come inside me. Jim arched his back and yelled, "Sweet Lord, thank you."

"Yes," I said. "I'm coming with you."

We must've both passed out 'cause when I came to, Jim was lying next to me, grinning in his sleep. He woke up and smiled and started kissing me all over. He kissed as high as possible, and as low as possible, then he kissed possible. I stood up and bent over, and we did what we both like. We made love all day long. I fell asleep in between lovemaking, and I saw my ancestors.

"Girl, you was supposed to wait," Aunt T said. "You never did know how to wait."

My grandma smiled. "Girl, hush, sometimes rules are made to be broken. Besides," she added, "y'all been waiting over twenty years to get it right."

"Thank you," I told them.

Jim must've thought I was talking to him 'cause I heard him say, "You wait, you ain't had nothing to thank me for yet. Come here, woman. Let me taste you."

The Haunting of Hip Hop

A Reading Group Companion

Bertice Berry speaks to many generations in *The Haunting of Hip Hop*. Weaving together the lives of Ngozi, who was violently robbed of his ability to communicate, and Freedom, the king of chart-topping sounds, Berry raises provocative questions about the ageless importance of dialogue. We hope that the following topics will help your reading group give voice to new ideas and enjoy a spirited discussion.

1. Ngozi embodies incredible strength of character: determination, integrity, a loving heart, responsibility, respect for his family. Who are the Ngozis (male and female) in your life and community?

2. Although he named himself Freedom, Harry Hudson faces numerous obstacles, even when he is a little boy. It's only through the spirit world that he can truly set himself free. What constraints are imposed by the modern world? Can ancestors really liberate their descendants?

3. Do you share Ava's opinion of Chucky Campbell? Did he sell out?

4. The heart of the novel deals with desecration of the sacred drum: "The beat, the rhythm, the words of hip-hop music rarely spoke the truth of the drum" (Chapter 30). What is your opinion of hip-hop culture? Do raw rap lyrics contribute to violence, or do they expose a painful way of life that would otherwise go unaddressed?

5. What does the drum represent to you? How can you honor it in your own life?

6. From ragtime to jazz, doo-wop, and rap, white culture has often appropriated black musical innovations. Discuss the exploitation issues that Ava and Freedom cleverly defeat.

7. Describe the hypnotic music that Ava hears on the night of Freedom's death. If the book had come with a recording, what do you suppose this music would have sounded like?

8. From the day he is born, Ngozi's mother has many visions about his future. She tells him, "Your life here will be short, but your task is great" (Prologue), and he carries this knowledge with him into the "beast" that entombs him during the Middle Passage. In modern society, what does it take to give a child that same sense of purpose and self-worth?

9. Ngozi has no frame of reference for the kind of cruelty he sees in America, perceiving his situation as a battle of the spirits: "Once their hatred matched that of their captor, they would

have forgotten the proverb: The only weapon that can do battle with hatred is the weapon of love and peace [page 41]. . . . Ngozi was certain that the blood of the lost would be on the heads of those traitors for generations to come [page 51]." How does this philosophy relate to the daily battles in your life and to the wars being waged around the world?

10. The grandmothers represent a bridge between the novel's two main male characters, Ngozi and Freedom. How do your aunts, mothers, and grandmothers provide a link to your ancestry? How do they interact with the men in your family?

11. The brownstone sits at the corner of West 138th Street and Harriet Tubman Terrace, in a "gentrified" stretch of Harlem. What is the significance of the brownstone's location? Why do you suppose Bertice Berry included a Southern connection for so many of the characters?

12. Why did Freedom have to join the spirit world? What effect does this have on the tone of the book's final chapters?

13. The brownstone ghosts cope with a variety of unfulfilled quests. What keeps the spirits from finding peace? Which quests were you most able to identify with?

14. Are you skeptical about the existence of a spirit world, or do you feel a connection to it? Discuss any dreams, intuitive thoughts, or visions that have made a difference in your life.

15. The novel ends on a note of triumph and unity. What can be done to make this vision, Ngozi's vision, a reality?

about the author

BERTICE BERRY, Ph.D., is an inspirational speaker, sociologist, former stand-up comedian, and the host of an eponymous talk show that debuted on the Hallmark Channel in spring 2002. She is the author of four works of nonfiction and the novels *Redemption Song*, *The Haunting of Hip Hop*, and *Jim and Louella's Homemade Heart-Fix Remedy*. She lives in El Cajon, California.

TREASON IN AMERICA

DISLOYALTY VERSUS DISSENT

Jules Archer
History for Young Readers

TREASON IN AMERICA

DISLOYALTY VERSUS DISSENT

JULES ARCHER
Foreword by Brianna DuMont

Sky Pony Press

NEW YORK

Copyright © 1971 by Jules Archer
Foreword © 2016 by Sky Pony Press, an imprint of Skyhorse Publishing, Inc.
First Sky Pony Press edition, 2016

Sky Pony Press books may be purchased in bulk at special discounts for sales promotion, corporate gifts, fund-raising, or educational purposes. Special editions can also be created to specifications. For details, contact the Special Sales Department, Sky Pony Press, 307 West 36th Street, 11th Floor, New York, NY 10018 or info@skyhorsepublishing.com.

Sky Pony® is a registered trademark of Skyhorse Publishing, Inc.®, a Delaware corporation.

Visit our website at www.skyponypress.com.

10 9 8 7 6 5 4 3 2 1

Library of Congress Cataloging-in-Publication Data is available on file.

Series design by Brian Peterson
Cover photo credit Associated Press

Print ISBN: 978-1-63450-628-1
Ebook ISBN: 978-1-63450-198-9

Printed in the United States of America

To Kerry Russell Archer at Harvard.

CONTENTS

FOREWORD

Treason may be the most dangerous word in the dictionary. It's hard to define, easy to accuse, and always accompanied by a noose—or a firing squad or an electric chair. You get the picture. On the surface, it seems black and white: either a person has betrayed their country or not. Either they will die for it or not. Yet, by highlighting specific events in American history, especially during tense times, Jules Archer shows us treason has plenty of gray areas and is often a matter of perspective. Sounds like a dangerous distinction when the penalty is so high, doesn't it?

Over the years, shades of gray have come from many sources, like where you lived in America during the Civil War or your ethnicity during World War II. If that all seems too murky and distant, you may have wandered closer to treason than you realized. Today, we call it internet trolling. Thanks to being born into freedom, nothing's stopping you from hopping on any form of social media and denouncing all of America as a mismanaged, mangled mess. That's just good old fashioned dissent, right? Actually, there's a thin line between traitor and patriot, and not everyone agrees on where it should be drawn. If this were 1950s Hollywood, you might find yourself bunking up at the nearest federal prison for your crazy tweets.

Beginning with the American Revolution, we see from America's own Founding Fathers how razor-thin that treasonous line could be. Who were the traitors? If you lived in Boston but still loved to drink tea while singing "God Save the King," then the British certainly wouldn't have you hanged, drawn, and quartered. But, after they were booted, the new government might. Now they were the guys in charge, and winners are never traitors.

After the revolution, the budding republic had a lot to figure out, as one can see by the passage of the Alien and Sedition Acts or the federal government's swift response to Shays' Rebellion and the Whiskey Rebellion. Even though the American Patriots began their rule with an uprising, they didn't want to be overthrown by the newest one on the block.

Moving on to the Civil War, the line between traitor and patriot became murkier than ever for the young country. The killing of President Lincoln, for example, was treated as an assassination in the North and a patriotic act in the South. After the war, America needed time to suss out what being a traitor meant in order to heal.

Throughout his book, Archer is an equal opportunist when it comes to his traitorous examples, highlighting many convicted women. Iva Toguri (a.k.a. Tokyo Rose) is a special favorite of his, having listened to her smooth radio broadcasts in the Pacific during his military service in World War II. Iva, a Japanese-American who defected during the war, detailed death and destruction to homesick American soldiers, trying to scare them into submission. Pointing to innocent Japanese-Americans being confined, Archer shows why this American woman would have defected and raises important questions about the effect of wartime hysteria. He shows how easy it was to throw around the word "traitor" and the damage it did.

Maybe a little too easy, since the definition regularly changed from year to year. Much like hairstyles, what's out of fashion one year can come back the next. Formerly attacked right-wing Fascists were giddy during the 50s as their left-wing enemies were suddenly the hunted under McCarthyism. Archer warns us to avoid condemning political opposition, however, since it might cycle back. He uses the Vietnam War as his example; those who opposed it were traitors during the Johnson Administration and purveyors of truth during the Nixon years.

Perhaps it's in the turbulent 60s where Archer best puts on display the many shades of gray of dissent. When Archer reaches this era, rife with civil rights protests, anti-establishment movements, and the divisive Vietnam War, it feels as if he's speaking directly about issues facing us today. He could be discussing the War on Terror or race riots in Ferguson, Missouri, proving just how timely this book is to our generation. His discussion at the end—on how each new generation of Americans will need to decide how much opposition is our Constitutional right versus how much threatens the security of our government—rings especially true today.

Is it First Amendment–protected dissent to "Occupy Wall Street" or is it disloyalty? Should you be worried about police manhandling you to the nearest jail cell if you choose to join activists protesting Michael Brown's death in Ferguson? Should riot police be worried for their own safety while watching over angry citizens? How far should you be able to take your discontent?

He outlines the risks of "cracking down hard on dissent" and quotes Thomas Jefferson, third president of the United States and an original traitor to the British crown, who said, "A little rebellion now and then is a good thing." It may seem as if Archer is urging us to fight against complacency—the death of any good idea. He certainly would have had a field day with current traitor/hero, Edward Snowden, who stands accused of espionage for leaking government documents concerning the US's broad-reaching surveillance system. Was Snowden a traitor or a patriot? Perhaps only time will tell.

In the heat of our protest-crazy nation, we should do well to remember Archer's advice: To disagree with the law is your right. To disobey the law will incur penalties. If enough people believe the law is unjust, they can rise up and change it. That is the power and promise of a democracy. A good government recognizes the need to be shaken up every now and then.

As Archer ended with a call to action, so will I. Educate yourself, get involved, and make America the place you are proud to pledge your allegiance to. Just don't sing traitor to those who feel the opposite of you. Tomorrow, the future may prove them the winners.

—Brianna DuMont

TREASON IN AMERICA

DISLOYALTY VERSUS DISSENT

ONE

What Is Treason?

"Treason," according to the *Encyclopedia Americana,* is "the breach of the allegiance which a person owes to the state under whose protection he lives, and the most serious crime known to the law." But exactly what does it mean to be guilty of a "breach of the allegiance" owed to your country? Since treason is punishable by the death penalty, the prosecution is required to prove that anyone indicted as a traitor is indeed an enemy of his country, both by intention and deed, not simply an idealistic patriot who wants to oust the incumbent administration because he sincerely believes it is misruling the country he loves.

Should our view of treason, and the punishment we prescribe, distinguish between those who are disloyal out of high motives and those who are traitors for greed or ambition?

Should we condemn as base not only Aaron Burr and Benedict Arnold, who were traitors for personal gain, but also those Americans who collaborate with a foreign power because they sincerely believe in the superiority of the principles espoused by that alien nation?

Should we punish equally the government employee who sells military secrets to foreign spies for large sums of money and the physicist who reveals atomic secrets to scientists outside the country because he believes in international scientific cooperation as the only path to world peace and progress?

Every major power in the world operates a secret intelligence service to pry out the secrets of unfriendly nations. Ours is the CIA. No country, including our own, lacks some citizens who are willing, for a price or out of hostility toward their government, to turn over its secrets or to engage in subversive activities under foreign direction.

In determining whether an American citizen has committed treason, we require valid evidence, as well as two witnesses or a confession in open court; knowledge of the reasons for such treason; and also knowledge of how much harm it has actually done the country.

It is not always as simple as it seems to decide what is, or is not, treason. Let's become jurors considering some typical cases drawn from real life.

Imagine that the citizen who comes before us admits that during the recent war he had blown up one of the nation's munition factories. An obvious act of treason!

But what if this is now postwar France, and the defendant has been a guerrilla of the French underground, sabotaging the collaborationist Vichy government? True, he was a traitor to Vichy France. But in our eyes he was a patriotic Frenchman fighting French traitors who had sold out his country to the German enemy. Our whole perspective about the case is now dramatically reversed. Not guilty!

The next case on our docket deals with a soldier in the field who has refused to obey government orders and has even killed the officer who tried to compel him to obey. Treason!

But what if this is Germany during World War II? The Nazi government has ordered the mass extermination of all Jews and

Slavs, including women and children. The defendant is a German soldier who puts loyalty to his God and his conscience above loyalty to the state. Is he a traitor to his country? Or is he a patriot who refuses to besmirch German honor by obeying an order to commit crimes against humanity?

The judges at the Nuremberg Trials declared that it is not treason to defy a government order to commit atrocities, but it is in fact treason to humanity to carry out such orders.

Let's consider a few other paradoxes that indicate the importance of motivation in deciding what we can justly label as treason.

In the dark a man suddenly springs out of some bushes and without warning kills three men strolling along a road. Murder! But wait—he wears an American officer's uniform. He has just slain three enemy soldiers in a country we are fighting. A hero!

But the light is better now, and we discover our mistake. The officer belongs to the enemy; the three soldiers he has ambushed are ours. Treachery!

Then it turns out, after all, that he *is* one of our officers. He has thwarted the attempt of three American deserters to escape to the enemy. A patriot!

But we next learn that he attacked the soldiers because they had discovered his plan to lead a military putsch to take over the US Army and were about to expose him. Traitor!

Motivation, obviously, has a great deal to do with whether someone can be considered a traitor or patriot. What is considered treason in one light can be recognized as patriotism in another. Much depends on *who* is doing the judging—also where; also when. The reasons why a man turns against his government may range all the way from the sordid motive of selling out his country for a bribe to opposing the administration for what he believes to be betrayal of his country's traditions and ideals.

The problem of defining treason is so complicated that many Americans confuse it with political opposition to the government, especially when dissent takes the form of breaking the law as a symbolic protest.

In a country which guarantees freedom of speech and dissent to all citizens, the limits to which dissent may be carried before an American is subject to arrest are problematical. But so is the question of treason when applied to a manufacturer who seeks excess profits by supplying the Army with inferior weapons that malfunction in battle.

Treason, obviously, would seem far too serious a charge to be leveled at any American except for the gravest of reasons. Yet it has often been hurled, as we shall see, for the political purpose of character assassination.

Abraham Lincoln had some thoughts on what is *not* treason in his first inaugural address. "This country with its institutions belongs to the people who inhabit it," he told the American people. "Whenever they shall grow weary of the existing Government, they can exercise their constitutional right of amending it or their revolutionary right to dismember or overthrow it."

We are, after all, a nation founded in revolution, which is justified in the Declaration of Independence. Many other governments in the world also hold power today because of revolutions against previous regimes. A few of these are the Soviet Union, Spain, Yugoslavia, Greece, Cuba, Mexico, Indonesia, Red China, France, Germany, Italy, Ireland, South Vietnam, North Vietnam, the Philippines, Egypt, Iraq, Cambodia, the Congo, and almost all of Central and South America.

Traitors, ironically, are considered traitors only so long as their treason is unsuccessful. "Treason doth never prosper," noted English writer Sir John Harington in 1613. "What's the reason? For if it prosper, none dare call it Treason!"

Those British subjects who wrote the Declaration of Independence were only traitors until their treason succeeded. Then they became the new authority in America, clothed in every bit as much respectability as the British governors whom they overthrew. And we now respect them as our great patriots.

Many Americans today feel, however, that revolution is no longer necessary or justified since we now have a two-party political system, in which the party out of power becomes the legitimate focus of grievances against the government. Certainly our history proves that the minority party has functioned as a bitter critic and foe of the administration in power.

But sometimes *both* major parties support a controversial venture, such as the Vietnam war. At such times the frustration of large numbers of Americans becomes so great as to explode in violent opposition to the government, as occurred during the turbulent election campaign year of 1968.

The citizen driven to defiance of the government out of dedication to principle does not regard himself as disloyal but as a true patriot. When Brutus joined the plot to assassinate Caesar, he insisted, "Not that I loved Caesar less, but that I loved Rome more."

Often when a revolutionist wins power, he sets up revolutionary courts to try those government officials he has overthrown as "traitors to the country." (Fidel Castro, Francisco Franco, Marshal Tito, and Ngo Dinh Diem all set up such courts.) In some countries treason is the name applied by politicians to the tactics of their rivals in a power struggle. The label of traitor sticks only to the losers.

Irish history is full of revolutionists condemned as traitors by English judges in English courts but who were exalted to the status of patriot martyrs when Ireland finally won her freedom from England. Today's Eire considers as traitors only those Irishmen who remained loyal to the British government during the Irish uprisings.

When the Nazis occupied Norway, their Norwegian puppet, Major Vidkun Quisling, arrested as traitors all of his countrymen who sabotaged the German occupying forces. But after the war Quisling was executed by his fellow Norwegians for high treason. Similarly, French Premier Pierre Laval punished opposition to the German war effort as an act of treason to the Vichy government. After the war the de Gaulle government sentenced Laval to the firing squad as a traitor to France.

Secession poses baffling questions of treason. Were the Biafrans who felt oppressed and revolted against Nigeria traitors? Was it treason for an outraged South to secede from an abolitionist-minded North? Are we dealing with traitors or patriots in the Puerto Rican Revolutionary Armed Independence Movement, which in 1969 bombed American hotels on their island, seized a radio station, and called on all Puerto Ricans to join "patriots in a revolution against Yankee imperialism"?

Are we on solid moral ground to insist that our government is *always* right ("Our country, right or wrong!") and that those citizens who disagree are traitors to the nation?

This book attempts the difficult task of exploring what is or is not treason, as illuminated by dramatic cases from American history. Baffling questions require answers:

Does the American government have the right to use repressive measures to protect itself from overthrow? How far can it legally go—against whom and under what circumstances?

Is the Communist party, or any group dedicated to the overthrow of the government, as entitled to advocate its policies as the Republican or Democratic parties?

Are Fascist groups that seek to turn the United States into a right-wing dictatorship, in the style of Hitler, Mussolini, and Franco, superpatriots or supertraitors?

Are Americans of foreign ancestry disloyal for feeling and maintaining cultural ties to the country of their fathers?

What is the dividing line between dissent and disloyalty? Is it treason for Americans to oppose a war in which the United States is involved?

Should a minority be allowed to decide which laws of a majority they will obey as just and which they will disobey as unjust?

How should treason be judged and punished?

How can all of us strengthen the bonds of loyalty we feel toward each other as Americans and help to prevent the development of situations that create disloyalty?

In the final analysis, each new generation of Americans must decide for itself how much opposition to the government is every American citizen's right and how much is unsafe for the security of the whole society.

This book suggests guidelines for reaching your own conclusions about disloyalty and dissent. With other Americans of your generation who agree with you, you are free to urge those views upon your representatives in Congress in order to redefine American duties and liberties for our own day.

TWO

"We Shall All Hang Separately"

In earliest times any threat to, or attack on, the state or head of state was punished as treason. A monarch or judicial tribunal decided just which acts of opposition were traitorous. It was far from unusual for the charge of treason to be made for the purpose of political punishment.

The most open-and-shut cases of treason were those in which a citizen or soldier was found to have been paid by an insurrectionist, or agent of a foreign power, to commit an act of treachery against sovereign or state.

Yet at least one great Roman monarch saw nothing wrong in wider loyalties than those prescribed by national boundaries.

"My city and country . . . is Rome," said Marcus Aurelius, the brilliant Roman emperor and Stoic philosopher, "but so far as I am a man, it is the world." Early Christians also subscribed to the brotherhood of man as a paramount patriotism that came before loyalty to Rome.

In ancient Rome treason usually involved only the military. Accused men were charged with bearing arms against the state; communicating with the enemy; betraying a citizen to the enemy; desertion; or surrender to the enemy. Torture was sometimes used to extract confessions, but men accused as traitors were seldom put to death unless they confessed or there were two or more witnesses to their guilt.

The Romans were apparently more interested in exposing treason than in punishing it. A condemned traitor was often allowed to flee the country before the date set for his execution. Banishment from the Rome he had betrayed seemed to many citizens a more appropriate punishment, and indeed a more terrible one, than death.

The scope of treason was vastly increased in the sixth century under Justinian, when Roman emperors were declared divine. The Justinian Code, the basis for all later Western law, called it treason to question an emperor's choice of his successor; to plot the murder of high magistrates; to meet in a mob with weapons or stones; to set prisoners free illegally; to incite others to sedition; and to falsify public documents.

The intention was considered equivalent to the actual deed if either could be proved. A convicted traitor was stripped of his property and beheaded.

Under King Edward III, England basically adopted the Justinian concept of treason. The Treason Act of 1351 provided death for "high treason," defined as offenses against the Crown. Lesser penalties were prescribed for "petty treason"—offenses against private "superiors," such as disloyalty of wife to husband, servant to master. Petty treason later became defined as the crime of murder.

Today's British law still retains four early definitions of high treason: plotting or even "imagining" the death of any member of the royal family, having illegal sexual relations with any female member of the royal family, levying war against the king, and giving aid and comfort to his enemies.

It was left "in the breast of the judges to determine what was treason, or not so." The looseness with which the Statute of Treasons was often applied is exemplified in the fifteenth-century case of Walter Walker, who lived at a Cheapside inn called the Sign of the Crown.

Walker was overheard telling his little son that if he would be a good boy and go to sleep, his father would make him heir to the Crown—meaning the inn at which they were living. Arrested and accused of sinister intentions against the royal family, he was executed as a traitor.

During the reigns of Queen Anne and King George III, new definitions of treason were specified: attempting to prevent the king's chosen successor from coming to the throne and plotting to harm or kill the king and his heirs.

The earliest British penalties prescribed for a convicted traitor were barbaric. He was dragged to the place of execution by a horse, hung long enough to agonize him, cut down, disembowelled, then beheaded. Afterward his body was cut into quarters and "disposed of as the King might see fit."

Women found guilty of treason were often burned alive until 1790, after which they were usually beheaded or hanged. In 1848 most acts once branded as high treason were reduced to "treason felony," for which a convicted traitor could be sentenced to prison for anywhere from five years to life.

In the American colonies, as hostility deepened toward the Crown, colonists uneasily demanded that the scope of treason be limited only to levying war against the king or giving aid and comfort to his enemies. But King George III preferred the broad English law that left the power to determine what acts of opposition or dissent were treason in royal hands.

One of the earliest Americans charged with treason to the Crown was Nathaniel Bacon, a young Virginia plantation owner and member of the Governor's Council. He was indignant at the high-handed rule of Governor William Berkeley, especially at Berkeley's refusal to take action against Indian raids on border settlements.

Arming three hundred followers, Bacon led an authorized attack on Indians in 1676, slaughtering 150 men. Governor Berkeley angrily charged him with treason and ordered his arrest. Bacon attacked and burned Jamestown, the capitol, putting Berkeley and the colonial government to flight. British troop reinforcements were rushed to Virginia. The rebellion collapsed with Bacon's death from malaria. Berkeley vindictively ignored pardons for Bacon's followers signed by the king and hanged twenty-three of them as traitors to the Crown. He was ordered back to England but died before he had to answer for his own insubordination.

As the colonists grew increasingly dissatisfied with British rule, defiance bordering on treason became highly popular and was considered evidence of personal courage. Patrick Henry, a struggling, twenty-seven-year-old Virginia lawyer, won fame and clients in 1763 by a speech attacking the king's right to set aside laws passed by the popularly elected assemblies.

Pleading a case, Henry cried, "A king by annulling . . . laws of this salutary nature . . . forfeits all rights to his subjects' obedience!" Shocked cries rose in the courtroom: "Treason! Treason!" But his challenge to Crown arrogance proved so popular that he was elected to the Virginia legislature. In 1765 Henry authored the Virginia Resolutions, defying Britain's Stamp Act and reasserting the right of the colonies to legislate for themselves.

"Caesar had his Brutus," Henry told the legislature, "Charles the First his Cromwell, and George the Third—"

Again cries of "Treason! Treason! *Treason!*"

"—George the Third," he finished defiantly, "may profit by their example! If *this* be treason, make the most of it!"

Defiance of the Crown grew increasingly common in the decade preceding the American Revolution. King George III and Parliament, as well as the royal governors of the colonies, strove desperately to turn back the mounting tide of rebellion. Sometimes they appeased the colonists, sometimes they took a firm stand, and sometimes they punished them. But there were few arrests for treason, for fear of provoking an uprising.

American dissenters had some staunch supporters in the British Parliament itself, men such as Isaac Barre, for whom Barre, Vermont, was later named. Barre fondly called them "Sons of Liberty," a name adopted by colonial firebrands Samuel Adams and Paul Revere for a secret society they organized in the summer of 1765. The Sons sabotaged the unpopular Stamp Act, then went on to organize a boycott of British imports and spur the colonies to cooperate in fighting for self-government.

The result was the Stamp Act Congress that condemned taxation without representation and declared the Stamp Act illegal. American leaders in the colonial assemblies passed bills refusing to pay for troops quartered upon them or to collect royal taxes. The British Parliament angrily dissolved the New York and Massachusetts legislatures, calling them seditious. But no arrests were made.

The Sons of Liberty organized mob clashes with British troops in New York and Boston in 1770. The Boston riot was exaggerated and exploited by Sam Adams and Paul Revere as the "Boston Massacre" to stir revolutionary fervor throughout the colonies. Sam Adams organized the Committees of Correspondence to keep the colonies in touch with each other about new "outrages" by British authorities and to report measures of resistance taken by the colonies affected.

In February, 1772, the Boston assembly threatened secession from Britain unless the rights of the colonies were respected. That June eight boatloads of Sons of Liberty from Providence boarded the British customs schooner *Gaspee,* which had run aground at Namquit Point. Putting its officer and crew ashore, they set the schooner afire. Despite huge reward offers, only one witness could be found to accuse anyone, and his testimony was so contradictory as to be worthless.

The *Gaspee* incident clearly indicated to Parliament the extent of popular support enjoyed by American "traitors."

England was kept informed of treasonous moves in the colonies by Dr. Benjamin Church, chief surgeon of Washington's army, an informer who succeeded in winning a place on the twenty-one-man executive board of the Committees of Correspondence. It thus came as no surprise to the British when the tax imposed by Parliament's Tea Act resulted in a boycott of British tea.

But Church didn't find out until the British did that Sam Adams had sent Sons of Liberty disguised as Mohawk Indians to raid tea ships in Boston Harbor and dump their cargoes overboard. The Boston Tea Party provoked a stormy debate in Parliament.

Many members demanded that known leaders of the Sons such as Sam Adams, Paul Revere, and Patrick Henry be arrested and brought to England to stand trial for treason. Some insisted that entire colonies, which obviously supported these acts of defiance, be drastically punished. King George agreed with this latter view as the only way to teach the Americans a lesson.

Ignoring pleas by Chatham and Edmund Burke for a conciliatory policy, Parliament passed the Boston Port Act. Boston

Harbor would be blockaded until Bostonians made restitution for the losses suffered by the East India Tea Company because of "dangerous commotions and insurrections." Further punitive laws were also decreed by the royal governor of Massachusetts.

Colonial indignation exploded. Only Georgia failed to send a representative to the first Continental Congress of thirteen colonies that met at Philadelphia in September, 1774. The Congress voted to boycott all British goods until Parliament agreed to give Americans a voice in their own affairs.

By April, 1775, colonial treason had gone so far that a New England militia was organized to resist British troops sent to enforce Parliament's decrees. The colonial guerrillas at Lexington and Concord "fired the shot heard round the world." One month later Benedict Arnold was authorized to raise a force to attack Fort Ticonderoga on Lake Champlain in order to capture armaments needed to resist the British Army.

The American Revolution had begun. In June, two days before the disastrous rout at Bunker Hill, George Washington was appointed commander in chief of the American forces.

Now, suddenly, the awkward decision about treason could no longer be avoided. Who were the traitors in the colonies—those disloyal to the British Crown or those disloyal to the American insurrection? On June 30, 1775, the Continental Congress passed the Articles of War, governing the conduct of soldiers enlisted in the rebellious Continental Army. Articles 5 and 6 authorized the punishment of any "mutiny and sedition" against the Revolution.

In August, King George III issued a Proclamation of Rebellion condemning the North American colonies for "traitorously preparing, ordering and levying war against us." Accusing many Englishmen in London of having carried on a "traitorous correspondence" with the rebels, the king forbade any further commerce with Americans guilty of "treasonable Commotions."

"I desire what is good," said George III; "therefore, everyone who does not agree with me is a traitor."

Toward the end of 1775, colonial leaders of the rebellion, who now called themselves patriots, began suspecting that Dr. Benjamin Church was the informer in their midst. Doubt became certainty when his mistress smuggled a coded letter through patriot lines to his brother-in-law in British-held Boston. Intercepted, it revealed that Church had been acting as a spy for British General Thomas B. Gage.

The Continental Congress, thunderstruck, ordered Church arrested as a traitor. He denied that he was guilty of treason since they were all still under British law, which defined treason as a betrayal of allegiance owed to the king. Baffled, Congress removed him from office, jailed him, then permitted him to leave the country. His ship was lost at sea.

At the insistence of the Revolutionary Army, Congress now passed a bill calling it treason, and prescribing the death penalty, for any American soldier to collaborate with the king's forces.

The new law was cited in June, 1776, when Thomas Hickey, a member of Washington's personal guard, unsuccessfully conspired to lead a force of patriots over to General William Howe's forces as they landed in New York. Washington court-martialed Hickey, who was hanged for "sedition and mutiny" and for holding a "treacherous correspondence with the enemy."

Washington told Congress that New York's mayor, David Mathews, had also been implicated in the plot. As a civilian, however, Mathews could not be prosecuted under the military-treason statute. The colonies, fighting for the right to self-government, were sensitive about giving Congress any federal power over civilians. So Congress simply passed a resolution stating that all colonists owed allegiance to the "United Colonies of America" and asking each colony to formulate its own laws punishing civilian traitors.

In January, 1776, as the fighting expanded from revolutionary resistance to a desperate full-scale civil war, Tomas Paine called for a declaration of independence from Britain in his widely circulated pamphlet, *Common Sense.* Congress passed the Tory Act, requiring local patriots to explain the American cause to all Tories and to disarm any who refused to pledge fealty to the colonists. The word "traitor" was now applied to any American disloyal to the rebellion.

In British and American Tory eyes the Declaration of Independence, adopted on July 4, 1776, was the ultimate act of treason. When any people "suffer a long train of abuses and usurpations," declared the colonists, "it is their right, it is their duty to throw off such government."*

Having openly announced their treason to the British Crown, the Americans at Philadelphia were under no illusions about what would happen to them if their revolution failed.

"We must, indeed, all hang together," warned Benjamin Franklin, "or most assuredly we shall all hang separately."

It now became more important than ever to weed out from their midst those countrymen still loyal to the Crown.

---

* Almost two centuries later Americans were reminded of these words by the Smothers Brothers, who had been dropped from CBS-TV programming because of their anti-Establishment humor. In a special Washington's Birthday show on NBC-TV, they quoted from the Founding Fathers. "We want to show," explained Tom Smothers, "that these great men defended the rights of dissent and free speech, and that to criticize your government does not make you a traitor. It makes you a modern patriot."

THREE

Traitors against Treason

Few voices denouncing treason to the Revolution were louder than that of Major General Charles Lee, a fire-eating professional soldier who had fought in the French and Indian War, married a Seneca chief's daughter, and campaigned with Washington.

When Howe's forces threatened New York in the autumn of 1776, Lee won Washington's permission to defend that sector and to deal harshly with the Tories of Long Island.

"Not to crush those Serpents," Lee warned, "before their rattles are grown, would be ruinous." He assured Congress that he would purge New York and its environs of traitors.

His troops raided the homes of suspected Tories, packing off prisoners to Connecticut. But when Howe took New York, forcing Washington to retreat across the Delaware, Lee was captured by a British patrol. Threatened with hanging, he saved his neck by promising Howe to betray Washington, a secret later revealed by British historians.

Unaware of Lee's defection, Washington ransomed him from the British by freeing some Hessian officers. Lee, restored to his command while secretly pledged to work "sincerely and zealously" for a British victory, sabotaged his orders to engage British forces near Monmouth, New Jersey, in support of an attack by Washington. His order to his troops to retreat instead resulted in a court-martial for cowardice. Unsuspected of treason, he was simply removed from his command.

When he eventually died on his Virginia estate, he was buried with honor as "a great American soldier and patriot."

The British scrupulously distinguished between the acts of military spying and treason. When they caught twenty-four-year-old American Captain Nathan Hale, disguised as a schoolmaster, gathering military information behind their lines in Long Island, he was hanged as a spy. It was as an American patriot, rather than as a traitor to the Crown, however, that he was allowed to utter his famous last words, "I only regret that I have but one life to lose for my country."

In British eyes the real traitors were the civilian leaders of the Revolution. To negotiate a treaty with the Dutch in 1780, Congress sent Henry Laurens, the South Carolinian who had been president of the Continental Congress two years earlier. Captured at sea, he was brought to England and clapped in the Tower of London on charges of high treason.

The British offered to spare his life if he confessed that he was a traitor to the Crown and transferred his allegiance. Laurens defied his captors. He was no British traitor, he insisted, but an American civilian prisoner of war. Two years later he was finally exchanged for a celebrated British prisoner in America, Lord Cornwallis, in time to join Franklin, Jay, and John Adams in signing a preliminary peace treaty.

The most celebrated traitor of the American Revolution was, of course, Benedict Arnold. From 1775 to 1778 Arnold fought so bravely that he won promotions from captain to major general. Twice wounded, he was the last American anyone would have suspected of treachery. But Arnold was a vainglorious, overambitious man for whom honors and promotions never came soon enough or often enough.

He had constant run-ins with his superiors, who found him imperious and difficult to get along with. Appointed commander of Philadelphia in 1778, he rode into the city as a military hero but a social zero. Taking over the fine mansion Howe had vacated, Arnold set about making an impression socially on the city's elite by entertaining extravagantly.

Soon deep in debt, he paid off Tory creditors with political favors. He married eighteen-year-old blond Tory socialite Margaret Shippen, whose expensive tastes plunged him even more deeply into debt. In 1780 he was court-martialed because of charges brought by the Council of Philadelphia that he was abusing his military authority. Found guilty, he was sentenced to be reprimanded by General Washington.

Washington, who respected Arnold's military abilities, rebuked him mildly. The proud Arnold was outraged by his humiliation at the hands of fellow citizens who, he felt, owed him a debt of gratitude for his heroic services on their behalf.

He was still brooding when his wife, Margaret, showed him a letter from British Major John Andre, an old beau of hers from the days of the British occupation of Philadelphia. Andre was now with Howe's forces in New York, serving as adjutant general to General Henry Clinton. The letter offered Margaret's husband twenty thousand pounds if he could obtain command of West Point and turn it over to the British. Arnold could also expect a high command with Howe's forces if he succeeded.

Still debt-ridden and bitter at his treatment, Arnold agreed to turn his coat. Washington offered him another field command, but Arnold pleaded that old wounds were bothering him and asked for the West Point command instead. When Washington consented, Arnold notified Andre at once. He also informed the British where Washington would be sleeping one night, but the information reached Clinton too late to be of use.

The British sloop *Vulture* brought Andre up the Hudson at night for a rendezvous with Arnold to arrange the surrender of West Point to the British. He was wearing a British uniform, but daybreak made it advisable for him to get back to the *Vulture* in civilian clothes with a pass signed by Arnold.

As he went through the American lines, his aristocratic manner made three American militiamen suspicious. They turned him over to their lieutenant as a possible spy with a forged pass. The lieutenant suspected that Andre was someone important because of wig powder in his hair, and notified Major Benjamin Tallmadge, of the new American Secret Service.

Tallmadge notified Washington, who was preparing to visit West Point. Word also reached Arnold that Andre had been taken. Arnold at once fled for refuge aboard the *Vulture,* lying in the Hudson, only hours before Washington reached his house for a breakfast appointment. Washington was confused by Arnold's mysterious absence, but all became clear when papers found in Major Andre's boot were rushed to him. He at once set about strengthening the sabotaged defenses of West Point.

On September 26, 1780, General Nathaniel Greene grimly issued general orders to the American troops, revealing to them that they had been betrayed by a top commander:

Treason of the blackest dye was yesterday discovered! General Arnold, who commanded at West Point, lost to every sentiment of honor, of public and private obligation, was about to deliver up that important post into the hands of the enemy. Such an event must have given the American cause a deadly wound, if not a fatal stab. Happily, the treason has been timely discovered. . . . Great honor is due to the American Army that this is the first instance of treason of the kind.

Andre asked to be shot, as that was a suitable military execution, but was sent to the gallows instead, where he coolly fixed the noose around his own neck. The British paid Arnold £6,315 for his unsuccessful treachery and gave him a field commission as a brigadier general. He fought against the Continental Army at Richmond, Virginia, and burned New London, Connecticut, massacring the defenders of Fort Griswold when they surrendered. British officers loathed him as an "ungentlemanly brute and traitor."

"General Arnold is a very unpopular character in the British army," observed the London *Lloyd's Evening Post* on October 11, 1780, "nor can all the patronage he meets with from the commander-in-chief procure him respectability. . . . The subaltern officers have conceived such an aversion to him, that they unanimously refused to serve under his command."

When the war was over Arnold sought to cling to his British commission, but the British had had enough of him. In 1783 he went to New Brunswick, Canada, where he became a merchant in the West Indies trade. Four years later accusations of dishonesty drove him to London, where war had broken out with France. He sought to fit out privateers but was so shunned and despised that he suffered what amounted to a nervous breakdown. He literally welcomed death on June 14, 1801, less than two months after the inauguration of a new vice president of the

United States who would soon rival Arnold in popular infamy as a celebrated traitor—Aaron Burr.

Americans were shocked when another Revolutionary hero was also revealed to be engaged in treasonable intercourse with the enemy. Connecticut-born Ethan Allen had moved in 1769 to that part of the New Hampshire Grants that became Vermont. The New York legislature charged that many settlers in western Vermont were actually on the New York side of the border, and insisted they must repurchase their property from Albany.

Indignant, Ethan Allen and his younger brother, Ira, organized the Green Mountain Boys, sworn to resist any attempt to drive Vermonters off their lands. The quarrel was momentarily forgotten with the outbreak of the Revolution. Allen became a hero when he led his Green Mountain Boys, under Benedict Arnold, to capture Fort Ticonderoga in May, 1775. He also won fame as a rough, fearless leader in expeditions against Canada under Schuyler and Montgomery.

The British finally captured him near Montreal in September, 1775. Imprisoned for two and a half years, Allen was released in an exchange of prisoners in May, 1778, after Washington warned that if he were executed for treason, the Americans would execute British prisoners as traitors.

A grateful Congress brevetted Allen colonel in the Continental Army and a major general in the militia. He returned home to the New Hampshire Grants, where his brother Ira had led a movement that broke away their section as the separate state of Vermont.

But congressional opposition blocked recognition of Vermont as a state. Ethan Allen angrily decided that if the United States could secede from Britain to win independence, then Vermont could secede from the United States for exactly the same reason.

Entering negotiations with Sir Frederick Haldimand, Governor General of Canada, Allen proposed making Vermont a Canadian province. He warned Congress bluntly in March, 1781, "I am as resolutely determined to defend the independence of Vermont as Congress that of the United States, and rather than fail will retire with the hardy Green Mountain Boys into the desolate caverns of the mountains and wage war."

Furious congressmen demanded Allen's arrest for treason. But cooler heads prevailed, suggesting that his dealings with Sir Frederick and his defiance of Congress were not intended as treachery, but only as pressure upon the Congress.

On March 4, 1791, after Ethan Allen had died at Burlington, his "constructive treason" was restored to the columns of patriotism by Vermont's admission to statehood.

It was not until fully two years after the Declaration of Independence that Americans had a national definition of treason. Until then treason had been a matter for each state to deal with separately. When the Constitution was ratified on September 13, 1788, the crime of treason—the only crime defined in the Constitution—was finally spelled out. Article III, Section 3, declared:

Treason against the United States shall consist only in levying war against them, or in adhering to their enemies, giving them aid and comfort. No person shall be convicted of treason unless on the testimony of two witnesses to the same overt act, or on confession in open court. The Congress shall have power to declare the punishment of treason, but no attainder [deprivation of civil and legal rights] of treason shall work corruption of blood, or forfeiture except during the life of the person attained.

The attainder clause was intended to prevent extension of punishment to a traitor's heirs. "Levying war" has been construed by Constitutional authorities to mean defiance of the government by armed force but more than just rioting or interfering with execution of the law. "Adhering to their enemies, giving them aid and comfort," has been interpreted as giving material assistance, voluntarily, to countries with which the United States is at war.

The First Congress, meeting on March 4, 1789, set the penalty for treason as death or imprisonment and fine, at the discretion of the court. The minimum penalty was five years' imprisonment, a ten-thousand-dollar fine, and inability to hold public office. An alien temporarily residing in the United States may be as guilty of treason as a citizen, on the theory that he owes a duty of allegiance to the country because he is sheltered under the protection of its laws while he is here.

In 1790 Congress decreed that the penalty for treason would be death by hanging. An accused person had to be given a copy of the indictment and a list of witnesses and jurors at least three days before trial. He was guaranteed counsel and the right to challenge thirty-five selections for the jury panel. If he chose to be mute at the trial, he would be considered as having entered a plea of "not guilty."

The treason clause did not become national law until after the war because otherwise it would have been necessary for the government to execute or imprison up to two hundred thousand Loyalists. Instead they went into exile, forcibly or voluntarily.

Unlike the bloodthirsty leaders of the French Revolution, American Revolution leaders were reluctant to execute fellow citizens who had aided the British or opposed the Revolution. Many of the Founding Fathers themselves had not reached the decision to be disloyal to the Crown without great anguish.

John Adams later confessed that he would have given anything he owned during the Revolution if somehow it could have been magically erased and the old colonial system restored. Relatives of Washington, Franklin, John and Samuel Adams remained loyal to the Crown. In many families there were similar divisions between father and son, brother and brother.

Understandably, many states preferred to pardon acts of treason by "acts of grace" when apprehended Loyalists agreed to take an oath of allegiance to the United States. Likewise, many British leaders were equally loath to regard the Americans in arms against them as guilty of treason.

"We do not call you rebels or traitors," Edmund Burke had told them from Parliament in January, 1777. "We do not call for the vengeance of the Crown against you. . . . On the contrary, we highly revere the principles on which you act, though we lament some of their effects."

Disloyalty to the new Republic was sometimes inspired less by allegiance to the Crown than by simple war-weariness. After four years of a revolt that had bled the country white of men, money, and goods, there was widespread unrest not only among the troops, many of whom were deserting, but also among the civilian population.

In Virginia, attempts to draft more men for Washington led to statewide riots. One riot leader, John Claypole, of Hampshire County, defied the sheriff, cursed Congress, and drank a public toast to the king. He and forty-one other rioters were arrested by state militia and charged with treason. But all were pardoned when the court selected to try them failed to convene because the commissioners prudently neglected to arrive.

At the end of the war the treason law took on a different coloration because of the new Republic's problems. Now it was no longer a question of allegiance to an external enemy but of rebellion against the authority of a weak new government. The Federalists in power were extremely sensitive to criticism and saw opposition to government edicts as the forerunner of treason, if not treason itself.

Shays' Rebellion in Massachusetts in 1786 was the first major armed insurrection that sought to prevent the enforcement of federal laws. After the war poor farmers were stripped of their farms, cattle, and possessions for inability to pay heavy taxes and debts. Many were thrown into debtors' prison by the wealthy merchants of Boston and Salem who controlled the Massachusetts legislature.

Mobs of farmers prevented courts from sitting so that no judgments could be passed against them. Issuing a proclamation against unlawful assemblies, Governor James Bowdoin called out the militia in September, 1786. The Regulators, as the poor farmers called themselves, elected war hero Daniel Shays as their leader. Shays, too, was in trouble because he could not pay a twelve-dollar debt. He led 1,100 men in shutting down the State Supreme Court at Springfield, which was preparing to indict him and other leading Regulators for treason.

After freeing imprisoned debtors, they sought to raid the federal arsenal for arms. But militia led by Major General Shepherd scattered them with artillery, killing four. Later a force led by General Benjamin Lincoln pursued them through the countryside. Shays escaped to Vermont, but fourteen of his followers were caught and sentenced to die as traitors.

A storm of public protest, however, forced the authorities to pardon some Regulators and let others off with short prison terms. Indignation swept the old legislature out of office. The new one granted some of the Regulators' demands and permitted Shays to return home.

Washington and his Federalists were deeply worried about the explosive instability of the new Republic. The same oppressive conditions of the poor that had provoked Shays' Rebellion existed in all states of the Union. Thomas Jefferson, now American minister to France, was certainly not helping matters by declaring cheerfully from Paris: "A little rebellion now and then is a good thing; the tree of liberty must be refreshed from time to time with the blood of patriots and tyrants." Did *all* governments, indeed, become tyrannies?

Was permanent treason the obligation of patriots?

FOUR

The Incredible Aaron Burr

The apprehension of the Federalists was intensified one year after Jefferson resigned from Washington's Cabinet to organize an opposition to Alexander Hamilton's policies. Hamilton saw Jefferson's influence in the outbreak of the Whiskey Rebellion.

When Hamilton had passed an excise tax on whiskey-making in 1791, Jefferson had predicted that it would be defied as "odious" by backwoods Scotch-Irish farmers of the Monongahela Valley in western Pennsylvania. They depended upon marketing their grain in the form of more easily transportable whiskey. Every farm had its own distillery. The tax was unwise, Jefferson warned, because collecting it would commit "the authority of the government in parts where resistance is most probable and coercion less practicable."

His predictions proved accurate. The whiskey farmers, viewing the tax as just as oppressive as the British Stamp Tax had been to all Americans, organized to resist it. Distillers who paid it were threatened. Revenue officers who entered Monongahela Valley were driven off bodily.

Washington and Hamilton angrily insisted that Pennsylvania governor Thomas Mifflin put down the insurrection. A Jeffersonian Republican, he refused. If anyone was going to be unpopular for using force against the whiskey farmers, let it be the Federalists. It was *their* law!

Hamilton warned the president that federal power and determination were being tested. If the government did not act vigorously to enforce the laws of Congress, then state power would be recognized as paramount. Americans in any state would be free to defy any federal laws they opposed.

Convinced, on August 7, 1794, Washington called out and federalized fifteen thousand militia troops from Virginia, Maryland, and Pennsylvania. This army was led across the Alleghenies by Generals Daniel Morgan and Henry Lee, accompanied by Alexander Hamilton in uniform. It was an absurdly large force to put down some regional rioting—as large as the army that had captured Cornwallis. But it suited Hamilton's purpose to demonstrate the great power of the federal government.

The whiskey rebels fled and the disorders were quickly quelled. Hamilton ordered eighteen farmers seized for trial in Philadelphia as traitors. Only two were convicted, however, and Washington pardoned both when it became embarrassingly apparent that raising an army against the desperate farmers of western Pennsylvania had been a serious political mistake.

There was widespread indignation against the Federalists in power for this flexing of military might against the people. The Jeffersonians soared in popularity as a new "party of the people" opposed to an aristocratic federal bureaucracy.

When Adams succeeded Washington as president in 1797, it was not lost on him that Jefferson, as his closest rival, had been elected vice president. Adams had to respect Jefferson's views on what to do about French interference with American shipping during the Franco-British war. Hawk Federalists in the Cabinet demanded war against France, but Jefferson's Republicans were vehemently opposed.

Adams discreetly compromised. He ordered strong defense measures but left the decision for war or peace up to the French. An undeclared naval war began in July, 1798. Hamilton increased his pressure on Adams for a declaration of war. He was infuriated by opposition from French-speaking Americans, considering them traitors. The Federalists also worried about the voting power of Irish immigrants, who were likewise flocking into Jefferson's Republican party.

Hamilton finally prevailed upon Adams to act against "treasonable activities against the United States" by sponsoring the Alien and Sedition Acts of 1798. On June 18 the Naturalization Act blocked immigrants from exercising their vote by requiring fourteen, rather than five, years of residence for citizenship. One week later the Alien Act authorized the president to deport all aliens suspected of "treasonable or secret" activities.

Two weeks later the Alien Enemies Act authorized the president, upon declaration of war, to arrest, imprison, or deport aliens still citizens of the enemy power. The following week the Sedition Act imposed fines and imprisonment on any citizens or aliens who participated in "any insurrection, riot, unlawful assembly, or combination." Anyone convicted of publishing "false, scandalous, and malicious writing" was subject to a fine of up to two thousand dollars and two years in jail.

Vigorously enforced by the Federalists to destroy Jefferson's Republican party, the new laws branded all political opposition as treason. Some twenty-five leading Americans, all Jeffersonians, were arrested, and ten were convicted, including one member of Congress.

Lyon Matthew, an Irish immigrant who edited a paper called *The Scourge of Aristocracy,* denounced President Adams as a bully. Arrested in Vermont, he was fined one thousand dollars and sentenced to four months in a miserable dungeon. The Green Mountain Boys rallied to his cause, forwarding petitions signed by thousands of Vermonters to Adams, who spurned them.

Indignant Vermont Republicans paid Matthew's fine and ran him for Congress. Elected by an overwhelming majority, he was sent to Washington in a sleigh at the head of a twelve-mile procession of jubilant Jeffersonians.

In Kentucky, Jefferson took the lead in passing state resolutions branding the Alien and Sedition Acts unconstitutional, while in Virginia James Madison did the same. The laws were defied by a new uprising in February, 1799, against a federal property tax levied by Hamilton to raise money for the war he was confident of inciting against France.

Tax collectors who went into Pennsylvania Dutch regions were forced to duck hot water poured on them from upper farmhouse windows by farmers' wives. When marshals arrested some of the farmers, seven hundred men led by former Continental Army officer John Fries forced their release. They drove the marshals off, crying, *"Ddmm de President, ddmm de Congress, ddmm de Arischdokratz!"* Ironically, John Fries had been an ardent supporter of John Adams.

The president, calling a Cabinet meeting, issued an angry proclamation against "certain acts, which, I am advised, amount to treason, being overt acts of levying war against the United States." A cavalry and artillery force of two thousand militia from New Jersey was dispatched in a new show of federal force. Fries was seized, tried for treason, and sentenced to hang.

He won a retrial when his lawyers proved that one of the jurors had concealed prejudice against him. But they withdrew from his defense when a second trial before "hanging judge" Samuel Chase, of Philadelphia, made it impossible for them to defend him fairly. Condemned again, Fries begged the president to spare him. But the Federalist Cabinet unanimously insisted that he must hang as an example.

Adams, an austere man but not without conscience, felt that martyring Fries was not only unjust but likely to provoke more revolts. Knowing his action would infuriate Hamilton and split the Federalist party seriously, he nevertheless insisted upon pardoning Fries. His courage shattered Federalist unity, letting the Jeffersonians win the White House. The Jeffersonians quickly saw to it that the repressive Alien and Sedition Acts were rendered inoperative.

"I discharged every person under punishment or prosecution under the sedition law," Jefferson said, "because I considered . . . that law to be a nullity, as absolute and palpable as if Congress had ordered us to fall down and worship a golden image."

In December, 1801, when Republicans Jefferson and Aaron Burr were tied for the Presidency in electoral votes, the House of Representatives decided in Jefferson's favor. The crucial vote was cast by Hamilton, who hated Jefferson but loathed Burr.

The brilliant, witty, and charming Aaron Burr was bitterly disappointed at being nosed out of the Presidency. Driven by an all-consuming hunger for power, he was galled at having to serve in Jefferson's shadow. Jefferson, in turn, soon found himself irked by Burr's disloyalty to the Republican party.

In January, 1802, Burr broke a tie vote in the Senate to vote with the Federalists in defeating an important Republican judiciary-reform bill that Jefferson wanted. Weeks later Burr was the sole Republican attending a Federalist dinner, at which he proposed a toast to "the union of all honest men." Burr's flirtation with the Federalists was unmistakable; he wanted their nomination to oppose Jefferson's reelection. Jefferson privately called Burr "a crooked gun . . . whose aim or shot you could never be sure of."

When Jefferson purchased the Louisiana Territory in 1803, Federalist leaders in New England assembled in a secret conclave called the Essex Junto. They were afraid that the Louisiana Territory would give southern agrarian states a balance of power over New England's manufacturing states.

Led by Adams's former secretary of state, Timothy Pickering, of Massachusetts, the Essex Junto plotted a secession of New England, New York, and New Jersey from the Union. The conspiracy called for establishing, with British support, a northern confederacy "exempt from the corrupt and corrupting influence and oppression of the aristocratic democrats of the South." British minister Anthony Merry pledged cooperation.

Control of New York was vital to the plot. The Essex Junto sought Alexander Hamilton as their candidate on the Federalist ticket for governor, but he spurned their conspiracy. So Pickering offered the role to Burr, whom Jefferson was dropping from the Republican ticket in the presidential elections of 1800. Burr promptly accepted.

He lost the campaign after bitter opposition to him by Hamilton as "a dangerous man, and one who ought not to be trusted with the reins of government." Once more Hamilton's enmity had frustrated Burr's ambitions. His political career wrecked, Burr forced Hamilton into a duel and killed him. Public indignation was so great that Burr was indicted for murder in New Jersey and felt compelled to flee.

During his last days as vice president, Burr had made a desperate offer to British minister Anthony Merry to split the Louisiana Territory from the Union and put it under the Union Jack. The price he asked was $500,000 and the loan of a British naval force. Merry relayed the offer to London, but the British Foreign Office considered Burr a lost, and extremely unreliable, cause.

Debt-ridden from living beyond his means, his reputation ruined on the eastern seaboard, Aaron Burr conceived a daring plan to retrieve his fortunes. The Louisiana Territory and Spanish Mexico were poorly defended lands. Why not turn land pirate, seize them with a private army, and proclaim himself emperor? He could then induce the vast Mississippi Territory to join him and so would rule an empire far greater and richer than Jefferson's miserable little seaboard republic!

Major General James Wilkinson, an old war comrade who was now commander in chief of the US Army as well as governor of the Louisiana Territory, was induced to support Burr's conspiracy. Like Burr an unscrupulous opportunist, Wilkinson was even on Spain's payroll as a secret agent. He supplied the former vice president with a military escort and a houseboat equipped with sails to take him down the Mississippi.

Among the influential Americans Burr solicited for support was Andrew Jackson, who at first cooperated under the impression that war with Spain was imminent and that Burr had been secretly authorized by the White House to organize a filibustering expedition to seize the Floridas.

Harman Blennerhasset, a wealthy Irish landowner, was thrilled with Burr's offer to make him Grand Chamberlain of the proposed empire and became an ardent supporter. By 1806 they had recruited a small private army of adventurers, assembling them on ten flatboats in Kentucky's Cumberland River.

Joseph H. Daveiss, US district attorney for Kentucky, accused Burr of seeking to mount an unauthorized expedition against Mexico. Burr brazenly confronted him in Frankfort, demanding that he prove the charge. Twice Daveiss empaneled a grand jury; twice Burr was acquitted for lack of evidence.

Jefferson observed these developments from Washington in worried silence. Many Americans thought that the silence from the White House meant that Burr was acting with the president's knowledge and secret consent, a notion Burr's hints encouraged. But Jefferson finally sent an emissary to the governors of Ohio and Kentucky to urge seizure of Burr's flotilla.

A worried General Wilkinson reached the conclusion that Burr's flamboyant venture was doomed to failure. Deciding not to risk swinging beside Burr for treason, he covered his tracks by writing a letter to Jefferson revealing his old friend's "deep, dark, wicked, and widespread conspiracy."

Burr, he warned, was planning to seize New Orleans, plunder bank funds, take over the arsenal and military stores, then raid Mexico. The buccaneer was also spreading the impression that his schemes were secretly endorsed by the federal government. Wilkinson had gone to New Orleans, Jefferson was assured, to marshal the city's defenses against Burr's treachery.

By this time all kinds of wild rumors were agitating Congress, which demanded that the president reveal what was going on. Jefferson sent them word on January 22, 1807, that "an illegal combination of private individuals against the peace and safety of the Union, and a military expedition" against Mexico had been uncovered. The traitor responsible, Jefferson revealed, was Aaron Burr, whose "guilt is placed beyond question."

Announcing a reward for Burr's arrest, Jefferson praised General Wilkinson for his patriotic exposé of the former vice president.

The news reached Burr in Mississippi. He at once fled on horseback, disguised as a backwoodsman. Even more than the bounty-hunters, Burr feared the military escort Wilkinson had given him, dreading that the commander in chief would order him killed to seal his lips about Wilkinson's complicity.

Burr was captured in Alabama and brought to Richmond, Virginia, to stand trial on two counts—high treason against the United States and a high misdemeanor for plotting the Mexican invasion. William Eaton, a former American consul, testified that Burr had confided to him the plot to set up a midwest empire with its capital in New Orleans, from which Mexico would be added by conquest. Wilkinson was to overthrow the government with the Army, assassinate Jefferson, and add the eastern states to Burr's new empire. Eaton further testified that he had warned the president, who had refused to believe Burr and Wilkinson would betray their country.

Burr, a lawyer, joined the defense as his own counsel. He accused Wilkinson of having frightened the president into alarming the American people. There was not a shred of evidence, he insisted, other than the affidavits of Wilkinson and Eaton, which were "abounding in crudities and absurdities."

The arraignment was held before Chief Justice John Marshall, sitting in Richmond, Virginia. Marshall found grounds for a charge of high misdemeanor in the matter of planning to invade Mexico but questioned the evidence for a charge of high treason. The prosecution had failed to produce the two witnesses required by the Constitution to testify to Burr's assemblage of forces to levy war on the United States.

Jefferson expressed doubts about the impartiality of Marshall, who disliked the president as much as Jefferson disliked him. Had not Marshall even attended a dinner with Burr at the home of Burr's defense counsel, John Wickham, while waiting for the trial to begin? Another Burr lawyer, Virginia's Edmund Randolph, argued that the prosecution had simply not proved the use of force against the government or even the intent to commit treason. Burr's trial, Randolph charged, was political persecution.

Justice Marshall cautioned the jury that Burr had to be given the full benefit of his constitutional rights before he could be found guilty of treason. The jury found Burr not guilty "by any evidence submitted to us."

He was then tried for a high misdemeanor—violating the 1794 Act of Congress forbidding any American to mount a military expedition against a country with which the United States was at peace.

Once again Marshall warned that the jury must accept only the strictest legal evidence, with the benefit of the doubt properly belonging to Burr. The jury took only half an hour to return another not-guilty verdict. General Wilkinson indignantly protested to Jefferson that Burr's acquittal was nothing less than the work of a "corrupt judge."

"The scenes which have been acting at Richmond," Jefferson wrote gloomily to a close friend, "are sufficient to fill us with alarm. We supposed we possessed fixed laws to guard us equally against treason and oppression; but it now appears we have no law but the will of the judge."

Despite his belated return to loyalty, Wilkinson did not escape arraignment before a grand jury for "misprision of treason"—the hiding of a crime by one who knows about it. But by a narrow vote of 9 to 7, his initial lapse of patriotism was not prosecuted. The grand jury was not allowed to know that during the Revolution Wilkinson had also been a conspirator in the

Conway Cabal, an unsuccessful intrigue to overthrow Washington and replace him with General Horatio Gates.

Although two juries had acquitted Burr of the charges against him, most Americans were convinced with Jefferson that he had indeed been a traitor. Later revelations in the 1890s from British and Spanish archives bore out this conviction.

British minister Anthony Merry's reports revealed that Burr, driven by ambition and spite toward Jefferson, had asked the British for £100,000 to finance an army that would seize Louisiana and the American West for the British flag. The British had ignored him as a flamboyant and irresponsible adventurer.

Spanish minister Marquis de Casa Yrujo's reports revealed that Burr had sent an emissary, New Jersey senator Jonathan Dayton, to ask forty thousand dollars for vital information involving Spanish interests. Dayton had revealed to Casa Yrujo the Burr plot to seize the Spanish Floridas and Mexico, capture the White House, imprison Jefferson, and plunder the US Treasury.

Had their respective governments permitted Merry and Casa Yrujo to testify at the treason trials, it is quite likely that Burr would have been hanged as a traitor. Freed instead under a cloud of suspicion, he fled to Europe in 1808. For four years he vainly sought to interest the British Parliament in his wild schemes. The scornful British finally lost patience and ordered him out of the country, as contemptuous of his treason as they had been of Benedict Arnold's.

Nearly destitute, Burr borrowed money from loyal friends and wandered disconsolately through Europe in search of a government willing to back his military fantasies. All monarchs, including Napoleon, scorned his powerless promises. Dejected, Burr tried to return home but was refused a passport by the

American ministry in Paris—the Jefferson influence exerted through the Madison Administration.

The outbreak of war with Britain in 1812, however, softened the American memory of Burr's treachery, and he was permitted to return to New York City. Giving up all schemes for power and glory, Burr prudently set himself a more practical goal— marriage to the rich widow Jumel. When he died at the age of eighty in 1836, Burr left many believers still convinced that he had been unjustly accused of treason.

FIVE

"Showers of Blood"

The prelude to the War of 1812 was the outbreak of the Napoleonic wars that led both England and France to seek to control American shipping lanes for their own advantage. The Jeffersonians were forced to impose a series of Embargo Acts between 1807 and 1809 forbidding trade with any power refusing to respect American rights at sea. The acts were bitterly opposed by the mercantile Federalists of New England.

Timothy Pickering, who four years earlier had masterminded the unsuccessful Essex Junto plot, now threatened New England's secession once more. He assured British envoy George Rose that there would be no second war against England, because he, Pickering, would soon lead a new American revolution. As president of a New England confederation, his first act would be to nullify the Embargo Acts and resume trade with England.

Pickering called upon the New England states to defy the Embargo Acts as unconstitutional. All Federalist leaders supported his proposal. New England legislatures and towns announced their refusal to cooperate in enforcing the acts; governors refused to furnish militia officers for enforcement. Pickering then proposed a New England convention to nullify the Embargo.

The arrest of Pickering and other Federalist leaders for high treason was demanded by infuriated Republicans in President

Madison's Cabinet and by war hawks in Congress anxious to go to war with England to seize Canadian territory. But Madison, recalling the arrests of Republicans under the Alien and Sedition Acts, refused to persecute political opponents.

Pickering's drive for secession was restrained by the powerful leader of the Federalist party, George Cabot, who insisted that they wait until the strategic moment—the new war with Britain he foresaw. The government would then be too involved with the foreign enemy to prevent the breakaway of an independent New England confederation.

On June 1, 1812, Madison asked Congress to declare war on Britain. New England (except Vermont), New York, New Jersey, and Delaware voted for peace, but the war hawks of the South and West prevailed.

Some conservative Republicans angrily supported Federalist opposition to "Mr. Madison's war." They forced an adjournment of Congress without voting a single bill to increase the tiny American Navy, which would now have to fight the world's greatest sea power.

"It is not the Federalists who are the party of treason," flared one indignant war hawk. "It is Madison's own party who are proving traitors to the nation in its hour of dire peril!"

The Federalists did everything they could to obstruct the war effort. The Massachusetts legislature, proposing the organization of a new peace party, urged citizens not to volunteer for a war "against the nation from which we are descended." Three New England governors would not call the state militia into national service. Federalist merchants refused to buy war bonds or fit out privateers for the government.

"Blue-light Federalists" actually signaled British blockaders offshore to alert them to the presence and impending attacks of American warships. Federalist newspapers spoke out against the war. Madison's own former secretary of state, Robert Smith, attacked the war in a public speech. Chief Justice Marshall called it a "base submission of the United States to Napoleon's wishes."

Madison still refused to take action against such "aid and comfort to the enemy" by ordering arrests for treason. He dreaded splitting and polarizing the country more than it already was. Besides, how could he accuse Federalist leaders of treason for opposing the war, when they could quote his own attack on advocates of an enlarged military as treasonous? When Hamilton and the Federalists had sought to increase the standing army, Madison had found it monstrous "that the traitors should . . . pursue some fixed plan for the extension of the military establishment."

The case of the New England governors who refused to call up the state militia for federal service did not reach the Supreme Court until 1827. In *Martin v. Mott* the Court agreed with Madison that the president, acting under congressional authority, was sole judge of emergencies that required the calling up of state militia, and that his decision was binding on all state officials.*

But on December 15, 1815, when the British launched attacks on the Maine coast, there were no federal troops stationed on the New England seaboard to resist them. At Hartford twenty-six delegates from New England states met behind locked doors in a secret convention to decide on steps for ending the war and the Embargo Acts.

---

* Whether it is equally binding in cases of undeclared wars such as Vietnam is still not clear. The Massachusetts legislature raised the question for the Supreme Court by passing a bill in April, 1970, holding it illegal to draft any citizen of Massachusetts for an American war that had not been declared by Congress.

A committee was dispatched to Washington to negotiate their demands. If those demands were rejected, Cabot hinted, the northern seaboard would consider Pickering's plan of seceding as a northern confederacy. But by the time the committee reached Washington, the country was celebrating Jackson's victory in New Orleans and the war was over.

The Federalist party was widely castigated for its role in sponsoring the Hartford convention. The Republicans accused Pickering, Cabot, and other Federalists of "conspiracy, sedition, and treason," but no arrests were made. The Federalist party was so discredited, however, that it did not survive the presidential election of 1816 but eventually reemerged as the Whig party.

During the Tyler Administration (1841–45) the question of treason to a state government became a stormy issue.

When Rhode Island had been granted a charter by King Charles in 1663, it had restricted the vote to property owners and their eldest sons. In 1776 a majority of these Federalist agriculturists had simply adopted the charter as Rhode Island's state constitution. As the state gradually became industrialized, foreign-born workers who flocked into the cities—mostly Irish Catholics—found themselves voteless and at the mercy of the rural Protestant minority.

Thomas Wilson Dorr, a brilliant young lawyer who had been admitted to Harvard at the age of fourteen, published an *Address to the People of Rhode Island,* challenging the legality of the Whig state government. Although the American Revolution had severed all state ties to England, Dorr pointed out, Rhode Island had illegally continued to base its government on a British charter.

In October, 1841, a citizens' convention of Democrats under his leadership framed a "People's Constitution" that gave voting rights to all adult white male citizens. The new constitution was overwhelmingly approved by fourteen thousand Rhode Islanders, who voted for it in extralegal gatherings.

Governor Samuel W. King immediately denounced the Democratic referendum as illegal. Confusion reigned over who now had the right to vote in Rhode Island elections. The King (Whig) and Dorr (Democratic) factions held separate elections for governor on April 18, 1842. Each side won its own election, and both claimed victory. King was reinaugurated at Newport. Dorr, whose strength was in the northwest, was inaugurated as governor in a Providence foundry.

King angrily rammed the Algerine Law through the legislature. This bill decreed all unauthorized public assemblages to be illegal and branded as traitors all men who assumed state office by authority of the alleged people's constitution. They were to be punished by life imprisonment at hard labor.

When the State Supreme Court invalidated the people's constitution as illegal, King asked President Tyler for federal troops to put down the Dorrite rebellion as treason. Dorr appealed to Tyler for troops to arrest King as a traitor.

The Whig president replied to King in a cautious letter expressing hope that the controversy could be settled locally. If the Dorrites resorted to open insurrection, however, he promised that the federal government would intervene on behalf of the old charter regime. He cited as his authority Article IV, Section 4, of the federal Constitution:

> The United States shall guarantee to every State in this Union a republican form of government, and shall protect each of them against invasion; and on application of the Legislature, or of the Executive . . . against domestic violence.

In May 1842 the King legislature proclaimed the Dorrites to be in a state of insurrection. Martial law was imposed and the state militia called out. In desperation, Dorr led his insurgents in a raid on the state arsenal at Providence to arm his followers. As the militia raced to beat them off, President Tyler alerted federal troops to stand by.

But the Dorrites were easily driven off by the artillery of the state militia. The rebellion collapsed, and Dorr fled to Connecticut. The King forces took revenge against his supporters, charging two in the legislature with treason and throwing dozens of others into jail without trial.

Hoping to rally his forces, Dorr stole back into Providence and ordered a faithful handful to dig trenches to stand off a militia attack. When the news reached King, he rushed three thousand militia to Providence. But they found only a few empty trenches; the Dorrites had melted away. So the militia arrested and jailed three hundred Providence citizens instead.

By April, 1843, however, Dorr's fight began to bear fruit even during his exile in Connecticut. The Rhode Island legislature finally adopted a new constitution with liberalized voting provisions.

Dorr made the mistake of thinking it was now safe for him to return. He was promptly arrested and on June 25, 1844, tried for treason to the state under the Algerine Act. Making certain that the jury was stacked against the defendant, Governor King also ensured the verdict by refusing to let Dorr subpoena defense witnesses because he now had no money to pay for the subpoenas. The jury sentenced him to life imprisonment.

The verdict infuriated Rhode Island's Democrats, who organized liberation societies to free Dorr. Their pressure was so successful that he was pardoned and freed a year later.

The Democrats struck back by challenging the legality of the King legislature's declaration of martial law in the crisis, as well as President Tyler's intervention on King's side. But in the Supreme Court decision of 1849, *Luther v. Borden,* the Court upheld the power of both the state legislature and the president to decide, in case of armed conflict within a state, which of two factions was the lawful government.

Dorr had one bittersweet taste of victory before ailments contracted in his foul prison dungeon caused his early death at age forty-nine. The legislature now numbered many Dorrites, elected as a result of his fight for democratic suffrage. On his deathbed, Thomas Wilson Dorr was brought word that the legislature had voted to annul the jury's verdict that had branded him guilty of treason.

Important questions of federal treason were raised again when President James Polk, infuriated by Mexico's refusal to sell the territory of New Mexico, determined to annex it forcibly. Sending American troops into the disputed area between the Nueces and Rio Grande rivers, Polk provoked a military skirmish that he used as a pretext for calling for war against Mexico for "shedding American blood on American soil."

On May 13, 1846, Congress voted Polk his war. Americans opposed to it continued to speak out vehemently. Whig congressman Abraham Lincoln branded the war as "unnecessarily and unconstitutionally begun by the President," to pursue "that rainbow" of military glory "that rises in showers of blood." He accused Polk of lying in claiming that the skirmish with Mexican troops had occurred on American soil.

Lincoln's home-town newspaper denounced him as "the Benedict Arnold of our District," and the Whigs refused to support him for renomination to the House. Another future president, Congressman Andrew Johnson, of Tennessee, accused Lincoln and other congressional opponents of the war of lacking the courage of their convictions.

If they condemned the war as wrong, Johnson challenged, why had they voted the men and money to prosecute it? He charged them with disloyalty for encouraging the Mexicans to believe that if they continued to resist, a peace party would come to power in Washington and end the war.

But the antiwar radicals persisted in their attacks on the invasion of Mexico. Horace Greeley, powerful editor of the New York *Tribune,* called General Zachary Taylor's battles "border ruffian aggressions . . . acts of a drama of naked villainy" intended to strengthen "the Slave Power."

Angry abolitionist William Lloyd Garrison, editor of the biting weekly *Liberator,* accused Governor Briggs, of Massachusetts, of "treacherous" conduct in summoning citizens to arms for a war by a slave power against slave-free Mexico. He publicly prayed for the defeat of his own country:

> May Mexico be victorious in every conflict, until not an invading foot treads upon her soil. . . . This is for Mexico strictly a war in self-defense . . . she deserves to be crowned with success, and the United States to be covered with defeat, as a matter of justice, and for the preservation of liberty.

Polk glumly recognized the unpopularity of the Mexican War not only in New England and the North but also in some regions of the South. He dared lift no finger to punish Lincoln, Greeley, Garrison, Sumner, Parker, Emerson, and other respected Americans for treason to the war effort.

One famous New Englander, Henry David Thoreau, invented a new way to publicize antiwar sentiment and sabotage the war effort—civil disobedience. He went to jail rather than pay his Massachusetts poll tax, in order not to contribute a penny toward the war. Thoreau wrote:

> I have heard some of my townsmen say, "I should like to have them order me . . . to march to Mexico—see if I would go"; and yet these very men have each . . . by their money, furnished a substitute. The soldier is applauded who refuses to serve in an unjust war by those who do not refuse to sustain the unjust government which makes the war.

Even though Polk's strongest support for the war was in the South, two Georgia congressmen denounced it, and South Carolina's John Calhoun demanded that all American troops be brought back to the Rio Grande. Protesting "the attainment of mere military glory," he blamed the war for damaging American prestige and violating our traditional concepts of liberty.

It was obviously impossible to sentence to death for treason hundreds of thousands, perhaps millions, of good citizens for speaking or acting against a war they considered unjust. The British Parliament, watching the acrimonious quarrel across the Atlantic, prudently decided to make their own treason laws more flexible. In 1848 the British made it more difficult to put anyone to death for idealistic opposition to his country's acts. A lower category of crime called "treason felony" was decreed, punishable by as little as five years and as much as life imprisonment. High treason was now the charge reserved for citizens accused of treachery for base motives.

The United States lacks any law distinguishing treason felony from high treason. For this reason there have been very few prosecutions under Article III, Section 3, of the Constitution. Most alleged traitors are generally prosecuted under other statutes, usually violations of laws of Congress which carry limited penalties and which juries are therefore more willing to enforce.

Americans have been reluctant to condemn legally as traitors fellow citizens whose ideas about what is patriotic differ from those of any administration in office. The requirements of patriotism often change from one administration to another. In 1856, a writer named Samuel G. Goodrich reminded Americans that not too long before, those who believed in democracy were suspect:

> We who are now familiar with democracy can hardly comprehend the odium attached to it . . . in the minds of the sober people in our neighborhood. They not only regarded it as hostile to good government, but as associated with infidelity in religion, radicalism in government and licentiousness in society. It was considered a sort of monster, born of Tom Paine, the French Revolution, foreign renegades and the Great Father of Evil, Mr. Jefferson.

Ironically, when the fashion in patriotism had changed with the War of 1812, the very Federalists who had accused Mr. Jefferson of treason were themselves accused of the same thing.

SIX

Civil War Treason

A new question of treason arose in the decade of the 1850s. Were the Utah Mormons traitors for fighting a small war against the United States out of religious principle?

Because of the unpopular practice of polygamy, the Church of Jesus Christ of Latter-Day Saints had been persecuted in the East and Midwest. Its leader, Joseph Smith, had been brutally murdered. His successor, Brigham Young, led the Mormons west in 1847 to the valley of the Great Salt Lake, the Mexican territory later to become Utah. Here, at the settlement they called Deseret, they felt free to follow their religious practices outside the jurisdiction of the United States.

The end of the Mexican War, however, had put the territory under the American flag. Eastern wagon trains were soon clattering through Salt Lake City on their way to newly discovered goldfields. The Mormons found themselves once more harassed by American authority. In self-protection they applied for statehood. But at congressional hearings, anti-Mormon Christian sects opposed their admission to the Union, charging them with treason, polygamy, and ritual human sacrifices.

The Mormons were accused of forcing fifteen hundred would-be immigrants to Salt Lake City to take this oath:

You do solemnly swear, in the presence of Almighty God, his holy angels, and these witnesses, that you will avenge the blood of Joseph Smith upon this nation, and so teach your children; and that you will from this day henceforth and forever begin and carry out hostility against this nation, and keep the same a profound secret now and ever. So help you God!

Denied statehood by an indignant Congress, Utah was made a territory instead. President Millard Fillmore appointed Brigham Young as governor. Non-Mormon federal officials began arriving in Utah. Many were alcoholic hack lawyers appointed to the Utah judiciary under the spoils system, and most were hostile to the Mormons. Relations between the federal appointees and the Mormons grew bitter rapidly.

In September, 1851, Utah Associate Justice Perry C. Brocchus addressed a Mormon congregation and upbraided the Mormons for their dubious loyalty to the government. Scolding Mormon women for accepting polygamy, he advised those in his audience to "become virtuous" instead. An uproar silenced the tirade.

Calming his furious followers, Brigham Young faced Brocchus and told him wrathfully, "Sir, if I had but crooked my finger, these good people would have torn you limb from limb—and our women would have been foremost among them!"

The Mormons were hard workers who made the desert bloom with irrigation canals and ditches, used water for the public benefit, forbade speculation in land, dealt fairly with the Indians and were respected by them, lived harmonious family lives based on the plural-wife system, and were in their own way as pious a people as any other religious sect.

Feeling persecuted by federal authority and American bigotry, however, they resisted cooperation with Washington. One Mormon band of desperadoes known as the Wolf-hunters joined Indian raiders in attacks on immigrant wagon trains en route to California. In the eyes of their fellow Americans, the real crime of the Mormons was their refusal to limit themselves to one wife apiece like other Americans.

In the elections of 1856 both Democratic and Republican candidates thundered against Mormon polygamy as a popular campaign issue translatable into votes. This agitation convinced the Mormons that a military campaign was being prepared to destroy their church. Fuel was poured on the fire when 120 immigrants in a wagon train rolled through Mormon territory abusing the Latter-Day Saints, poisoning their wells, and burning their fences. Pioneer leaders threatened to return from California with reinforcements to wipe out the Mormons.

On September 7, 1857, at Mountain Meadows in southwest Utah, a wagon train was attacked by an Indian band accompanied by Mormon Wolf-hunters. A three-day siege brought casualties to both sides. A truce was arranged when Mormon militia under John Doyle Lee appeared with a white flag. The immigrants accepted Lee's offer to escort them to safety.

But the entire company, with the exception of some children, was then brutally massacred. An outraged President Buchanan told Congress that Young and his followers apparently were determined "to come into collision with the Government of the United States." Young was removed as Utah's governor, and Buchanan ordered fifteen hundred troops, under Colonel Albert Sidney Johnson, into the territory.

Young defied the president. Declaring martial law, he ordered all Mormons to arms to keep federal troops off Utah soil.

Mormon cavalry burned three wagon trains of federal supplies and captured eight hundred oxen from a fourth. Johnson captured Lee and executed him for the Mountain Meadows massacre. But the onset of winter forced both sides into bivouac until spring.

By then Buchanan had managed to reach an accommodation with the Mormons through their spokesman in Washington. He was anxious to extricate himself from the uncertain expedition to Utah that political foes were mocking as "Buchanan's blunder." The Mormons were induced to save face for the president by making a formal acknowledgment of Washington's authority in Utah and allowing federal troops to remain for a while as long as they did not attack any Mormons.

In the summer of 1858 a peace commission from Washington brought the Mormons a presidential pardon for their treason. Brigham Young went to prison several times before he died in 1877, survived by twenty-five wives and fifty-six children, but never once for treason. His crime was a stubborn refusal to pay alimony to his nineteenth wife after she had divorced him.

Treason of another sort by fanatical abolitionists was also a government headache. Kansas sheepman John Brown conceived the idea of carving an independent republic of fugitive slaves out of the southern Appalachians to serve as a refuge and fortress for blacks escaping from the South.

He drew up a constitution for the proposed republic and was chosen by eleven white and thirty-five black followers as its commander in chief. To get the arms the new republic would need, Brown led eighteen followers, four of them black, in a guerrilla raid on the federal arsenal at Harper's Ferry, Virginia. On the night of October 16, 1859, they seized the arsenal, killed the mayor, and took sixty leading citizens as hostages.

Calling out the Virginia militia, Governor Henry Wise frantically wired President Buchanan for federal troops. John Brown urged slaves in the town to join his ranks, but none dared fire a gun beside him. They remembered too well the hundred blacks who had been shot and the twenty who had been hung when Nat Turner and only six fellow slaves had run amok in Virginia twenty-eight years earlier.

Before dawn one of Brown's sons was dead and another wounded. When Colonel Robert E. Lee arrived with a company of marines from Washington and forced Brown's surrender, they found only Brown and six other survivors in the locomotive-roundhouse to which the raiders were forced to retreat.

Panic spread through a South frightened of a slave uprising, then quickly gave way to vengeful wrath. John Brown, wounded after his capture, was rushed to trial only eight days later. His counsel urged him to plead insanity. Many abolitionists, in fact, were convinced that his fanaticism and wild schemes indicated mental instability. But Brown refused to save his life by discrediting the soundness of his cause.

The jury found him guilty of "treason and conspiring and advising with slaves and other rebels, and murder in the first degree." Writing to his children that he was content "to die for God's eternal truth on the scaffold as in any other way," Brown was hanged on December 2, 1859.

Millions of conservative northerners defended his execution by the South, arguing that he had not been hanged as an abolitionist but as a traitor to the laws of the United States. Every American owed his loyalty to the government, they insisted, however much he might hate some of its institutions.

But Ralph Waldo Emerson predicted that "that new saint . . . will make the gallows glorious like the cross."

"In firing his gun," cried William Lloyd Garrison, "John Brown has merely told us what time of day it is. It is high noon . . . thank God!" Garrison himself had risked arrest for treason by publicly burning copies of the Fugitive Slave Act and the Constitution, which he renounced as "a covenant with death and an agreement with hell!"

The Civil War raised questions of treason more profound than any since the founding of the Republic. Did states alienated from the federal government have the right to secede to form their own independent nation? Or was this a conspiracy forbidden by the Constitution, making all Americans who joined it traitors to the Union, not southern patriots?

Southerners pointed to the agitation of radical abolitionists such as Garrison, who for years had been demanding that the North secede from the Union, casting the South and slavery adrift. None of *them* had ever been punished. Why should secession be treason only when the South wanted it?

Ironically, General Robert E. Lee had insisted that every southerner's first loyalty ought to be to the federal government.

"I wish to live under no other government," he insisted, "and there is no sacrifice I am not ready to make for the preservation of the Union." He added, "I wish for no other flag than the Star Spangled Banner and no other air than 'Hail Columbia.'" He considered secession "nothing but revolution!"

Yet once the fat was in the fire, Lee asserted that his "loyalty to Virginia ought to take precedence over that which is due the Federal Government." Far from enthusiastic about the rebel cause he had been prevailed upon to lead, he admitted sadly to General William S. Harney, a southerner loyal to Washington, "I had no idea of taking any part in this matter. I wanted to stay at Arlington and raise potatoes for my family, but my friends forced me into it."

Plots to slay Abraham Lincoln were assessed as either high treason or southern patriotism, depending on the geography of the judgment. Lincoln protested the close escort of Pinkerton police assigned to him as president-elect, forcing Allen Pinkerton to reveal that there were several serious conspiracies afoot to kill him. Lincoln was astonished.

"Why would anyone want to do that?"

"Mr. President," Pinkerton sighed, "you simply cannot comprehend the mad, hysterical feeling prevailing against you in and around Baltimore."

But Lincoln could not take seriously the threats on his life. That was why he was insufficiently protected at Ford's Theater the night John Wilkes Booth made history. Lincoln appreciated the wrath of southerners frustrated by northern policy against slavery but could not bring himself to believe that they would assassinate him for it.

On July 17, 1862, an act of Congress prescribed a ten-thousand-dollar fine and punishment of from five years at hard labor to execution for anyone convicted of insurrection, conspiracy, or treason against the government. Now every American who aided the Confederacy by either word or deed was put on notice that he could pay for his political sympathies with his life.

SEVEN

"A Scurvy Lot They Are"

Southern spies scorned northern treason laws. Rose Greenhow, an attractive, socially prominent Washington widow, declared, "Instead of loving and worshipping the old flag of the Stars and Stripes, I see in it only the symbol of abolition—of murder, plunder, oppression, and shame."

Learning of a federal plan to attack the Confederate Army at Manassas, she rushed a secret warning to General Pierre Beauregard. His subsequent victory led Confederate President Jefferson Davis to acknowledge the South's debt to her. She charmed military secrets out of vulnerable Union satraps until caught by Allen Pinkerton and jailed. Her influence in Washington society was so great that plans to try her as a spy were dropped, and she was released in a prisoner exchange.

Another celebrated female traitor was Belle Boyd, a beautiful young Virginian girl. At seventeen she shot and killed a Union sergeant for trying to force his way into the Boyd home. Gallant federal officers, smitten by her crinoline charms, decided that Belle's offense had been "justifiable homicide."

A passionate Confederate, she carried secret intelligence through Union lines dozens of times. The quartering of northern officers in the Boyd home under martial law provided her with vital information for the Confederate Army. Once she braved heavy fire from both sides to cross a battlefield with a warning for Stonewall Jackson that enabled him to save his forces from a Union trap.

"I thank you for myself and for the army," Jackson wrote her, "for the immense service that you have rendered your country today."

When Belle sent Jackson a new warning via a Rebel soldier who was actually a Union secret agent, it fell into the hands of Secretary of War Edwin M. Stanton. Jailed, she was freed in a prisoner exchange with Richmond, where she was welcomed by the city band and where Confederate troops presented arms in her honor.

The Conscription Act of March 1, 1863, made it an act of disloyalty to refuse to be drafted for the Union Army—unless you could afford to pay three hundred dollars for a substitute. Northern workers considered the bill discriminatory against the poor. Irish-American laborers especially resented being drafted to fight a war they saw as freeing the black man to compete with them for jobs. Draft officials were driven off the Pennsylvania coalfields by the tough Molly Maguires.

The first draft lottery in New York touched off wild rioting and violence. A mob of thousands broke into an arsenal, passed out carbines, and surged through the streets, burning buildings and smashing draft offices. They cut down telephone poles, tore up tracks, and overturned horse-cars. Bodies of lynched Negroes swung from lampposts all along Clarkson Street, flaming human torches in the night.

Thirteen regiments of federal troops had to be taken out of the war from General George Meade's army at Gettysburg. Rushed to New York on express trains over cleared tracks, they arrived just in time to prevent the burning of the *Tribune* building. Mobs sought to lynch editor Horace Greeley, blaming him for championing the cause of emancipation.

Throwing up breastworks along Ninth Avenue, the rioters fought the Army until their ammunition was exhausted. When Meade's troops finally restored order, over fifteen hundred rioters and troops lay dead.

Lincoln was forced to take other fighting units away from Meade to prevent similar explosions in other cities. Meade had to put off pursuing Lee and the badly battered Confederate Army as they retreated from Gettysburg, possibly robbing the North of a quick victory.

The draft rioters of New York had unquestionably violated the treason statute of the Constitution—"levying war against" the United States and "giving aid and comfort" to their enemies. They were also in violation of Lincoln's own Treason Act of 1862. But no charges of treason were brought.

Lincoln also had his hands full with citizens known as Copperheads—northerners with southern sympathies. Because they were so numerous and some held high office, Congress set up a committee to investigate the loyalty of all federal employees. It soon became known as "the office of secret accusations." Government clerks, terrified of losing their jobs, agreed to spy on fellow employees and department heads, reporting all "suspicious" talk or contacts.

In September, 1862, Lincoln issued a proclamation suspending the writ of habeas corpus that allows lawyers to free illegally detained defendants under the Sixth Amendment. Lincoln wanted the power to keep Copperheads and draft opponents in jail to restrain their damage to the war effort. The alternative was clogging the courts with difficult-to-prove treason trials.

Lincoln was promptly attacked as a military despot who was violating the Bill of Rights out of expediency. Public indignation mounted when loyal northerners were mistakenly arrested and jailed along with draft resisters, Copperheads, and spies. The War Department was forced to free all those arrested under Lincoln's decree who agreed to take a loyalty oath.

Perhaps the most important Copperhead was Ohio's Clement L. Vallandigham, congressman, lawyer, and newspaper editor who had opposed the Civil War bitterly from the start. He even entered secret negotiations with the French to get Napoleon III to force peace talks upon the North.

In 1863, General A. E. Burnside angrily issued a general order stating, "The habit of declaring sympathy for the enemy will not be allowed" in his military district. Violators, he warned, would be arrested for treason and executed. Vallandigham defied him.

Continuing to denounce Lincoln, the Union, and the war, the Copperhead leader called upon midwesterners to ignore Burnside's order. Arrested, he was court-martialed and sentenced by Burnside to imprisonment in Fort Warren for the duration of the war. But Lincoln changed the sentence to a more appropriate and humane one— "deportation to Confederate territory." Vallandigham approved his banishment, announcing scornfully, "I do not *wish* to belong to the United States!"

His defiance inspired Edward Everett Hale to write the famous novel *The Man without a Country*. Appearing in the *Atlantic* for December, 1863, it inspired a surge of patriotic feeling throughout the North. Vallandigham, however, was convinced that the tide of public sentiment was turning against Lincoln, the Republicans, and the war. He assured Confederate President Jefferson Davis that the Democrats stood a good chance of winning the 1864 elections on an antiwar platform.

Making his way to Canada, Vallandigham sought to help organize the opposition to the Republicans from there. New York's Governor Seymour echoed his charges that the real treason to America was the Administration's destruction of free institutions in the North to put down rebellion in the South. At public meetings Seymour and other Copperheads denounced arbitrary arrests, Lincoln's suspension of the Sixth Amendment, and Vallandigham's deportation. The Democratic State Convention of Ohio defiantly nominated Vallandigham for governor.

Lincoln defended his policies by pointing out that if such outspoken "traitors to the Union" as Lee and Breckinridge had been arrested for treason before the war, "the insurgent cause would be much weaker." He predicted, "I shall be blamed for having made too few arrests, rather than too many." And he asked, "Must I shoot a simple-minded soldier-boy, who deserts, while I must not touch a hair of a wily agitator who induces him to desert? . . . To silence the agitator and save the boy is not only constitutional, but withal a great mercy."

He did not order Vallandigham's arrest, however, when the latter returned to Ohio in 1864 to wage an unsuccessful campaign for governor. The Copperhead vowed that he was not trying to aid the Confederacy, simply to restore "the Union as it was." He appealed his arrest and military trial as a civilian by Burnside, but the Supreme Court refused to hear the case in order not to undermine military authority.

Two years later, however, in a decision called *Ex parte Milligan,* the Court ruled on the issue in the case of Lambdin P. Milligan. Arrested in 1864 and charged with "conspiracy, affording aid and comfort to rebels and inciting insurrection," Milligan and three Indiana Copperheads had been found guilty of treason and sentenced to hang by a military commission.

Lincoln had put off signing the order for execution, but President Andrew Johnson had signed it after Lincoln's assassination. Milligan's lawyer appealed to the Supreme Court on grounds that he had been unlawfully tried by a military tribunal while civilian courts were available and open. By a vote of 5 to 4, the Supreme Court agreed, finding that neither the president nor Congress had power to suspend the constitutional safeguards of citizens during time of war.

When the Civil War was over and the dead counted, the awkward question rose of who should then be arrested for treason. The vengeful cry, "Hang Jefferson Davis!" rang through the North. President Johnson promised, "I'm going to hang that traitor to a tree!"

The sacrificial scapegoat was captured by Union soldiers in Georgia on May 10, 1865. Jailed at Fort Monroe, he was kept in leg irons by Major General Nelson A. Miles for four days. Guarded day and night, he was proudly exhibited by Miles to visitors like a rare captive tiger. The government indicted him for treason, but two years went by without a trial.

Johnson knew that there was no evidence linking Davis to Lincoln's assassination. Whether the southern rebellion could be made to stick as a treason charge in court was a moot question which, incidentally, was never settled judicially.

Horace Greeley was indignant at the injustice of keeping Davis under lock and key so long without his day in court. He forced the government to set a bail bond of $100,000 under the prisoner's right to a "speedy and public trial by an impartial jury" (Sixth Amendment). The money was raised from a group of prominent Americans, and the ex-president of the Confederacy was set free in May, 1867.

A storm of angry northern criticism blasted Greeley for his act of humanity. He replied defiantly, "So long as any man was seeking to overthrow our government he was my enemy; from the hour in which he laid down his arms, he was my formerly-erring countryman." In the South, of course, Jefferson Davis continued to be revered as a great patriot; only those who had refused to support the Rebel cause were regarded as traitors.

The bitterness of the treason question did not die easily after the war. In 1865, Missouri, where Copperhead sentiment had been strong, passed an amendment to the state constitution requiring citizens wishing to teach, preach, or vote to swear that they had been loyal to the Union. Congress compelled all attorneys practicing in federal courts to take a similar oath vowing past loyalty.

Two years later, in the cases of *Cummings v. Missouri* and *Ex parte Garland,* the Supreme Court ruled both requirements unconstitutional in a 5 to 4 decision. Nevertheless, almost a century later, similar federal and state loyalty-oath requirements were again demanded to determine political purity.

In 1872, the Republican party under President Ulysses S. Grant was badly split. Its liberal wing attacked the administration for seeking to grab Santo Domingo. Feeling they could not support Grant for renomination, the radical Republicans broke away and ran their own candidates. They were denounced as traitors by party regulars, who reminded them of Decatur's famous toast: "My country, right or wrong!"

Carl Schurz replied, "Our country, right or wrong! When right, to be kept right; when wrong, to be put right!"

The debate over those two points of view was still as hot as ever almost a century later when superpatriot groups, angered by opposition to the Vietnam war, used Decatur-inspired car stickers reading: "America—Love It or Leave It!" Dissenters replied with their version of Schurz's sentiment: "America—Love It and Change It!"

Schurz, along with celebrated Americans such as William Jennings Bryan, Mark Twain, Samuel Gompers, and Harvard president Charles Eliot, formed the Anti-Imperialist League in 1898 to oppose the Spanish-American War. Jingoists defended the war on grounds that it was obviously America's Manifest Destiny to civilize countries that "practised barbarism."

The Anti-Imperialist League observed caustically that when "civilizers" stooped to barbarism to end barbarism, it was hard to tell the barbarians apart. "Imperialism is hostile to liberty and tends toward militarism," the league declared, "an evil from which it is our glory to be free."

No treason charges were brought against the war dissenters, who were simply swept aside as cranks and crackpots.

After only ten weeks of fighting, Cuba and the Philippines were in American hands, while the Anti-Imperialist League pondered the futility of their dissent.

Violent clashes between labor and capital around the turn of the century introduced new concepts of treason. The radicalization of the labor movement, with the rise of Socialists, anarchists, and Wobblies (Industrial Workers of the World, IWW), frightened the big corporations. The newspapers they controlled began attacking labor militants as dangerous traitors plotting revolution.

When three men were jailed for bombings in labor battles in the western minefields, President Theodore Roosevelt declared that, guilty or not, they were "undesirable citizens." Thousands of angry labor sympathizers began wearing buttons inscribed: "I Am an Undesirable Citizen."

Jack London gave his version of treason: "A strikebreaker is a traitor to his God, his country, his wife, his family and his class."

Muckraking journalists branded as traitors the robber barons who perverted the government for their own ends, along with the elected and appointed officials who served them as hirelings. In 1906 David Graham Phillips wrote a stinging exposé for *Cosmopolitan,* called "The Treason of the Senate." He accused Rhode Island's senator Nelson W. Aldrich of leading a conspiracy to betray the American public, manipulating legislation to enrich powerful special interests.

"A scurvy lot they are . . . with their smirking and cringing and voluble palaver about God and patriotism," Phillips wrote angrily. They were, he said, traitors not only to all the people but also to the political parties that had elected them to the Senate.

Although no tycoons were indicted for treason, Roosevelt assumed the mantle of a social reformer. Calling himself a "trust-buster," he began introducing bills to put mild curbs on the more outrageous buccaneering of the big corporations. But the trusts continued to prosper by controlling legislation through big political contributions.

"That's the system," Lincoln Steffens, most famous of the muckrakers, explained in 1920. "It's an organization of social treason, and the political boss is the chief traitor. . . . They buy the people's leaders."

The big corporations waited for an opportunity to counterattack those they considered traitors to the American free enterprise system—muckrakers, Socialists, anarchists, and labor radicals. Their chance came with the outbreak of World War I. Public wrath was aroused against pacifists and the political Left, who were lumped with German spies and sympathizers as dangerous traitors.

The most celebrated case was the arrest and trial of radical labor leaders Tom Mooney and Warren Billings. They were charged with exploding a bomb on a crowded street corner during a Preparedness Day parade on San Francisco's Market Street on July 22, 1916. Ten persons were killed, forty others maimed. The defendants were prosecuted by District Attorney Charles M. Fickert, who knew that the San Francisco Chamber of Commerce was anxious to discredit strike organizers. A conviction could win its support of his nomination for governor.

Tom Mooney's friendship with anarchist Alexander Berkman, Fickert charged, indicated his terroristic and antimilitaristic motives in bombing the parade. William Randolph Hearst's *Examiner* demanded the arrest of all known or suspected radicals in California. The press carried distorted and fabricated stories, planted by the city's Bomb Bureau and by Fickert, to incriminate Mooney and Billings and prejudice any jury against them.

At the trials the chief prosecution witnesses were obvious perjurers and people with shady pasts. Almost all contradicted themselves, and each other, under cross-examination. Several later recanted their testimony, admitting they had been told what to say. With no reliable evidence to offer, Fickert sought to win a conviction by waving the flag.

"This American flag was what they desired to offend," he cried. "They offended that by killing the women and men that worshipped it. Here is another photograph of Mrs. Van Loo dying on the streets of our city, and in a feeble hand she holds the American flag, and if that flag is to continue to wave, you must put an end to such acts as these!"

He demanded the death penalty. "Gentlemen, the very life of the nation is at stake. No foreign foes were on our land at this time; some traitor, some murderous villain, with his associates, perpetrated this crime. . . . The crime was against the flag; the crime was against the Constitution of the United States; the crime was against the laws of this government."

The defendants were tried separately. The jury brought in a verdict against Billings of murder in the first degree, recommending life imprisonment. When Mooney was brought to trial in January, 1917, the United States was on the verge of war. Peace sentiment was already suspect as treason.

Prosecutor Edward A. Cuhna, Fickert's chief assistant, accused Mooney of being part of an anarchist conspiracy to weaken America by sabotaging "Preparedness"—the catchword signifying national defense. Proof against Mooney rested largely on the eyewitness testimony of Frank C. Oxman, alleged to be a wealthy Oregon cattleman.

"Oxman was by far the most important of these witnesses," Judge Franklin A. Griffin later declared. "There is no question but that he made a profound impression on the jury. . . . He is the pivot around which all of the other evidence in the case revolves." When the jury found Mooney guilty of murder in the first degree, Griffin ordered him to hang.

But attorneys of the two convicted men were convinced that there had been a terrible miscarriage of justice. There was good reason to believe that the bombs had actually been the work of either German agents or Mexican revolutionaries, but neither lead had been diligently pursued. Evidence was found that Mooney could not have been anywhere near the bomb when it was thrown: a photo showing him with other spectators watching the parade from a rooftop a mile from the explosion. A jeweler's street clock established the time.

Fickert's office had suppressed this photo. Witnesses who had come forward to prove Mooney's innocence had been gotten rid of. Then it was found that Oxman had committed perjury at a previous trial. Evidence grew that his testimony against Mooney had also been false and that Fickert knew it.

Fremont Older, editor of the San Francisco *Bulletin,* tried to reveal these facts, but the paper's publishers refused to let him. He quit and became editor of the rival *Morning Call* in order to expose the legal conspiracy against the convicted radicals. A nationwide uproar led to demands for Fickert's ouster.

"The people leading this fight against me are the anarchists," Fickert accused. "Their main reason for wanting me out of office is that they fear prosecution. There were more than a hundred people concerned in the Preparedness Day bomb plot, and it is this anarchist element . . . that seeks my recall."

Growing wartime hysteria over radicalism and disloyalty helped smother the facts. Theodore Roosevelt rushed to Fickert's defense with a published telegram calling the issue one between patriotism and anarchy: "ALL WHO DIRECTLY OR INDIRECTLY ASSAIL YOU FOR ANY REASON SHOULD BE PROMPTLY DEPRIVED OF THEIR CITIZENSHIP." Roosevelt was soon attacking all radical labor and peace groups as "the Bolsheviki of America."

On the eve of a referendum to decide the recall of Fickert, a bomb exploded outside the Governor's Mansion in Sacramento. Next day the recall motion was voted down. Although no evidence linked fifty-three Sacramento members of the IWW to the bombing, they were jailed and eventually prosecuted by the federal government for violating the wartime Sedition Act.

Fickert won his nomination for governor, campaigned promising "complete suppression of sedition on the home front," and lost. When the war ended, Mooney's execution was only a month away. Then Fremont Older's *Call* published a bombshell— transcripts of conversations taken from Fickert's "bugged" telephone.

They proved all the charges made against him by Mooney-Billings sympathizers. In a wild fury Fickert confronted Older in San Francisco's Palace Hotel and assaulted him.

Governor Stephens now acted to save Mooney from the gallows, commuting his sentence to life imprisonment. Not at all grateful, Mooney wrote the governor angrily:

> It is my life you are dealing with. I demand that you revoke your commutation of my death sentence to a living death. . . . I am innocent. I demand a new and a fair trial or my unconditional liberty through a pardon. If I were guilty of the crime for which I have been unjustly convicted, hanging would be too good for me. Then why commute my sentence to life?

The Colfax *Record* had an answer:

> The reason that Mooney and Billings are in prison is because a majority of the people of the State of California want them there and the Supreme Court and the Governor dare not disobey that majority. It is quite beside the point whether or not they are guilty of the particular crime of which they were charged and convicted. The question is: Are Mooney and Billings the sort of people we want to run at large? We have decided this in the negative and we have locked them up.

The crusade to free Mooney and Billings grew steadily after the war and was part of every labor and radical rally. Mounting labor unrest, a Seattle general strike, and a labor-sponsored Mooney Congress alarmed big-business interests.

They were convinced that a Bolshevik plot of revolution was afoot when unknown persons mailed bombs to many prominent symbols of the Establishment on the eve of May Day, 1919. Two bombs went to Fickert and Cuhna, who, like the other targets, did not open them and were unhurt. Two anarchists were arrested, but no charges were filed. One suspect was simply deported; the other was alleged to have fallen out of a fourteenth-story window while in custody, under unexplained circumstances.

Fickert sought to win reelection as district attorney on the slogan, "American Flag or the Red Flag," but lost.

As new evidence kept turning up to prove the innocence of Mooney and Billings, even seven of the jurors who had convicted Mooney appealed to the governor to pardon them.

Mooney was offered a parole in 1927 but refused it: "I am absolutely innocent. I will not accept anything short of Pardon."

A National Mooney-Billings Committee—sponsored by such famous Americans as Roger Baldwin, Clarence Darrow, John Dewey, Arthur Garfield Hays, Sinclair Lewis, Lincoln Steffens, and Rabbi Stephen Wise—now demanded absolute pardons for both prisoners.

"Mooney can stand prison," Socialist leader Norman Thomas said, "better than we can stand having him there!"

Now a worldwide cause celebre, the case began making new headlines in the *Manchester Guardian, The New York Times,* and other major organs of international influence. Albert Einstein, Bertrand Russell, and H. G. Wells pleaded for the prisoned martyrs. Over five hundred ministers, the Federal Council of Churches of Christ in America, the National Catholic Welfare Council, dozens of governors, mayors, and congressmen added their voices.

"If Tom Mooney is not freed," declared Theodore Dreiser, "he should, by rights, be taken out of prison by force!"

President Herbert Hoover appointed the Wickersham Committee to study the case, then suppressed its findings. In 1932, a Democratic Congress demanded that the report be made public. It revealed that the impartial government investigation had found the two radicals to have been victims of a gross injustice. But they were still not freed.

The California State Assembly itself passed a resolution in 1937 declaring Mooney innocent and demanding a full pardon. A Gallup poll one year later showed that 66 per cent of Americans agreed. But it was not until January 7, 1939—five days after the election of Culbert L. Olson, California's first Democratic governor of the twentieth century—that Tom Mooney was declared innocent and freed from San Quentin Prison.

He was now partly deaf, in ill health, divorced, penniless, and unemployed. In October, Billings also was set free. They had spent a total of twenty-two years of their lives behind bars for a "traitorous crime against the flag and the Constitution and the laws"—a crime they had not committed but had been punished for in a climate of wartime hysteria.

EIGHT

Treason in World War I

Another labor martyr of World War I was Socialist leader Eugene V. Debs. On June 16, 1918, while addressing a labor rally in Canton, Ohio, on behalf of Mooney and Billings, Debs made no bones about his opposition to the war, even though he knew Secret Service agents were taking notes in the crowd.

"You need to know that you are fit for something better than slavery and cannon fodder," he declared. "I am opposed to every war but one. I am for that war with heart and soul, and that is the worldwide war of social revolution. In that war I am prepared to fight in any way the ruling class may make it necessary, even on the barricades!"

Arrested, he was sentenced to ten years in jail and deprived of his citizenship. "The government has made me a citizen of the world," he observed dryly. Running from prison as the Socialist candidate for president in the 1920 elections, he received almost a million votes. President Woodrow Wilson, who could not forgive Debs's refusal to support the war, would not pardon him, insisting, "This man was a traitor to his country!" It was president Warren Harding who pardoned Debs in 1921, although he did not restore his citizenship.

Ironically, while campaigning for the League of Nations after the war, Wilson admitted to a crowd in St. Louis, "Who does not know that the seed of war in the modern world is industrial and commercial rivalry? The real reason that the war . . . took place was that Germany was afraid her commercial rivals were going to get the better of her, and . . . they thought Germany would get the commercial advantage of them."

Yet Wilson had jailed Debs for saying exactly the same thing—that World War I had been an imperialistic conflict for markets, not a crusade to save the world for democracy.

On April 6, 1917, ten weeks after Congress declared war on Germany, it passed an Espionage Act. Conviction for aiding the enemy, obstructing recruiting, or sabotaging military discipline carried punishments of up to a twenty-thousand-dollar fine and twenty years in prison. The postmaster general was authorized to exclude from the mails newspapers, periodicals, and all printed matter alleged to be treasonable or seditious.

A Socialist named Schenck was the first to be convicted on a charge of impeding recruiting by writing pamphlets condemning the war as an imperialist struggle in which workers of the world could have no interest. His case was appealed to the Supreme Court as a violation of his right to free speech. But Justice John Haynes Holmes upheld the legality of the Espionage Act on grounds that encouraging draft resistance was a "clear and present danger" to the nation in arms.

"When a nation is at war," Holmes declared, "many things that might be said in time of peace are such a hindrance to its effort that their utterance will not be endured as long as men fight, and that no court could regard them as protected by any constitutional right."

The American Civil Liberties Union, organized during World War I to protect the constitutional rights of Americans opposed to the war, sharply dissented. Holmes himself later agreed that the "clear and present danger" doctrine could not be used to choke off radical ideas, no matter how unpopular or how uncomfortable the government found them.

Not until over a year after the Espionage Act did Congress pass an amendment called the Sedition Act. The new law was aimed specifically at Socialists and pacifists, prescribing severe penalties for interfering with the war effort; using "disloyal, profane, scurrilous or abusive language" about the American government, Constitution, flag, or armed forces; or urging a cutback in production of war materials.

Used to imprison Debs and other Socialist leaders, the Sedition Act was first challenged when a young Russian-born immigrant named Abrams, with four coworkers in a New York hat factory, printed and distributed leaflets attacking the government for sending an American expeditionary force against the new Red Army in Siberia. Arrested, they protested that they supported the war against Germany and considered it weakened by diverting troops to interfere with the revolutionary struggle in Russia. But they had urged workers to strike rather than produce arms for use against the Soviet Union.

Found guilty, they were sentenced to twenty years in jail. The Supreme Court upheld their conviction, but Justices Holmes and Brandeis dissented. There was no "clear and present danger" to the war effort in this case, Holmes wrote, so it amounted to a violation of the First Amendment.

"I believe the defendants had as much right to publish [their leaflets] as the Government has to publish the Constitution of the United States now vainly invoked by them," Holmes argued.

He added, "We should be eternally vigilant against attempts to check the expression of opinions that we loathe and believe to be fraught with death, unless . . . an immediate check is required to save the country." In 1921, President Harding commuted the defendants' sentences, but they were deported to Russia.

For several years before America went to war with Germany in April, 1917, millions of Americans of German and Irish extraction had bitterly opposed any aid to Great Britain. Wilson, who at first tried to keep the United States neutral, nevertheless detested them as "hyphenated Americans."

The leader of the anti-British movement was a well-to-do Irish-American lawyer, Jeremiah O'Leary, who had been president of the American Truth Society. He offered Wilson the society's support in the 1916 presidential elections if Wilson stuck to his neutrality policy. Wilson wired him contemptuously: "I WOULD FEEL DEEPLY MORTIFIED TO HAVE YOU OR ANYBODY LIKE YOU VOTE FOR ME. SINCE YOU HAVE ACCESS TO MANY DISLOYAL AMERICANS AND I HAVE NOT I WILL ASK YOU TO CONVEY THIS MESSAGE TO THEM."

Soon after America entered the war, O'Leary organized an American branch of the anti-British Sinn Fein society. He was indicted for "conspiracy to commit treason" in violation of the Espionage Act. Britain was now America's war ally; thus anti-British agitation was now disloyal.

At the trial the government proved that O'Leary's propaganda had been financed from Germany but could not prove that he knew it. A defendant indicted with him, Madame de Victorica, turned state's witness, but her testimony was discredited when O'Leary proved that she was an admitted spy and dope addict. Another witness was exposed as a perjurer. Deciding that the case had not been proved, the jury freed O'Leary.

These were dangerous times for dissent. Superpatriotic mobs frequently took the law into their own hands. Any public criticism of the war or of war profiteers often brought the cry of "Traitor!" Six victims were painted yellow; many were hung until almost dead (three were cut down too late); sixty-four were tarred and feathered; fifty-five kidnapped and whipped; eleven hundred were forcibly driven out of the country.

Government punishment was no less severe. A St. Louis woman went to jail for ten years for writing in a letter to a newspaper, "I am for the people and the Government is for the profiteers." There were sentences of fifteen years for talking against the draft; ten years for opposing the Liberty Loans; twenty years for calling the government a liar, for approving of the sinking of the *Lusitania,* and for predicting a German victory.

Sabotage of the war effort by corporation executives received gentler treatment. In order to conserve steel for guns, tanks, locomotives, and ships needed for the war, the War Industries Board ordered Detroit's industrial leaders to cut back the production of cars. They refused, informing board head Bernard M. Baruch that they would use all the steel and coal they wanted for cars, and he couldn't stop them, war or no war. They gave in only when he threatened to seize all their coal and shut down their plants.

Baruch also clashed with the steel industry, which was gouging the government on defense orders. Baruch deplored the fact that profits were immense. But the steel barons would not stop war profiteering until President Wilson, at Baruch's appeal, warned that the government would take over steel production.

The labor unions, forbidden to strike for the duration of the war, protested the disinclination of the Justice Department to prosecute striking industrialists for sedition.

Western nations were seriously worried by the emergence of the Russian Revolution during the war. In 1919, Britain, France, and the United States mounted a joint, unsuccessful expedition to Siberia to overthrow the new Soviet regime. Leaders of the USSR grew convinced that the West would not allow a Communist government to survive as a threat to world capitalism.

So they developed the Comintern, a Communist international organization. Its representatives organized Communist parties directed from Moscow. The Kremlin planned to use them as centers of subversion and espionage against nations hostile to the Soviet Union.

In January, 1919, Ludwig C. A. K. Martens, a member of the Russian Communist party, was sent by the Comintern to help organize the Workers' (later the Communist) party in the United States. Members recruited from the radical labor movement were encouraged to feel that anything they could do to help the Soviet Union, the new "workers' paradise," automatically helped the cause of the working class everywhere.

Attorney General A. Mitchell Palmer took the view that *all* "radically-inclined individuals," not only Communists, were dangerous to the security of the United States. In August, 1919, he created a General Investigation Division (later the FBI) of the Department of Justice. J. Edgar Hoover, a young operative who headed it as Palmer's special assistant, was ordered to compile a list of sixty thousand "suspected radicals."

On the night of January 1, 1920, Palmer-ordered raids in thirty-three cities and seized over four thousand political and labor militants in mass arrests. Labor saw the raids as an attempt to intimidate its organizers from calling strikes because of low wages, high prices, and unemployment. After being jailed for up to a week, almost all the "radically-inclined individuals" arrested had to be released for lack of any valid evidence against them.

Felix Frankfurter, who had been chairman of the War Labor Policies Board, joined a dozen prominent lawyers in condemning the Palmer raids as illegal. Palmer called the lawyers "Communists," and Frankfurter's name was added to the G.I.D.'s list of suspected subversives. By the time the raids stopped in May, the list had grown to 450,000.

Yet in his own book, *Masters of Deceit,* J. Edgar Hoover noted that Communist-party membership was still under 12,400 even two years later. And Communist candidates in the presidential elections eight years later still could not attract even fifty thousand votes. Referring to the Palmer raids, a later president, Harry S. Truman, called them "a terrible thing . . . the 'Communist hysteria' program of its day."

The raids probably radicalized many workers who until then had regarded their grievances as directed only against big business, not against the government. When citizens are oppressed by a majority, Lord Acton warned in 1877, "there is no appeal, no redemption, no refuge but treason."

During the 1920s American industrialists, worried about the spread of the Communist movement, watched with deep interest the steps taken by their counterparts in Europe to develop an anti-Communist force. First in Italy, then in Germany, big business interests financed a militaristic movement called fascism. Led by Mussolini in Italy and Hitler in Germany, Fascist storm troops terrorized all opposition in order to seize power in the democracies and establish a dictatorship.

On November 25, 1922, Benito Mussolini led his Blackshirts in a march on Rome, overthrew the government, and declared himself dictator. Two weeks later the Scripps-Howard press featured an interview with the newly elected commander of the

American Legion, Alvin Owsley, who declared that the Legion likewise stood ready to take over the American government if necessary. He warned that the world spread of revolutionary doctrine had to be taken seriously, and the Legion was fighting every element threatening democracy.

"Should the day ever come," he declared, "when they menace the freedom of our representative government, the Legion would not hesitate to take things into its own hands—to fight the Reds as the Fascisti of Italy fought them."

Edward A. Rumely served as an American link to the Nazi (National-Socialist) forces in Germany, who, under Adolf Hitler, sought to emulate Mussolini's coup d'etat in Italy. Rumely had been arrested in July, 1918, on charges of perjury, for concealing the fact that he had been an agent of Imperial Germany in buying and publishing the New York *Evening Mail* with German funds. A famous American, Henry Ford, had rushed to Washington to try to save him from indictment, but Rumely was sentenced to a year and a day in the Atlanta Penitentiary.

"Edward A. Rumely was for years the secret paid agent of the German Government," declared George Harvey, American ambassador to England. "Rumely's close, if not closest, friend during the past six years has been Henry Ford."

Ford's sympathies with Germany persisted in his postwar support of Hitler's anti-Semitic Nazi movement. When Ford was being boomed as a presidential candidate in 1923, the Chicago *Tribune* quoted Hitler's tribute: "We look to Heinrich Ford as the leader of the growing Fascist movement in America."

At the 1923 trial of Hitler for his unsuccessful Munich beerhall putsch, Herr Auer, vice president of the Bavarian Diet, testified: "The Bavarian Diet has long had the information that the Hitler movement was partly financed by an American anti-Semitic chief, who is Henry Ford. . . . Herr Hitler openly boasts of Mr. Ford's support. . . . A photograph of Mr. Ford hangs in Herr Hitler's quarters." The charge was frequently reported in the *Manchester Guardian, Berliner Tageblatt,* and *the New York Times.*

It was never denied. In a book he wrote in 1938, / *Knew Hitler,* Nazi agent Kurt K. W. Luedecke related how Hitler had sent him to America in 1924 to obtain funds for the Nazis. When Hitler came to power in Germany in August, 1934, he awarded Ford a swastika decoration, which Ford never returned or repudiated even after war was declared. Prior to 1941, however, it was not treasonable to give aid and comfort to the Nazis.

For seven years Ford distributed Nazi-originated anti-Semitic propaganda through a newspaper he published, the Dearborn *Independent.* It was edited by his public-relations counsel, William J. Cameron, who published the *Protocols of the Elders of Zion.* These discredited forgeries, slanders against the Jews, created such indignation that many Jews filed libel suits and the Jewish community organized a boycott of Ford cars.

On June 30, 1927, Ford made a public apology to Jews, pleading that it was Cameron, not he, who had been responsible for the anti-Semitic campaign of the *Independent,* which he claimed not to have been informed about. He admitted that the slander "justifies the righteous indignation entertained by Jews everywhere toward me." Also acknowledging that the *Protocols* were proved "gross forgeries," he stopped publication of the *Independent.* The boycott against Ford cars ended.

During the twenties three consecutive Republican administrations refused to recognize the Soviet Union. Colonel Raymond Robins, wartime head of the US Red Cross mission in Moscow, felt that this policy was shortsighted. He enlisted the aid of Idaho senator William Borah and Nebraska senator George Norris to change it, but their efforts failed.

The Hearst press, which had vastly increased its circulation with sensational headlines about the Red Peril, published "Soviet" documents indicating that Senators Borah and Norris had been paid $100,000 each by the Comintern through the Soviet ambassador in Paris. Outraged, Borah initiated an investigation that proved the documents to be forgeries.

They had been promulgated by White Russian refugees, who had also cajoled Henry Ford into paying $7,000 for forged documents. The swindlers were arrested in Germany, sentenced to jail, then expelled instead as "undesirable aliens."

In 1928 the Hearst press used more forged documents to accuse Borah, Norris, and Senator Robert LaFollette of receiving more than a million dollars from the "revolutionary" Mexican government. Hearst was mad at Mexico for expropriating his properties there. The Senate investigated. Even the "experts" Hearst produced to validate the documents were compelled to admit that they were, indeed, forgeries.

The Red-baiting of the Hearst press only obscured the fact that there were genuine acts of disloyalty by American citizens who considered their first allegiance to Moscow, not to Washington. William Odell Nowell, a Georgia Negro who came to Detroit for an auto job, was recruited for the Communist party. In November, 1929, he was invited to Moscow with twenty-six other recruits for training and returned to further Soviet objectives as president of the American Negro Labor Congress. Moscow instructed Nowell to prepare a Negro revolt in the South to coincide with a hoped-for uprising of northern workers.

Both projects fizzled, however, because of working-class distaste for communism and black fear of white terrorists in the South. Nowell took advanced training at Lenin University but grew disillusioned with Communist tactics and quit the party. Finding himself discredited as a labor organizer, he testified against accused Communist spies for the House Un-American Activities Committee (HUAC) and was rewarded by a job with the Ford Motor Company.

When the nation fell into the Great Depression in October, 1929, with unemployment quickly soaring to a total of fifteen million, industrialists were worried by the angry mood sweeping over the country. The conservative press denounced dissenters and demonstrators against the government as Reds.

In July, 1932, angered by the failure of Congress to vote a bonus promised them, seventeen thousand desperate, jobless veterans and their families marched to Washington. Camping on the edge of the city, the Bonus Army vowed to remain until Congress passed the Patman Bonus Bill. President Hoover ordered Chief of Staff General Douglas MacArthur to evict the veterans forcibly.

The use of troops, cavalry, and tanks outraged the veterans, who threw bricks. Tear-gas shells were lobbed back. A stampede among a crowd of ten thousand injured many spectators. At bayonet point the troops forced the Bonus Army back and burned down their shacktowns. National indignation burst over the heads of Hoover and MacArthur, who were charged with "murdering veterans on the streets of Washington."

It should be noted that the *Official Training Manual* (No. 2000-25) of the US Army of that day taught soldiers this definition of democracy: "A government of the masses . . . results in mobocracy. Attitude toward property is communistic—negating property rights. . . . Results in demagogism, license, agitation, discontent, anarchy."

Conservatives labeled the Bonus Army a Communist plot to provoke the calling out of troops so that the Hoover Administration could be denounced as "Fascist." But Hoover's heavy-handed blunder in antagonizing the nation's veterans counted heavily against him in the elections of November, 1932. Franklin D. Roosevelt and the Democrats were swept into office in a landslide victory, and a new era began.

The decade of the 1930s saw a sharpening of conflict between the American forces of Left and Right, intensified by hard times. Roosevelt's New Deal program sought to reform the weaknesses of laissez-faire (unrestricted) capitalism, which he blamed for the Depression. Accused of seeking to scrap the capitalist system, Roosevelt explained that on the contrary, he was seeking to save it from revolution because of its excesses. Nevertheless the Right, including most big-business leaders, regarded him as a Communist or radical whose policies amounted to "creeping socialism."

The pro-Roosevelt forces, including both liberals and leftists, tended to be sympathetic toward the Soviet Union. The anti-Roosevelt forces looked toward Nazi Germany and Fascist Italy for their inspiration. Each camp accused the other of treason to American ideals. Out of their clash would come the stormy episodes of the thirties, climaxed by the explosion of the mightiest clash of world powers in history.

NINE

The Fifth Column

The American anti-Semitic movement of the thirties was fueled from Nazi Germany. Using the Jews as a scapegoat for Germany's troubles, Adolf Hitler rode to power on a wave of anti-Semitic hatred. It was the emotional cement he used to glue together his Fascist-minded supporters overseas.

His plan for piecemeal conquest of the world by his Nazi "super-race" required that the major powers be kept passive and in awe of Germany as he took over smaller countries one by one. To assure this paralysis, he established a "fifth column" of pro-Nazi traitors or sympathizers in each country, working for Hitler's interests against their own government's.

His supporters in the United States and other countries included anti-Semites, antilabor businessmen and politicians who saw in fascism a tool for handcuffing unions, extreme right-wingers who hated democracy and wanted a dictatorship, criminal classes and racketeers who saw the Fascist movement as an opportunity to exploit gullible followers, and those German-Americans who admired and were loyal to the Fuehrer.

This fifth column was directed from Germany through various channels, with the objective of encouraging isolationism ("Keep America out of Europe's wars!"). Many prominent isolationists were sincere, patriotic Americans, some of them pacifists, who wanted to spare the United States the cost in blood and treasure of a second world war. Hitler's agents skillfully exploited this sentiment for Nazi ends.

They worked to discredit Americans who wanted to aid Hitler's victims as the Nazis swallowed Austria, the Sudetenland, Czechoslovakia, and Poland; challenged England and France; then finally attacked the Soviet Union. German propaganda spread the idea that only American Jews were behind demands to boycott Germany, help the Allies, and eventually join them.

Some big-business leaders were persuaded to look upon Hitler as the world savior of Christianity, in a struggle against "Jewish" communism and liberalism. Uneducated masses were encouraged to believe that Hitler was going to free them from "the oppression of the Jewish bankers"—despite the fact that only a tiny percentage of United States bankers were Jewish.

That was why Wendell L. Willkie, nominated by the Republican party to oppose President Roosevelt in the 1940 elections, declared, "I consider . . . every anti-Semite as a potential traitor to America." When pro-Fascist Father Charles Coughlin tried to support him in the weekly newspaper, *Social Justice,* Willkie icily repudiated him.

"I am not interested," he declared, "in the support of anybody who stands for any form of prejudice as to anybody's race or religion, or who is in support of any foreign economic or political philosophy in this country."

The extent to which the pro-Nazi movement on the American Right constituted treason or conspiracy to commit treason was a question difficult to settle while the United States was still at peace. After Pearl Harbor, however, arrests of many fifth columnists followed swiftly, particularly of those who persisted in championing the cause of Nazi Germany.

What about the Left during the thirties? American Communists, whose first loyalty was to Stalin and Moscow, were only a small minority at the beginning of the decade. Their ranks grew rapidly, however, during and following the Depression. They also exerted great influence in the militant labor movement and among the nation's liberals and intellectuals.

American Communists believed in world revolution by the working classes and in Stalin as the leader of that revolution. But Stalin, unlike Trotsky, whom he exiled and then murdered, was far less interested in world revolution than in the security of the Soviet Union. He suspected a plot by the capitalist powers of the West to destroy Russia, secretly building up Hitler's war machine for that purpose.

The major goal of Stalin's foreign policy during the thirties was to thwart that plot. He used the Comintern to help mobilize the liberal and labor forces within the democracies to press for stopping fascism as a threat to world peace. Independently, this was also the policy of American liberals, who saw Hitler as a menace not just to the Soviet Union but eventually to the United States.

Hard-core Communists fanatically obeyed every directive from Moscow and had no scruples about committing treason if and when directed. Among them were actual Russian agents, just as there were German agents among the American Fascists. But many Communists were simply "true believers"—idealistic intellectuals, socialists, and labor leaders who felt that the Soviet Union offered the only real hope of stopping Hitler.

Some Americans sympathized with Communist objectives, but not wholly; or they refused to put themselves under party discipline. Others supported the anti-Fascist movement but wanted no part of the Communists. The Comintern encouraged the organization of many "united front" groups in which "fellow travelers," as well as anti-Communist liberals and labor leaders, could wage their own fight against fascism.

The extent to which the pro-Soviet movement on the Left constituted treason or conspiracy to commit treason was even harder to determine than among the pro-Nazis. Communist policy attacked Nazi Germany up until 1938, when Hitler and Stalin signed a nonaggression pact, then divided up Poland.

American Communists were stunned but quickly fell into line by stopping all agitation against Hitler, switching the line to keeping America out of an "imperialist" war on the side of Britain and France. But after Hitler broke the pact with Stalin and attacked the Soviet Union, American Communists once more crusaded for all aid to the Allies to "stop Hitler."

It was painfully obvious that their policies were blueprinted in the Kremlin. Many disillusioned liberals and laborites dropped out of the Communist party and out of some united-front groups they controlled.

"When I'm told it's great to boo Hitler on Monday, then not to boo him on Tuesday," said one defector wryly, "I know I'm in the wrong outfit."

Pearl Harbor ended the confusion, however, by making Germany our enemy and the Soviet Union our ally along with England and France. American Communists instantly won respectability and American Fascists lost it. There were no prosecutions of American Communists for treason during World War II; there was no reason for it. Few Americans worked more energetically for an Allied victory.

The day after Hitler first seized power in Germany, an organization of American storm troopers called the Silver Shirts was organized by William Dudley Pelley. Running afoul of the law, he was convicted of a felony and given a five-year suspended sentence. In 1936 he received Nazi funds to run for president on a "Christian party" ticket.

"The time has come," he declared, "for an American Hitler and a pogrom." He promised to do away with the Department of Justice, using his Silver Shirts as an army and police force.

The goateed American fuehrer was indicted for sedition when he continued his work as a Nazi agent after the war began.

"You are a traitor to your country, the arch-Quisling of America," US District Attorney J. Howard Caughran accused him, "parading under a false flag of patriotism while you stabbed your country in the back. You will go down in history with Benedict Arnold and Aaron Burr!"

Protesting that he was being persecuted "by the Jews," Pelley was found guilty and sentenced to fifteen years.

Leader of the first Silver Shirt squad of storm troopers was Gerald L. K. Smith, a pastor who gave up the pulpit to follow first Huey Long, then Pelley. Breaking with the American fuehrer, he subsequently allied himself with other leaders of the extreme Right—Coughlin, Francis E. Townsend, and William Lemke. His newspaper, *The Cross and the Flag,* urged all anti-Semitic, ultranationalist groups to unite in a single American Fascist movement for greater strength.

In September, 1940, most right-wing organizations flocked into the America First Committee, which opposed Roosevelt's policy of increasing aid to the Allies.

Smith urged his followers to be "ruthless," and according to *the New York Times,* made no secret of his intention to "seize the government of the United States." Declaring his candidacy for the Senate, he told a Detroit rally that God had ordered him to save "this glorious Republic from ruin."

Although the outbreak of war with Germany shattered the America First Committee, Smith sought to revive it in January, 1943, as an America First party to "win the peace." What this meant became clearer after the war when it was discovered that America Firsters had accepted financial support from Nazi Germany. Smith, however, was not indicted with other pro-Fascists.

James True, a virulent American Fascist of the thirties, actually patented a kind of policeman's nightstick for killing Jews. Distributing Nazi and British Fascist propaganda, he vowed, "Fascism is the answer . . . it is the last defense of Christian capitalism." He sought to further his goal by selling firearms to American Nazi groups.

The chief Nazi agent in the United States during the decade was George Sylvester Viereck, who had been propaganda adviser of the German embassy since the First World War. In a book written after that war Viereck explained, "Every propagandist drapes himself in the flag. The objective of German propaganda was . . . to strengthen and replenish Germany; to weaken and harass Germany's foes; and to keep America out of war."

When Hitler came to power, Viereck sought to use Congress itself as an agency for disseminating Nazi propaganda in the United States. Founding a publishing house called Flanders Hall, he contracted for books from congressmen who promoted isolationism, defeatism, and anti-Communist and pro-Nazi policies.

He worked out a scheme to have the American government subsidize bulk mailings of his pro-Nazi propaganda through the office of Congressman Hamilton Fish, Sr., who had headed the first congressional committee to investigate "subversive activities" in 1930. Fish allowed his House Office Building facilities to be used as Viereck's Washington headquarters.

After war broke out, Viereck was arrested as a Nazi agent along with Fish's office clerk, George Hill, who confessed the scheme. Viereck would write pro-Nazi speeches for Fish and some twenty other congressmen and senators who were willing either to deliver them or insert them in the *Congressional Record* as "printed remarks." Viereck would then order reprints delivered to Hill, who mailed them out postage-free in bulk, in addressed envelopes bearing a congressional frank, to Fascist organizations throughout the country.

Hill testified that Fish had introduced him to Viereck and told him to collaborate with the Nazi agent. Viereck had paid Hill for these services and had also given him money to bribe congressmen into cooperating. Almost a million pieces of Nazi propaganda had been mailed at government expense.

A grand jury ordered Fish to explain his involvement. He denied knowing that Viereck was in the pay of Hitler, calling him "an American citizen of long standing and good standing." His memory failed him in answering other embarrassing questions.

Viereck was convicted, but the Supreme Court reversed his conviction on March 1, 1943, on the technical ground that he was not compelled to report to the State Department any of his activities except as "agent of a foreign principal."

The rise of pro-Fascist agitation in the United States led the House of Representatives in 1934 to appoint a McCormack-Dickstein Special Committee on Un-American Activities to investigate Nazi propaganda. The committee uncovered a sensational Fascist plot to seize the government that involved many captains of industry. These industrialists, horrified by Roosevelt's "Socialist" New Deal and his encouragement of a powerful labor union movement, were convinced that the capitalist system could not survive four years of "That Man in the White House."

A putsch to seize control of the government by force was organized by pro-Fascist extremists during Roosevelt's first term. They hoped to capture the White House and establish a Mussolini-style dictatorship under distinguished war hero Major General Smedley Butler, ranking major general of the Marine Corps. The plotters made forty-two separate efforts to persuade Butler to lead the putsch.

A war hero twice awarded the Congressional Medal of Honor, Butler was their ideal choice for a "man on horseback" because of his great prestige among American veterans, who could be expected to rally behind him as an American dictator. Gerald C. MacGuire, former head of the Connecticut American Legion, offered Butler three million dollars to form the projected new "superorganization" of veterans and three million dollars more as needed. General Butler, an incorruptible patriot, pretended to play along with the plotters to get full details of the cabal.

MacGuire explained what they had in mind once the White House was captured: "Did it ever occur to you that the President is overworked? We might have an Assistant President. The dumb American people will swallow that. We have got the newspapers. We will start a campaign that the president's health is failing." Then the new "supersecretary" of the conspiracy would move up to become "Acting President," because Vice President John Nance Garner had no wish for that office.

MacGuire informed Butler that in two or three weeks a new organization "to maintain the Constitution and so forth" would be announced in the press and would contain many names important in American industry. This was the organization behind the putsch.

"In about two weeks," General Butler testified, "the American Liberty League appeared, which was just about what he described it to be."

Contributors to the league, as revealed by the Seventy-fourth Congress, included seven members of one of the nation's major corporations, the racist president of a leading oil company, partners of Wall Street banking firms, the head of a major steel company, the former chairman of a leading food company, the director of a southern railroad, and dozens of other important figures.

General Butler now felt that he knew the whole treason plot. Roaring a furious rejection of the offer to make him an American Mussolini or Hitler, he warned MacGuire and his backers not to try to get another general for their scheme.

"My one hobby is maintaining a democracy," he snapped. "If you get a half million soldiers advocating anything smelling of fascism, I am going to get a half a million more and lick hell out of you, and we will have a real war right at home!"

He went to Washington on February 15, 1935, and testified in secret session before the McCormack-Dickstein Committee.

"The whole affair," he declared, "smacked of treason to me. . . . I have one interest in all of this, and that is to try to do my best to see that a democracy is maintained in this country." Another witness, a newspaper man, corroborated his testimony.

"MacGuire denied these allegations under oath," noted the committee's official report (No. 153, 74th Congress, 1st Session, House of Representatives), "but your committee was able to verify all the pertinent statements made by General Butler, with the exception of the direct statement suggesting the creation of the organization. This, however, was corroborated in the correspondence of MacGuire."

It added, "Evidence was obtained showing that certain persons had made an attempt to establish a Fascist organization in this country. There is no question that these attempts were discussed, were planned, and might have been placed in execution when and if the financial backers deemed it expedient."

Significantly, the American Liberty League quickly dissolved after the McCormack-Dickstein report. None of the principals involved in the plot was indicted for treason, possibly because President Roosevelt was anxious not to widen the gulf between himself and big-business leaders, whose cooperation he needed to make the New Deal work. Besides, the country was not at war, and treason would be difficult to prove—especially against the best corporation lawyers in the nation.

In 1934 a noted anti-Semite, Mrs. Elizabeth Dilling, published the first "subversive list" since J. Edgar Hoover's list of the Palmer-raid days. In a book called *The Red Network* she named such dangerous radicals as Rev. Harry Emerson Fosdick, Mahatma Gandhi, Sigmund Freud, New York Mayor Fiorello La Guardia, Sinclair Lewis, Chiang Kai-shek, Mrs. Eleanor Roosevelt, and New Deal legal adviser Felix Frankfurter.

She labeled as "Communist institutions" the YMCA, the Federal Council of the Churches of Christ, and the Civil Liberties Union. Addressing students at the University of Chicago, she accused, "You're all guinea pigs of Stalin. The University of Chicago is a Red school!"

In her book Mrs. Dilling explained that fascism "seeks a harmony between all classes," a remarkable conclusion apparently confirmed by several trips to Germany. In a lecture tour during the thirties she attacked democracy as a system of "mobocracy," explaining that the United States was not a democracy but a republic. Winning support from some right-wing congressmen, senators, and wealthy New York superpatriots, she refused to stop recruiting for fascism after Pearl Harbor. The Department of Justice indicted her as a pro-Nazi propagandist.

"I am guilty only of pro-Americanism!" she cried.

The swastika flew boldly at all meetings of the German-American Bund, organized in 1933 under orders from Berlin. Its fuehrer was Fritz Kuhn, a Munich-born Nazi-party member who had entered the United States in 1926 as a chemist in the Ford plant. The Bund had its own private storm troopers wearing swastika armbands, who were necessary, Kuhn explained, to protect Bund rallies from being broken up by Communists.

A New York legislature investigative committee, under Senator John J. McNaboe, reported that the Bund's private army was "being trained to serve . . . a foreign dictator." Kuhn's demagogic speeches mimicked Hitler's, charging that all Communists and bankers were Jews, and that 60 percent of the government was Jewish.

"Free America!" he cried, giving the Nazi salute.

He established twenty-four Bund camps throughout the United States with Nazi funds. Bund cells received orders from Berlin on propaganda activities, espionage, and revolutionary preparations. Their mission was spelled out by Hitler: "National Socialism would be worth nothing if it restricted itself to Germany alone and did not seal the rule of the superior race over the whole world for at least one thousand to two thousand years."

The Nazis spent an estimated $300 million a year toward this goal on their foreign auxiliaries. Returning from a visit to Germany, Fritz Kuhn wrote, "We must impel American politics with a pure German feeling. . . . America, under all circumstances, must keep out of any European war. That is the greatest service we can show Germany." A special prayer was written for the Bund's youth groups. It began, "Adolf Hitler, we believe in Thee."

The Bund distributed Joseph Goebbels's propaganda vilifying President Roosevelt and Mayor La Guardia, who was called a "Jewish lout" and "chief gangster" for suggesting that Hitler belonged in a chamber of horrors. La Guardia replied dryly that while his mother had a slight infusion of Jewish blood, "I regret that it is not enough to boast of."

Throughout the thirties, as Fritz Kuhn and others on the extreme Right urged Americans to take the Nazi road to the future, the Jews in Germany were being terrorized, thrown into concentration camps, and murdered along with political opponents and Slavic people in countries Hitler overran.

As American outrage grew at these atrocities, Kuhn stopped displaying the swastika at Bund rallies, replacing it with American flags. But on November 29, 1939, the movement received a setback when Kuhn was convicted of larceny and forgery and was sentenced to up to five years in jail. The New York legislature then passed an act forbidding the use of uniformed storm troops at rallies.

The Bund continued under Gerhard Wilhelm Kunze, an ex-chauffeur, of Philadelphia. In 1940 Bund officials were indicted in New Jersey for violating a 1935 state law against inciting racial and religious hatred. Convicted and sentenced, they appealed to the State Supreme Court. A reversal was granted on the ground that the law violated the rights of free speech because there was no "clear and present danger to the State."

The jubilant Bund held a joint rally with the Ku Klux Klan in New Jersey. The legislature thereupon closed down the Bund's Camp Nordland as a public nuisance. Florida and other states passed statutes outlawing Bund activities. The Bund nevertheless held a national convention in September, 1941.

The war put the Bund out of business. In April, 1942, the FBI, arrested sixty-four alien members. Many were convicted and jailed; some who were naturalized citizens lost their citizenship for disloyalty. Kunze, tried as a spy for supplying military information to Germany, was sentenced to fifteen years, with five years added for fomenting resistance to military service in the American Army.

Japan, too, had its agents operating in the United States during the thirties. Typical was Cincinnati-born John S. Farnsworth, an Annapolis graduate who had served on destroyers in World War I and commanded a Navy air-squadron base at Norfolk. After marrying a society girl, he began to live above his means and was court-martialed for refusing to pay his debts.

Unable to get civilian employment with this blot on his record, he offered his services as an aviation technical adviser to other countries. Japan was interested, but only in naval secrets he could obtain for them. Farnsworth, who held a grudge against the Navy for "persecuting" him, agreed.

Calling on old friends in naval circles, he managed to steal confidential documents from their offices. One officer's suspicions were aroused by the large bills Farnsworth was flashing around. The FBI, alerted, put a twenty-four-hour watch on him.

They secured evidence that he was collecting Navy code and signal books, sketches, photographs, blueprints, maps, and ship models and was meeting secretly with the Japanese naval attache, Commander Akira Yamaki, and later with his successor, a Commander Ichimiya. Following the trail, the FBI, located firms that had photostated naval material for Farnsworth. This tactic had been abandoned as too risky; Ichimiya installed photostating machines in his own hotel quarters, which maids were forbidden to enter.

Through Farnsworth, eight years before Pearl Harbor, the Japanese learned the effectiveness of almost every gun in the US Navy and the capabilities of its aircraft carriers.

Arrested, Farnsworth insisted that he had only been pretending to spy for the Japanese in order to penetrate their espionage network, hoping that if he succeeded, the Navy would reinstate him. At his trial in February, 1937, however, he pleaded nolo contendere—neither an admission of guilt nor a plea of innocence. Found guilty, he was sentenced to four to twenty years in a federal penitentiary.

But the most dangerous treason, as war approached, continued to be that practiced by Hitler's American admirers.

TEN

The Language of Hate

Another important crusader for fascism in America was Lawrence Dennis, who had worked for the State Department for seven years. Switching to Wall Street, he became a leading intellectual spokesman for the far Right. In 1936, as "an important American Fascist," he was given an interview with Mussolini, and in Germany he met Baron Ulrich von Gienanth, who financed Nazi agents in the United States. Jailed Nazi agent Friedrick Auhagen later reported having given Dennis Nazi funds.

"I do not believe in democracy or the intelligence of the masses," Dennis wrote in a book predicting the coming of American fascism. "This book is addressed . . . to the ruling groups, actual and potential." He praised German and Italian aggression in the countries they overran and Japan's rape of China.

With the outbreak of war with Germany, Dennis applied for a commission in the US Army but was refused. He continued working discreetly for fascism by using important senators, representatives, publishers, businessmen, and clergymen to promote his views. When his activities came under fire from an investigative body of Congress, he did not hesitate to ask the Civil Liberties Union to defend his right to denounce democracy.

A year after Pearl Harbor he was still proposing that the Republican party speak out against the war effort and continuing to denounce the New Deal as a Communist plot.

The patriotism of some industrialists during the late thirties seemed as dubious as that of those involved in the abortive putsch plot exposed by General Butler. On November 23, 1937, when Hitler was testing his tanks and planes in Spain to overthrow that democracy for Franco's fascism, a curious meeting took place in a Boston hotel. Seven prominent American industrialists and congressmen reached a secret cartel agreement with two Nazi consul generals—Baron von Tippleskirch, of Boston, and Baron Manfred Freiherr von Killinger, of San Francisco.

They established joint monopolies of aluminum, synthetic rubber, tungsten, quinine, and other essential defense materials. The resultant shortages hampered American defense production to the point that a Senate hearing held by Senator Harry S. Truman branded Standard Oil and other important corporations involved as "traitors" to the war effort. The hearings also accused many American business leaders of refusing to cooperate with the government's request that they convert half their production to defense needs before Pearl Harbor and of balking even months afterward.

The same Nazi consul general who engineered the cartel agreement, Baron von Killinger, also blueprinted a plan for a revolutionary network to "liberate" Americans from democracy. A West Virginia engineer, George E. Deatherage, was a key figure in this conspiracy. In 1935 he had revived a defunct Ku Klux Klan organization called the Knights of the White Camellia to spread anti-Semitism. He also founded the American Nationalist Confederation, uniting seventy-two different Fascist groups.

Deatherage distributed propaganda shipped to him by the Nazi bureau, World Service. He also sought to frighten American Jewry by ordering his followers to spread "terror and fear" by burning swastikas on hills overlooking towns. When war broke out, he withdrew from the organizations he headed to avoid prosecution. But in February, 1942, he was fired from his job at the Norfolk Naval Base as an "undesirable" security risk and a year later was charged with sedition.

Another important pro-Fascist agitator was Joseph P. Kamp, who in 1935 began editing a newspaper called *The Awakener.* He abandoned it after two years when its virulent anti-Semitism began to run it into trouble and organized the Constitutional Educational League. It distributed over two million copies of a booklet called *Join the C.I.O. and Help Build a Soviet America,* in which Kamp charged that labor's sit-down strikes in Detroit were a Moscow-directed plot for revolution.

The Senate Civil Liberties Committee, headed by Senator LaFollette, began investigating the league. Kamp accused the committee of being "disloyal and un-American." Through his league, which had industrial support, he was instrumental in getting the House of Representatives to set up a new Un-American Activities Committee "to investigate subversion" under his friend, Martin Dies of Texas. It soon became clear that HUAC's target would be almost exclusively the Left, not the Right.

Edward Sullivan was appointed chief investigator of the Dies Committee. In addition to a record of nine police arrests and employment as a labor spy, he had directed a Fascist Ukrainian group, edited an anti-Semitic hate sheet, and been a speaker at German-American Bund rallies.

HUAC's second chief investigator was Dr. J. B. Matthews, whose writings were reprinted by the Nazi Foreign Office and who wrote in his autobiography, "America's answer to communism will be fascism." Years later Matthews became a close adviser of Robert Welch, founder of the John Birch Society.

When Dies took over HUAC in May, 1938, Congressman Dickstein, who had headed HUAC in the earlier investigation of the Fascist conspiracy exposed by General Butler, declared, "One hundred and ten Fascist organizations in the United States have had, and have now, the key to the back door of the House Un-American Activities Committee."

Three congressmen—Coffee, of Washington, O'Toole, of New York, and Hook, of Michigan—accused Dies of making HUAC "a sounding board for the un-American Fascist groups." Several congressmen charged that Gerald L. K. Smith was the secret director of HUAC.

"It seems to me," said Congressman Savage of Washington, "that all Gerald L. K. Smith has to do is yell 'sic 'em,' and the committee's counsel takes after whatever party Mr. Smith is peeved at."

The Dies Committee attacked New Deal projects, the National Labor Relations Board, the Department of Labor, the Workers' Alliance, and the American Youth Congress as "Communist-infiltrated." To charges that he was trying to silence the Left and help the Right, Dies replied, "What amendment in our Constitution protects these spies and agents of foreign governments?" HUAC produced political headlines, but no spies.

The Imperial Wizard of the Ku Klux Klan praised Dies, declaring that his program "so closely parallels the program of the Klan that there is no distinguishable difference between them." When Dies left Congress in 1945, he admitted to a St. Louis *Post Dispatch* reporter that his primary purpose had been to harass the New Deal by charges of Communist infiltration, which he knew were hurting the Roosevelt Administration.

A national poll in 1934 declared the second most powerful and popular man in the country, after Roosevelt, to be Father Charles E. Coughlin, the "radio priest." At first he supported the New Deal, thinking it would bring "social justice" modeled after Mussolini's corporate fascism. He soon found Roosevelt's policies too liberal for his tastes. When the president appointed some prominent Jews to public office, the anti-Semitic Coughlin turned against him fiercely.

Through radio broadcasts, his weekly paper, *Social Justice,* and mass rallies at which he made demagogic speeches, Coughlin peddled the Nazi line. When he attacked Roosevelt as "the great liar and betrayer . . . the Scab President," his bishop forced him to make a public apology.

In the 1936 elections he joined Gerald L. K. Smith and Francis Townsend in supporting Congressman William Lemke's Union party against Roosevelt. "One thing is sure . . . democracy is doomed!" he cried out on his radio program. "This is our last election. It is fascism or communism. We are at the crossroads. . . . I take the road of fascism!"

Lemke received only 900,000 votes, but Coughlin's National Union for Social Justice soon had almost 8,500,000 members. In 1938, he urged all Fascist groups to join in a "Christian Crusade against Communism." The result was the Christian Front, which used strong-arm squads and aspired to put in power a corporate-clerical state like Franco's.

Social Justice served as the Front's mouthpiece against what Coughlin called the "poppycock of democracy." He filled it with liberal quotes from Hitler's and Goebbels's anti-Semitic speeches; articles by George Sylvester Viereck, the registered Nazi agent; and even the forged *Protocols of the Elders of Zion.*

The Catholic Church made it clear that his views did not represent Church policy, and many prominent Catholic leaders denounced him. But Coughlin persisted in broadcasting Nazi propaganda, charging that it had been necessary for Hitler to take power to keep the Jews from communizing Germany, then the world. Meanwhile the Christian Front's street gangs grew more and more violent in breaking up anti-Fascist meetings.

Mayor La Guardia ordered the New York Police Department to crack down, and 233 of the Front's storm troopers were arrested in 1939. Seventeen members of the Front were indicted for conspiring to mount a Fascist revolution to take over the government. The prosecution accused them of seeking to "incite Jews to riot and then have a revolution and a counter-revolution." The jury disagreed, and the Fronters went free.

Coughlin was finally silenced on the air by his ecclesiastic superiors in 1940. He continued to publish *Social Justice,* however, even after Pearl Harbor. In April, 1942, the Attorney General banned it from the mails as "a systematic and unscrupulous attack upon the war effort."

As Coughlin's star faded, American Fascists found a new hero in Charles A. Lindbergh, the "Lone Eagle," who had become an American idol in 1927 by making the first nonstop solo flight over the Atlantic. Tall, blond, handsome, and modest, married to an ambassador's daughter, "Lucky Lindy" had been lionized everywhere. The whole nation had sympathized when a brutal kidnapping had cost his son's life, impelling him to take his family to live in England.

In 1938, Lindbergh made a trip through Europe, visiting Germany, the Soviet Union, and France. Returning to England, he joined appeasers in that country who insisted that Germany's air power was superior to that of the British, Russians, and

French combined. Outraged Britons accused him of trying to frighten the Western powers into appeasing Hitler.

"Those who are favored with his views," reported the *London Express,* "say that he never hesitates to voice his glowing admiration for Hitler and the German State." Eleven noted Soviet fliers who had been Lindbergh's hosts in Moscow charged, "He had an order from English reactionary circles to prove the weakness of Soviet aviation and give Chamberlain an argument for capitulation at Munich."

When Lindbergh returned to Germany, Hermann Goering enthusiastically decorated him with the Service Cross of the German Eagle as a "distinguished foreigner who has deserved well of the Reich." Supporters of Lindbergh later insisted that he had only been ingratiating himself with the Nazis under orders of the US Defense Department to gather intelligence for them on Nazi air strength, a claim never validated.

On April 25, 1941, President Roosevelt compared Lindbergh to a Civil War Copperhead for his isolationist stance. Lindbergh resigned his commission in the Air Force Reserve. Several months later, addressing a nationally broadcasted America First Committee rally, he parroted the Fascist line:

> The three most important groups who have been pressing this country toward war are the British, the Jews and the Roosevelt Administration. . . . [The Jews'] greatest danger to this country lies in their large ownership and influence in our motion pictures, our press, our radio and our government.

The New York *Herald Tribune* accused him of having "sinned against the American spirit." Secretary of the Interior Harold Ickes asked sarcastically whether anyone had ever heard

Lindbergh speak on behalf of democracy. William Allen White characterized his speech as "moral treason."

A controversial and tragic figure now scorned and denounced as a traitor by the majority of shocked and saddened Americans who had once idolized him as a great national hero, Lindbergh lapsed into brooding silence. One cynical radio wit asked, "What's everybody mad at Lindy for? He only followed Adolf's advice that if you're going to tell a lie, tell a whopper if you want to be believed. Look where it got Adolf!"

Once war was declared, however, Lindbergh's supporters saw to it that he was given some secret flying missions in the South Pacific, for which he was awarded the Congressional Medal of Honor and restored to the Air Force Reserve as a general.

John Roy Carlson, an anti-Fascist investigator who infiltrated the Fascist movements of the thirties, reported on a typical rally of the American Nationalist party. About four hundred people had crowded into a New York ballroom for the occasion.

"The whole country is overrun with foreigners, niggers, Jews," yelled a speaker. "Is this the white America of our fathers? Is this a land of Christian patriots or blood-sucking Communists? This here country has been stolen from us Christians by a bunch of conniving rats. What are we going to do about it?" The mob burst into an uproar.

"Kill the Jews! Hang them from lampposts!"

"Wipe every atheistic Communist off the face of the earth!"

Another speaker shouted, "Democracy, democracy, democracy! They throw it in our faces. You hear it on all sides till you get sick of it. What is this democracy? It is a rotten form of weakness." He called for an end to "absurd propaganda against

Germany." The mob enthusiastically applauded mentions of Father Coughlin, Hitler, and Franco.

The American Nationalist party organized a storm-trooper unit that taught the use of clubs, blackjacks, brass knuckles, and alley-fighting. Its recruits were part of the goon squads that joined the Christian Front to terrorize anti-Fascists.

The Front also enlisted the American Patriots, led by anti-Semite Allen Zoll, who applied unsuccessfully for a job as a Japanese propaganda agent. When New York radio station WMCA refused to carry Coughlin's inflammatory broadcasts, Zoll threw an American Patriots picket line around the station. Offering to call it off for $7,500, he was indicted for extortion.

Another prominent Christian Front group was the Christian Mobilizers, led by Joe McWilliams, who declared, "I'm going to have the greatest collection of strong-arm men in the city. And if anybody tries to stop us . . . they'll think lightning hit them." His followers included convicts, rapists, burglars, and street toughs, who did not hesitate to assault police.

"This is another revolution," McWilliams shouted at one street meeting. "It's a revolution against the Jew first, then against democracy, then against the Republican and Democratic parties. Both are rotten . . . useless. We are going to drive them both out and . . . run this country with an iron hand, the way Hitler runs Germany. . . . We are his fellow fighters."

The Christian Mobilizers crusaded against passage of the Lend-Lease Act, defense appropriations, and the Selective Service Act as "Jewish plots." McWilliams confessed to John Roy Carlson, "I don't believe half of this anti-Jew stuff I preach, but . . . it's the only language they understand—the language of hate. Hitler made it work and that's what I'm trying to do."

Another group known both as the American Fascists and Crusader White Shirts was led by a Tennessee fanatic named George W. Christians. He advocated seizing power by a military march to surround government buildings and "by sheer numbers and a patriotic appeal" to force officials to yield.

One night when President Roosevelt was expected in Chattanooga, Christians threatened to cut off the city's electric power. "Lots of things can happen in the dark," he hinted.

Most of the paramilitary groups in the Christian Front had plans for sabotage in the event of war with Germany. "In time of war we are all saboteurs," declared James Banahan, commandant of a secret Fascist Iron Guard unit disguised as the Midtown Sporting Club of New York. "We'll blow hell out of this country. We'll blow up docks, power plants, ships, bridges. . . . They'll blame the Communists. We'll spread confusion and chaos. . . . If they catch you with guns, we are members of the National Rifle Association, catch on?"

Banahan renamed his group the American Phalanx and affiliated it with the Ku Klux Klan. In January, 1940, the FBI, arrested seventeen members, charging them with conspiracy to overthrow the government. Tried in Queens, New York, then a strong center of Coughlinites, they were acquitted by a jury. Queens Borough President George U. Harvey defended the Christian Front as "Americans."

One of the most active workers in the American Fascist movement was Mrs. Leslie Fry, a paid Nazi agent. She worked with Baron von Killinger as West Coast organizer of the plot for a Fascist putsch. When it failed, she fled to Germany before the FBI could seize her. In 1942 she made the mistake of trying to reenter the country on a German ship and was taken into custody and indicted for sedition.

The Christian Front had its friends in Congress. Representative Jacob Thorkelson considered Joe McWilliams a "staunch American" and inserted in the *Congressional Record* quotations from many Fascist and anti-Semitic sources. He praised Hitler and Mussolini on the floor of Congress and scoffed, "There is not one democracy which has survived for any length of time."

Senator Robert Reynolds, chairman of the Senate's Committee on Military Affairs before Pearl Harbor, cooperated with American Fascist leaders and inserted their propaganda in the *Congressional Record.* As a military expert, he assured Americans that they were fortunate to have between them and the Soviet Union the protection of the islands of Japan.

Strong support for the extreme Right came from the Committee for Constitutional Government. Organized in 1937 by publisher Frank E. Gannett, it was headed by the same Edward Rumely who had been jailed as a secret German agent during World War I. The committee raised $210,000 to propagandize America First's policies. When the Senate Committee to Investigate Lobbying Activities called Rumely to testify in 1938, he removed his name from the organization's stationery.

William E. Dodd, America's ambassador to Germany from 1933 to 1938, warned Americans, "A clique of US industrialists is hell-bent to bring a fascist state to supplant our democratic government and is working closely with the fascist regimes in Germany and Italy."

Attorney General Jackson, speaking at the Boston Club on October 16, 1938, enumerated the names of the leading Fascists in America. The two largest press associations in the nation, the United Press and the Associated Press, reported the speech but for reasons best known to themselves omitted all the names except one. Boston's *Law Society Journal* published all.

Two months later Secretary of the Interior Harold L. Ickes followed Jackson's warning with a speech at Columbia University naming Lawrence Dennis as an American propagandist for fascism and Lindbergh and Coughlin as the nation's leading quislings—Vidkun Quisling was a Norwegian fifth columnist who had betrayed Norway to the Nazis.

After war was declared, Ickes attacked the big business firms that had sabotaged America's defense needs because of cartel agreements with I. G. Farben, the German firm controlled by Hitler. He pointed out that for over four months Alcoa had resisted expanding production of aluminum, depriving the country of the equivalent of ten thousand fighter planes. "If America loses the war," he said in June, 1941, "it can thank the Aluminum Corporation of America."

In May, 1940, British sympathizers in America rallied behind William Allen White in a Committee to Defend America by Aiding the Allies. That September, the isolationists and pro-Fascists united their forces in the America First Committee.

America First argued that the new world war was none of America's business, and that the United States should simply ignore it. After the war it was discovered that America Firsters had accepted financial support from Nazi Germany. Pearl Harbor exposed the bankruptcy of America First's insistence that American interests were not threatened by the spread of international fascism, and the organization collapsed.

Meanwhile, what about subversion on the left?

ELEVEN

"As Close to Treason as I Dare"

The Communist party grew stronger through the thirties by appeals designed to attract not only the working classes but also the intellectuals of America. New members were often recruited into the party through personal friendships.

The celebrated black novelist Richard Wright was a case in point. As a lonely young man in Chicago, he found a welcome in the Communist John Reed Club. White Communists showed him that they had no color bias, respected his talent, and were willing to form personal friendships with him.

"How different this was," he marveled, "from the way in which Negroes were sneered at in America. . . . I was meeting men and women . . . who were to form the first sustained relationships in my life."

It became an "in" thing for intellectuals to sympathize with the Reds, giving rise to the label of "parlor pinks." As during the sixties, radicalism on campus was a mark of distinction among the brightest members of the student body and faculty. This new left wing fully supported Roosevelt's New Deal as the first mild measures of social reform.

Many law-school graduates and other intellectuals flocked to Washington to work enthusiastically for the New Deal. Some of these civil servants were Soviet sympathizers; many were simply anti-Fascist; others were influenced toward the left by friendships with men they admired.

Whether some were disloyal, advancing the interests of the Soviet Union over those of the United States, was a question that would eventually be raised with dramatic consequences. Many government officials later accused by rightists of "treason" had sinned only in being active anti-Fascists before Pearl Harbor had made it patriotic. On the other hand, many American isolationists attacked by leftists as "Hitler agents" were actually only intent upon keeping America out of war.

Cooperation of fellow travelers with the Communists in anti-Fascist activities began to fall off in 1936, when Stalin began the strange Moscow trials of alleged Soviet traitors. For two years top Soviet officials accused themselves of monstrous acts of treason in open court and were led away to firing squads. Shocked American anti-Fascists suspected that the confessions had been procured by torture or threats to the defendants' families. Repelled by Stalin's paranoiac idea of "justice," they withdrew from cooperation with US Communists.

The American League Against War and Fascism, which represented a whole range of anti-Fascist sentiment from middle-of-the-road Democrats to Communists, fell to pieces in 1938 when Hitler and Stalin signed their nonaggression pact. American anti-Fascists wanted no part of a world leader who was willing to "shake hands with the devil" and join with him in invading and dividing Poland.

During the two years between the Hitler-Stalin Pact in August, 1939, and Hitler's attack on Russia in June, 1941, American Communists tried to close their dwindling ranks. Their speakers used Marxist rhetoric to justify the pact, urging an end to aid to the Allies and a new isolationism.

"We must have faith in the great Soviet Union as the only Socialist power in the world!" cried one party member at a 1940 streetcorner meeting witnessed by the writer. "Stalin has foiled the plot of the capitalists to drive Germany against Russia and has taken eastern Poland to protect the Polish people under a Socialist shield."

"That wasn't your line *last* year!" someone yelled.

"Stalin explained that dialectic materialism requires Communists to be flexible, according to the needs of changing events," the speaker replied. "The true enemies of working people everywhere are the imperialists of Wall Street and Ten Downing Street. Stop our rotten capitalists from dragging us into a dirty war! Down with Roosevelt, who has betrayed the New Deal to the munitions-makers who want blood money!"

Those Communists and fellow travelers who remained committed to the party during this period were almost wholly those who continued to have faith in Stalin, like Ossip Garber. A Bronx photographer, he was found to be operating a passport-forging ring for the use of Communist agents traveling abroad and was sentenced to prison for two years.

But as the war drew closer, the counterespionage branch of the FBI concentrated on the major threat to American security—Hitler's spies and seditionists. Early in 1940, William Sebold, a naturalized American visiting his family in Germany, was picked up by the Gestapo and detained until he agreed to train and serve as a Nazi spy. Returning home, he set up a shortwave radio transmitter in a house at Centerport, Long Island, operating a clearing-house for coded military information brought to him by other Nazi spies.

But Sebold was no traitor; he had notified the FBI of the plot. The station was under the control of G-men, who fed

Sebold misleading facts for transmission to Germany in code. Nazi spies who brought Sebold military secrets were photographed by a concealed camera. One spy bragged of having sold information on a top-secret US bombsight to Germany for four thousand dollars. In June, 1941, the FBI suddenly moved, and thirty-three men and women were arrested, cracking the major Nazi espionage ring in the United States.

With war an imminent possibility, in June, 1940, Congress passed the Smith Act, making it unlawful to advocate or teach the overthrow or destruction of the government by force or violence or to be part of any group advocating such doctrine. Rightist lawmakers who pushed the bill intended it for use against the extreme Left, not the extreme Right.

But war with Germany brought consternation to the forces of the Right. To persist in pro-Fascist, antiwar efforts was now, by the Constitution, open treason. The Fascist movement either became inactive or went underground. The few pro-Fascists who continued their activities were arrested.

HUAC, under Martin Dies, nevertheless persisted in searching for traitors only on the Left. President Roosevelt condemned the committee. Vice President Henry Wallace compared Dies to Goebbels. The FBI called HUAC's reports fake. Congressman Eliot, of Massachusetts, accused Dies of playing into the hands of the enemy and undermining the war effort. Letters poured into Congress demanding the abolition of HUAC, but Dies stubbornly insisted that the only real menace to an America at war with fascism was "communism."

Colonel Robert M. McCormick, powerful publisher of the Chicago *Tribune,* was an ardent supporter of rightist causes from the Dies Committee to America First. Together with his cousin,

Joseph Patterson, publisher of the New York *Daily News,* and Patterson's sister, Eleanor Patterson, publisher of the Washington *Times-Herald,* McCormick published daily items that were regularly used by Joseph Goebbels for Nazi propaganda.

Congressman Elmer J. Holland denounced the McCormick-Patterson papers in the *Congressional Record* as "the vermin press," whose aim was "to preach defeatism among our civilians and mutiny among our soldiers, to spread dismay among our allies, and to create joy in the hearts of our enemies."

Three days before Pearl Harbor the Chicago *Tribune* published a secret war-prospectus prepared by the Army and Navy Joint Board, outlining America's defense plans in case of war. The paper's headlines indicated that the plans proved the president's intention to drag America into the war against Germany. Secretary of War Henry Stimson was outraged.

"What would you think of an American General Staff," he asked Americans, "which in the present condition of the world did not investigate and study every conceivable type of emergency which may confront this country, and every possible method of meeting the emergency? What do you think of the patriotism of a man or a newspaper that would take those confidential studies and make them public to the enemies of this country?"

On April 17, 1942, Librarian of Congress Archibald MacLeish accused some publishers of treason without naming them. One publisher, MacLeish revealed, had told his staff that he intended to come "as close to treason as I dare." The American Society of Newspaper Editors was urged not to cross the line "where freedom of expression darkens into treason."

William Allen White, influential editor of the Emporia *Gazette,* called it a good speech, "but I wish he had named names—Coughlin, McCormick, Patterson, Pelley, et al."

"MacLeish," declared Colonel McCormick, "is a Communist." Conservative publishers called MacLeish's attack an attempt by the Roosevelt Administration to silence its critics.

Attorney General Francis Biddle urged the Senate Judiciary Committee to permit military censorship because "the most closely guarded military secrets of the government have come into the possession of newspapers and magazines and ultimately into the hands of agents of enemy governments." Among secret material leaked to Nazi Germany and Japan in this way, Biddle revealed, had been aircraft data, maps of Midway Island naval installations, Army codes, classified Navy communications, and photographs of Army camps and airfields.

The three McCormick family papers, undeterred even after Pearl Harbor, published a list of ships participating in the Coral Sea Battle against Japan. The dispatch carried a Washington dateline and quoted unnamed Navy officials as sources. The Administration angrily took the publishers to court for betraying military secrets to Japan.

Pleading not guilty, the Chicago *Tribune* admitted that their list had really been compiled in Chicago from a book on ships, with no information from the Navy. The case against the three papers was dismissed, but Congressman Holland called the two Pattersons "America's number-one and number-two exponents of the Nazi propaganda line . . . doing their best to bring about a Fascist victory." Radio Berlin sympathized with the McCormick-Patterson press as victims of "Roosevelt's dictatorship."

Some important industries were also unwilling to cooperate with the war effort. Most of Detroit's auto firms resisted the government's demands that they convert their production to defense needs. Standard Oil explained that its cartel agreement with I. G. Farben of Germany prevented its manufacture of synthetic rubber in the United States.

"This is treason!" Senator Harry S. Truman said angrily.

The War Production Board accused the Carnegie-Illinois Steel Corporation of refusing to fill government orders needed for shipbuilding while diverting iron and steel to favored customers for civilian use. President Roosevelt ordered the Navy to take over three plants of the Brewster Aero Company for refusing to cooperate with the government's aviation needs.

Diehard pro-Fascists continued their hate campaigns against the government even after Pearl Harbor.

In March, 1942, Edward Holton James, of Massachusetts, circulated a leaflet charging that the president had "plotted wars against nations which had done us no harm." He demanded Roosevelt's resignation and a peace bid to the Axis powers.

Awaiting trial for criminal libel, he declared, "I have no use whatever for this thing called democracy. . . . We should have storm troopers just like Hitler did. They must be brutal. . . . The only way to save America is for Hitler and Japan to smash us." He disseminated a series of *Grapevine Letters* urging the organization of seditious "Yankee Minute Men" groups.

"Of course I know the *Grapevine Letters* conflict with the law," he confided to John Roy Carlson. "And I know what it means if we're caught. But I'm within my constitutional rights in putting them out. It's the sedition laws which are unconstitutional." In January, 1943, he wrote a *Grapevine Letter* assailing President Roosevelt for provoking the war with Japan and in March declared, "He who resists the draft today, in the name of liberty, gains a place of honor by the side of the immortal heroes who founded this country."

Kurt Mertig, a Hamburg-American Line employee, continued to call meetings of the Citizens Protective League he had founded to promote the Fascist line. "This is nothing more than a Roosevelt war," he told followers one night. "All your money is being turned over to the Reds and the British." He blamed "the traitor congressmen and senators who passed the Lend-Lease Bill. They are traitors to America."

The meeting was also addressed by Mrs. Leonora Schuyler, an anti-Semitic superpatriot who had "revealed" that the Pope was Jewish when the Vatican had condemned Hitler. She defended Japan as "the only civilized nation in the Orient."

Mertig was ordered removed three hundred miles inland by the Army in 1942 under the Relocation Order allowing the secretary of war to exclude security risks from coastal regions.

Another war protester was Francis P. Moran, head of the New England Christian Front, who worked out of an office he claimed to use for "sociological research." His office was closed down by the FBI in November, 1942, and he was summoned before a Washington grand jury for writing in a leaflet: "Mr. Roosevelt has sent our citizens to their death. He is guilty of murder. . . . We advocate the refusal of all sincere and courageous American citizens to pay such taxes."

The war effort, said the president, "shall not be imperiled by a handful of noisy traitors . . . who in their hearts and souls have yielded to Hitlerism and would have this republic do likewise." But when the FBI arrested three men for "alleged seditious utterance," they were released by order of Attorney General Francis Biddle.

"At this time," Biddle explained, "every reasonable attempt should be made to maintain both free speech and public safety. . . . Freedom of speech should be curtailed only when public safety is directly imperiled." It was an interpretation of the "clear and present danger" concept which sought to protect the right of dissent. If a citizen could not depend upon his guaranteed rights under the Constitution, what was to distinguish American democracy from its foe, German fascism?

The released pro-Fascists jubilantly called an antiwar rally, stating in leaflets: "The US Attorney General says we have a PERFECT RIGHT to talk—AND WE WILL!"

Likewise, when the West Virginia State Board of Education sought to enforce a "patriotic" state law compelling school children to salute the American flag, Supreme Court Justice Robert H. Jackson wrote the majority opinion in 1943 *(West Virginia v. Bamette)* finding the state law in violation of both the First and Fourteenth Amendments.

"If there is one fixed star in our constitutional constellation," Jackson declared, "it is that no official, high or petty, can prescribe what shall be orthodox in politics, nationalism, religion or other matters of opinion, or force citizens to confess by word or act their faith therein."

The FBI tried to follow Biddle's guidelines in distinguishing disloyalty from dissent. It was not always easy.

The National Workers League was a Nazi-front organization seeking to erode morale among defense workers in vital war industries. It held rallies and flooded Detroit with pro-Fascist propaganda. Its secretary, Garland L. Alderman, wrote a letter published in the May, 1942, issue of *The American Mercury,* promising, "The peace will be negotiated by Hitler, Mussolini, the present Japanese government, and by Sir Oswald Mosley of England, and by patriotic Americans such as General Moseley, William Dudley Pelley, Father Coughlin, Colonel Lindbergh and Senator Nye."

Alderman managed to avoid indictment for sedition but made the mistake of leading a mob of twelve hundred people armed with knives, clubs, and guns against Negroes moving into a federal housing project. He was arrested for complicity in rioting.

Frank W. Clark, of Tacoma, a former lieutenant in Pelley's Silver Shirts, sought to build an underground army of pro-Fascist veterans armed with guns and knives. He used false names and letter drops to throw FBI agents off his trail.

"When the day comes to settle the score and I'm given a reward for my patriotism," Clark said, "I want to be made chief executioner of those guys who are now sticking up for democracy." He worked closely with socialite Mrs. Lois de Lafayette Washburn, who insisted that Japan was not really America's enemy but its ally, "helping us fight off the Jew and the Jewish capitalist system." Both Clark and Mrs. Washburn were arrested by the FBI for sedition on January 4, 1943.

In Utah, a religious fanatic and racist from South Africa, Ernest Hollings, headed the Christian party. Proclaiming Hitler "the Redeemer of the American Constitution," he called for reversing the war to ask Germany and Japan to send troops to the United States to help fight "American communism."

Ralph Townsend, a former consular official, was editor of *Scribner's Commentator,* which had been the voice of the America First Committee. Indicted for sedition, he fled, was caught, and confessed to being an unregistered paid propaganda agent for the Japanese. The magazine was shut down. Its publisher, Douglas Stewart, went on trial for perjury in a District of Columbia court in March, 1947.

Baron von Strempel testified that he had authorized Hans Thomsen, of the German embassy, to pay Stewart over ten thousand dollars to spread Nazi propaganda throughout the United

States. Thomsen's testimony confirmed this. The jury nevertheless acquitted Stewart, possibly because the Cold War was now raging.

One dramatic case of treason involved a twenty-two-year-old lens grinder named Herbert Haupt, son of a naturalized German inmigrant who was an ardent Nazi. Joining the German-American Bund and training weekends at a Nazi youth camp in Michigan, young Haupt enjoyed swaggering around in uniform. In 1941, to escape the draft, he fled to Germany.

In June, 1942, a German submarine put ashore two rubber boats on American beaches—one near Amagansett, Long Island, the other near Jacksonville, Florida. Each had a quartette of Nazi saboteurs with enough explosives to blow up bridges, tunnels, shipping locks, and defense plants. Herbert Haupt was part of the second squad.

One nervous saboteur lost his nerve and sought to save his skin by tipping off the FBI, making a full confession. Both squads were quickly rounded up before they could do any damage. Haupt was arrested at his parents' home in Chicago.

Five days later President Roosevelt appointed a secret military commission to hear the case. Haupt and the other seven defendants confessed, but their attorney argued that they had not committed a single act of sabotage and had not intended to. They had agreed to be Nazi agents, he claimed, only to escape from Germany and join friends and relatives in America.

"To accept the version of the defense, gentlemen," the judge advocate general told the eight officers on the commission, "is to conclude that the defendants came here not as invaders but as refugees." The verdict was life imprisonment for one defendant, thirty years for another, and death in the electric chair for Haupt and the others. They were executed at noon the same day and were buried in unmarked graves in Washington.

Haupt's father, Hans Max Haupt, was tried for "harboring an enemy of the United States." Convicted of treason, he was freed on appeal to the Supreme Court, which decided that the government had not proved his guilt fully enough to satisfy constitutional requirements. Ruled the Court: "The law of treason makes, and properly makes, conviction difficult, but not impossible."

The saboteur who had been sentenced to thirty years, a naturalized American named Anthony Cramer, also won his freedom on appeal because only one and not two witnesses, as required by the Constitution, had testified to his treason.

By eight months after Pearl Harbor, under the direction of Attorney General Biddle, Hoover's FBI had arrested and brought to trial a total of 9,405 Axis agents, both American- and foreign-born. One of the first sent to jail was Laura Ingalls, an aviatrix who had been an America First agitator. Found to be a paid but unregistered Nazi agent, she told the Court, "My motives were born of a burning patriotism and a high idealism. . . . I am a truer patriot than those who convicted me!"

Another American who sabotaged the war effort was Robert Jordan, Harlem's self-styled "black fuehrer." Employed as a sailor on a Japanese steamship line, he had organized the Ethiopian Pacific Movement, Inc., pledging its support to both Japan and Hitler. Embittered by American racism, he opposed fighting a war against Japanese "blood brothers of color."

"If American Negroes looked ahead," he declared, "they would fight for the interest of Japan, the leading dark nation." At street rallies in Harlem he promised that Japan would liberate the black man, and urged Negroes to organize a fifth column against the government. Indicted for sedition, he was sentenced to ten years in federal prison.

Early in 1942 a Nazi flier who was a prisoner of war in Canada escaped to Detroit with the aid of Max Stephan, a Detroit Nazi and America Firster. Charged with treason for supplying the escapee with money, clothing, and shelter, Stephan was sentenced to death.

John Eoghan Kelly, Christian Front organizer and promoter of Franco's brand of fascism in the United States, was indicted as a paid Franco agent in May, 1943, and convicted.

The Department of Justice indicted Mrs. Washburn, Frank W. Clark, Mrs. Leslie Fry, George Deatherage, and two others for sedition on January 4, 1943. Senator Nye, whose isolationism had led him into America First, declared, "They are no more guilty than I am." The charges against them, he insisted, were invalid because they were based upon the defendants' antiwar activity before Pearl Harbor.

Senator Robert A. Taft, of Ohio, agreed that the "indictments present a real danger to the continuance of freedom." McCormick's Chicago *Tribune* called the proceedings a "Moscow propaganda trial." The trials began on July 2 and continued through 1944. Five years after the first indictments, the Justice Department was still trying to collect enough evidence to convict them of wartime treason. In November, 1946, Chief Justice Bolitho L. Laws, of the Circuit Court of Appeals, finally ordered dismissal of the indictments against sedition defendants who had not yet been convicted.

The end of the war left an important category of obvious traitors still to be tried—those Americans who had been out of the reach of the Department of Justice because they had committed their treason from the lands of the enemy.

TWELVE

Day of Reckoning

Once the war was won, traitors who had been helping the enemy war effort from abroad were sought by the government. The most prominent were those who had broadcast Axis propaganda from Berlin, Rome, and Tokyo, seeking to demoralize American servicemen. They were often frustrated failures, misfits in their native land, who combined spite against the United States with enjoyment of power, comfort, and status in the service of the enemy.

Robert H. Best, an eccentric 220-pound southerner who dressed in high-laced boots and a Stetson, had been a foreign correspondent for the United Press in Vienna. He had stayed away from his own country so long, veteran correspondent William L. Shirer suggested in his book *Traitor,* that Best had lost touch with American thinking and been infected with the Nazi virus. When his dispatches became more propaganda than news, United Press ordered him home. Best procrastinated until he was fired for "insufficient work and performance."

After Pearl Harbor Best had been rounded up with over a hundred American correspondents and diplomats who were interned at Bad Nauheim. The Nazis quickly singled him out for preferred treatment, however, giving him comfortable quarters in a hotel and fine meals. When the internees were repatriated as a group in May, 1942, Best chose to stay behind.

He began broadcasting propaganda for Goebbels, exalting Hitler as "a crusader for civilization" and trying to persuade GIs preparing to invade Hitler's "Fortress Europe" that they were fighting the wrong enemy. Captured when American forces overran Germany, Best came to trial in Boston in 1948.

He testified that he had never meant to betray his countrymen, only to warn them against the dangers of "bolshevism, Jewry and Roosevelt's warmongering." Found guilty on all charges, he was sentenced to life imprisonment. He declared defiantly, "If I had to do it again, I would!"

One of the more astonishing traitors to be arraigned was the influential poet Ezra Pound. Idaho-born, the red-bearded eccentric, who wore long hair before it was fashionable and dressed in Byronic collar and long-flowing cape, was arrested in Genoa in the spring of 1945. Pound had lived as an expatriate in Italy. He had detested pre-Mussolini Communist disorders in the cities and admired the dictator as an apostle of law and order.

He had also been naively impressed by the racist views of a German economist, Silvio Gesell, that all a country's economic troubles were caused by "usurious interest rates extracted by Jewish money lenders." Over Radio Rome, Pound made prewar speeches urging Americans not to support any war against Mussolini or Hitler, because it was a "Jewish plot."

When Pearl Harbor was attacked, Pound sought to return home but found his request for aid in being repatriated coolly ignored. Enraged, he went on Radio Rome to denounce the war, praise "Hitler the martyr," and urge Americans to accept the Fuehrer and Mussolini as their true leaders.

After the war he was imprisoned in a Pisa detention camp, then flown to Washington in February, 1946. Found mentally unfit for trial, he was sequestered in St. Elizabeth's Hospital, Washington, DC, as insane. Many Americans who respected his poetic talents were deeply upset by this judgment, even though they deplored his treason and knew he could be executed for it.

"I believe he should be freed," Ernest Hemingway said in 1954, "to go and write poems in Italy, where he is loved and understood." He labeled Pound's treason "errors of judgment and pride."

Another celebrated postwar trial was that of "Axis Sally," whose real name was Mildred Gillars. Maine-born, she was an actress, singer, and radio announcer so spectacularly unsuccessful that she had subsisted on crackers and apples for months. In a desperate attempt to win publicity, she had faked a suicide attempt after first notifying the press.

Unable to "make it" in the United States by her twenty-eighth birthday, she had left for Europe to try her luck there. In Germany she had formed an attachment to Max Otto Koischwitz, a former naturalized American who had taught German literature at Hunter College. Mildred imbibed his anti-Semitic, anti-Roosevelt, anti-British theories, and he got her a job at the *Rundfunk* radio station as a broadcaster of news overseas.

As Axis Sally, her voice was soon familiar to GIs in England, who were preparing to invade occupied France. She sought to destroy their morale by describing vividly the horrible fate that awaited them. D-Day, she warned, stood for "doom, defeat, and death." When they were fighting bloodily on Omaha Beach, she taunted them with doubts about the fidelity of the wives and sweethearts they had left behind in America.

After Germany's defeat, Axis Sally sought to escape into the Russian zone of occupation but was captured and brought back to the District of Columbia for trial. She protested that she couldn't be tried for treason, because she had sworn an oath of allegiance to Nazi Germany, making her German. But she could produce no proof. The jury found her guilty, fined her ten thousand dollars, and imposed a sentence of from ten to thirty years.

Her counterpart in the Pacific, "Tokyo Rose," was actually not one woman but as many as twenty who assumed the role. Only one was an American citizen—Iva Ikuku Toguri, of Los Angeles, who had been educated at the University of California. She had been visiting a dying aunt in Japan in 1941 when war broke out. The Japanese had offered her repatriation in the fall of 1942, but she had refused to go.

News from the United States revealed that 110,000 Americans of Japanese ancestry were being evacuated from their homes on the West Coast and sent to relocation centers inland as security risks. The evacuation was being carried out under General John DeWitt, who had declared, "A Jap is a Jap and must be wiped off the map."

Outraged that Japanese-Americans were being deprived of their rights as citizens, with no charges of any kind being filed against them, simply because of their ancestry, Iva felt no desire to return to a concentration camp. She later claimed that she had asked the Japanese to intern her, but they had refused. Instead, in 1943 she had gone to work for Radio Tokyo, broadcasting to American GIs in the Pacific.

Like Axis Sally, her propaganda on the Tokyo Rose show was designed to make American soldiers discouraged, homesick, worried that their wives and girl friends back home were untrue to them, and fearful they would never get home alive. The bait used to lure GIs to listen was popular music.

Introducing records, she would say cheerfully, "Enjoy them while you can, because tomorrow at 0600 you're hitting Saipan . . .

and we're ready for you. So while you're alive let's enjoy. . . ." After the battle of Leyte Gulf she purred, "Orphans of the Pacific, you are really orphans now. With all your ships sunk, how will you get home?"

In 1945 Iva married a Portuguese-Japanese employee at the Domei Japanese News Agency, Felipe D'Aquino. When she was apprehended and tried in a Federal District Court in 1949, she pleaded that this marriage canceled her American citizenship, but Chief Judge Michael J. Roche ruled out the plea because she had made treasonous broadcasts before the marriage.

Found guilty, she was sentenced to a ten-thousand-dollar fine and ten years' imprisonment. Released after serving seven years, Iva fought payment of the fine, claiming she had been unfairly convicted because of anti-Japanese prejudice. She also alleged that she had been made a scapegoat by the Japanese government for some of the Radio Tokyo broadcasts made by other Tokyo Roses because she was the only American.

She was not without her defenders among Pacific veterans she supposedly had subverted during the war. The writer recalls listening to her one time in the jungles of New Guinea when a fellow GI said, "We ought to write Tokyo Rose a fan letter. She sure plays great music. Makes you homesick, all right, but it passes the time real nice. And that bunk she peddles is always good for laughs. Besides, with no women around, that sexy American voice is sure nice on the ears!"

If Iva had accepted repatriation during the war, she would undoubtedly have been compelled to join other Japanese-Americans herded in camps situated in arid sections of the West. Hastily constructed, these centers were surrounded by barbed-wire fences, armed guards, and night-time searchlights—in effect, prison compounds. Shortages of food and medical supplies touched off a riot at one center.

A 1944 Supreme Court decision *(Korematsu v. US)* had upheld the government's right to move the Japanese-Americans inland as a security measure, although dissenting Justices Roberts, Murphy, and Jackson called it unconstitutional. The War Relocation Authority was warned, however, that it could not detain any person whose loyalty had been established.

The War Department set up registration procedures to "clear" loyal Japanese-Americans so that they could leave the centers. Those seventeen or over were asked, "Will you swear unqualified allegiance to the United States of America . . . and forswear any form of allegiance or obedience to the Japanese Emperor?"

The question was an intolerable affront to thousands of American-born citizens of Japanese descent, who resented the slur on their loyalty. Some had fought in the American Army during World War I. Others were second- and third-generation Americans (Nisei and Sansei) with as little as one-sixteenth Japanese ancestry.

They knew that a similar oath was not being required of the Kamps, Deatherages, Kuhns, Vierecks, Pelleys, McWilliamses, Trues, and other pro-Fascists, some of them German-born and avowed Hitlerites, who were allowed at liberty. For that matter, why weren't all Americans with German and Italian ancestry *also* being herded into concentration camps as security risks and compelled to take loyalty oaths? The Japanese-Americans could see only one explanation—racial discrimination against Asians.

"I will not forgive this government of the United States as long as I live," vowed one outraged Japanese-American. "Does the Government think we are without pride?"

Some thirty-one thousand internees took the oath, but over six thousand flatly declared themselves disloyal in protest. Many of these were older Japanese-Americans who had been compelled to sell their homes, farms, and businesses in California at a heavy loss and now had nothing to go back to after a lifetime of hard work in the country of their adoption. Deciding to return to Japan after the war, they made it necessary for their respectful American-born sons and daughters to choose family loyalty over loyalty to country.

About three thousand refused to register for military service, torn with doubt or embittered by unfair treatment. "We are Americans, not dual citizens," argued one Nisei. "But if we are citizens in the first place, then why are we in these camps?"

In January, 1943, however, the War Department decided to accept volunteers from the camps for all-Nisei combat units. The Nisei resented the "opportunity" offered them to serve their country, not as other young Americans did, but in a segregated Nisei command. The reason, apparently, was to isolate them to control any possible sabotage or treason. Many Nisei, nevertheless, swallowed their pride and enlisted.

Their units proved among the bravest and best American troops in the war, achieving an outstanding war record that did much to erase anti-Japanese prejudice after the war.

Some Japanese-Americans who renounced their citizenship in anger cooled off after the war and sought to compel the government to restore their status. The War Department, they charged, had subjected them to unfair intimidation and coercion. In some cases citizenship was restored. In others no clearcut decisions were reached, leaving them, as one Nisei wryly described their status, "native American aliens."

Among genuine traitors the government caught up with after the war was Jane Anderson, of Georgia. A pro-Fascist newspaperwoman, she had covered the Spanish Civil War not only as a reporter but also as a spy for Franco. Caught by the Loyalists, she had been tried and sentenced to death but was saved by the intervention of the US State Department.

In Berlin when Pearl Harbor was struck, she was hired by the Nazis to make short-wave propaganda broadcasts to America four times weekly over the *Rundfunk* under the pseudonym of Lady Haw Haw. The name derived from the nickname for William Joyce, Lord Haw Haw, another American traitor broadcasting to England for the Nazis.

In April, 1942, Lady Haw Haw made a bad tactical blunder. Seeking to paint a rosy picture of life under Hitler even after years of war, she broadcast a description of delicious meals being served in Berlin's cabarets. America's OSS (Office of Strategic Services) decided that front-line Nazi soldiers on field rations and rationed Germans in the countryside would also enjoy hearing how well the German 4-F's and bureaucrats were eating and enjoying the war back in Berlin.

So they translated her English broadcast into German and re-broadcast it to Germany and Nazi battle areas. Goebbels, apoplectic with rage, threw Lady Haw Haw off the air as a fool. The Department of Justice had declared her a traitor, but after the war the indictment against her was dropped because her brief fiasco as a Nazi propagandist didn't seem sufficiently important to be worth prosecuting as treason.

Lord Haw Haw was another matter, but one which the British handled. Fifteen days after Britain and France went to war with Germany, English short-wave listeners began to hear him speaking in impeccable British tones from Berlin. He described every German victory ecstatically, praised the power of Hitler's air force, and warned the Allies to sue for peace at once or face certain doom.

The owner of the beautiful British voice was not a British subject but an undersized, ugly, awkward American named William Joyce. His father, Irish-born contractor Michael Joyce, was a naturalized American citizen whose son had been born in the United States in 1906. Three years later the family moved to Ireland. Influenced by his father's antipathy to the Irish independence movement, at fifteen William Joyce served as a spy for the British Black-and-Tans. The Joyce house was burned down.

In 1922, when Ireland won her freedom, the Joyces left for England, where William attended Birkbeck College for Working Men at London University.

After graduating, he sought to become a British Army officer but was rejected because of doubts about his citizenship and also because in both appearance and lineage he did not pass muster with the officer class of "gentlemen." He joined the Conservative party but found the same social rejection.

Bitterly convinced that England was in the "wrong hands," he turned to Sir Oswald Mosley's British Union of Fascists, dedicated to making England a dictatorship. Although he became Mosley's deputy and propaganda director, Joyce was stung when Mosley, too, refused to accept him as a social equal.

Breaking with Mosley, he founded his own National Socialist League, looking to German rather than British fascism. In 1939, as war with Germany loomed, Joyce applied for a British passport and left for Berlin, determined to help Hitler conquer the England that had snubbed him. When Britain declared war, Joyce joined the *Rundfunk* as Lord Haw Haw.

Several times daily he delivered Nazi-colored newscasts so skillfully that Germany decorated him for his services. In 1940 he was granted German nationality. D-Day came as a shock to him, crumbling his dreams of returning to England as a deputy fuehrer. As Hitler's empire collapsed, Joyce fled Berlin disguised as a German but was caught and flown to England to stand trial as a traitor on September 17,1945.

His lawyers decided to defend him on the ground that he was actually an American citizen by birth and therefore could not be tried as a British traitor. "It will be amusing to see if they get away with it," he said. The prosecution insisted that, American or not, Joyce had claimed and received the protection of a British citizen by applying for a British passport. He therefore owed allegiance to the Crown.

The jury agreed, and Joyce was hanged as a traitor on February 1, 1946. Ironically, had he sought an American passport to go to Germany from England, the British would not have been able to try him for treason. And since he had accepted German naturalization before America entered the war, he would also have been immune to American prosecution.

The American and British postwar trials for treason were models of restraint compared to the hunger for revenge that swept over countries that had been invaded and kept under the Fascist heel during the war. In 1946, the French, purging citizens who had turned collaborationist during the Nazi occupation, arrested half a million men and women on charges of treason. Holland had 130,000 such arrests; Belgium, 60,000.

In France many suspected traitors were given "street justice" by enraged mobs who shaved the heads of women who had associated with Nazi troops, and beat and shot male collaborators. Thousands were executed in mass trials.

In 1946 *Time* marveled at the strange phenomenon that had led hundreds of thousands of people to betray and seek to destroy the institutions under which they had lived. "In the twentieth century," *Time* observed, "treason has become a profession, and its modern form is the betrayal of ideas."

In the United States the discredited and battered Right thirsted for revenge against the liberals and the Left. Swiftly changing world events restored their influence in Congress, and the pursuit of treason on the Left was soon in full cry.

THIRTEEN

"Twenty Years of Treason"

Even before the war ended, it became apparent that there would be a postwar struggle between the Soviet Union and the West for spheres of influence in Europe and the Pacific. The question of which side would replace the power vacuum left by the downfall of fascism in Europe and Japanese imperialism in Asia resurrected the anti-Communist movement in the West.

All through the war, enthusiasm for the Russians had been considered not only respectable but patriotic. Thousands of American leaders of Congress, industry, labor, education, the arts, and the military, including General Douglas MacArthur, lauded the heroism of the Red Army and the Russian people. Even Joseph Stalin, despite the infamous Moscow trials and the blood of millions of anticollective kulaks on his hands, was hailed as a great wartime Allied leader.

American celebrities socialized extensively with Russians visiting or stationed in the United States. In Hollywood many movie stars attended parties given by Russian film producer Boris Moros, unaware that he was not only a spy for the Soviet Union but also a double spy for the FBI, reporting on stars suspected of being Communist-party members.

What had been patriotic and popular from December, 1941, through August, 1945, quickly became subversive after the war.

Americans who continued to express Soviet sympathies after March 12, 1947, when President Truman enunciated the Truman Doctrine to contain Russian expansionism, risked investigation for disloyalty.

A revived American Right began to attack the government once more, this time accusing it of harboring a Communist conspiracy that had brought about the downfall of Generalissimo Chiang Kai-shek by Mao Tse-tung. The architect of this "treason," the Right insisted, was Secretary of State Marshall.

During the war both Chiang's Nationalists and Mao's Red Army were ostensibly allied forces fighting, with American aid, against Japan. But American General Joseph ("Vinegar Joe") Stilwell, in charge of American forces in Southeast Asia, had reported angrily that while Mao's forces fought superbly against the Japanese, Chiang's army was inactive and corrupt, using American aid only to enrich themselves and fight Mao's guerrilla forces. Asian experts in the State Department, after investigation, recommended that Chiang's aid be cut.

In 1949 Chiang's forces were overthrown by Mao's Red troops, mostly with arms captured from the Japanese and in battles with the Nationalists. Chiang withdrew to the island of Formosa. Still subsidized by extensive American aid, he paid for a "China Lobby" to agitate Congress in his behalf against mainland China under Mao. Pressure by the Pentagon silenced General Stilwell upon his return, so that he could not tell the press the truth about Chiang.

The China Lobby cooperated with American rightists in seeking to pin a label of treason on all who had opposed or criticized Chiang. John Stewart Service, an anti-Chiang State Department official who had served in China during the war, was arrested in 1945 under the Espionage Act. He was accused of revealing to

Philip Jaffe, editor of *Amerasia,* an American magazine critical of Chiang, classified information submitted to the State Department on the Chinese situation. A Washington grand jury voted unanimously against his indictment.

However, Jaffe and two other Asian experts were indicted and fined for "illegal possession of government documents." The New York *Herald Tribune* observed, "The State Department's action in calling in the FBI and bringing about arrests which resulted in headlines concerning 'spies' and 'espionage' was an extreme action."

A Senate subcommittee investigation headed by Senator Millard Tydings reported, "We have considered the evidence and concluded that John Stewart Service is neither a disloyal person, a pro-Communist, nor a bad security risk." But in December, 1951, with McCarthyism raging, a Presidential Loyalty Review Board found "reasonable doubt as to his loyalty," and Service was dismissed.

During the late summer of 1945, Igor Gouzenko, a twenty-six-year-old Russian cipher clerk with the Soviet embassy in Canada, decided to defect. He took with him files documenting a Russian spy ring in the West. As a result of his disclosures, twenty persons were arrested and eleven sent to prison.

The most important contact Gouzenko named was Dr. Allan Nunn May, British nuclear physicist, who had provided the Russian military-espionage apparatus, GRU, with a steady stream of nuclear information after the first atomic bomb was dropped on Japan. May, who had strong Communist sympathies, felt that the Soviet Union was entitled, as a war ally, to share in Allied nuclear research for its own protection. An even balance of nuclear power, he believed, would preserve world peace after the war by keeping the West from threatening nuclear warfare against the Soviet Union.

Placed on trial, May admitted his treason, explaining, "I only embarked on it because I felt this was a contribution I could make to the safety of mankind. I certainly did not do it for gain." Found guilty of communicating information that might be useful to an enemy, he was sentenced on May 1, 1946, to ten years in prison. He served six of them.

Gouzenko's exposure of a spy ring heightened the Red scare in the United States. Politicians began seeking subversives in every aspect of American life—schools, Hollywood, the universities, government, the Army, labor unions. Americans who had been anti-Fascist before the war, cooperating with the Soviet Union as a war ally, now found themselves smeared indiscriminately as "Commie traitors."

In 1945 Representative John E. Rankin, of Mississippi, whom *Newsweek* called "a militant racist and anti-Semite," took over the chairmanship of the old Dies (HUAC) Committee. He won headlines with a Red probe of Hollywood involving top stars. Full credit for the investigation was claimed by Gerald L. K. Smith, described in 1948 by the Illinois American Legion as "probably the most vicious of the rabble-rousing and sensational hate-mongers operating today."

Eight years later when Smith sought to campaign for Nixon, he was told, "There is no place in the Republican party for the race-baiting merchandisers of hate like Gerald L. K. Smith."

During the next two years Rankin, aided by New Jersey Representative J. Parnell Thomas, used HUAC to mount political attacks against American liberalism. They ran the committee as a kind of public court-martial, branding prominent Americans as traitors without giving them the right to cross-examine accusers and paid informers.

In 1946, when OPA Administrator Chester Bowles announced a price ceiling for the 1946 cotton crop, Rankin denounced him as a Communist. HUAC's chairman called the Fair Employment Practices Committee "the beginning of a Communistic dictatorship the like of which America never dreamed."

The postwar rise of the extreme Right in the United States was helped by Stalin's intransigence in retaining control of East Europe behind what Churchill labeled an Iron Curtain. When Secretary of Commerce Henry Wallace criticized the Cold War drift of American foreign policy under Secretary of State James Byrnes, President Truman requested Wallace's resignation, indicating that anticommunism was now the order of the day.

But Truman's new hard line toward the Left did not placate the Right, which now attacked the Democratic Administration as having been "soft on Communism" and "riddled with traitors." In the elections of November, 1946, they won control of both houses of Congress. Rankin demanded that a commission be set up to probe and fire every government employee whose loyalty was "found to be in doubt."

In March, 1947, to placate the Republican Congress, Truman issued a Loyalty Order subjecting two million federal employees to a purge of suspected Communists or fellow travelers, at a cost of twenty-five million dollars. That same year, ironically, in a congressional study called *Fascism in Action,* Representative Wright Patman, of Texas, found the real danger to American security still the threat of the extreme Right:

> We are forced to admit that fascism is today an ever-present danger to our democracy. . . . $100,000,000 per year is donated to propaganda organizations, some of which show very definite fascist tendencies. . . . Many persons feel that all

agreements between American firms and foreign firms should be made public. This would automatically expose attempts of foreign fascists to work through American sympathizers.

He quoted Dr. Douglas M. Kelley, a noted psychiatrist who had attended the Nuremberg Trials of Nazi defendants:

> We can find the same ideas thinly veiled in our public press today. Even worse, we find some of our top political men, members of our highest governing bodies, making statements which would do credit to Rosenberg, Hitler, or Goebbels. . . . I am convinced that there is little in America today which could prevent the establishment of a Nazilike state.

But HUAC and the loyalty probe operated solely on the premise of the "Red Menace." Under Truman's Loyalty Order, 570 civil-service employees were fired and 2,478 forced to resign. In the first two years of the Eisenhower Administration, with Senator Joseph McCarthy leading the witch-hunt, over 8,000 more government employees left public service.

The loyalty probes extended everywhere—into the armed forces, universities with government research grants, plants with defense contracts. On the most dubious circumstantial evidence —often "guilt by association" or on the word of paid informers with prison records—thousands of Americans were forced out of their jobs under a cloud of suspicion about their loyalty. Many were State Department officials who had been identified with our wartime pro-Soviet policy.

When one federal employee challenged the legality of his dismissal, the Supreme Court refused to overturn a lower court verdict against him, in effect upholding the constitutionality of Truman's Loyalty Order *(Friedman v. Schwellenbach,* 1947).

In October, 1947, Thomas initiated a new probe into Communist infiltration in Hollywood, guaranteeing front-page headlines for HUAC. Proceedings were halted to allow testifying right-wing stars such as Adolph Menjou, Gary Cooper, George Murphy, and Ronald Reagan to pose for movie, TV, and newspaper cameras. One of HUAC's committeemen was Richard M. Nixon, a new, young Republican representative from California.

Writers labeled Communists in the hearings sought to appear before HUAC to defend themselves against charges made against them, but were not allowed to make statements. Film writer Dalton Trumbo pointed out that Gerald L. K. Smith had been allowed to make a statement.

"That statement is out of order," Thomas snapped.

Several indignant writers who refused to be silenced were removed forcibly from the hearing. As he was dragged off, Trumbo shouted, "This is the beginning . . . of American concentration camps!" The mother of film star Ginger Rogers had testified earlier that Ginger had refused to speak the "subversive" line of a Trumbo script in a wartime film: "Share and share alike—that's democracy."

"The most un-American activity in the United States today," said a Detroit *Free Press* editorial, "is the conduct of the congressional committee on un-American activities."

"Neither Mr. Thomas nor the Congress," reminded the Republican New York *Herald Tribune,* "is empowered to dictate what Americans shall think." Under the pressure of intense press criticism, Thomas reluctantly let the next Hollywood writer testifying make a statement.

Albert Maltz accused HUAC of not permitting persons named as Communists to cross-examine witnesses who made the charges. Denouncing HUAC's bias, he cited a statement Thomas had made linking the New Deal with the Communist party and describing the Ku Klux Klan as "an acceptable American institution." He wound up with scornful defiance:

> If I were a spokesman for General Franco, I would not be here today. I would rather be here. I would rather die than be a shabby American, groveling before men whose names are Thomas and Rankin, but who now carry out activities in America like those carried out in Germany by Goebbels and Himmler.

Some of the hostile Hollywood witnesses were known Communists or former Communists; some were fellow travelers; some were simply liberals. But all argued that it was unconstitutional to compel them to reveal their political affiliations or beliefs, past or present. Ten refused on principle.

Maltz reminded HUAC of Thomas Jefferson's declaration that all Americans had the right to hold and maintain whatever opinion they chose—"which shall never be a crime in my view; nor bring injury to an individual."

Famous novelist Thomas Mann, a refugee from Nazi Germany, warned in November, 1947, against political inquisitions under the pretext of anticommunism: "That is how it started in Germany. What followed was fascism, and what followed fascism was war." But that month Thomas won citations for contempt of Congress against the "Unfriendly Ten" writers.

The Motion Picture Association of America held a secret meeting in New York at which producers agreed to fire the Ten and blacklist them from further employment. Sued by the writers, five years later four major studios made out-of-court settlements of $107,500 for breach of contract, conspiracy to blacklist, and damages for loss of employment.

On December 7, 1947, the Ten were tried on contempt charges. Five received the maximum sentence, a year in jail and a one-thousand-dollar fine; two got six months in jail and a five-hundred-dollar fine. Ironically, HUAC's chairman went to jail before any of them did. In 1948 Drew Pearson revealed that J. Parnell Thomas had put his relatives on the public payroll, accepting kickbacks for this nepotism. He was tried and sentenced to up to eighteen months in the Federal Correctional Institution at Danbury.

The Red hunt went on under other leaders, with little or no protection for the rights of persons whose reputations were impugned. After the press was given the names of 110 teachers summoned to appear before HUAC for interrogation, the hearings were never held, leaving the named teachers under a cloud of suspicion. Accusations were made on the basis of paid informers such as Manning Johnson, who had admitted publicly that he would commit perjury "a thousand times over" for the FBI.

Witnesses frightened by HUAC into incriminating others were praised as patriotic. Some former Communists, disillusioned with the party, turned informer for HUAC and the FBI, naming government officials they accused of being involved in a Soviet espionage system.

Connecticut-born Elizabeth Bentley, who drifted into the Communist party out of hatred for fascism in the 1930s, became the mistress of Jacob Golos, head of World Tourists, Inc., a front for Soviet espionage operations. When Golos died in 1943, Miss

Bentley continued to act as courier between American spies and NKVD (Soviet secret police) agents.

Growing disenchanted with the party as a Moscow puppet, she went to the FBI, in August, 1945. Two years later, having continued in the party as an FBI, operative, she testified before a New York grand jury that she had collected party dues from secret party members working for the Office of Strategic Services, the Department of Commerce, the Air Corps, and the Treasury.

HUAC sought fresh headlines by summoning Miss Bentley to testify before the committee. She named a number of government officials as Communist-party members. Nathan Gregory Silvermaster, an Agriculture Department official during the war, was labeled a spymaster whose influence with Lauchlin Currie, a Roosevelt adviser, had enabled him to place Communists in government jobs. Silvermaster called Miss Bentley a "neurotic liar," branding her charges "false and fantastic."

He exercised his right under the Fifth Amendment to refuse to answer questions that might tend to incriminate him.

Miss Bentley accused Harry Dexter White, assistant secretary of the treasury and author of the Morgenthau Plan, of giving Silvermaster classified information for the NKVD, relayed through her. White, ailing in health, accused HUAC of star-chamber proceedings (secret, unfair trials); he died shortly afterward of a heart attack.

Lauchlin Currie admitted having known Silvermaster and others accused by Miss Bentley but denied involvement with anyone he knew to be a Communist.

Another government witness, Whittaker Chambers, senior editor of *Time* and a former Communist, named Alger Hiss as a member of a prewar Communist apparatus in Washington. Hiss was a high-echelon official in the State Department, an ardent New Dealer, and adviser to President Roosevelt at Yalta. He had been made secretary general of the UN Organization at San Francisco under Truman and had become director of the Carnegie Foundation for Peace. Chambers's accusation created an uproar, and the issue quickly became a political one.

Administration supporters, believing in Hiss's innocence, lined up against New Deal haters, who saw in the Hiss case powerful proof of their charge that it had harbored Communists.

Philadelphia-born Chambers had drifted into the Communist party in 1925, convinced that Lenin had the right idea about gaining power to build a just society. He had worked as an editor for the *Daily Worker* and the *New Masses.* In 1932, he was told by a Russian agent that he had been selected for underground work, and was used as a courier of secret messages.

In 1934, J. Peters, Russian head of the underground in the United States, had introduced Chambers as "Carl" to Harold Ware in Washington. An adviser to the Department of Agriculture, Ware, like Peters, was a Comintern agent. His job was to organize important American Communists in the government into a Red cell under his control. One secret member of the Ware group, Chambers alleged, was Alger Hiss.

Hiss, who had once been secretary to Supreme Court Justice Oliver Wendell Holmes, had joined the Socialist party during the Depression years. He had gone to Washington to join other bright young Harvard lawyers working for the New Deal at the urging of his friend Lee Pressman, a lawyer with the AAA (Agricultural Adjustment Administration). His brilliance was quickly recognized, and his career began to soar.

What happened subsequently was a matter of controversy. According to Chambers's testimony, Hiss was brought into the Ware group through Pressman but did not attend gatherings to avoid suspicion. He received his orders from the Comintern through Chambers, who would give him State Department documents to microfilm for transmission to Moscow.

In May, 1939, shaken by the Moscow trials and having broken with the Communist party, Chambers decided to expose the Ware ring. He confided in anti-Communist writer Isaac Don Levine, who brought him to Assistant Secretary of State Adolf Berle. Berle had promised to investigate the matter, Chambers testified, but nothing had been done.

Berle later contradicted Chambers. "This was not, as he put it, any question of espionage," Berle testified. "There was no espionage involved in it. He stated that . . . a study group of some sort had been formed. . . . He did not make the direct statement that any of these men were members of the Communist party." Chambers was also shown to have given perjured and contradictory testimony.

There was reluctance to believe the word of a self-confessed former Red spy and informer against highly respected American officials, even after Chambers gave his testimony before HUAC. On August 5, 1948, Hiss voluntarily appeared before HUAC to deny every word of Chambers's allegations, stating that he had never even heard of Chambers until the previous year when the FBI had asked whether he knew him.

Representative Richard Nixon was not satisfied, however, and insisted on additional HUAC hearings at which he was an active interrogator. He believed Chambers's story. Democrats accused Nixon of persecuting Hiss in order to advance his political career with Red-baiting headlines, a technique that had won him election to Congress over Helen Gahagan Douglas.

President Truman contemptuously dismissed Chambers's charges of a Red plot against America among highly placed government officials as a "red herring," pressed by HUAC as a political issue for the forthcoming 1948 elections.

In subsequent hearings it developed that Hiss had known Chambers but under another name. As each man testified in turn, their stories clashed constantly. Someone was obviously lying. In a dramatic face-to-face confrontation, Hiss finally challenged Chambers to repeat his story outside the hearing room so that he could be sued for libel. Chambers, after some hesitation, did so, and Hiss sued.

On new evidence produced by Chambers to support his story, HUAC reconvened a grand jury, which indicted Hiss for perjury under oath before the committee. At the trial Chambers produced purloined State Department papers and microfilm he claimed to have obtained from Hiss. He had hidden them in a hollowed-out pumpkin on his farm, he had explained, and had forgotten about them. Hiss denied that he had been the one to give Chambers what were now famous as "the Pumpkin Papers."

The FBI located an old 1938 Woodstock typewriter, once owned by Mrs. Hiss, on which some of the stolen documents had apparently been copied. The defense held that the typewriter had been given away by the Hisses before the purloined documents had been copied on it, and that some documents had been stolen from Hiss's office. Hiss's attorney labeled the whole case a political stunt to hurt the Democrats.

The baffled jury could not agree on a verdict after five tries, and the case had to be tried again. By that time Chambers had dug up new witnesses, and so had Hiss. Nineteen character witnesses took the stand to vouch for Hiss's loyalty, veracity, and integrity. Hiss's lawyers introduced psychiatrists who testified that Chambers was "a psychopathic personality" whose symptoms were evidenced in repetitive lying, withholding the truth, and pathological accusations.

But the prosecution produced Republican Senator John Foster Dulles, who had helped make Hiss president of the Carnegie Endowment Fund. Dulles contradicted five different statements Hiss had made at the trial. Other witnesses backed up Chambers's testimony. The jury found Hiss guilty, and on January 25, 1950, he was sentenced to five years' imprisonment.

Secretary of State Dean Acheson, commenting on the case, declared, "I will not turn my back on Alger Hiss." Republicans charged that this proved that the Democrats were "the Party of Treason."

Nixon, who had played a leading role in the investigation and prosecution of Hiss, declared, "I think the entire Truman Administration was extremely anxious that nothing bad happen to Mr. Hiss. Members of the Administration feared that an adverse verdict would prove that there was a great deal of foundation to all the reports of Communist infiltration into the Government during the New Deal days."

Years later he said, "Looking back, I suppose the great lesson of the Hiss case is the personal tragedies involved for both Hiss and Chambers. . . . Both were, I think, sincerely dedicated to the concepts of peace and the concept of bettering the lot of the common man, of people generally. They were both idealists. Yet, here are two men of this quality who became infected with Communism . . . willing to run the risk, as they did, of disgrace in order to serve the Communist conspiracy."

Nixon's success in putting Hiss behind bars catapulted him into national prominence. He won the Republican nomination for vice president in 1952 under Eisenhower, who introduced him to the National Convention as "a man who has shown . . .

an ability to ferret out any kind of subversive influence wherever it may be found, and the strength and persistence to get rid of it." Nixon campaigned warning that a Democratic victory would bring "more Alger Hisses, more atomic spies," and attacked the Democratic candidate, Adlai Stevenson, for having been a character witness for Hiss.

Alger Hiss served forty-four months at the federal prison in Lewisburg, Pennsylvania. Released, he went quietly to work in New York as an office-supply salesman for a stationery company. He continued to assert his innocence and his belief that his name would eventually be cleared. Whittaker Chambers died in July, 1961, a bitter, enigmatic figure to the end.

The Hiss-Chambers case was only the beginning of a Republican attack on Democratic liberalism for what Senator Joseph McCarthy began calling "twenty years of treason."

FOURTEEN

Climate of Fear

The mounting tensions of the Cold War, inflamed by the testimony of former Communists like Chambers and Elizabeth Bentley, led to the indictment of eleven top leaders of the Communist party in January, 1949, on charges of violating the Smith Act by conspiring to teach the overthrow of the government.

The nine-month trial was a stormy one. In violent outbursts, the defendants accused Judge Harold Medina of "railroading" them to prison on government orders. All were convicted and ten received five-year jail sentences.

The extreme Right was well-pleased with the new political climate in which treason was now found only on the Left. In 1948, Allen Anderson Zoll set up the National Council for American Education, dedicated to censoring "subversive" textbooks and demanding loyalty oaths from school and university faculties. Once described by Senator Estes Kefauver as "a notorious hatemonger," Zoll had formerly headed the American Patriots, cited as Fascist by former Attorney General Biddle.

Zoll's council worked closely with HUAC in mounting an investigation of "academic treason." The fallout produced the 1949 New York State Fineberg Law, and similar laws in other states, requiring the firing of any teachers who uttered "treasonable" or "subversive" words. "Is it all right," one teacher asked, "to quote the Declaration of Independence?"

The National Education Association found that by July, 1949, twenty-two states were requiring loyalty oaths, and a dozen states had fired teachers for "disloyalty—undefined." When J. B. Matthews, HUAC's chief investigator, left the committee, he took with him a suspect list of three thousand teachers, one thousand clergymen, and half a million other Americans, which he turned over to Republican Senator Joseph McCarthy, of Wisconsin.

McCarthy, ex-chicken farmer, ex-Marine, and part-time lawyer, was an unpleasantly aggressive but effective demagogue looking for a headline-winning crusade that would advance his political fortunes. He stumbled upon it in a speech he made on the Hiss case at Wheeling, West Virginia, in February, 1950.

"In my opinion," he declared, "the State Department . . . is thoroughly infested with Communists. . . . The Secretary of State proclaimed his loyalty to a man guilty of what has always been considered as the most abominable of crimes—of being a traitor. . . . It awakened the dormant indignation of the American people."

When he found his attack widely quoted, McCarthy began wildly attacking all Democratic leaders, accusing them of "twenty years of treason." He called President Truman "a . . . who ought to be impeached." He made a practice of holding up a piece of paper dramatically for news photographers, intoning, "I have in my hand a list of two hundred and five names that were known to the Secretary of State as being members of the Communist party and who are still working and shaping policy in the State Department."

He never showed the list and often cited a different number of names. Senator Millard Tydings, of Maryland, summoned

McCarthy before a Senate subcommittee and demanded that he reveal his list. McCarthy stalled, then finally submitted a list that had abruptly shrunk from 205 to 4 names. And he no longer charged that they were "Communists" or "card-carrying Commies," but simply "pro-Communist." Only two worked for the State Department. Next day he offered four more names, but only one was a State Department employee.

Senator William Benton accused McCarthy of having "borne false witness and deliberately and repeatedly corrupted facts." McCarthy countered with a libel suit, meanwhile continuing his campaign of character assassination and smear by innuendo that gave rise to a new term for irresponsible accusations against innocent people—"McCarthyism."

Describing the McCarthy inquisition, Gustavus Myers wrote in *The History of Bigotry in the United States:*

> McCarthy himself was to insult and defame Presidents Truman and Eisenhower, Cabinet officers, generals, ambassadors, fellow Senators and Americans from every walk of life. Nor was the extent of the witch hunt restricted merely to the activities of Senator McCarthy. A spirit of fear and dread blanketed the nation, and everywhere "little McCarthys" sprang up to accuse, threaten and terrorize their fellow countrymen.

Even the man General Eisenhower had called the greatest American of his century, General George Marshall, commander of the US Army in World War II and secretary of state under Truman, was described by McCarthy as part of a "conspiracy so immense and an infamy so black as to dwarf any previous such venture in the history of man."

McCarthy found no treason on the extreme Right, where American Fascists flourished in the anti-Communist hysteria he whipped up for them. The anti-Communist Korean War provided the emotional climate in which his attacks thrived.

Harvey Matusow, a professional Red-hunter for McCarthy, described how they mounted a headline-winning crusade against "subversive" books:

> McCarthy's plan was simple and also dramatic: take a book, show that a Communist sold it to a Communist in a Communist bookstore, or a bookstore located in a school declared Communist by the Attorney General . . . and in that way convince all who were watching the TV show that the sale of such books was one of the reasons that 500,000,000 Chinese were now living under a Communist Government.

As a result of McCarthy's crusade, US information libraries overseas were ordered to remove books that did not meet with his approval. In Indiana, a lady member of the State Textbook Commission demanded the banning of all books about Quakers as Communist because "they don't believe in fighting wars." She also sought to ban Robin Hood, explaining, "There is a Communist directive in education now to stress the story of Robin Hood. They want to stress it because he robbed the rich and gave to the poor."

The Rockhill (South Carolina) *Herald* gleefully suggested that undoubtedly the real name of the folk hero of Sherwood Forest had been "Robinoff Hoodski." The present-day Sheriff of Nottingham, England, observed derisively, "Robin Hood was no Communist. She's undoubtedly thinking of Little Red Riding Hood."

As head of the powerful Permanent Senate Subcommittee on Investigations, McCarthy played to the TV cameras and made headlines in right-wing papers by denouncing as "Comsymps" (Communist sympathizers) leading Democrats, Republicans, and Protestant clergymen who advocated peace, civil rights, or social reform. His greatest support came from the least-educated Americans, who believed his slander of even the mildest liberals as "treasonous agents of Moscow." A Gallup poll showed a majority of Americans supporting his crusade.

Professor Owen Lattimore, of Johns Hopkins University, was named by McCarthy as America's "top Russian agent," responsible for withdrawal of support from Chiang Kai-shek and so "turning over China to the Reds." This interpretation was peddled by the China Lobby—heavily financed by millionaire Alfred C. Kohlberg, an importer who had made a fortune out of Nationalist China—which wanted to influence American financial and military aid for Chiang. The China Lobby also worked through Joseph P. Kamp's Constitutional Educational League, which had been named in the mass sedition indictments of 1942 and 1943.

McCarthy made his accusation against Lattimore on the floor of the Senate, where he could not be sued for libel. He produced another former Communist turned informer, Louis Budenz, who gave hearsay testimony (inadmissible in any court of law) that he had been told by other Communists that Lattimore was a party member. Under later questioning, Budenz admitted having previously discussed Lattimore with Alfred Kohlberg.

McCarthy refused to allow Lattimore's lawyers to introduce in evidence an affidavit from Bella V. Dodd, a former leading Communist expelled from the party, that she had never once heard Lattimore's name mentioned. A Senate Foreign Relations subcommittee investigated and cleared Lattimore.

"We find no evidence to support the charge that Owen Lattimore is the 'top Russian spy' or, for that matter, any sort of spy," the report said; adding, "The Lattimore case affords an opportunity to reaffirm this nation's determination to protect its citizens when they . . . express freely their honest views and convictions."

In his book, *Ordeal by Slander,* Lattimore declared,

> The witch-hunting of which McCarthy is a part is recruited from ex-Communists and pro-Fascists, America Firsters, anti-Semites, Coughlinites and similar fringe fanatics of the political underworld. It was groups like these that Hitler used to run interference for him, causing the confusion and dismay that he and his real backers, the big-time reactionaries, needed in order to take over the state.

That McCarthy was a demagogue did not change the fact that some Americans had, or were still, engaged in treason for the Soviet Union. But these individuals were more likely to be under the professional observation of FBI operatives than McCarthy's headline-hunters. J. Edgar Hoover noted that the genuine traitors were usually only a handful of party members, carefully and secretly selected by Moscow. Some had been compelled to spy because of threats to relatives in Russia; most served the Soviet Union for ideological reasons.

All of Moscow's American agents were made to sign incriminating papers and reports. "If the initial ideological enthusiasm wears off, as it probably will," Hoover explained, "the agent is trapped . . . he cannot break away."

Soviet spy Colonel Rudolph Abel operated for over seven years as chief of an espionage ring before he was caught. Typical of his American contacts were Manhattan teacher Morris Cohen and his Polish wife, Lola. Seven forged passports under a variety of names took them to different countries as Soviet agents. A CIA tip to Scotland Yard brought about their arrest in England under the name of Kroger. Their suburban house was found full of espionage gadgets, a high-frequency transmitter, and micro-dot equipment to transmit British naval data. Each received twenty years in prison.

In March, 1950, a former Justice Department employee, Judith Coplon, and her sweetheart, Valentin Gubichev, a Soviet consular official, were indicted for conspiracy and attempted espionage. She was found guilty of copying FBI reports on espionage and turning them over to Gubichev. He was expelled; Miss Coplon's conviction was set aside because of the illegal use of wiretapping evidence against her.

One of the most sensational series of espionage cases developed out of the arrest in Britain of physicist Klaus Fuchs, a German refugee who supplied information about American and British nuclear weapons to the Soviet Union. His data helped Moscow produce their own A-bomb some months earlier than they would have developed it on their own.

Ordered to the United States with other British physicists to work with American scientists during the war, he had relayed atomic data to Moscow through Harry Gold, a naturalized American of Russian parentage. Returning to England after the war, Fuchs continued to turn over atomic data to Russian agents but now accepted payment from them. In 1949, he was arrested by British security agents, tried, and sentenced to fourteen years in prison.

His confession implicated Harry Gold, who had been serving the Soviet Union as an industrial spy in America for fifteen years. Gold was a spy not because he was a Communist but primarily because he enjoyed espionage and liked inventing romantic lies about himself. He confessed his treason to the FBI and promptly sought to win a lighter sentence by turning government witness against others he named.

Chief figures of the spy ring, Gold said, were Ethel and Julius Rosenberg, a radical New York couple. Ethel's young brother, David Greenglass, was employed as a machinist in the atom-bomb project at Los Alamos, New Mexico. Gold alleged that Greenglass had been persuaded by the Rosenbergs to turn over A-bomb secrets to a spy courier who would be sent to him by a Soviet consular clerk. Gold was the courier.

Greenglass and the Rosenbergs were arrested by the FBI. Turning state's witness, Greenglass testified against his sister and her husband. Largely on his testimony and Gold's, the Rosenbergs were found guilty and sentenced to be electrocuted.

"I consider your crime," Judge Irving Kaufman told them, "worse than murder. . . . I believe your conduct in putting into the hands of the Russians the A-bomb . . . has already caused, in my opinion, the Communist aggression in Korea, with the resulting casualties exceeding fifty thousand and who knows but that millions more of innocent people may pay the price of your treason."

The case created a storm of controversy among millions who considered the Rosenbergs innocent. Some atomic scientists stated that the American public had been misled into believing in atomic "secrets," whereas the scientists of any major power could build an A-bomb exactly as the American physicists had done without any outside help.

Liberals worried that the Rosenbergs had been victims of a frame-up because of their radicalism in a Cold War climate of fear and hysteria. Doubts were raised over the testimony of

Gold, who was a self-confessed imaginative liar, even under oath. Some critics were convinced that he had offered perjured evidence, full of holes and contradictions, in return for a promise of leniency in his own prosecution.

David Greenglass was also suspected of having been coached in the story he told, sacrificing his sister and her husband in a desperate attempt to save his own skin and spare his wife from prosecution. Throughout the trial the Rosenbergs steadfastly maintained their innocence, despite clear hints by the prosecution that they could avoid the death penalty by admitting guilt.

"Free the Rosenbergs" committees formed in London, Paris, Rome, Vienna, Copenhagen, and other cities. Appeals for clemency flooded into the White House from all over the world, including the Vatican. Even those who believed the Rosenbergs guilty felt that the death penalty had been too severe. But President Eisenhower refused to halt the execution.

As the hour of electrocution drew near, crowds gathered in dozens of major cities around the world to hold public prayer vigils for the Rosenbergs. In Paris, the American embassy, fearful of huge crowds gathering in the Place de la Concorde, called for protection. The embassy was surrounded by French troops armed with machine guns and tear gas.

The Rosenbergs died at Sing Sing on June 19, 1953, protesting their innocence to the last. Several subsequent investigations reached the conclusion that their guilt had not been proved; but that guilty or innocent, they had died as victims of political persecution.

Joseph P. Morray, visiting professor of law at Berkeley, raised some thoughtful questions: "What is the reason for our fury against Hiss, the Rosenbergs, Fuchs . . . ? Is it because they have refused to share with us a hatred for the Soviet Union? These people did wrong in violating the laws of their states. But the laws themselves and we who support and enforce them are not blameless. . . . We ought therefore to enforce them reluctantly and seek to avoid punishing acts done in good conscience."

When one of those laws, the Smith Act of 1946, was challenged in *Dennis et al v. United States,* the Supreme Court upheld the act in 1951. Justice Hugo Black dissented, stating that the Smith Act violated the First Amendment. He called for a return to Justice Holmes's "clear and present danger" doctrine before advocacy of revolution could be punished.

Justice William O. Douglas agreed, finding that the teaching of "Marxist-Leninist doctrine" was not necessarily "conspiracy to overthrow" the government. Justice Robert Jackson also suggested that Communists represented little threat to any stable government: "The Communist recognizes that an established government in control of modern technology cannot be overthrown by force until it is about ready to fall of its own weight."

Nevada senator Pat McCarran, chairman of the Senate Judiciary Committee, originated much of the "antitreason" legislation. In September, 1950, his McCarran Act required the registration of Communist and "Communist-front" organizations and the internment of Communists during a "national emergency" in six concentration camps with a capacity of 100,000 persons.

President Truman vetoed the bill, declaring: "The application of the registration requirements to so-called Communist-front organizations can be the greatest danger to freedom of speech, press and assembly since the Alien and Sedition laws of 1789." The bill was passed over his veto.

"It is enough to make Jefferson and Madison and Lincoln rise from their graves," declared the Pulitzer Prize–winning St.

Louis *Post Dispatch.* Added the *Christian Century,* "Jefferson would have gone to jail."

In June, 1952, the McCarran-Walter Act changed US immigration laws to screen out "subversives" and provide for deportation of immigrants and naturalized citizens for Communist and "Communist-front" affiliations.

McCarran, like other congressmen on the far Right, found no subversion among Fascists or pro-Fascists. After a visit to Franco Spain, he urged American loans to the dictator as a fine "anti-Communist" and ruler of "a civilized Christian nation." McCarran also urged that Jewish displaced persons be barred from the United States. "On the basis of my investigation," he claimed, the United States was admitting "persons who will not become good citizens and who will become ready recruits in subversive organizations."

The Anti-Defamation League accused him of "essential hostility toward Jews." Father Joseph L. Lamb, director of Social Service of the Rhode Island Diocese, said of the McCarran-Walter Act, "I am quite shocked and surprised in seeing Hitler's principles retained in our immigration legislation."

In 1954, an extension of the McCarran Act, the Communist Control Act, was introduced in the House. It required any person or organization cooperating with any Communist goals to register under the McCarran Act. The *Wall Street Journal* observed, "For all we know, the Communist party may be against juvenile delinquency. So is this newspaper."

But the bill passed, along with two more restrictive measures that year, the Espionage and Sabotage Act and the Immunity Act. Senator McCarthy, whose persistent and shrill Red-hunts continued to set the emotional climate for "national security" legislation, boasted, "There won't be enough cells in federal prisons when I get through!"

To McCarthy, almost every intellectual, every liberal, every Democrat, was an actual or potential traitor. He used his growing power to create panic and confusion in the government itself, calling upon its two million employees to inform on each other and on department heads if they had any information about suspected Communist beliefs or tendencies.

During 1953 and 1954 McCarthy held a long series of hearings at which irresponsible attacks were made on the loyalty of respected Americans. President Eisenhower, increasingly outraged, began speaking out against McCarthy's squads of "book-burners," unfair conduct at the hearings, and attempts to saddle "thought control" on the American people.

McCarthy finally went too far when he staged televised hearings attacking the US Army for concealing and protecting subversion. Forcing Army Secretary Robert T. Stevens and Brigadier General Ralph Zwicker to testify, McCarthy insulted Zwicker, telling him contemptuously he was not fit to wear the uniform. The American people, a majority of whom had until then supported McCarthy, were shocked as the TV cameras exposed him as an arrogant bully who bluffed, lied, distorted, sneered, and used outrageously unfair tactics.

The reaction was swift. Stunned Americans, ashamed of having thought of McCarthy as a hero, turned their backs on him. McCarthy was bewildered. He could not understand that he had made a serious tactical blunder in letting the public see him in action as he really was instead of letting them read glorifications of him in the right-wing press.

Republican Senator Ralph Flanders, of Vermont, comparing McCarthy to Hitler, introduced a resolution of censure against him, declaring, "Were the junior senator from Wisconsin in the pay of the Communists, he could not have done a better job for them." After an investigative committee reported, the Senate formally voted condemnation of McCarthy by a vote of 67 to 22.

His power broken at last and his dreams of becoming an American fuehrer in the White House destroyed, McCarthy rapidly slipped into oblivion and died soon afterward.

McCarthyism had been dealt a crushing blow—but not a fatal one. The far Right had other strings to its bow.

FIFTEEN

Vietnam: The Price of Dissent

On the Atomic Energy Commission, one of the "security chiefs" in charge of evaluating the loyalty of atomic scientists such as Harold Urey, Leo Szilard, and J. Robert Oppenheimer was Medford Evans, who had written an article called, "Why I Am Anti-Intellectual." Evans later became Birch Society coordinator for Texas and an adviser to General Edwin Walker, who was relieved of his command for subverting his troops.

Perhaps one of the most celebrated victims of McCarthyism was J. Robert Oppenheimer, a nuclear physicist internationally acclaimed for his brilliance. In 1936 he had found himself deeply disturbed by current events. His students were finding it difficult to get suitable jobs because of the Depression. His Jewish relatives in Germany were being threatened by the Nazis. Germany and Italy were sending troops, planes, and tanks to help Franco overthrow democracy in Spain.

Tens of thousands of American intellectuals were becoming political activists. Among those who joined the Communist party were Oppenheimer's wife, brother, and sister-in-law. He, however, like the great majority of liberal intellectuals, simply joined the anti-Fascist movement. President Eisenhower later described him as politically naive but certified that he had not been involved in any subversive movement.

The Hitler-Stalin Pact of 1939 disillusioned the Oppenheimers. He was further dismayed by Stalin's purge of three Russian physicists he respected. His wife dropped out of the Communist party, and he left the anti-Fascist United Front.

After Pearl Harbor Oppenheimer did such valuable work for the government defense effort that he was asked to take charge of building an American atomic bomb. He revealed his former membership in left-wing groups but was assured that this would not deny him security clearance for the project.

Gathering about him the top physicists in America, Oppenheimer became the guiding genius of the stupendous secret research and development project at Los Alamos. He saw no reason to discontinue seeing close personal friends who had been, or still were, Communists or leftists; the Soviet Union was now America's war ally and "respectable."

Through George Eltenton, British chemical engineer, Soviet scientists suggested to Oppenheimer that informal exchanges of atomic information could help the Allied war effort against Germany. Upset by this unofficial approach, Oppenheimer warned Colonel John Lansdale, project-security officer at Los Alamos, that Eltenton might bear watching. However, he concealed the name of the friend who had conveyed Eltenton's message to him, not wanting to get him in trouble.

Oppenheimer was one of the scientists who recommended dropping the A-bomb on Japan to end the war quickly. President Truman awarded him the Medal of Merit, declaring, "More than any other one man, Oppenheimer is to be credited with the achievement of the atomic bomb." He cited the scientist's "outstanding service to the War Department . . . and his unswerving devotion to duty." Oppenheimer was appointed adviser to the

UN Atomic Energy Committee Scientific Panel as well as to the US Atomic Energy Commission.

But he became increasingly uneasy about leaving atomic weapons in the hands of the generals and urged that they be put under civilian control. He also pleaded for international control of the weapons to prevent a terrible nuclear-arms race. These views infuriated powerful figures in the State Department and the Pentagon, coming as they did in the midst of the deepening Cold War. Rumors began to circulate that Oppenheimer was secretly sympathetic to the Russians.

Eminent Americans such as Dr. James Conant and Bernard Baruch and many indignant nuclear physicists rushed to his defense, branding the rumors absurd. Oppenheimer persisted in advocating international cooperation on atomic energy so that it might be used for the peaceful benefit of all mankind. There were no such things as "atomic secrets," he warned; any major nation's physicists could develop an A-bomb. In August, 1949, Americans were stunned when the Soviet Union exploded theirs.

The Pentagon demanded that American scientists quickly press ahead and develop a super-bomb—the H-bomb—which Dr. Edward Teller assured the generals could be made. Oppenheimer and the General Advisory Committee to the Atomic Energy Commission warned that it could only lead to a deadly arms-race that might end in the destruction of the world.

But Cold War hysteria prevailed; the H-bomb was built and exploded in November, 1952. Less than two years later Russia had its own hydrogen bomb, and the atomic race skyrocketed as each side kept perfecting delivery systems.

McCarthyism led to a challenge of Oppenheimer's right to access to American atomic secrets. "More probably than not," declared his accuser, William L. Borden, a former minor official, "he has acted . . . [as] an espionage agent." At an Atomic Energy Commission hearing, Oppenheimer's security clearance was revoked, and he was denied access to restricted atomic data as a "security risk." It was tantamount to a civilian court-martial branding him guilty of disloyalty.

Not until December, 1963, when Cold War hysteria had abated, did the Atomic Energy Commission seek to apologize by presenting Oppenheimer with the highest honor it could bestow—the Enrico Fermi Award. President Lyndon B. Johnson made the presentation at the White House. When Oppenheimer died three years later, representatives of twenty-five nations of the world halted an international conference on nuclear arms control to pay tribute to the man his country had labeled a "security risk."

In 1955, Attorney General Howard J. McGrath, speaking to the American Bar Association, said, "We appear to be going through a period of public hysteria in which many varieties of self-appointed policemen, and alleged guardians of Americanism, would have us fight subversion by proscribing an orthodoxy of opinion, and stigmatizing as disloyal all who disagree with them."

Robert Williams, an African American ex-Marine, was so angry at the treatment of blacks in America that he wrote to President Eisenhower in 1955, expressing his desire to renounce his citizenship. Four years later, as head of the Monroe, North Carolina, NAACP, he began to arm its members, insisting, "Negroes . . . must henceforth meet violence with violence." Suspended by the NAACP, he went to Cuba and returned a confirmed "Fidelista."

In 1961 he was charged with kidnapping and holding a white couple as hostages until police rescued them. Fleeing to

Cuba, Williams was given asylum as a political refugee. He told American blacks over Radio Havana, "Not only does freedom require the will to die, but it also requires the will to kill. . . . Let us meet violence with violence."

He formed an organization called RAM—Revolutionary Action Movement, Black Liberation Front of the USA— which helped train African Americans in Cuba in guerrilla warfare and sabotage. When Cuban Communists cooled toward Williams, he left in the spring of 1966 for Red China.

Two RAM members were subsequently arrested in New York for conspiring to murder moderate black leaders Roy Wilkins and Whitney Young; fifteen others were arrested for violating the New York State criminal-anarchy law. In Philadelphia RAM members were arrested for plotting a riot at which the lunches of policemen sent to fight would be poisoned.

In December, 1967, Williams, now in Africa, declared that he planned to return home to face charges against him, clear himself, and run as a black-power candidate for president. Four months later the Malcolm X Society held a convention in Detroit, signing a declaration of independence calling for a separate African American nation in the South. Robert Williams was elected president and H. Rap Brown minister of defense.

When Williams sought to return home in 1969, Trans World Airlines refused to let him board its plane in London, claiming "such transportation would or might be inimical to the safety of the flight." Upon protest by the Civil Liberties Union, TWA finally flew him to the United States as the sole passenger of a plane that normally carried 130 passengers.

In the late 1950s the Supreme Court began administering some stinging rebuffs to McCarthyism. *Pennsylvania v. Nelson* (1956) held the state's antisubversive legislation unconstitutional for usurping the federal right to determine and suppress subversion. *Watkins v. US* (1957) set aside the contempt conviction of a labor-union official for refusing to name other Communist-party members he had known in earlier years.

Yates v. US (1957) put a stop to over one hundred indictments and convictions under the Smith Act since the imprisonment of the Communist-party leaders. The Court held that no one could be charged under the Smith Act if he simply advocated or taught forcible overthrow of the government as an abstract principle, with no proven effort to incite a specific act.

The Court also sought to stop discrimination against Americans who considered compulsory loyalty oaths degrading and unconstitutional. In *First Unitarian Church v. Los Angeles* (1958), the Court ordered restoration of tax-exemption rights for Unitarian church property, which had been denied the Unitarians for refusing to take oaths swearing they did not advocate violent overthrow of the government or support of any foreign government. The Court found that they had been denied their rights under the Fourteenth Amendment.

Such decisions, following the historic 1954 decision of the Court, *Brown v. Board of Education of Topeka,* which held school segregation to be illegal, infuriated the extreme Right in America. The principal targets of their wrath were Supreme Court Chief Justice Earl Warren and Justice William O. Douglas.

The Birch Society was formed in Indianapolis in December, 1958, by Joseph Welch, a retired candy manufacturer. Dedicated to the principles of McCarthyism, the Birchites revived the Christian Front spirit of the Coughlinites, attracting the cooperation of other far-Right extremist groups.

Founder Joseph Welch attacked democracy as "merely a deceptive phrase, a weapon of demagoguery, and a perennial fraud." He denounced President Eisenhower as "a dedicated, conscious agent of the Communist conspiracy," along with other such "Red" agents as Milton Eisenhower, John Foster Dulles, and General George Marshall. President Roosevelt had been guilty of "plain unadulterated treason." And Justice Warren had to be impeached for "converting this republic into a democracy."

Thomas Anderson of the Birch Society National Council proposed, "Why not hold some treason trials? The perfect site for treason trials would be Hyde Park." Those who should be put on trial at Roosevelt's homesite, he hinted, included Presidents Truman, Eisenhower, and Kennedy, along with their respective secretaries of state.

In July, 1961, the *Birch Society Bulletin* estimated that there were "300,000 to 500,000 Communists in the United States" and "not more than a million allies, dupes and sympathizers." Liberals were included in the society's private lists of "subversives" because they were "trying to change the economic and political structure of the country so that it could be comfortably merged with Soviet Russia."

Another far-Right voice warning of a Red takeover was that of the Reverend Billy James Hargis, who conducted a million-dollar Christian Crusade against Communism from Tulsa, Oklahoma. Hargis denounced the UN as "that traitorous outfit in New York City" and named as the "betrayers" of America *"Time* magazine, National Council of Churches hierarchy, Washington *Post,* NAACP, and all other liberals and internationalists."

Major General Edwin A. Walker, who was removed from his command for propagandizing his troops with Birchite materials, appeared before Congress to assail many distinguished public figures as "soft on Communism" and charge that a mysterious "control apparatus" linked to Secretary of State Dean Rusk was working on behalf of the Soviet Union.

These charges raised questions of his sanity and caused even ultra-conservative William F. Buckley, Jr., to admit, "The verdict is that General Walker be consigned to history's ashcan, and that henceforth his name call forth the roars of contempt and ridicule." Walker incited a racist mob at the University of Mississippi against permitting the registration of its first Negro, James Meredith. Arrested, he was charged with inciting rebellion and insurrection, and the government ordered him to be given a psychiatric examination.

Walker later turned up to lead a turbulent demonstration in Dallas against the United Nations; next day a screaming mob of his followers physically attacked Adlai Stevenson when he attempted to speak in that city. They also distributed "Wanted" posters with president John F. Kennedy's face and the headline: "WANTED FOR TREASON against the United States." Four weeks later the president was assassinated in Dallas.

Birch Society member Robert Bolivar DePugh founded a group called the Minutemen, with units in forty states and all major cities. His troops had hidden field pieces, machine guns, and other weapons and held "Guerrilla Warfare Seminars" regularly as a "patriotic duty."

DePugh justified his private army by citing HUAC's 1960 report stating that since Communist tactics were designed to render conventional military forces ineffective, the American people might have to rely on other forces for defense against armed subversion. Former Governor Pat Brown warned that there were twenty-four hundred of DePugh's "armed rightists" in California alone.

In 1968, HUAC issued a report called *Guerrilla Warfare Advocates in the United States.* It listed dozens of Communist, black-nationalist, and other left-wing groups but made not one mention of the Minutemen or any of the other innumerable private far-Right guerrilla armies in the nation.

Nazi leader Hermann Goering once explained how to saddle a dictatorship on a country: "Tell the people they are threatened. Throw the pacifists in jail for threatening the security of the nation. It's as simple as that and it works in any country."

Throughout the decade of the sixties and into the seventies, the burning question of treason centered around the highly controversial Vietnam war, perhaps the most unpopular war in all American history. It was an undeclared war, so that technically the statute of treason could not be applied.

But the issue was nevertheless one of treason versus patriotism. Those who supported the government insisted that it was the duty of all Americans to support the war ("My country, right or wrong"). Those who opposed the war as immoral, unjust, and a tragic blunder declared that the true course of patriotism lay in opposing the war in every way possible, to get America out of its unfortunate involvement in Asia.

Anti-Vietnam demonstrations involved burning draft cards, burning the American flag, sitting-in at induction centers, lying down in front of troop trains, breaking into draft centers and burning files, and protesting against ROTC and Defense Department research projects at the nation's universities.

Taking part in antiwar demonstrations were ministers, priests, rabbis, doctors, professors, scientists, Nobel Prize winners, and such celebrated national figures as Dr. Martin Luther King, Jr. A leader of the anti-Vietnam movement emerged in

Senator Eugene McCarthy, of Minnesota, who challenged President Johnson's renomination in the election campaign of 1968. He scored upsetting successes in the primaries, causing Johnson to decide against running for reelection.

In November, 1965, Republican Senator Thomas Kuchel excoriated "the vicious, venomous and vile leaders of this infamous movement who attempt to influence young people of this country to evade the draft by fraud and chicanery." He demanded an investigation by the Justice Department, insisting, "What has gone on sows the seeds of treason!"

HUAC hearings on antiwar demonstrations at Berkeley spotlighted student publications that advocated sabotage against the Vietnam war as "the only remaining route to peace." *Open Process* urged:

> Break war-related laws: draft, security, federal trespassing. Damage war equipment. Join with your fellow workers in strikes, slowdowns, and "botching the job" in key war industries. . . . Publish state secrets you have access to. . . . People have a right to know what "their" government is up to.

Most antiwar protesters, however, were nonviolent, limiting their protests to demonstrations and symbolic acts of civil disobedience in the tradition of Thoreau and Gandhi. They demanded an end to the bombing of North Vietnam; of the use of napalm bombs against peasant women and children; of the burning of "suspected" villages; of the torture of captured Viet Cong soldiers; of the massacre of women and children in territory controlled by the Viet Cong.

In opposing the Vietnam war for humanitarian reasons, they insisted, they were simply living up to the principles established by the United States government at the Nuremberg Trials in condemning "crimes against humanity." The dissenters cited world condemnation of the United States' role in Vietnam, pointing out the irony of an American government, born in revolution, seeking to put down a patriotic revolution against the unpopular dictatorship of the South Vietnam regime.

In May, 1967, Representative L. Mendel Rivers, chairman of the House Armed Services Committee, demanded prosecution of Americans counseling, aiding, and abetting avoidance of the draft. Assistant Attorney General Fred M. Vinson, Jr., replied that the First Amendment barred such prosecutions.

"Let's forget about the First Amendment!" snapped Representative Herbert, of Louisiana. In October, antiwar demonstrations at the Pentagon angered General Lewis B. Hershey, selective service director, who ordered the nation's draft boards to call up immediately any registrant who interfered with the draft or was involved in antiwar demonstrations.

The Justice Department informed Hershey that punitive reclassification was illegal and unconstitutional and that no registrant could be punished for protesting against the war or the draft. Hershey refused to rescind his order, stating that it had been authorized by the White House. But local draft boards soon learned to disregard it whenever they were challenged by the Civil Liberties Union, which took such cases up to the Supreme Court and won them.

The Johnson Administration felt that it had to do something to stop the mounting draft resistance. In January, 1968, Dr. Benjamin Spock, the renowned baby doctor, the Reverend William Sloane Coffin, of Yale, and three colleagues were indicted, charged with conspiracy to "counsel, aid, and abet" violations of the draft law.

The defendants argued that they had been within their rights of freedom of speech and assembly. As for "conspiracy," it was pointed out that all the acts complained of by the government were done openly in front of TV cameras, including their issue of a "Call to Resist Illegitimate Authority." The trial was obviously a political one, they charged, meant to intimidate other leaders of the antiwar movement.

The Boston trial judge went out of his way to influence the jury by giving them ten guidelines to use in deciding the guilt of the accused. The jury freed one defendant, found the other four guilty. Each received a two-year jail sentence.

But the First US Circuit Court of Appeals in Boston soon overturned the conviction, finding that the lower-court judge's guidelines to the jury had been prejudicial. The defendants had also been right in stating that "vigorous criticism of the draft and of the Vietnam war is . . . protected by the First Amendment, even though its effect is to interfere with the war effort." Dr. Spock and one defendant were freed; charges against Dr. Coffin and another were later dropped.

"It seems to me absolutely tragic," Dr. Spock declared after his release, "that young Americans will continue to die in Vietnam . . . and that young men have been imprisoned for being opposed to it and doing as their consciences dictated."

Another trial of anti-Establishment dissenters was soon to shake and confuse Americans even more.

SIXTEEN

"A Police Riot"

In the summer of 1967 President Johnson reactivated the Subversive Activities Control Board, which had performed no functions for the past eighteen months. But two years later a unanimous Court of Appeals decision invalidated the board as unconstitutional, along with the board's required registration of alleged Communists.

Turbulence marked the election year of 1968. There were civil disorders, ghetto riots, antiwar and antidraft protests, student revolts, a poor people's march on Washington, and the shocking assassinations of Martin Luther King, Jr., and Robert Kennedy.

An alarmed Congress saw these chaotic developments as signs of a left-wing conpiracy, instead of as symptoms of widespread frustration and anger over the Administration's persistence in waging the Vietnam war while neglecting the urgent problems of the black, the poor, and the young at home.

After a race riot sparked by black militant H. Rap Brown, Congress added an antiriot clause to the Civil Rights Act of 1968, making it a crime to cross state lines with the intention of provoking a riot. The law did not intimidate the nation's antiwar dissenters into giving up their plan for a confrontation with the Administration at the Democratic National Convention scheduled for Chicago in late August.

Their intention was to influence the delegates, by demonstrations outside the convention hall, to reject the Administration's policies and deny the presidential nomination to Vice President Hubert Humphrey. Their choice was Senator Eugene McCarthy, whose candidacy had become the symbol of the antiwar movement. His young, idealistic supporters were joined by more radical anti-Establishment hippies and yippies.

Mayor Richard J. Daley, of Chicago, denied the demonstrators places to hold rallies or demonstrations and turned the convention hall into an armed fortress. Anti-Administration Democratic delegates, as well as members of the press, were roughly handled by the Chicago police. Daley augmented the police force with National Guardsmen and Army troops, insisting that they were needed to preserve law and order in the face of threatened violence.

There were bloody clashes between police and demonstrators. Young people were attacked and beaten up, subjected to tear gas and Mace, and dragged into police vans. TV cameramen filming some of these scenes were also attacked by police. Indignant delegates at the convention angrily denounced Mayor Daley for using "Gestapo tactics."

Daley defended the police by insisting that they had been provoked by insults and filth hurled by some of the demonstrators, although he admitted that "some" police might have "overreacted" to the provocation. Ironically, millions of Americans who were shocked at the scenes of violence in Chicago they saw on TV were not indignant at the clubbing of McCarthy's young supporters but at the TV networks for showing it.

An impartial commission was appointed by the president to investigate the Chicago riots. The resultant Walker Report concluded, "To read dispassionately the hundreds of statements describing at first hand the events of Sunday and Monday nights is to become convinced of what can only be called a police riot."

The New York Times blamed the Daley regime for causing the disorders in the first place by denying the right of assembly to protesting groups and for using excessive and indiscriminate force to stifle the dissent that was obviously doing serious political damage to the Democratic party.

Eight young "New Left" leaders of the demonstrators were indicted in Chicago for conspiracy to cross state lines to incite a riot. No Chicago police were indicted for assaulting demonstrators and spectators. As the Walker Report noted, "There has been no public condemnation of these violators of sound police procedures and common decency by either their commanding officers or city officials."

HUAC held hearings on the "Subversive Involvement in Disruption of 1968 Democratic Party National Convention," seeking to prove that the young dissenters under indictment had conspired to cause the trouble in Chicago and disrupt the convention. Thomas Hayden, former president of the Students for a Democratic Society (SDS), was interrogated by HUAC counsel Frank Conley.

Hayden accused HUAC of trying to paint the antiwar movement "as somehow being an aggressive, violent movement. It is a case of the criminal calling the victim the criminal." He admitted having gone to North Vietnam to meet with Communist officials, stating that he wanted "to try to understand the outlook on peace and war that the other side held."

He added, "My Government, which I don't think represents me, is wrong in Vietnam." Accused of trying to destroy the present American democratic system, he replied, "That is a joke. . . .

I don't believe the present American democratic system exists. . . . You have destroyed [it] by the existence of a committee of this kind."

Asked whether he believed that the young revolutionary movement he represented really expected to succeed, he brought laughter by replying dryly, "Well, I think we will at least outlive you." He added calmly, "Probably much of our time will be spent in penitentiaries."

Hayden considered support of the Vietnam war to be "patriotic in the worst sense." He said, "I think the symbols of patriotism have been stolen by the Right, and they have to be regained by those people who are working to make freedom and peace in this country consistent with American interests."

The Chicago Eight were put on trial in that city before Judge Julius Hoffman. It was a political trial that brought the Justice Department under Attorney General John Mitchell into stark confrontation with the New Left. The proceedings were kept in an uproar from start to finish by clashes between the unruly defendants and the prickly judge.

When one defendant, black militant Bobby Seale, refused to be silenced, Judge Hoffman ordered him bound to his seat and gagged. The spectacle was so repellent to ideas of American justice that the judge sentenced him instead to four years in jail for contempt of court and remanded him for separate trial at a later date.

For five months the other seven defendants continued to disrupt the trial. They challenged Judge Hoffman as a biased judge who granted every motion of the prosecution and denied every motion of the defense. When former Attorney General Ramsey Clark and Rev. Ralph David Abernathy, Martin Luther King's successor, sought to testify in their behalf, Judge Hoffman refused to allow them to be heard.

The defendants made no secret of their contempt for the brand of justice dispensed in Chicago. While the jury was out deliberating on a verdict, Judge Hoffman sentenced all the defendants and their attorney, William Kunstler, to a total of over fifteen years in jail on 160 separate counts of contempt.

After four days of deliberation, the jury returned a verdict acquitting two defendants and finding the other five innocent of conspiracy but guilty of crossing state lines with the intention of inciting to riot. Three of the jurors considered the law unconstitutional but were persuaded to agree on a compromise verdict so that the law could be tested by a Supreme Court review of the case on appeal.

Judge Hoffman sentenced each of the convicted five defendants to the maximum term of five years, with a five-thousand-dollar fine plus court costs. At first he tried to keep them in jail on exorbitant bail, pending appeal, as men "too dangerous" to be at large, but he was finally compelled to free them on lower bail on condition they stay out of further trouble.

The trial shook the judicial system of the United States, worrying the bar associations. The Seven had entered Judge Hoffman's courtroom convinced that the Establishment they opposed would not give them a fair trial. Feeling they owed it no respect, they had yelled, hooted, laughed, and clowned all through the proceedings.

Many bar associations felt that the government should never have put on what was obviously a political trial. While condemning the actions of the defendants in turning the courtroom into a propaganda platform, they deplored equally the violations of fair judicial practice by the presiding judge.

Professor Larry Nachman, a political scientist at the City College of New York, observed in the *Nation:*

The weight, authority, and legitimacy of the United States Government was put behind Daley and the Chicago police. This action instantly distorted history. Once the trial began, one could retain one's original view of the Chicago violence only at the cost of raising some deep and ugly questions about the nature of the United States Government that was prosecuting the case. . . . The primary wrong in the trial was not the partiality, unfairness and vindictiveness of the judge but his willingness to permit the Government to use a federal court to legitimatize violence against its opponents.

As the trial ended, the chief question was whether the Court of Appeals would overturn Judge Hoffman's sentences on the basis of judicial errors. If it did not, the case would go to the US Supreme Court, which would then decide whether the federal law against crossing a state line with intent to create a riot was a violation of the First Amendment.

Meanwhile, a 1970 Supreme Court decision upheld the right of judges to use whatever means of restraint were necessary to maintain decorum in the courtroom, even to banning a defendant from attending his own trial, if necessary.

The violence in Chicago seemed to signal the end of an era of political confrontation and the beginning of revolutionary opposition to the government. Millions of youthful dissenters were disillusioned with their inability to "change things around" by working within the political system.

"We're convinced now," one militant said, "the Establishment is deaf to any argument except an exploding bank."

Serious clashes began taking place between the outspoken revolutionary Black Panthers and the police departments of various cities. Police raids on Panther headquarters resulted in shoot-outs during which both Panthers and police were killed and wounded. Many Panther headquarters proved to be heavily stocked with weapons, which the Panthers insisted were solely for self-defense. They saw the raids as part of a plan by Attorney General Mitchell to wipe out the black-militant movement. The Justice Department denied it.

Police quoted Max Stanford, of the Black Panther party, at a 1966 rally, according to an Associated Press dispatch:

> Stanford took the podium. Flanked by members of the Black Panther group, he said "black men" must unite in overthrowing their white "oppressors," but must do it "like panthers—smiling, cunning, scientifically . . . striking by night and sparing no one." Stanford said the US could be brought down with "a rag and some gasoline and a bottle"—the ingredients of a fire bomb.

If the Panthers were using fire bombs in race riots or against police cars, other bombs were the weapons of a militant faction of SDS called the Weatherman. Giving up all hope of "reforming the system," the Weatherman took to the tactics of blowing up symbols of capitalism. On the West Coast, a Bank of America building was destroyed by bombing, and in New York City the General Telephone and Electronics, General Motors, and IBM buildings were bombed. The bombers gave advance warning of their targets so that no persons would be hurt.

When Rennie Davis, one of the Chicago Seven, was asked how he felt about these bombings in a TV interview, he replied that the radicals had destroyed only a few "capitalist buildings," whereas the American government had bombed and destroyed over a million men, women, and children in Vietnam and still had not stopped. Which, he demanded, was more violent?

He was answered by New York *Post* columnist James Wechsler, who pointed out that by the tactics of anarchy, the New Left would only provoke heavy repression in reprisal from the government. Not only would New Leftists be crushed, but they would at the same time badly hurt the chances of persuading the American people to correct the injustices that were alienating the young, the black, the poor, and the liberal.

The big question for the seventies was whether the American government could or would move swiftly enough to reform the system, as the New Deal had done in the crisis of the thirties.

The Bank of America bombing, cautioned University of California sociologists Richard Flacks and Milton Mankoff, "ought to warn this country's managers that they have just about exhausted the loyalty of the country's youth. . . . Once they have lost faith in legitimate authority and see normal channels blocked, the political newcomers express their rage in ways less tempered by questions of proper strategy and tactics."

They foresaw a rapid radicalization of middle-class youth unless the government soon ended the war in Vietnam and solved America's desperate problems at home.

New York mayor John V. Lindsay also saw the problem as one of the nation's institutions failing the hungry, the poor, the black, and the young, creating anger among them. "I share that anger," he said. He did not, however, justify terrorism because of valid grievances. "It is cowardly," he declared, "and it is immoral. If you claim to believe the Vietnam war is immoral—if you understand why the burning of a village and the slaughter of civilians is an abhorrent act—then your job and my job is not to open up a new frontier for bloodshed, but to stop it everywhere, once and for all."

But Lindsay also warned of allowing the government to use repression to crush dissent: "We have seen all too clearly that there are men—now in power in this country—who do not respect dissent, who cannot cope with turmoil, and who believe that the people of America are ready to support repression as long as it is done with a quiet voice and a business suit. And it is up to us to prove that they are wrong."

SEVENTEEN

Disloyalty versus Dissent

Now it is time to try to answer some of the questions about disloyalty and dissent raised in the first chapter; or at least to recognize guidelines for an intelligent approach to the problems raised.

Does the government have the right to use repressive measures to protect itself from overthrow? How far can it legally go—against whom, and under what circumstances?

Certainly every government in the world seeks to prevent its own overthrow from within or without. It claims the loyalty of its citizens in exchange for the rights and privileges they enjoy under its aegis. Trouble arises when a group of citizens feels that a law or action of the government is so unjust or bad that they, like Thoreau, must disobey it.

The government has sought to punish them by legal prosecution, as in the cases of Debs, Spock, and the Chicago Seven, or to combat them with congressional or security-agency probes, as in the cases of Hiss, Oppenheimer, and the Hollywood Ten.

The needs of national security need to be weighed against the dangers of treating dissent as disloyalty. The loyalty probes of Oppenheimer and other scientists who disagreed with government policy in the fifties made many American scientists afraid to offer constructive criticism of the nation's military research.

Some refused to attend important international scientific conferences for fear of being suspected of contact with Communist scientists. Others quit government service rather than curb their free scientific inquiry.

Another risk of cracking down hard on dissent is that the dissenters, like the Weathermen, of SDS, are driven underground, where they are far more dangerous to the government. When the Johnson and Nixon Administrations took repressive measures against the protests led by SDS against the Vietnam war, the organization split into nonviolent and violent (Weatherman) factions. The Weatherman then began to protest by bombing banks, business buildings, and police stations.

Americans alleged by the government to be disloyal or treasonous may actually be so, like Benedict Arnold or William Dudley Pelley. But it must also be kept in mind that throughout American history the cry of treason has been raised as a political weapon to silence embarrassing questions about an administration's failures or shortcomings, as the John Adams Administration did against the Jeffersonians and the Lyndon Johnson Administration did against antiwar senators.

To prevent the political misuse of the treason charge, the Founding Fathers carefully defined the crime, and the proofs required, in Article III, Section 3, of the Constitution. Some Congresses, however, have evaded this restriction by punishing alleged treason under different names in such loosely drawn legislation as the McCarran, McCarran-Walter, Communist Control, and Smith Acts.

At the height of Cold War hysteria in the early fifties, Congress debated whether to outlaw the Communist party as subversive, in order to protect American security.

"If we outlaw the Communist party," said Representative Emanuel Celler, of New York, "there is no reason why if the Republicans are in control they could not outlaw the Democratic party. . . . You could say that any party that opposes high tariffs or believes in deficit spending is subversive."

In point of fact, Senator Joseph McCarthy had crusaded against the liberal record of the Democratic party as "twenty years of treason," and at the height of his power public-opinion polls showed that a majority of Americans supported him.

Unless we violate the Bill of Rights, we cannot single out any political group and declare it illegal, no matter how much we detest its policies. The rights of dissenters are what distinguish our democracy from Communist or Fascist dictatorships. We might also question the wisdom of harassing unpopular political minorities by either punitive legislation or police action.

France, England, Italy, the Scandinavian countries, and many others permit the Communist party and all other radical parties to operate openly in opposition to the government. The result is that their dissent is peaceful and works for change within the political system.

But what about Fascist groups like the Christian Front, the Silver Shirts, and the Minutemen, who seek a right-wing dictatorship in the style of Hitler, Mussolini, and Franco?

Fascists have the same political rights under the Constitution as Communists or any other radicals. If they are guilty of treason, the Department of Justice has an obligation to bring such charges in court. If they are not guilty of treason, they are protected by the Bill of Rights.

It is true that both the far Right and the far Left are dedicated to undermining our democracy. The far Left has been urging violence and revolution as the only way to bring about needed change, insisting that the government will neither listen to nor act upon grievances.

Abraham I. Pomerantz, who was deputy chief counsel of the American legal staff at the Nazi trials in Nuremberg, explained far-Right tactics:

> The approach, copied from the Nazis, works this way: The press and radio first lay down a terrific barrage against the Red Menace. Headlines without a shred of evidence shriek of atom bomb spies or plots to overthrow the government, of espionage, of high treason, and of other bloodcurdling crimes. We are now ready for the second stage: the pinning of the label "Red" indiscriminately on all opposition.

American security may be better protected from extremist propaganda by open and searching discussion of the claims made by the far Right and the far Left than by jailing the propagandists. On June 14, 1953, President Eisenhower denounced Senator Joseph McCarthy's attempt to outlaw books discussing communism in a speech at Dartmouth. "How will we defeat communism," the president demanded, "unless we know what it is, and what it teaches, and why does it have such an appeal for men?"

Is it disloyal for Americans of foreign ancestry to maintain cultural ties to the country of their fathers?

As a nation of immigrants, it would be surprising if Americans of Italian descent did not feel a kinship with Italian relatives, those of Irish descent with Irish relatives, those of German descent with German relatives, those of Jewish descent with Israeli relatives, those of Japanese descent with Japanese relatives. Their cultural heritage and sympathies have little to do with their basic loyalty to America.

As we saw, the John Adams Administration directed harsh alien and sedition laws against French immigrants during a time of strained relations with France. American Catholic immigrants in the nineteenth century were often persecuted as traitors because of their religious allegiance to Rome. Patriotic Nisei were put in World War II concentration camps simply because of their Japanese ancestry.

Reason and justice would suggest that in time of crisis, all Americans should be considered equally loyal, regardless of their cultural or blood ties to a hostile nation, until there is legal evidence to prove that they are not.

How can we determine the dividing line between dissent and disloyalty? There is perhaps no thornier question.

It is, first of all, important to distinguish between disloyalty to the nation and total opposition to the policies of a particular administration. The Jeffersonians were not traitors because they wholly opposed the anti-French war policies of the Adams Administration, although the Federalists insisted that this opposition was treason. Likewise, when the Jeffersonians took over the White House, the Federalists were not traitors for wholly opposing the anti-British war policies of the Jefferson Administration, although the Jeffersonians insisted that *their* opposition was now treason.

Perhaps all of us could agree that political opposition of any kind should never be regarded as treason, since today's government policies may be proved to be wrong tomorrow and changed around completely. No better modern example can be cited than the Vietnam war. The Johnson Administration branded as traitors those who called it a mistake and demanded that American troops be withdrawn. The Nixon Administration agreed it was a mistake and reversed American policy by gradually withdrawing our forces from Vietnam.

Assuming that the Vietnam war and drafting troops for it was a mistake, was the American minority that opposed it justified in breaking the law to try to stop what they considered an illegal and immoral war? This question inevitably raises a deeper problem. Can a minority be allowed to decide which laws of a majority they will obey as just laws and which laws they will defy as unjust?

"Are laws to be enforced simply because they were made, or declared by any number of men to be good," Thoreau asked in opposing the Mexican War, "if they are *not* good?"

But the very meaning of democracy is that the laws of the majority must prevail. If each individual is free to obey only laws he likes, there is no rule of law but only anarchy. To *disagree* with any government law or policy, and agitate for its repeal, is every citizen's right. But he does not have the right to disobey a law unless he is willing to pay the prescribed penalty for his defiance.

On the other hand, many dissenters feel that it is wrong for the majority to force a minority to obey laws the minority considers unjust. During the fifties some scientists broke national security laws to share atomic knowledge with other scientists abroad in the interest of world peace.

"Where does a man's loyalty lie?" asked British biologist Michael Amrine in his book, *Treason*. "Is loyalty to the race larger than loyalty to the nation? . . . If I lie, I am false not only to you, but to myself, to my science, to my civilization, and, as I believe, false to the best interests of my country. . . . It is madness."

Deeply religious persons have also been prosecuted and jailed for activities opposing the draft, a war, or laws discriminating against blacks or the poor. Among them have been Quakers, priests, ministers, and rabbis convinced that they had no choice but to place their beliefs about God and a "higher morality" above the demands of the state.

Perhaps if such Americans must be arrested to uphold the authority of the law, their arrests should be made with a public acknowledgment that they are regrettable. Those willing to go to jail out of the convictions of their conscience also deserve, at least, to have their beliefs fully reported to the American people. If enough of us are convinced that they are right, we owe it to our own consciences to insist that Congress change the unjust law.

How should treason be judged and punished?

American justice requires that anyone accused of treason be presumed innocent until proved guilty in court after a fair trial on the basis of factual evidence. As we have seen, however, many Americans have been persecuted as "traitors" through the device of a one-sided congressional-committee hearing, with no opportunity to cross-examine witnesses against them. Condemned by hearsay evidence inadmissible in any court of law, they have also been smeared by such police-state principles as "guilt by association."

The need for such congressional inquisitions to protect American security is questionable, at best. Almost all real cases of treason, espionage, and sabotage have been uncovered, and successfully prosecuted, by the FBI and the intelligence sections of the armed forces.

Any government has the right to protect itself against revolutionists who seek to overthrow it by violence. In view of our own history, however, one wonders if American revolutionists can be prosecuted for treason. Were the American revolutionists of 1776 traitors for conspiring to overthrow the legal British government they were sworn to uphold? Were American southerners traitors in 1861 when they conspired to rebel against the federal government?

Many antisubversive laws have tried to make it a crime to teach, study, or predict revolution. In his Dartmouth speech President Eisenhower said, "We have got to fight it with something better, not try to conceal the thinking of our own people. They are part of America. And even if they think ideas that are contrary to ours, their right to say them, their right to record them, and their right to have them at places where they are accessible to others is unquestioned, or it isn't America."

Few Americans realize that revolution is justified in the Declaration of Independence under special conditions—when a government becomes despotic and refuses to heed the peaceful petitions of its people for a redress of just grievances. "It is their right, it is their duty," states the Declaration, "to throw off such government and to provide new guards for their future security."

Those citizens who have advocated revolution in twentieth-century America, however, are only a small if highly vocal minority. They have not convinced the vast majority of Americans that their government is despotic, or that it is unwilling or unable to correct injustices in our society. But they serve the purpose of spotlighting those injustices and goading the government to corrective action.

Most of us feel revulsion at genuine traitors who sell out their country to foreign powers, like Robert Best, Axis Sally, Lord Haw Haw (William Joyce), and Harry Gold. Often, however, they are emotionally warped individuals, frustrated in their lives and ambitions, and socially maladjusted. Perhaps it would be more humane to punish all such convicted traitors by imprisonment rather than by execution.

Sometimes, too, treason represents an unbearable choice between disloyalty and signing the death warrant for a man's family. Both Nazi Germany and the Soviet Union have forced American citizens to become spies on the threat of otherwise torturing or killing their relatives still in Europe.

Another argument in favor of flexible prison terms for treason is that the law can make mistakes, but a mistake cannot be corrected once a convicted defendant has been executed. If the Rosenbergs had been innocent, as they insisted and many investigators believed, a jail term instead of the death sentence would have given their defenders a greater opportunity to prove their innocence.

The value of the death penalty as a deterrent to treason has its defenders as well as its critics. It would be as difficult for either side to prove its case as to prove that the death penalty does or does not prevent murders.

Few lawyers would disagree, however, that it is harder to get a jury to convict a traitor if they know he may be put to death for what some may see as political reasons. Ironically, more real traitors would probably be prosecuted and convicted if the death penalty for treason were abolished.

Finally, how can all of us strengthen the bonds of loyalty we feel to each other as Americans, helping to reconcile the differences that polarize us and drive some dissenters to despair, others to acts of disloyalty?

It will certainly help if the government regards dissenters as the "loyal opposition," listens respectfully to their arguments, and tries to accommodate their point of view at least to some extent. National unity is hardly helped when government spokesmen attack dissenters as unpatriotic or traitorous or when police or National Guard troops use unwarranted force against protest demonstrations or kill students on campus.

At the same time responsible leaders of dissent need to police their own ranks to keep protest demonstrations nonviolent. A few hotheads throwing stones or breaking windows can provoke official violence and turn public sympathy away from the demonstrators. Change is far more likely to come about by means of dissenters who work peacefully within the political system than through the violence of revolutionaries.

All of us can help, too, by "cooling the rhetoric"—refraining from name-calling. To refer to the police as "pigs" or to dissenters as "a bunch of effete intellectual snobs" only intensifies the hostility on both sides.

We can also strengthen the bonds of loyalty in America by avoiding any insulting references to ethnic minority groups. Some German-Americans who had been insulted and derided during the hysteria of World War I became, in bitterness, fifth columnists for Nazi agents during the thirties and forties.

Some Italian Americans sneered at as "wops" or "dagoes" by fellow Americans became angry supporters of Mussolini. Some Nisei, treated contemptuously as "Japs" and thrown into American concentration camps, indignantly refused to swear loyalty to the United States during World War II. The race riots of the sixties and the rise of black militants sworn to violence against the white Establishment were in large part the fruit of two centuries of white oppression, insult, and scorn.

We must work harder at being Americans in the best sense, and that means becoming more tolerant of each other's different ethnic backgrounds and different views. We must not fall into the trap of confusing dissent with disloyalty or of defining only conformity as patriotism. The American flag belongs to all who live under it—those who support the government as well as those who oppose the government.

"We are a rebellious nation, our whole history is treason," abolitionist Theodore Parker reminded his fellow Americans. "Our blood was attainted before we were born; our creeds are infidelity to the mother church, our constitution treason to the fatherland."

Our Founding Fathers were never apologetic for their treason to England, considering it a glorious rebellion in the name of freedom. Had they lost the War of Independence, they would not be remembered today as great American patriots but only as unsuccessful British traitors. Well aware of this, they wrote the treason clause into the Constitution to make it extremely difficult to convict any American of treason.

"God forbid," wrote Thomas Jefferson, "we should ever be twenty years without such a rebellion. . . . What country can preserve its liberties if its rulers are not warned from time to time that this people preserve the spirit of resistance?"

It will always be arguable as to where dissent ends and disloyalty begins. We might suspect that any country that prosecutes too many citizens for conspiracy or treason tends to be totalitarian, whereas any country that prefers to engage dissenting citizens in public debate so that their arguments and proofs are compelled to survive or fall on their own merits is likely to be a free society.

Jeremy Bentham, the great English jurist who helped codify Britain's laws, declared that the way to tell a free government from a despotism is "the security with which malcontents may communicate their sentiments, concert their plans, and practice every mode of opposition short of actual revolt, before the executive power can be legally justified in disturbing them."

Perhaps that is the kind of perfect society all of us should strive for—a nation in which there is no need for violent protest, revolutionary activity, or disloyalty because every citizen has full opportunity for patriotic dissent, with the assurance that he is being heard and that the majority fully respects the rights of the minority.

Voltaire suggested the spirit of such a democracy when he wrote the beautiful oath of the free citizen: "I disapprove of what you say, but I will defend to the death your right to say it."

Bibliography

(* Indicates Recommended Reading)

*Archer, Jules, *Angry Abolitionist: William Lloyd Garrison*. New York: Julian Messner, 1969.

*———, *The Extremists: Gadflies of American Society*. New York: Hawthorn Books, Inc., 1969.

*———, *Hawks, Doves, and the Eagle*. New York: Hawthorn Books, Inc., 1970.

*———, *Laws That Changed America*. New York: Criterion Books, 1967.

*———, *The Unpopular Ones*. New York: Crowell-Collier Press, 1968.

*———, *World Citizen: Woodrow Wilson*. New York: Julian Messner, 1967.

Baruch, Bernard M., *Baruch: The Public Years*. New York: Holt, Rinehart and Winston, 1960.

*Beirne, Francis F., *Shout Treason: The Trial of Aaron Burr*. New York: Hastings House Publishers, Inc., 1959.

*Bessie, Alvah, *Inquisition in Eden*. New York: The Macmillan Company, 1965.

Blackstock, Paul W., *Agents of Deceit*. Chicago: Quadrangle Books, 1966.

*Boveri, Margret, *Treason in the Twentieth Century*. New York: G. P. Putnam's Sons, 1963.

*Bulloch, John, *Akin to Treason*. London: Arthur Barker Limited, 1966.

*Carlson, John Roy, *Under Cover*. Cleveland and New York: World Publishing Company, 1943.

Carr, Albert Z., *The World and William Walker*. New York: Harper & Row, Publishers, 1963.

*Chambers, Whittaker, *Witness*. New York: Random House, 1952.

*Chapin, Bradley, *The American Law of Treason*. Seattle: University of Washington Press, 1964.

Chevalier, Haakon, *Oppenheimer: The Story of a Friendship*. New York: George Braziller, 1965.

De Toledano, Ralph, *Spies, Dupes, and Diplomats*. New Rochelle, New York: Arlington House, 1967.

————, and Lasky, Victor, *Seeds of Treason*. New York: Funk & Wagnalls Company, 1950.

Ducann, C. G. L., *Famous Treason Trials*. New York: Walker and Company, 1964.

Dulles, Allen, *The Craft of Intelligence*. New York: Harper & Row, Publishers, 1963.

*Forster, Arnold, and Epstein, Benjamin R., *Danger on the Right*. New York: Random House, 1964.

*Gentry, Curt, *Frame-Up: The Incredible Case of Tom Mooney and Warren Billings*. New York: W. W. Norton & Company, Inc., 1967.

*Grodzins, Morton, *The Loyal and the Disloyal*. Chicago: The University of Chicago Press, 1956.

*Hiss, Alger, *In the Court of Public Opinion*. New York: Alfred A. Knopf, 1957.

Holbrook, Stewart H., *The Dreamers of the American Dream*. Garden City, New York: Doubleday & Company, Inc., 1957.

*Hoover, J. Edgar, *Masters of Deceit*. New York: Henry Holt and Company, 1958.

Klapp, Orrin E., *Symbolic Leaders*. Chicago: Aldine Publishing Company, 1964.

Krock, Arthur, *In the Nation: 1932-1966*. New York: McGraw-Hill, Inc., 1966.

Lamparski, Richard, *Whatever Became Of. . . ?* New York: Crown Publishers, Inc., 1967.

*Lattimore, Owen, *Ordeal by Slander*. Boston: Little, Brown and Company, 1950.

Legislative Reference Service, Library of Congress, *Fascism in Action*. Washington: US Government Printing Office, 1947.

Long, David F., *The Outward View*. Chicago: Rand McNally & Company, 1963.

*Markmann, Charles Lam, *The Noblest Cry: A History of the American Civil Liberties Union*. New York: St. Martin's Press, 1965.

Mazo, Earl, *Richard Nixon*. New York: Avon Books, 1960.

*Morray, Joseph P., *Pride of State*. Boston: Beacon Press, Inc., 1959.

*Myers, Gustavus, *History of Bigotry in the United States,* revised edition. New York: Capricorn Books, 1960.

*Newberry, Mike, *The Yahoos.* New York: Marzani and Munsell, 1964.

Reader's Digest, Secrets & Spies. Pleasantville, New York: The Reader's Digest Association, 1964.

*Root, Jonathan, *The Betrayers: The Rosenberg Case.* New York: Coward-McCann, Inc., 1963.

Rosner, Joseph, *The Hater's Handbook.* New York: Dell Publishing Co., Inc., 1967.

Rowan, Richard Wilmer, *The Story of Secret Service.* Garden City, New York: Doubleday, Doran and Company, Inc., 1937.

*Seldes, George, *Facts and Fascism.* New York: In Fact, Inc., 1943.

*————,*One Thousand Americans.* New York: Boni & Gaer, 1947.

Seth, Ronald, *Secret Servants.* New York: Farrar, Straus and Cudahy, 1957.

Spolansky, Jacob, *The Communist Trail in America.* New York: The Macmillan Company, 1951.

*US House of Representatives, Committee on Un-American Activities (HUAC), *Guerrilla Warfare Advocates in the United States.* Washington: US Government Printing Office, 1968.

*————, *Subversive Influences in Riots, Looting, and Burning, Part 6 (San Francisco-Berkeley).* Washington: US Government Printing Office, 1969.

*————, *Subversive Involvement in Disruption of 1968 Democratic Party National Convention, Part 2.* Washington: US Government Printing Office, 1968.

*West, Rebecca, *The New Meaning of Treason.* New York: The Viking Press, 1964.

*Wexley, John, *The Judgment of Julius and Ethel Rosenberg.* New York: Cameron & Kahn, 1955.

*Weyl, Nathaniel, *Treason.* Washington: Public Affairs Press, 1950.

*Wise, David, and Ross, Thomas B., *The Espionage Establishment.* New York: Random House, 1967.

Young, Kimball, *Isn't One Wife Enough?* New York: Henry Holt and Company, 1954.

Also consulted were issues of the *Nation, Newsweek,* and other periodicals, including publications of the American Civil Liberties Union, the far Right, and the New Left.

Index

Smith, Joseph, 50, 51

Smith Act, 113, 149, 158, 167, 184

Smothers Brothers, 16n

Sons of Liberty, 12, 13

Spanish-American War, 64

Spock, Benjamin, 172, 173, 183

Stalin, Joseph, 86, 87, 111, 112, 134, 138, 163

Stamp Act, 11, 12

Standard Oil, 99, 115

Stanford, Max, 180

Stanton, Edwin M., 58

Steffens, Lincoln, 65, 70

Stephan, Max, 122

Stevens, Robert T., 160

Stevenson, Adlai, 148, 169

Stewart, Douglas, 119

Stilwell, Joseph, 135

Stimson, Henry, 114

Strempel, Baron von, 119

Students for a Democratic Society (S.D.S.), 176, 180, 184

Subversive Activities Control Board, 174

Sullivan, Edward, 100

Szilard, Leo, 162

Taft, Robert A., 122

Tallmadge, Benjamin, 20

Taylor, Zachary, 47

Tea Act, 13

Teller, Edward, 164

Thomas, J. Parnell, 137, 140–142

Thomas, Norman, 70

Thomsen, Hans, 119–120

Thoreau, Henry David, 48, 171, 183, 188

Thorkelson, Jacob, 108

Tippleskirch, Baron von, 99

Tito, Marshal, 5

"Tokyo Rose", 126, 127

Townsend, Francis E., 88, 102

Townsend, Ralph, 119

Treason laws, 9, 24, 26, 37, 48, 49, 57, 121, 188, 191

Trotsky, Leon, 86

True, James, 89

Truman, Harry S, 78, 99, 116, 135, 138, 144, 145, 147, 150, 151, 158, 163, 168

Trumbo, Dalton, 140

Turner, Nat, 54

Twain, Mark, 64

Tydings, Millard, 136, 150

Tyler, John, 43–45

"Unfriendly Ten", 141

Union party, 102

United Nations, 169

Urey, Harold, 162

Vallandigham, Clement L., 60, 61

Vichy Government, 2, 6

Viereck, George Sylvester, 89, 90, 102, 128

Vietnam, 4, 5, 42n, 63, 162–173, 177, 181, 184, 187, 188

Vinson, Fred M., 172

Virginia Resolutions, 11

Voltaire, Francois, 194

Walker, Edwin, 162, 168

Walker, Walter, 10

Walker Report, 175, 176

Wallace, Henry, 113, 138

War of 1812, 40, 49